THE EN
DREAMS

The continuing voyages of HMS SURPRISE

Welcome aboard!

Alan Lawrence

Feb. '24

ALAN LAWRENCE

THE END OF DREAMS

The continuing voyages of HMS SURPRISE

They went with songs to the battle, they were young,
Straight of limb, true of eye, steady and aglow.
They were staunch to the end against odds uncounted;
They fell with their faces to the foe.

They shall grow not old, as we that are left grow old:
Age shall not weary them, nor the years condemn.
At the going down of the sun and in the morning
We will remember them.

They mingle not with their laughing comrades again;
They sit no more at familiar tables of home;
They have no lot in our labour of the day-time;
They sleep beyond England's foam.

For the Fallen *(Extract)*
By Laurence Binyon

A tale of the struggle for Greek independence by
ALAN LAWRENCE

Mainsail Voyages Press Ltd
Hartland Forest, Devon
https://alanlawrenceauthor.wordpress.com

THE END OF DREAMS
The continuing voyages of HMS SURPRISE

ISBN-13   979-8-8738543-5-6
Story text typeset in Times New Roman 11 point.

The continuing voyages of HMS SURPRISE
The series thus far:

diverse reader reviews of the first seven titles:

"a riveting series of seafaring novels"
"I devoured this book in three days"
"another triumph for Alan Lawrence"
"the characters become friends you care about deeply"
"a brilliant work"
"truly great stuff, back to a quality absent since O'Brian"
"one of the most gripping and captivating of this genre"
"difficult to put down"
"the next page is pulling me to read it!"
"a masterfully crafted novel"
"superlatives are quickly exhausted"
"a cracking read - compulsive"
"another engrossing read in this enjoyable series"
"I found myself reliving the O'Brian experience"

THE END OF DREAMS

The continuing voyages of HMS SURPRISE

A FOREWORD BY THE AUTHOR

This is the eighth book in this series, all of which are consecutive stories. Almost all of the historical happenings described within them are a catalogue of true events, upon which the fictional return to sea of *HMS Surprise* (which was about to be converted to a prison hulk in 1823) is superimposed. All the books may be read as standalone tales but each follows on closely from its predecessor as the essential story develops from its beginnings in the first title with the enthusiastic return to sea of veterans and follows their experiences and the powerful influences exerted upon them as the Greek war at sea develops. However, all of the titles are, essentially, stories about *people* rather than *events*.

Before concluding the writing of this book I made something of a lengthy diversion to study with great fascination the history of the U.S. Civil War, the trilogy written by Shelby Foote being the most impressive account of any war that I have ever read; meticulous in detail, comprehensive in every respect, and only the merest scintilla of a sympathy for the Confederate cause allowed to escape the author's lips, *for so it seemed to me,* in his charming and softly spoken Southern voice in the TV series "The Civil War". The student of that conflict may discern that I have, myself, allowed a few famous words of that luminary of the Confederate cause, General Thomas "Stonewall" Jackson, to slip into my own tale; and, to counterbalance any suggestion that I possess even the least sympathy for the Confederate cause (which was never the case), I have also drawn inspiration from that undoubted genius of the Union side and the most wondrous and able man of that conflict, President Abraham Lincoln, to shape a few words of my own fictional hero, as the reader may discover.

The words of the song in Chapter Ten are Sandy Denny's *"At the end of the day"*; a more sublime song will never be found.

I would like to extend my thanks to Maarten Platje for his generous consent to use his wonderful painting as the basis for the book cover. I have diverged from the wonders of Ivan Aivazovsky throughout my series only once before, and that for a Greek artist (Konstantinostis Volanakis, 1837-1903) for the cover of my seventh title, but the cover of this book (my eighth), a superb work of Maarten's, is nothing less than the equal of those historical marvels of Aivazovsky.

Visit Maarten's website here: https://maartenplatje.com/

This book is dedicated to all those veterans of all conflicts who struggle with PTSD. My brief note on that subject is followed by poignant and moving words by one particular WWII veteran, Patrick Thomas, a Royal Navy sailor and survivor of the sinking of a Landing Craft (LCH 185) at the Normandy beaches, and whose story was the subject of a fascinating TV documentary, one which is well worth watching: *"No Roses On A Sailor's Grave"*.

Finally, thanks are due to Sally, my love and great supporter, for stoically enduring my long spells of 'focus' whilst writing these tales.

Alan Lawrence, January 2024

PTSD

There surely comes a moment in all bloody conflicts when each and every military man realises that he has done enough, has done as much as he can, when he knows that he can do no more, when he has struggled too long with the increasing and desperate burden placed upon him, when he realises that the load is crushing his mind, bearing hard down upon his spirit, and - *little by little* - destroying his essential soul, the person that he is, the person that he struggles to avoid leaving behind, as that bleak prospect looms large and personal resolve crumbles into deep distress; a lack of patience, a swift anger and a recurring despond are all symptoms of that long-lasting affliction. However, perhaps the worst aspect is that the horrible memories linger for so long, perhaps for ever.

There are, of course, other events, not necessarily military ones, which can oppress people with similar feelings, and the recognition of this has come only in relatively more recent times; but that of the soldier, fundamentally, was studied in a degree of detail only as late as the Second World War, when the terrifying experiences of U.S. soldiers in Normandy and, later, the breakout into a wider France brought many to the verge of a mental collapse, the widespread evidence of which was ultimately brought to the notice of the academic.

In the military context, it is rarely understood - *that is to say, in the sense of the vast majority of the general public realising it* - that war is the most brutal extension of politics; as Carl von Clausewitz famously stated. That tragedy of ignorance is, sadly, often the most dreadful shortcoming of, not the public, but the (national) leadership of many belligerents, most particularly those who *initiate* military conflict. Relatively few such national leaders have experienced the dreadful terrors of the combat soldier. The glaring question, therefore, *one which cannot be avoided by any responsible person, or at least those with an unbiased knowledge of events,* is to what extent such initiators give prior thought to the countless unfortunates who will suffer the consequences of their actions, of their jingoism, and that *usually calamitous* prejudice they oft possess which is nationalism, most often in the form of expansionism, the wildest notions of such being an ill-considered lust for empire (whether past or future), and always without regard to the cost - *the cost to others, that is.*

How, one might ask, do such monsters attain the pinnacle of state control? How do they maintain such control? How do they manage, seemingly, to carry the populace with them and to keep that support when they embark on their violent and unjustifiable ventures?

The answers seem invariably to lie in populism and nationalism, the regrettable combination of which is a reflection of a general absence of wider (political) understanding, essentially a failing of education in such societies. Of course, the absence of a free press is a hugely influential factor, but in that event and at that stage the rot (of such a society) has long set in.

But, enough of that; such rambling serves merely to place the reader's thoughts in an awareness of all that lies behind that most dreadful of all experiences: war.

The political drivers and the psychological construction of tyrants both lie far beyond a book of fiction such as this, as are the traumatising effects on the man at the front, the man subject to the fall of the rocket or artillery shell, the smashing impact of the bullet, the man who sees his comrades-in-arms pulped by a shot or explosion.

However, these issues rarely, if ever, make an appearance in fiction, and that hardly does justice to the story or delivers authenticity for the reader. In my own books I have therefore strived to write with a degree of attention to these cruel realities.

The characters of this, my own, story are immersed in their own realisations, weighing their personal interpretations of what is happening to them and all about them. They are losing comrades, friends; they have arrived in Hell.

"Over all these years, of course,
I've never given a thought about "185";
It wasn't until I came to Normandy in 2013
To see Jeff Beringer's grave;
And having visited that, it resurrected memories.

You can't live in the past,
But I like history;
Because it's quite simple,
People learn from history.

There are other stories to be told, of land, sea and air;
And probably many that will never be told;
But this memorial is for a particular ship,
Not generalising, it was one for LCH185;
One ship and its crew.

And as I said in my speech,
That the crew were my family;
I mean, I have gazed on memorials before;
I can only say, an emotional moment.

Once in a while your thoughts can go back,
And mine went back all those years;
I saw the sea, an empty sea;
But when I was here, that sea
Was full of ships and landing craft."

Patrick Thomas

Veteran survivor of LCH185,
sunk off Normandy June 25th 1944,
at the unveiling of a memorial to the ship.

Lion-sur-mer, June 2018

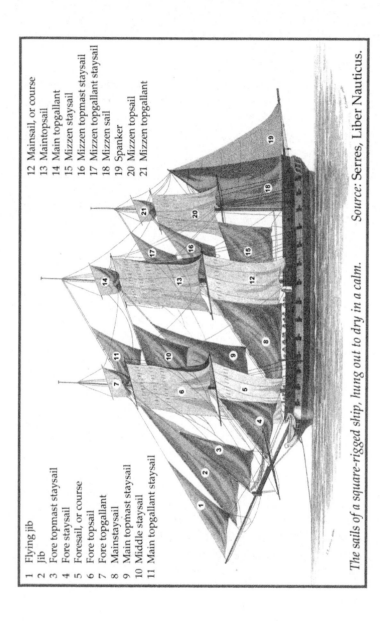

1 Flying jib
2 Jib
3 Fore topmast staysail
4 Fore staysail
5 Foresail, or course
6 Fore topsail
7 Fore topgallant
8 Mainstaysail
9 Main topmast staysail
10 Middle staysail
11 Main topgallant staysail
12 Mainsail, or course
13 Maintopsail
14 Main topgallant
15 Mizzen staysail
16 Mizzen topmast staysail
17 Mizzen topgallant staysail
18 Mizzen sail
19 Spanker
20 Mizzen topsail
21 Mizzen topgallant

The sails of a square-rigged ship, hung out to dry in a calm.   *Source:* Serres, Liber Nauticus.

Chapter One

Saturday 6th May 1826 10:30   Argostoli Port, Cephalonia

Mid-morning and five bell strikes of the forenoon watch rang out with shrill, discordant resonation; however, the bleak, aural reminder of time passing was entirely ignored by the veterans of *HMS Surprise* as they shifted about the decks of the frigate, seemingly without the least sense of urgency, under a deep-blue sky, the great expanse broken by only the merest wisps of distant white cloud; indeed, every man actually moving appeared to do so with an indolence verging on sloth, for such was how it seemed to the casual observer; for all the barky's old tars were perfectly aware of their promised departure for home on the morrow, and they basked in that glorious thought. Home! At last! That sweet prospect, as much as the radiant warmth of the bright morning sun, scarcely a breeze in the air, warmed their hearts as they toiled, exceedingly slowly, about their duties and preparations amidst a loud backcloth of talking, shouting, cursing, grumbling, whistling and even singing; all of which was expressed within a perfect amity.

For three years the ship's experienced crew, every one of them a volunteer, had fought *their* prized ship - *for that was how they considered her to be* - alongside a disparate collection of armed Greek merchantmen against the overwhelming superiority of the Turk navy, and in so doing they had suffered a great number of casualties, many of whom had been killed; *too many*, for so it seemed to weary men who had lost long-term shipmates, close friends and even family members, all of them precious brothers-in-arms; for the vast majority of the crew hailed from Falmouth town, a tightly-knit community where everyone was familiar to everyone else, where pious, God-fearing families worshipped together with unfailing regularity at the town's Methodist chapel in Killigrew Street, and where the loss of even a single man was

1

a deeply wounding and heartfelt calamity for all of the close congregation; and so it was too aboard the frigate.

However, this day was different, spirits were high; for the men readying the ship for departure believed with a profound intensity that their own fighting was done, finished; they would fight no more bloody battles, would suffer no more fatalities; they would be homeward bound in the afternoon, and that was just a few hours away. Home! The sensational anticipation had pulsated throughout their minds in every wakened minute for days; indeed, it had long been the cherished subject of their dreams for many a month; and now the exciting moment was near arrived at last, and they revelled in the so sublime pleasure of that glorious thought.

Captain Patrick O'Connor, a man who hailed from Galway, prematurely greying with scarcely a trace remaining of his former full shock of red hair, contented himself with thoughtful immobility whilst standing on his quarterdeck, satisfied for once with being a mere observer, all organisation left to his lieutenants: Pickering, Codrington and Mower. For his own mind and body had been sorely taxed, most acutely of late during several bloody battles; in fact, he was recuperating from a severe leg wound, and the day represented a welcome respite, a relief, from prolonged, severe strain. Although not deliberate, for such could never be the case, his mind wandered as if his conscious thinking had paused, and he relaxed into that rare, pleasurable sensation of repose, revelling in it: responsibility had faded away for just a short spell, the most invaluable of moments; for so it seemed to his tired mind. His nose subliminally registered the tangy smell of salt air and the customary, deep, rich odour of the tar and resin which abounded from the deck caulking and the myriad ropes of the rigging, and both his ear and eye caught the occasional slap of canvas sailcloth in the weak breeze. More minutes of indistinct musing passed with an infinite slowness until, at last, he blinked, his sore eyes ranging wide once again all over his ship, looking here, there and everywhere in turn, passively taking in the disparate movements of all kinds, but wholly ignoring the calling, swooping flight of inquisitive gulls, a flock of them hopping about the masts and the deck, scavenging, seeking some cast-away tidbit to eat; but his eyes and thoughts were without the least focus, a welcome placidity displacing long-held, disturbing anxieties and deep-seated disquietude; for in that moment, relaxation and respite were the most valuable, the most precious, of all friends.

'Mr Tizard!' O'Connor eventually stirred with reluctance from his private contemplations to interrupt the ship's carpenter as he passed by the compass housing, 'How are you faring... the repair of the shrouds and stays... the last of the hull damages... and the leaking holes?'

'All be well, sir; the rigging has been replaced, and as for the holes, every one of 'em be fixed up right well tight,' the reply came back in definitive voice, borne of long experience, and greatly reassuring at the same time to all in earshot. 'There be no more water coming in; you can be sure of it, sir.'

'Very good,' murmured O'Connor, mildly relieved, albeit he had been expecting nothing less than a positive report from the experienced carpenter, himself a longstanding veteran of *Surprise*. 'Carry on.'

The morning thus far had seen a constant stream of small boat traffic between the frigate and the quay, many local people and great quantities of foodstuffs making the short passage aboard numerous small fishing vessels across the harbour to *Surprise's* deep-water anchorage, a constant shouting abounding between the crew aboard ship and the ferrying boats. Those men toiling with the considerable loading noted with keen anticipation the wonderful aroma of fresh-baked bread, such a joy to contemplate after weeks of the hard tack which was dry ship's biscuit; many wide eyes marvelled at the casks of local wine and the sweet-scented kegs of delicious, ripe raisins, cultivated from the Black Corinth grape since the days of Homer and the perfect protection against the perils and ills of scurvy; for so the ship's surgeon, Dr Simon Ferguson, had most earnestly assured them. It was a valuable staple of local agriculture and

3

commerce, its local production near unique in all of the eastern Mediterranean since the Greek war had effectively ended mainland cultivation; but Cephalonia offered the delicious fruit in a bountiful plenty, and the embargo on trade with the mainland, forbidden by the Ionian authorities because of the endemic plague there, had ensured that the sweet grape had become a favoured staple aboard the frigate.

On the gun deck, Duncan Macleod, a Scots compatriot of Simon Ferguson, strode up and down, fore and aft, repetitively and without pause, checking everything coming aboard, issuing stowage instructions, scolding lazy men who inclined towards idleness with shouts of, 'Look alive, Look alive there!', all of which were ignored; which he understood very well and with which he entirely sympathised; for the happy day was a rare event, and the entire ship's company was immersed within it; even the sick and wounded below were much cheered. Macleod was himself ranked captain, but he had long served aboard *Surprise* as First Officer. He was a physically imposing man, a robust figure, stocky even, with short, grizzled grey hair, and seemingly possessed of all the confidence of the world. He had also acted in the role of an intelligence officer for the British government for some years, serving in Greece at the Patras consulate when the Greek insurrection had first begun. More recently, when in England, he had been consulted by no less a person than the Foreign Secretary, George Canning, who had sought his advice on the prospects for Greek endurance in the war against the Turks. However, Macleod himself firmly considered that his own role and duty was to serve with his close friend, O'Connor, for the duration of *HMS Surprise's* service in the Greek conflict, to the extent that he had always demurred from all thoughts of command of any other vessel.

The bosun appeared on the quarterdeck, stepping up towards the helm. 'Mr Sampays!' Pat called out; for his mind, long years of experience and responsibility deeply engrained within it, could not consciously avoid enquiry, and the many and varied mutilations of his ship, consequent to the recent

4

battles against fully three Turk frigates, were only being remedied to his satisfaction in the recent days since escaping from the fray. 'The boats; will you care to tell me how we stand?'

'Certainly, sir.' The bosun was a Portuguese who had served with Pat aboard *HMS Tenedos* before *Surprise*, and was one of Pat's most valued non-commissioned officers. 'The cutter has been in the water all morning, fetching the fresh water from the town - *doubtless you have seen her, sir* - she was the least struck of all. The launch is near ready, and I venture she will float right d'reckly... before the first dog watch; but the pinnace will take some further hours. Be assured we will press on, sir. Mr Tizard is attending... until she is finished... maybe tomorrow...' Sampays paused, as if sensing that Pat did not care to receive even the least bad news.

Pat sensed this, 'Come on, Mr Sampays, spit it out; let's not be barking about the mulberry tree.'

'Very well, sir; I regret to say that the jolly boat is smashed beyond... that is to say... we have broken her up... for her timbers... to fix the damages to the others... Mr Tizard said we had no choice... not the least...' Sampays halted and stared at his captain, Pat's unblinking face betraying his evaluation.

In that slow moment of lingering assessment, Pat ignored the pressing interruption of his steward, Murphy, who had appeared and was standing close by to ask his captain's wishes for his second breakfast. An irritated Pat offered only a shake of his head towards him by way of reply, but Murphy lingered, as if to press his case, as Pat returned his attention to the bosun. 'So... the jolly boat is lost to us... I see; well, that is a pity, for sure,' he pronounced eventually in a voice of mild dismay; 'However, I am reminded of what my old grandma used to tell me... the dear that she was... *Better one good thing that is... than two things that were.*'

'Yes, sir,' mumbled Sampays, digesting Pat's conclusion; 'That is... is... *the most sensible of advice...*'

'Indeed, it is... *and a trout in the pot is better than a salmon in the sea.*' Pat smiled wide and Murphy nodded his own emphatic affirmation in the background as Sampays stared, seemingly searching for similar inspiration. 'So I have always thought,' added Pat, nodding to Sampays. 'I venture we must content ourselves with what we *do* have.' The bosun could find no suitable answer and moved off without further ado.

Pat continued to ignore a visibly impatient, even vexed, Murphy and turned to stare, rather absently, over the side at the approaching cutter. He reminded himself to be thankful for the weather, a hot day with little wind and consequent calm water; for the small boat's heavy burden of freshwater barrels was plainly most severely taxing both the capacity of the cutter and the strength of its oarsmen to fetch such a heavyweight cargo from the quay; but not a single man rowing minded his hot and strenuous exertions in the least, for a sense of great happiness had permeated the frigate since yesterday, and everyone, both the crew and the town's inhabitants, had embraced the glorious occasion with joy, with exuberance and, not least, deep satisfaction.

A large number of excited townsfolk had thronged the quay all morning to offer their most cordial farewells, *Surprise* having been a frequent visitor for three years; but for some of them the parting of the ways was, sadly, something of a black cloud on the bright horizon which was the end of the frigate's warlike duties; in fact, the continuation of more than a few valued friendships was thrust, most pointedly, into an unwelcome doubt, a significant proportion of those affected being both young and - on the town side at least - female. And although such friendships were not strictly of the monogamous kind as far as several of the old tarpaulins of the barky were concerned, Pat had countenanced such liaisons on account of the barky's long spells at the town during her three years of service in Greece; and so all such goodbyes were sincere and therefore heartfelt and distressing; more so for the hopeful damsels of the town, for the sense of inevitability and permanent separation was powerful and emotional; because for the poorest of the people of Argostoli, many of whom had become impoverished since war and disease had ravaged the mainland, far distant Falmouth was as inaccessible as the mountains of the moon; and they knew, they understood, that it would ever be so.

Pat's gaze turned away from the cutter and he looked all about him until his eyes fell upon his closest friend in all the world: Doctor Simon Ferguson was a slightly older man, in his late forties and somewhat wizened in his appearance, but physically unprepossessing and rather shabby in his attire, all of it being visibly worn and much of it bloodstained to the careful eye. He was leaning over the stern rail, unmoving, and looking down into the water as if in the most thoughtful introspection and oblivious to the cacophony of noises all about him.

Pat stepped slowly across his quarterdeck to stand alongside his friend. A few seconds passing and no acknowledgement from him, Pat ventured a few words, 'Good morning, Simon. It is the grand day today, what with our departure nigh upon us.' No reply other than a grunt, and so Pat persevered, 'At what are you staring, may I ask?'

'The *caretta caretta*,' Ferguson replied quietly but did not stir, his head unmoving; 'Down there.'

'The car... caretta?'

'Turtles, the Loggerhead. I am feeding them with the final remnants of the salted sardines. The taint of age has long rendered them unpalatable... at least to my own taste.'

'Yes, I have much the same feeling about the salt pork... too long in the cask, no doubt. Oh, for a fine beefsteak, eh? When we fetch home to Falmouth, I promise you we will enjoy a prodigious grand one in the Royal Hotel; what do you say?'

'That will be most welcome, thank you. For my own part I confess a longing for the plainest of dishes... for porridge... *with salt*. In the Isles... in Tobermory in my childhood... I grew up on plain fare, and porridge was my customary

7

breakfast every morning... and - *I recall* - it was often also served for my dinner... Yes, I will ever be mindful that we were poor.'

'As was I, brother; in Connemara it was the rare sight to see a child with shoes; and as for food, well, allow me to say that I had my fill of the potato a deal of years ago! And now... and now, I am a potato farmer!' Pat laughed aloud. 'On my fifteen acres of peat bog... A potato farmer of all things!'

'Oh, come now; let us attend to reality, Patrick O'Connor,' retorted Simon, plainly not in the mood for humour; 'You are no more a potato farmer than I am Lord of the Isles!' He looked up and stared at his friend. 'You are a *mariner*, a man whose aspirations, *whose very essence*, will ever be served by the sea; in fact, I am sure that your entire existence... *your essential spirit*... has been founded upon Neptune's watery realm. Indeed, does not the sea call to your very soul? Is that not the case? No reply is required, I assure you, for I will never believe a word to the contrary.'

'Perhaps there is something in what you say, for I have been afloat since I was but thirteen...' Pat sighed even as he smiled again, trying to shake his friend's demeanour to something more convivial, '... and even before that I fished the waters off Cleggan... for my dinner... sometimes venturing far out... to Inishbofin and Inishark... *if the weather was fair*. It has always seemed the natural thing.' A sigh of reminiscence, of nostalgia even, and Pat continued in good voice, sweet memories of old flooding back into a mind most grateful for the recollection, 'There is a deep channel between the two islands where plentiful cod and pollack are to be found... great shoals of fish... boundless stocks of herring... and salmon too... a great plenty of them all.'

'I do not much care to hear any mention of the last species you refer to,' Simon spoke still in acerbic voice as he turned away to throw the last of the sardines into the water, the splash being followed by the brief flurry of three turtles breaking the surface and fighting for the food.

Pat stared closely at his friend: *what did Simon mean? Why was there an aura of dismay about him, a dissatisfaction even, and why so on such a grand day as this?* Such discontent seemed scarcely credible when they were imminently quitting bloody, beleaguered Greece to return home. He pondered what to say, eventually offering the most innocuous of questions, one which he felt sure would fall on safe ground, 'What will you be doing... tell... on a morning such as this... when you fetch home?'

'Oh, I aspire only to a simple life... *the simplest...* a routine - *yes, a routine* - when I will serve patients in my village and the wider Mull... *ten thousands of good and honest people are in want of a surgeon on the island...*' Simon spoke hesitantly and in low voice as if his words, his plans, in some way offered something of an alleviation from an inner distress, a heartfelt one, 'I care nothing for the strong winds there, which might carry a careless soul away when they blow, nor the omnipresent rain, which will be a blessing after the heat of Greece; neither will I be disturbed by the infernal midge... No, I will study the tern, the sea eagle - *how I yearn to see one again... the majesty of the bird* - and the chaffinch... and a myriad others... and the furthest sea passage I care to contemplate will be a mere few miles... Jura and Islay being the most distant islands in my thinking... from my own home in Tobermory. That is to say, *if* I possess of a home when I return...' Simon frowned as his voice tailed off.

'What do you mean? Has something happened?' asked Pat anxiously; 'I do recall that your landlord was pressing you for funds.'

'Indeed, he is. I received a letter only yesterday - *the mail packet ship arrived at Corfu on Thursday* - from Flora - *Mrs MacDougall...*' Simon hesitated.

'Please to explain.'

'It seems that the vulpine rogue - *my landlord, Salmon* - has written formally to request that I vacate my house...' Simon's voice carried the merest audible tremor but flagged a world of concern. 'I will have no abode, I will possess no home, Pat... when I return to the village; *worse:* Mrs MacDougall and her bairns... *the two young lassies...* will be homeless, no roof over their heads... We must quit the house by the end of this month.' Pat stared, floundering and speechless, until Simon resumed in scarcely more than a whisper, 'I do not care to sound discontented, but what am I to do?'

Pat's own confusion, a hiatus of incomprehension, nothing constructive coming to mind, was broken by the welcome interruption of a mildly excited Tom Pickering, 'Sir, Doctor Ferguson... I beg pardon for my intrusion.' Pat nodded and the lieutenant continued, 'Mr Mower has returned from the quay with a note from Captain Kennedy.'

'Please; go on, Mr Pickering,' Pat spoke slowly, a rising sense of dismay gradually settling upon him, a minor apprehension gradually dawning; something unknown and unwelcome was closing in and registering within his tired mind.

'Colonel Napier requests your permission to come aboard, sir... to bid you farewell... to do the civil. Captain Kennedy asks that you reply at your earliest convenience.'

'Why, of course; that will be... *we will be...* delighted to welcome the Resident aboard... *and* Captain Kennedy. Please reply forthwith... with my compliments.' Pickering saluted and hastened away. Pat turned back to Simon, 'Dear friend... I beg you will set aside your... *your disconsolation...* at least for the moment. We will speak later, but now I must attend the Resident and his deputy; I must away to prepare, to set Murphy in train... rouse him to duty... before Napier arrives. *Hold fast*, for things are rarely as black as they might seem; no, they ain't, not by a chalk as long as your arm.' Pat seized Simon by his shoulders, 'Hold fast... hold steady, I beg you will... and please to remember... as the old folks say back home... *when you put a horse out, he'll always find grass.*'

Simon gazed deep into his old friend's eyes and spoke in firmer voice, 'Patrick O'Connor; that is, perhaps, not the most... *appropriate* turn of phrase in the circumstances, and it does not quite serve to quash my anxieties, no; but I thank you for the precious sentiment, brother; I do.'

Pat nodded but turned away with reluctance. He hastened to descend the companionway steps to the gun deck where he looked all about him at the continuing hive of activity: the repair of the pinnace was proceeding just forward of the coach, water casks were being lowered on ropes to the deck, numerous crates of foodstuffs were strewn everywhere, and all about the turmoil of disarray a hundred and fifty men and more were conversing; for the most part happily, but loud shouts also abounded, a few curses more strident than everything else and resonating the length of the deck when fingers and toes were crushed in careless handling; but nothing of such struck Pat as serious, for the garrulous banter was a most satisfying chorus, as cheerful as anything that he could recall hearing for several years, certainly so whilst serving in the Greek conflict; and that lifted his spirits from the small dismay he had felt when trying but failing to find something, some few words at least, of consolation for Simon. He turned towards Tom Pickering; the lieutenant was known as the jester in the gun room, but sadly nothing of mirth had been heard from him for a considerable time, 'Mr Pickering, I think we may leave until the afternoon watch all thoughts of holy-stoning.'

Pickering looked aghast, for the deck was strewn everywhere in the most ramshackle fashion with barrels, boxes, casks, butts, hogsheads, puncheons, great swathes of canvas, timbers and a plethora of detritus left by the carpenter's workings; and then he noticed Pat's smile and realised the joke at his expense; he smiled wide and shook Pat's proffered hand, a mutual nod offered and no further words required.

As Clumsy Dalby rang out loud six bells of the forenoon watch, the bosun called out, 'UP SPIRITS!' and all work on deck was paused for the customary grog issue, a very welcome refreshment in the baking heat of the day. The happy banter of the men continued whilst queuing for and enjoying their grog, scores of happy old tars sitting on casks, tea chests and the deck itself, an atmosphere almost of festival abounding.

Pat passed quickly through the coach, the ante-room before his cabin. His steward, Murphy, was already at his table, attending to Pat's clothing with a flat iron, a second one warming on the stove. The temperature therein was consequently stifling hot despite the paucity of glass remaining in the stern gallery, almost all of it shot and smashed away during the recent battles. Pat immediately began to sweat profusely, nothing of a breeze to offer the least of small relief. Murphy, noting Pat's haste and discomfort, looked up with eyes of staring inquisition.

'Murphy,' declared Pat in a voice that declared he would brook not the least obfuscation from his servant, for such was not unusual, 'Colonel Napier will be coming aboard in a short while, perhaps within the hour. Please to stand by with the coffee pot and rouse out a brace of madeira and port wine and... and look to Wilkins to see if there is the least prospect of some modest comestibles. Perhaps a basket of marchpane biscuits can be found?'

Murphy sniffed most emphatically, 'Well, sorr, and begging your honour's pardon, but will 'ee care to shift your clothes? You mayn't greet the Colonel's presence in them old rags; that is to say, in your *second-best* uniform... sorr.' Murphy, despite his many and varied shortcomings, for there were many such, was nothing if not fastidious in all matters relating to his master's clothing.

Pat stared at his steward, an abrasive rebuke immediately coming to mind, but then he cautiously looked to his jacket and then to his trousers; sure enough, he could hardly argue to the contrary: both vestments were stained with a variety of blemishes; those marks which were obviously long-dried blood he did not care to dwell on, and a number of ripped gashes and torn holes were plain to see with only cursory scrutiny. 'Very well, you have the advantage of me, and I concede the matter,' he declared with a sigh and in sour voice, much to Murphy's satisfaction. 'We will look to whatever else can be found in the line of a better - *a cleaner* - uniform.'

A gentle knock on the cabin door and Pat's second steward, Freeman, appeared, bearing a silver tray and a coffee pot. 'Massa, will 'ee want for coffee?' Freeman was a strong, tall, black African who had escaped the dire horrors of a slave ship by swimming to the barky; a quite incredible feat whilst burdened by the iron bilboes which had shackled his legs. It had been a physical triumph which had greatly impressed his eventual rescuers when they hauled him aboard the ship's boat. Subsequently, he had been adopted and christened by the crew; and with his genial good nature he had become a well-liked and greatly-respected shipmate, having most closely attended to help the surgeons' endeavours during several bloody battles to defend the Greek island of Samos. He had rarely left the sickbay in recent days, serving as nurse and caring for those unfortunates who had been wounded fighting three pursuing Turk frigates as *Surprise* rescued her own men from the recent fall of the long-besieged Greek town of Missolonghi in the final desperate hours of conflict, fire and death when it was sacked by the invading Turks.

The coffee aroma registered instantly and Pat brightened; even small cheer was valuable in his present uncertainties and much appreciated; so much so that he had wondered in recent days as he himself recovered from his leg wound and the ship's repairs were carried out whether he had finally reached his own limit of fortitude, of endurance; eventually deciding that such was certainly possible, perhaps even probable. It had been a profoundly shocking conclusion, a heartfelt and deeply dismaying one, humbling even; but it was not wholly unexpected, for his mind had struggled for a long time with persistent doubts and anxieties which he had not been able to shake off, most acutely so as casualties had mounted and faithful long-term shipmates had been lost. The most unpalatable and haunting question of all recurred once more, his gloomy thinking on an utterly reluctant path: *had he reached the end of his sea-going career in the Royal Navy?* It was the most unappealing prospect and he tried hard to put it out of mind. He looked up at Freeman and spoke with emphatic gratitude in his reply, 'I think that might answer tolerably well. Thank you, most kind.'

An ever-attentive Murphy was perfectly well aware that his captain was not in best spirits, in the pink of composure, and had not been so since even before the return to Greece; in fact, Murphy recalled very well that Pat's decision to embark upon the latest Greek voyage had been a difficult one, painful even; and he knew that it had been reached only after a hard-fought struggle between Pat's opposing feelings of anguish and conscience; the former was founded on a deeply-felt reticence to see his crew, *his valued shipmates*, experience further bloodshed, together with his revulsion at that vile commonplace which was the many atrocities perpetrated by both sides in the war; however, the other side of the painful, cerebral coin had been *the call of his conscience*, the latter being, primarily, a duty of care to his precious friends and veterans; for he could never contemplate their dangerous tribulations in a bloody war without him to lead them, to protect and preserve them; for that was the true depth of his feelings after all the years of fighting together.

A greatly sympathetic Murphy, always in close attendance, contented himself with the happy thought that all the fighting was over: *they were going home and his captain's spirits would no longer be so cast down*; and he hoped with a fierce passion that it would be so. He set down his iron on the stove and hastened to pour Pat's coffee, a nod to Freeman sending the second steward on his way. Pat looked carefully and with rare appreciation at his compatriot; for Murphy too hailed from Galway, from the county town itself. Eventually, a few sips enjoyed and a modicum of composure recovered, a seated Pat offered his gentle enquiry in ribald voice, 'Murphy, from where exactly did you gain your dedication for washing clothes... *excessive washing*, if I may say so?'

Murphy managed the beginnings of a smile as he replied in the Gaelic tongue, 'Is uaigneach an níochán nach mbíonn

14

léine ann.'* He chortled out loud, much to Pat's astonishment, before adding, 'That's what *my* grandma used to say, sorr.' The humour and its homespun origin registered with both men as a welcome flush of delight, and Pat laughed with him, which much pleased his steward.

* *It's a lonely washing line that has no man's shirt on it.*

A peremptory knock on the door was followed by an excited Lieutenant Pickering entering, 'Sir, Colonel Napier is climbing the ladder... *and I do believe General Adam is with him!'*

Pat leaped up from his chair with a degree of panic, 'Quickly, Murphy; the Governor of all the Ionians himself is here; lose not a moment; my best uniform, if you please! Bear a hand there!'

'Well, 'ere it be, sorr; right d'reckly pressed.'

A frantic three minutes of the utmost haste, and Pat fidgeted to find comfort in his clean full-dress uniform, the rigidity of the starched white lapels, the stiff collars and tidy cuffs seeming so utterly alien after such a long time in undress uniform, in his "second best" as Murphy termed it. Of all things the pristinely clean white breeches and long stockings seemed wholly incongruous in that moment, and his shoes, which had not seen the light of day for an age, had been blacked to a shine by his steward. Murphy thrust the black cocked hat upon Pat's head as the visitors swept through the door without the least ceremony. Pat felt the warm sweat rivulets accumulating on his back as he took a deep breath, 'Welcome, Colonel Napier; I hope I see you well.' Pat turned to shake his principal visitor's hand; 'Welcome, General Adam... sir,' he declared as Adam advanced to greet him; 'I am most heartily glad to see you again.' Pat turned briefly towards the Resident's aide at the rear; 'Captain Kennedy, a pleasure.' He waved towards his table, 'Gentlemen, please, I beg you will be seated.' A brief nod towards Murphy and the steward hastened away.

Cordial pleasantries followed after all were seated about the table until a silent hiatus descended, when a curious Pat invited comment, 'Sir Frederick, to what do I owe the honour, the... *the pleasure...* that it is?'

'The pleasure is all mine, Captain O'Connor, I do assure you. I am pleased to see you in better health than the last time. How is your leg?'

'Oh, the wound is all healed now, never better; thank you, sir.' Pat did not believe that the lie sounded convincing in the least, for the truth of the matter was that his severe leg wound, whilst looking healed to his eye and notwithstanding the bright scar and still-present stitches, still gave him considerable pain.

'That is very good to hear.' Adam got straight to the point, 'I am led to understand by Colonel Napier that it is your intention to depart this very day, to return to England; hence I have hastened here with the utmost celerity. Is that the case - *your departure today?*'

'Indeed, it is, sir; once we have completed our watering and the last man is returned aboard.' Pat wondered where the Governor's enquiries were leading. At least he no longer felt apprehension about conversing with him; for Sir Frederick, within the confines of the cabin, had expressed a degree of support and sympathy for the Greek cause when last they had met, when Pat had returned from the last-minute evacuation of his officers from Missolonghi after fighting off three attacking Turk frigates, destroying one of them; it had been the occasion when he had been very severely wounded in his right leg.

Adam spoke up with an immediate return to his interest, 'Captain, I could not but observe the... *the damages* to your vessel from the quay, more greatly evident as my boat approached, and most particularly so as I climbed the ladder. Is she fit to sail? Are you sufficiently prepared to depart... with the uncertainties of... and the... the *potential* for a furious Biscay and suchlike before you?'

Pat sighed inwardly and could not conceal his frown of dismay. 'I greatly regret, sir, that she looks to be in a right lubberly state... much like the end of a riotous day of revelling at the Bartholomew Fair... and, I confess, our repairs may seem to the... *the untutored* eye to be a trifle on the... *the primitive* side, but my people are working double tides... as busy as right proper bees - *worker bees*,' declared Pat, temporizing, 'and no doubt by the time we fetch Malta... and later, when we gain the Rock... although it would never please such as the Devonport shipwrights - *the particular fellows that they are* - we will have remedied much that you saw.'

Murphy and Freeman returned in that moment, hastening to deposit coffee pots, cups, glasses and fortified wines upon the table. Wilkins too, Pat's cook, set down a large silver tray of marchpane biscuits. All the servants stood back, awaiting Pat's instruction; a nod from him and the stewards poured coffee and wine for all.

Adam resumed, 'Naturally, we are here to offer our own farewells and, of course, our best wishes for a swift voyage home... *the swiftest.*'

'Thank you, sir,' Pat whispered, waiting for something more substantive; for he was never more sure than then that there was something of that ilk to follow, something which he innately feared he would not welcome.

'I have received enquiries...' Adam continued quietly, '... during these recent two weeks since you... *since you returned* from... *from that place*... indeed, the Turk representative to the Ionians - *a Swiss merchant, the gentleman resides in Corfu* - would appear to be most interested in ascertaining precisely the events as... as Missolonghi finally succumbed... and I do detect a most particular interest on his part as to the... *the fighting* between an unidentified naval vessel and that Turk squadron which was tasked with preventing further provisions... *powder and sustenance*... from reaching the town. In fact, I believe it is conceivable, perhaps even likely, that he was referring to that very same Turk squadron which your own vessel engaged. What do you say?'

Pat nodded, but offered only a cautious affirmation, 'Most likely it was, sir.'

'Naturally,' Adam continued, 'His Majesty's Government, the Ionian representatives of which are my staff

17

and I, has disavowed all knowledge of such events; for such would undoubtedly create - *will I say* - friction... extreme friction... *the most extreme...* in Constantinople. The Sublime Porte is already suspicious of our... our leanings, *our possible intentions...* in this matter... and in the war generally.' Pat nodded but remained silent as Adam pressed on, 'Captain O'Connor, was it the case that *all* your people, officers and men alike, were evacuated from the town? No one was left behind... no one at all... *alive or dead?*'

'Not a one, sir,' Pat swallowed and felt the tightening of his throat as his mouth dried in an instant. He took a hasty gulp from his wine glass.

'Very good,' pronounced Adam. 'Then we may hold to our statement to the Swiss gentleman that His Majesty's Government denies that any Royal Navy ship... or even any with a British registration... is interfering in the war, most particularly so in the final days of Missolonghi; and should any report to the contrary emerge... and with the least credibility... then we will refer to the possibility... *the mere possibility* of an unknown... *an unidentified...* vessel... a *privateer...* being the foundation for all rumours and suchlike.'

Pat gulped only air and felt the dryness of his mouth once more; he was perfectly aware of the status of *Surprise* as a privateer, for such had been explicitly explained to him at the outset, three years previously, by no other than the First Lord of the Admiralty, Lord Melville himself; indeed, the recent resupply mission had also mandated adhering to that unofficial or private standing. Consequently, it had been Pat's cherished hope that *Surprise* and her men would not have to fight at all, that they would simply deliver the donated supplies to the besieged town and swiftly depart; but that had not, unfortunately, been the case, for the charitable concerns of his surgeons had compelled them to aid the wounded defenders within the town in the final bloody days before it was overwhelmed.

A unanimous, silent pause followed as all reflected on Adam's enquiry and reminder, the Ionian Governor no doubt

18

considering the matter most carefully. The hot coffee was ignored as it cooled but the wine was gratefully appreciated in the enduring heat of the cabin. A still apprehensive Pat was becoming ever more aware of the unwelcome warm streams of sweat that coursed from his armpits and the damp rivulets that increasingly trickled down his chest and back, a discomfort that no one else seemed to be suffering from; at least, not that he could readily perceive. He silently cursed Murphy for lighting the cabin stove, and he scowled at him even as the steward fussed all about the table, refilling glasses at every opportunity whilst listening attentively to every word uttered.

Eventually, Adam resumed once more, 'It is perfectly plain to the Philhellenes about this table, *for we are all such,* Captain... *it is perfectly plain...* that the efforts of you and your men... and of your gallant vessel... have been much appreciated by such Greek authorities that we... in the Ionians... are in contact with. Your departure will surely be much lamented by them, for the war is not going well for the Greeks.' A meaningful pause, 'However, your much-valued contribution is ended.' Pat found himself nodding emphatically, perhaps more than might be perceived as polite affirmation, as Adam continued, 'Allow me to bring one further matter to your attention.' Pat simply stared, a paralysing flush of apprehension seizing all his thoughts, and no words could he find. 'You may be aware,' declared Adam, 'that the mail packet arrived in Corfu from Malta late on Thursday. The captain of said ship attended my office early on Friday morning... which was certainly unusual... *not the norm*; and he explained that he had been followed - *pursued even* - by two Turk frigates as he approached the Ionians. In fact, he remarked that they had ventured so close that he could make out their officers on deck with his glass. They shied off - *for so he said - only as the packet entered Corfu's waters*. Hence, I am come here today, O'Connor, and at my earliest convenience, to advise you of this event and to urge caution - *the utmost caution* - when you depart this place.'

A surge of alarm flooded Pat's thoughts in an instant; the prospect of encountering Turk warships once more was not something he wished to contemplate ever again; indeed, he shrank from the very notion, offering only a few words of acknowledgement to Adam in a low voice, 'Sir, I thank you for bringing this to my attention with such express; I am most uncommonly glad that you did so.' He sat back in his chair to reflect and was plunged into a feeling of gloom, remaining silent and reflective for the most part even as several further jugs of the madeira and port wine continued to be consumed and more comfortable exchanges flowed across his table, a considerable pleasure found by his visitors in the marchpane biscuits, a plentiful supply of which had been baked in haste. The attentive and curious stewards, keen to eavesdrop, never relented from keeping glasses topped afresh at the least indication from anyone present or, for that matter, without any indication whatsoever.

Later, the visitors having departed, the frigate finally hauled up her cables and inched away from her anchorage as her sails grasped wide to catch and fill with the feeble zephyr of a *Levanter*, slowly gaining way as she left behind a thousand and more locals, all of them shouting and waving reluctant farewells from the quay, a cable away, the minds of many gripped by an uncomfortable amalgam of wonder, excitement and sadness. By the time that precious Cephalonia had finally slipped away to disappear in the distant wake of the frigate some three hours later, the day had slipped into the relative cool of the evening, and a mixed mood of lethargy and relief abounded amongst all the ship's company, both officers and men. In the great cabin the ambience was the strangest of melds; a general uncertainty was palpably visible in the seemingly preoccupied faces of the three friends, Pat, Duncan and Simon, sitting mute therein around the captain's table. The relief that war-torn Greece would soon be left far, far behind was certainly discernible, for such feeling was endemic to everyone throughout the decks of the frigate. It was certainly prevalent in the thoughts of Pat, for the memories of the most brutal, the most violent, of recent events persisted and could not be wholly dispelled; the anxieties of that unnerving horror gnawed at an unsettled mind, and such deep-rooted consternation hung low in all his reflections, like an unwanted black cloud on a day of little wind: palpable, hovering and threatening.

'Will I offer you one of these fine cigars?' volunteered Pat to his silent friends, striving to find some good cheer, anything; 'It is the rare treat to find such fine tobacco in these parts. I bought them only yesterday from a merchantman arrived from Charleston and laden with Sea Island cotton plants for Egypt; her captain vouched that they were Cuban... *the cigars*; there's glory for you! Ain't that the grand pleasure? He - *the Yankee* - declared he had put in here to water and to speak with anyone with knowledge of the war. Of course, I was able to help him in that line... but I regret to say he was never a generous man, he would not budge on the price. I will have you know that I threw all caution to the wind and spent my precious last five shillings to buy them.' Pat persisted, no response from his friends, 'For sure it is an uncommon black day when I can afford only such as these three cigars and nothing more. Here, take one, if you will; I dare say the taste of a such a divine tobacco will answer the case... will do wonders to lift the spirits.' Both Simon and Duncan accepted but with no more than a grunt in response. Still no reply was returned as Pat and both his friends lit up, three billows of smoke erupting. At least - for so Pat contented himself - there was a smile of satisfaction evident in his companions' gaze.

Relapsing into introspection as he enjoyed his own cigar, Pat reminded himself once more that the barky had, thankfully, finished her duty, had done what little that could be done for the doomed defenders of the besieged Greek town of Missolonghi. The end had come when the ship's surgeons and others had been hastily evacuated from the beach, quite literally in the final, frightening minutes before the raging crescendo of blood and terror of the raging Turk army which

21

swept in at the brutal finale of the siege to put the terrified and despairing inhabitants to the sword in a frenzy of slaughter during the fading light of the gloaming. Many massacres had continued all throughout the night against a backcloth of flaming fires and terrifying screaming, the night air filled with unceasing cries for help that would never come; it would forever remain a truly horrific burden within the minds of all who had witnessed it and escaped.

'Sorrs, will 'ee care for coffee?' Murphy's customary whining voice broke the silence, for he was trying his best to lift the languorous mood in the cabin. Pat simply nodded, resigning himself to the absence of sociable exchanges.

Concurrent with the frantic rescue of the ship's surgeons from the beach in small boats and their escape through the surrounding salt lagoons towards a hoped-for sanctuary aboard the barky, a protracted sea chase and duel between *Surprise* and three pursuing Turk frigates had resulted in the first of the Turk ships suffering considerable damage from *Surprise's* guns and falling away from the battle; that was followed by a cataclysmic magazine explosion aboard the second of them, the titanic scale of the eruption prompting the third Turk frigate, until then waiting for an opportunity to engage *Surprise*, breaking off to sail away in apparent retreat, for she had also been previously and partially disabled by the barky's guns, and had struggled to catch up with the pursuit and the eventual final engagement.

The horrifying sight of the huge explosion of the powder magazine and its absolute destruction of the Turk frigate had stunned everyone aboard *Surprise* and her nearby boats who had witnessed it, shocking all to the very core of minds already shattered by prolonged sights of bloody death and widespread destruction; for such dire recollections were the stuff of nightmares for every man aboard, an oppressive mental dark sky which they could not shake off, a persistent and frightening seizure of the mind which would not go away, and likely never would, as many of them, despairing, were reluctantly beginning to realise.

22

Pat's listless thinking wandered back to the present, and he stared at his friends in scrutiny, in concerned evaluation. The customary supper of toasted cheese was long finished and a brace of empty port wine bottles awaited Murphy's collection as the three satiated companions seemingly sat in somnolent anticipation, as if awaiting something, something unexpected, something dangerous, frightening even, to happen; but for minds that had long been immersed in terror, that nothing did happen, nothing at all, seemed so hard to come to terms with, and such confusion blighted all attempts to think positively, constructively, every attempt seemingly thwarted within a mental vacancy, frozen in an uncomfortable hiatus of confusion from which concentration could not break free for more than mere brief moments.

The delectable and fragrant smoke of cigars, a rare treat for many months, permeated the cabin, three butts still smouldering in the ashtray, Murphy's covetous eyes frequently flickering towards them as he continued, unfailingly, to pour coffee, a fresh pot following the first. Occasional discreet glances were directed by all towards friends around the table, seeking the least thing, any vestige of significance, or even of insignificance, to escape sealed lips; but inexorable slow minutes slipped by and not the least murmur disturbed the solitary introspection which filled tired, exhausted minds; indeed, Simon appeared, to Pat's gaze, to have fallen asleep.

'I fear we have been sorely tested... these three years gone,' murmured Pat eventually and in low voice to no one in particular.

'Aye,' declared Duncan, looking up; 'It is the most dreadful of conflicts, for sure, and it strikes hard on the poorest of folk. I cannae conceive of why any person possessing of the least humanity would engage in the terrible slaughter which we have all seen; 'tis the world's pity.'

'Perhaps it is well that war is so... *so terrible*,' Pat sighed deeply, resignation writ large on his face, '... else men might grow fond of it.'

'Reflection is a flower of the mind...' Simon stirred at last from his own somnolence, speaking in little more than a bleak whisper, which carried a world of despond, 'And war is delightful... for those who have no experience of it.'

'We are both coming it the philosopher tonight, Simon,' replied Pat, striving for a warm voice to cheer his friend.

'Not I; would that I might boast a mind of such profound and succinct clarity; Erasmus, it was.'

'Erasmus? I am not familiar with the name. Is he a notable in the medical line... or a friend of yours... from Mull perhaps?'

'Sadly not; I regret to say that I am three centuries too late to make his acquaintance.' Simon's reply brought only a frown from Pat.

With that, the three friends lapsed once more into silence and further contemplation, further words seemingly unappealing to all. Pat, seeking something of distraction from his low spirits, picked up his pen, dipped it into the ink bottle, and looked to his log.

Chapter Two

In the background the soft, soughing noises of a gentle wind brushing against the sails and the rush of the water churned in the frigate's wake were just faintly audible through the gaping, open wounds inflicted upon the stern gallery as *Surprise* ploughed on in her watery furrow, westward towards Malta; for she was, it seemed at last, *truly* homeward bound; and that was the fragile straw which indistinct thoughts clutched so hard to grasp. The customary creaking of the coach partition with the rise and fall of the hull on the most insignificant of wave crests, scarcely more than ripples, was the only other noise to leaven the enduring silence.

Pat sat at his table and scribbled intermittently, the quill scratching with irritating friction on the crisp paper, frequent refreshment at the ink bottle resulting only in expanding blots, each one invariably accompanied by grunts of rising, audible dissatisfaction until, his tiniest of remaining reserves of patience utterly finished and seized by angry exasperation, he ceased writing and hurled the pen to the deck with a loud exclamation which echoed all around the cabin, 'Damn it! Damn it to hell! Enough of such drivel!'

The nearest of his friends, Simon, looked up from his own thoughts with a face visibly filled with a world of concern, which was echoed in his softly-spoken voice, 'Brother, will you care to enlighten us? What troubles you so?'

No reply forthcoming, Duncan leaned forward within his chair to peer closely at Pat, opposite, before turning his head and switching his close gaze towards Simon, staring directly at him. Duncan shook his head very slightly but chose to remain silent, for he knew the unspoken answer, he understood it perfectly well.

Murphy, long-accustomed to the usually more comfortable rites of his revered Captain's table and much used to a customary banter and informality when the three friends were together - a concord which was so markedly absent in the present bleak ambience - stared silently too. He was not an educated man but he was by no means unintelligent; he stood close by, unmoving, pondering, wondering, puzzled; for things were surely not as they seemed. Silence most assuredly did not signify contentment on this occasion. Certainly, there had previously been indications of a welcome satisfaction during supper, perhaps too some tiny signs of relief in the earlier banter across the table during the modest meal; for, he reassured himself once more, the barky *had really finished* with her mission in the hell that was Greece and - Murphy shuddered with the memory - Missolonghi having fallen in an orgy of bloodletting there was no purpose in remaining any longer; and yet, to Murphy's way of thinking, the mental strains, the weight of obligation, the deep sense of fear and all-consuming despond plainly all still lingered in the minds of every person present. Such former blight of spirits that had long persisted had not been sloughed off; that seemed plain to his searching eye. Something of anguish, unspoken, something of a weighty burden, continued to oppress his charges, the tired trio of friends; for Murphy too recognised it without the least doubt and, after the briefest of considerations, he understood, he too saw it with clarity; for the same strange air of doubt, a despond nigh on despair, abounded throughout all the ship despite the relief of quitting the torment and trials of the Greek war; and he wondered with a passion: *when would such gloom be cast off?*

Murphy admitted to himself with a great sigh that he shared the very same disquieting concerns, and the same questions railed against his own efforts to convince himself that the war was in the past: *but was it really the case? Was it the end of sudden death? Was the barky truly now on her way home, home to Falmouth town, to that longed-for sanctuary?* Murphy could only admit to himself that he could not be wholly sure; for something, something deep-rooted within, would not allow him to unreservedly accept it; and he could not understand that, he did not know why such should be so. Certainly, he concluded, he was sure of one thing: it was the very same concern which oppressed his captain. The fighting had been long endured, the barky had been amidst the worst of it for three years, and many shipmates, so many of them valued friends, had been lost; consigned to forgotten, watery graves; most of them simply thrown over the side in great haste during the heat of battle; but now the barky was going home: Home! But no, he could not quite bring himself to truly believe it; nor could he shake off the painful torment of memories. He sighed once again and tried, valiantly, to succour his captain from his obvious dismay with all that he could think of in the moment, 'Well, sorr, will 'ee care for more port... brandy perhaps... or... or I dare say a bottle of whisky might be found?'

Murphy's enquiry, so softly spoken it was scarcely more than a whisper, broke the enduring stare of O'Connor, who looked up and towards his Irish compatriot, a silent minute passing as if a mind of focused concentration could not quite accept the distraction, could not absorb the question. 'Eh? Whisky?'

No more words were forthcoming, none could be found, and Murphy stared with a rising sense of concern verging on distress at his captain, whose shrunken eyes and deeply-lined face betrayed the ingrained fatigue and mental exhaustion so representative of everyone aboard, officers and men alike. Pat had immediately relapsed into silence and allowed his chin to sink back to his chest, another minute elapsing before he spoke again and in a timbre which reverberated with anxiety, even with fear, and there was too a discernible note of horror in his shrieking exclamation, 'DAMN IT! We were lucky... we were so very lucky!'

'To what do you refer?' ventured an alarmed Duncan cautiously in puzzled voice.

Pat stared up, up towards the deckhead, seeing nothing at all, before he replied, 'I think we had the blessing of Saint

Patrick and all the saints to escape those three Turk frigates... and - *to be sure* - all the luck in the world.'

From the far side of the table the diminutive figure of a concerned Doctor Simon Ferguson stared at his friend and interjected in a voice which conceivably strived to project confidence, emphatic assurance, perhaps even a note of command, 'No, no; that is certainly not the case; I beg to contradict you. I have heard the story from Mr Codrington; indeed, Mower and Pickering too are all in accord: you defeated the first opponent with a most skilful engagement in which she shied off, considerably damaged; and subsequently you placed *Surprise* in the most favourable location from which to defend her whilst waiting to rescue Duncan, Marston and I... *and I beg to thank you for that once more*.' Simon raised his voice and spoke with heartfelt emphasis, 'It was *your* actions, *your* resolve and *your* fortitude which saved us and our fellow shipmates from the sack of Missolonghi!' Simon spoke further and with a loud passion, 'And whilst there... waiting for us... you fought and destroyed - *utterly* - the second of the Turk frigates; in fact, I myself witnessed the explosion from the small boat I was in whilst striving to regain the sanctuary of our beloved *Surprise*... and it was a shocking explosion, of such magnitude that it left nothing - *nothing at all* - remaining of the Turk... save for wreckage... for burning fragments... *and bodies... scores of them*... I doubt I will ever forget *that* sight. No man... no captain... *no friend*... could have done better, Patrick O'Connor, and I beg you will hold firm to that thought... and cast aside any other notion; it was not *luck*, it was no such thing!'

'Aye, and the third Turk plainly took fright and fled. There isnae doubt that he didnae fancy his chances against the man he saw fighting that action,' added Duncan with grave emphasis. 'It was quite the famous victory for the barky.'

Pat's eyes flickered as if weighing the merit of his friends' words; he looked first to one and then the other but said nothing.

Simon persevered, 'Our escape from that sad desolation... with the town afire... and beserkers raging throughout the burning streets... would not have resulted without *your* courage... and *your* dedication... to save your shipmates... and whilst we may have enjoyed the blessing of Saint Patrick... *and I will concede that may have been the case...* luck played not the least part in it; none, none whatsoever... and that is plain to the meanest understanding.'

'Aye, and there isnae a man aboard of a different persuasion,' Duncan added in a voice which carried not the least doubt.

Pat hesitated for a minute whilst reflecting until, his thoughts gathered, he spoke in low voice, one which was filled with bitterness and doubt, 'So many men lost... a score and more of the hands wounded... Yet we are no longer facing Boney's fleet, there is no prospect of an invasion... across the Channel... but here we are... in the service of a country which is no more than the disparate fiefdoms of warlords, none of whom seem to be better than brigands; certainly there is no apparent organisation... and we are at sea whilst bereft of any flag and fighting Turks - *TURKS!* Upon my word...' Pat's feelings and voice were rising, '... what will the men think of me were we to face the enemy once more... to fight another such battle... What will our people think, eh?'

'Pat, dear friend,' Duncan spoke up in determined tone, 'You are to consider that before this damnable war there was no national Greek organisation, merely Ottoman provinces; for such as a government takes many years of evolution before an answer emerges; and in *our* province - *at sea* - there was ever little love lost between those separate fleets of Psara, Hydra and Spetses; in fact, there was a deal of skirmishing... *provocations perhaps...* between them when they encountered each other *before the war*. It was nothing of note but certainly exhibited a deal of unpleasantness. Yet now, and despite this void... *this absence of any Greek government...* bereft of an Admiralty and without the least of assured funds, the sailors of all three islands will readily follow Admiral Miaoulis, a

29

Hydriot, and against far greater a fleet that the Greeks can assemble when all together. Hydriots, Spetziots and Psariots will follow that man because he is trusted... respected... *indeed, he is revered...* by all Greek seafarers. *They know* that they possess a great leader, one for whom they will fight battles and risk their lives.... and - *will I say* - so do *our* men, for they all consider themselves followers of that leader whom *they* trust and respect, *which is you.* You are nae Captain Pigot, the deplorable cockalorum that he was, and *Surprise* is nae *Hermione*; indeed, I cannae recall the last flogging aboard *this* barky.'

Silence; several minutes passed without a word from Pat, his friends' compliments seemingly not accepted. From near the door, Murphy stared with a face of abject shock and horror, for nothing of this ilk had ever before been heard in the cabin.

'It is my considered belief, brother, that your apprehensions in respect of any potential concerns of our shipmates are ill-considered; that is to say, *ill-founded*. If you hold to them you are quite mistaken,' ventured Simon; 'Duncan is in the right of things; I am sure of it.' A pause. 'Why, I doubt Nelson himself could have done more to inspire his men.' It was Simon's last throw, but in this he failed, utterly; his quiet words betrayed the hesitancy of his own profound weariness. The cabin fell into silence once more until he spoke up after a minute, 'I venture a pot of coffee may serve... will do all that is required... If you please, Murphy.'

'And perhaps we *will* look to a wee dram of the whisky,' declared Duncan emphatically, looking up once more from his own reflections. In much louder voice, as if trying to lift the general ambience, to drag his friends' spirits out from something akin to depression, he added, 'Aye, I venture there isnae anything better to close the day... 'tis the long night we will be in our cots.'

Murphy, pleased and relieved to receive orders, *any orders*, hastened away after a brief nod towards the table.

'I beg your apology for my ill-temper,' murmured a crestfallen Pat quietly after a minute, looking towards Simon and then Duncan; 'For some time I have been feeling a little hipped... and I have, I confess, sunk into a most uncommon giddy melancholy... and that will serve none of us well; and so I will endeavour to throw off the infernal despond. I thank you most heartedly, both of you, for your warm words; I am in your debt, I am so.'

'Not in the least!' declared Duncan with loud conviction.

'Never in life, soul,' followed Simon. 'It is *we* who are in *your* debt; of that there can be no doubt.'

Pat replied to Simon in quiet voice, 'What are you thinking of... *yourself*? Do tell.'

'Efficacy.'

'Eh?'

'The low efficacy of the lamentable stock of medicines I possess with which to treat the wounded.' Simon spoke with exasperation, 'Lamentably, *and to their enduring shame*, the Sick and Hurt still foists upon us much of physic that is proven useless - *at least to my way of thinking*. One such *concoction,* which Marston enquired of this morning for a man sorely burned about his legs, is Mullins Patent Balm; but there are a whole host of such quack remedies in the medicine chest which the Board persists with... I am reminded of Gregory's Liquid and Carey's Warranted Arrowroot being only two such which have recently been discredited... and as for Mungo's Cordial - another damnable, so-called staple of the medicine chest - such will serve well - *very well* - only those who may be incommoded by those irregularities as may be pertinent to their digestion... *their movements, will I say*... but it is of precious little other use... and we have not a one at present who is so afflicted.'

Pat groaned inwardly, for the remedies mentioned had long been esteemed as potently effective by many of the old hands aboard ship, along with others which were still liberally dispensed on the lower deck and without Simon's sanction, but he managed, with a degree of difficulty, to prevent thought

31

reaching visible expression, 'How are our lads... below... the... the injured?' He found that he could not quite bring himself to utter the term *wounded*, for the very word itself was distressing to even think of; and he wondered, he searched, but without the least success and not for the first time, for why that should be so profoundly difficult in his thinking and for how long such might continue to oppress him.

'My stock of laudanum is replenished... *thankfully*... and there is at least a surfeit of bandage... but I am ever in fear of the prospect for... for the onset of *infection* in wounds... for the more serious cases,' declared Simon in a voice which carried a world of concern; and he added, hastily, 'That is to say, in the case of those most severely set back of our shipmates. I speak not of those unfortunates who have lost a limb... the amputation of which is as easy as kiss my hand... that is to say... procedures with which we are well accustomed to. No, such is perfectly within the capabilities of Michael Marston and myself.... save for the exceptional cases... a leg coming off at the hip... and... *and suchlike...*' Pat and Duncan shuddered and swallowed but said nothing. 'My fears are most particularly for those with chest wounds. In such cases - for Marston and I are ever in fear of infection - *we* are introducing iodine as substitute for the old customaries which are vinegar and wine. Yet I hold a weight of anxiety for such unfortunates and hope - *that precious standby* - that such treatment will prove worthwhile.

Pat reflected upon his original reluctance, three years previously, to countenance a minister of the church coming aboard; indeed, he had been in dread of a devotee of the pulpit sitting at his table, and it was only Simon's influence that had carried the day, had enabled Marston, a friend of Simon and an unbeneficed clergyman, to join the ship's complement. He felt a rush of self-condemnation for his own petty prejudice, for so it now seemed, and he felt obliged to interject with all that he could think of in the tide of coruscating dismay that assaulted his mind, 'Marston is assuredly a most accomplished surgeon.'

'Aye, he is certainly nae tub-thumper,' added Duncan in hopeful reinforcement.

Simon resumed, 'Marston is rarely away from the cockpit... Jason too... and they are ever at the cots with comforting words and with what little else we can offer...' Simon's voice tailed off, '... but I confess that I do not entirely share Marston's faith and perfect conviction that the Lord will help those particular unfortunates.'

Simon's bleak and halting litany of his own despair plunged everyone back into solitary reflection and more silence, neither Pat nor Duncan able to comment in the cruel moment of the cold reminder that many of their longstanding shipmates remained in the most acutely painful physical discomfort as well as suffering that burden which was the mental distress that all aboard so stoically endured.

Ten minutes passed before the loud, perhaps deliberate, crash back of the cabin door which announced Murphy's return. Tired faces lifted and weary eyes looked with a degree of intrigue towards the silver plate with the finest crystal glass tumblers that Pat possessed upon it. They were set down upon the table by Murphy with resounding determination, the whisky bottle swiftly uncorked with an almost ceremonial flourish, and bountiful measures of a generosity never before seen in the cabin were poured with not a moment lost, and an astounded Pat choked back his remonstrations as the whisky perilously neared the rim in each case.

'Bumpers it is!' declared Duncan with satisfaction.

Three hands tentatively gripped brimming glasses, carefully drawing them through the gentle rise and fall of the deck towards awaiting mouths. Rekindled red eyes and somnolent, fatigued minds for the first time appreciated the gesture that was Murphy's benevolent purpose.

All raised their glass as Pat offered the anticipated Sunday toast in heartfelt voice, a tidal wave of brutal memories, both recent and painful, instantly surging to the fore for all; acid bile was rising in a flood tide of unwelcome anxieties, 'Absent friends!'

'And those at sea!' Duncan added in a louder, most emphatic voice. The whisky, fiery that it was, fiercely burned throats as it went down with glorious ritual and determination; not that anyone could down it in one, the excessive measure that it was; indeed, Simon was wracked by coughing for a minute until Murphy passed his coffee cup.

The familiar and following coffee was well received, in small fashion bestowing a modicum of normality, of blessed relief even. Tentative smiles were offered across the table as the three friends clutched once more for the smallest straw of normality. More silent minutes passed in thoughtful reflection, the toast to absent friends so deeply resonating in wounded minds; and then Pat's ears unexpectedly caught the faint drift of music, the gentlest of strings, the delightful sound so seemingly incongruous in the poignant moment, the music wafting as if some ethereal, acoustic zephyr from beyond the coach. 'Murphy... the music?' he ventured.

'Well, 'tis Mr Marston, sorr... and Mr Mower be with him; they be abaft the helm, near the rail.'

Pat's face brightened; 'I see; then perhaps it's time for us to take the air. Gentlemen, what do you say?' Pat's apparent and unexpectedly rapid uplift in spirit and his suggestion were seemingly very well received; Duncan and Simon were nodding emphatically, and both immediately rose from their chairs. Without further ado the three friends walked out through the coach to the companionway and stepped up to the quarterdeck where all turned about to stare towards the foc'sle, into the near sunset, as if to take stock, a little of the warmth of the day still lingering. All were immediately appreciative of the gentle air current about their heads, something of a cool and refreshing saviour.

The early evening light was subdued but the low sun was still bright below the main and fore courses on the larboard bow, the radiant bright globe beginning to settle in its graceful descent, as if about to kiss the surface of the sea at the far distant horizon. The movement of the deck was gentle, insignificant in that moment; the faint breeze bestowed the most innocuous of lee heel, near indiscernible, upon the ship; so much so that the scene before them, the absolute tranquillity of it, was hard to accept; and it only slowly registered as such after several slow minutes staring, whilst its benign embrace slowly infiltrated long-distressed minds which were still tortured and afflicted by the most brutal and horrific of experiences; and then came the moment, the instant of realisation: the surging floodtide of relief was tangible, powerful, all-engulfing: Greece and the bloody war really was in the past and, at last, that flash of understanding struck home, like a mental hammer blow upon the mind, as a sudden and wholly overwhelming catharsis; and the three friends stood transfixed. No words could be found; it was plain to all that none could conceivably be adequate for such a sublime moment; and so they simply stared at each other as if seeking much-needed mutual confirmation; but, as a further minute trickled by, the precious wash of rescue, of relief, receded a very little; but there remained in the visible gaze of uncertain eyes a recognition of engrained, deep discomfort, a raw residue of torment, an understanding that three minds alike were still troubled; and that was an equally profound and shocking comprehension.

'Well, sorr, Mr Marston sends his compliments,' Murphy's familiar voice interjected, most pointedly, to rescue his charges from their obvious locus of dismay; '... and would 'ee care to join him? That is to say... if you are at leisure.'

'What? What was that, Murphy?' mumbled Pat, his focus still upon Simon who stood, immobile, one arm around the mainmast and staring at the sunset. The sun was ever lower, as if falling into the sea on the western horizon, despite which the heat lingered even so late in the day, and Pat felt it in the sweat on his brow, his shirt already become exceedingly damp and sticking with determination to his back.

'Mr Mower, sorr, aft... at the rail... and will 'ee care to play music with him?'

'With all my heart!' exclaimed Pat, a rising sense of relief stirring within him.

Duncan, the most resilient of men, interjected, 'Aye, I will... with pleasure. I found an old tin whistle... *a flageolet*... in Argostoli before we departed. Simon, what do you say? Will we make our attempt upon music?'

'That is an excellent notion,' murmured Simon somewhat vacantly, his mind also striving to focus; 'Indeed, I rather think we will. Yes, yes... certainly; a better notion cannot be imagined. Murphy, bear a hand there; be so kind as to fetch our instruments from the cabin. Here, up here, in the air, in the fresh air... I am sure we will play... *play well*... here... upstairs.'

Duncan was already stepping aft, around the gratings and so to the helm, where he acknowledged Barton's knuckle at his forehead and his cheerful greeting, 'Evening, sir,' with a broad smile and a nod as he strived to find again something of that so precious feeling of relief.

The master, Jeremiah Prosser, was more emphatic with his greetings to Simon and Pat; 'Good evening, sirs! All's well, she's making near five knots, and nothing to report.' Pat, who was trailing his friends and still beset by a degree of uncertainty, nodded vacantly but could find no words.

Only the upper half of the distant sun remained visible above the horizon as the trio reached the stern rail, both Marston and Mower rising from the tea chests upon which they had been sitting to greet them with broad smiles and effusive words of welcome. The three friends at last replied in good voice, for they were determined to reach for and grasp every conceivable comfort, for the least thing that precious company, benevolent words and a delight in music might afford them. Within minutes three chairs were fetched from the cabin by Freeman, and Murphy presented Pat's 'cello and Simon's viola.

'Mr Marston, this is an unexpected but surely pleasant turn of events,' declared Pat cautiously, gathering his sensibilities and with the beginnings of a smile, his right hand caressing the body of the 'cello in his lap, his left fingers already at the pegbox, a small sense of routine, of familiarity, the merest hint of a pleasure, near-forgotten, all dawning within his mind; 'What do you propose that we play?'

'Sir, do you recall our attempts upon the work gifted to me by Paganini in Genoa... when we were there to visit Lord Byron? We endeavoured to grasp the makings... *the essentials...* of the composition... on New Year's eve.'

'Certainly, I do; and it is the most beautiful piece; it is so. There is a deal of... *of body... substance...* in it, a powerful plenty; as was certainly the case with that man. Oh, how I would love to hear him play once more... such a delight, so greatly moving; it is a sure thing that even the very thought will ever bring tears to my eyes. I am sure we will find his music again... *in Heaven.* I wonder: will we be so fortunate as to hear his playing again *in this life?*' Not a word of reply was forthcoming from anyone present, for all were much taken aback by the contemplative nature of the remarks from the stoic man they were accustomed to. The pause, an expectant vacancy, registered with Pat, and so he resumed in firmer voice, 'I dearly hope so. But surely our... *our unfamiliarity with it...* it's complexity... will be our undoing?'

'Not at all, sir. Mr Mower and I have enjoyed many an hour striving to master it, and we have devised several variations for the paucity of our orchestra. It is, as you may recall, a piece written - *in C* - for a trio of viola, 'cello and guitar... and we are surely blessed with all such instruments being present for the first time.' Mower nodded in emphatic encouragement and Marston pressed on, 'I will substitute for the viola with my violin until Dr Ferguson introduces his instrument... perhaps in harmony with the violin... at least to begin with.' Simon stared and nodded, a degree of interest registering within his own discomforts. Marston continued, 'I have transcribed the music upon these sheets.' Marston passed them round, each pinned to a shard of broken tea chest, and each man placed one upon his knee.

Pat looked doubtful but strived to reply as best he might, 'Doubtless it is an excellent idea, a... *an admirable notion*; yes, very well. I do recall the... *the basis* of the piece, if my memory does not deceive me. Please, give the note. Wait! Murphy, be so kind as to bring us a lamp from the coach... and stand above us; you may attend and...' Pat actually grinned, '... and with the blessing of Saint Patrick you may even enjoy our endeavours.' Pat smiled again and even Murphy managed a weak grin.

'Brother, will we long have light enough to read the music sheets?' Simon still held to his hesitations; that was plain for all present to see.

Pat put his hand on his friend's shoulder and smiled, 'Firelight - *or moonlight for that matter* - will not let you read fine stories, but it's warm, it's entirely satisfactory, and you won't see the dust on the floor.'

'Your grandma, no doubt?'

Pat nodded and smiled. 'We will make our best endeavours... and that will content us; I'm sure of it.'

The sun finally blinked out its farewell, but the western sky remained filled by the brightest, the most vividly radiant, red to pink afterglow, a most spectacular illumination which filled the whole horizon from north to south, capturing the attention of everyone on deck, all marvelling at the glorious panorama, five more minutes passing with everyone silently enraptured and enjoying the still-lingering small warmth whilst the dusk light lasted. The wake was faintly audible in the background, the creaking of the rigging was near indiscernible to minds long accustomed to it; and the occasional slap of the sails, under the lightest of loads, offered not the least distraction as a silent Pat stared intently with lingering hesitation into the darkling sky, all the while wondering if, perhaps, it signified in some grand fashion that the curtain had truly and finally come down on the violent horrors of the Greek venture.

For several minutes the invited string musicians rubbed the familiar rosin block on their long-unused bows, each man looking to his fellows as if waiting for someone to take the lead, a hesitation lingering as if akin to uncertainty, almost a wavering of conviction: *was music truly appropriate to the*

38

moment? It was Simon, resolution and determination firming within his mind, who eventually broke the ice and prompted the ensemble, 'Gentlemen, let us avail ourselves of what small benefit we may gain from the twilight before it entirely fails us. Will we begin?'

Marston, an exceptionally talented violinist, began to play, slowly at first, exhibiting an intense concentration as he delivered the unhurried but flowing notes with great accomplishment; for by any measure he was himself verging on the skill of a maestro. Within a few seconds Mower followed with the subdued but smooth strings of his guitar, adding a soft rhythm, an audible comfort of secondary reinforcement in the background, complementing the classical brilliance of Marston. A few seconds more passed before Pat, marvelling at and delighting in the sounds so unexpectedly presented to him, made his tentative attempt upon the composition, his 'cello bringing a low foundation, an anchor even, in subtle contrast with the other two instruments but without the least conflict as he restrained the volume so as to accord with the violin in perfect harmony. Both Marston and Mower nodded to him in recognition of his contribution, so greatly pleasing to the ear of all the musicians.

Enthralled, Simon simply observed and marvelled; the wash of small pleasure rising within him seemed so incongruous after the dreadful tribulations of recent weeks, for the sound of music had become almost alien to him; but he studied his sheet even as he listened with rising fascination, discreetly glancing at the musicians from time to time: *was Pat, his closest friend in all the world, relaxing for the first time in many months?* Despite the picture of absolute concentration on Pat's face, his vigorous fingering and bowing, so visibly all-consuming, that did seem to be the case, as Simon, still unmoving himself, discerned whilst observing; and he began to slowly rejoice, for that profound thought, that tiny glimmer of his friend's relief, was deeply moving, hugely significant and all-important to him in that moment; and, the unexpected pleasure that it was, the feeling slowly blossomed until it subsumed within it every fibre of his concentration, his very being; and so he sat, utterly immobile, mute in blessed relief, with tears forming in his eyes, blinking rapidly in a vain attempt to dispel them even as they began dribbling down his cheeks, and he stared in abject fascination.

From the corner of his eye Marston was pleased to see that Freeman had returned once more after a brief return to the cockpit, and he too seemed to be much enjoying the music. It was a joy to all to see him, away from his wounded charges and taking pleasure, and surely also respite, in the rare, precious moment.

Pat had waited a long time for Simon to join in, many quick glances ventured towards his friend, still immobile and merely watching, until Pat prompted him with a gentle toe, a nod and a smile, which lifted Simon's heart in an instant, sent his spirits soaring; and with a surging sensation of happiness he opened his own endeavours, resolutely following Marston's lead, the sweeter-sounding viola and the delightfully mellow violin coming together as near seamless twins of harmony as the music slowed for the opportunity for all to re-establish an accord, a concurrency, which was achieved after scarcely a minute more.

As time passed by and the competency of the musicians incrementally exerted its influence over the playing, a rising consolidation was found by them all, until they had firmly mastered the glorious, musical masterpiece and the intentions of its creator. The music had also seized the attention of most of the crew, and a large crowd had gathered on the quarterdeck, their faces revealing that the aural infusion was very welcome, had seemingly or at least momentarily dislodged the longstanding and engrained spectres of fear within their own seared minds; for at least two score of them practised with an instrument, at least a pipe or a fiddle; and thrice that many enjoyed singing, even if it was only the familiar old shanties.

With a rising sense of joy, all of this background scene of widespread satisfaction amongst their audience registered with the musicians, and so they played on, more precious minutes passing in great pleasure as diversions upon variations flowed; and, as the former, glorious radiance in the western skies eventually faded to leave only the faintest remnant of pink remainder low across the horizon before the foc'sle, the lingering vestiges of dusk light finally faded; but Murphy's close attendance with the lamp continued to illuminate the music sheets and the concentration on the close faces of the musicians, all of them utterly focused on and striving with determination to play more of Paganini's marvel as best they could; indeed, their efforts were perfectly satisfactory, were all that was necessary; an oasis of relief had been found; and so the string trio played on and on, for another half-hour into the deepening darkness, for the sublime ambience on the quarterdeck was gathering an intensity which had plainly gripped them all. Duncan, utterly absorbed, had long cast off all fears of intruding with his shrill flageolet and was contributing as he thought fit, all caution cast aside, adding an extra dimension to the paragon which Paganini had never conceived of.

The enduring breeze from across the stern rail ruffled hair, which passed unnoticed; the gentle rise and fall of the deck was scarcely discernible; and the quiet background noises from the helmsmen and the crew gathering were all ignored as the musicians revelled in the wondrous pleasure, so gratefully found. Clumsy Dalby, on duty, had been halted by Sampays from ringing the bell throughout the last dog watch, and so time slipped by in blissful serenity, every man on duty and formerly working on deck having suspended all work tasks to sit on deck as quietly as quietly could be to enjoy the rare and precious event.

For all present, the simple delights discovered in the rising and falling notes were so utterly beatific for minds long accustomed to the most dreadful and bloody horrors, witnessed over many months and never to be forgotten; but now, in the sublime relief found in the music, something profound had registered in stricken minds; something beautiful was here before them, within their grasp, and not a man wished the music to ever reach its end; and so the musicians played on and on, until the sheet was eventually forgotten as further and increasingly reckless improvisations followed more undreamed-of variations. String fingers had long become sore when the last feeble glimmer of the dusk light was long gone and the Argand lamp was guttering, running low on oil. A very few more minutes of rising volume followed, a vigorous crescendo was reached, the four friends seizing what joy might be found in the lingering last moments, all persons present so very reluctant to let go the blessed solace, until the music finally ended as the lamp too expired to leave the quarterdeck in momentary silence, in near complete darkness save for the merest scintilla of light from the new moon; and everyone present was simply overwhelmed in a flood tide of absolute relief; and for long seconds, as the majesty of their achievement dawned on shattered minds, no one was able to speak a single word.

The silence endured only momentarily, until a delighted Pat looked up and towards the wheel to see near two hundred men of the crew, all staring, fascinated, having been in thrall to the music; and then came the loud applause, every man hurriedly rising to his feet to deliver a barrage of frenetic hand-clapping, foot stamping and joyous shouts of greeting, which went on for a full five minutes, unceasing, the crew too basking in the mood of salvation; until Pat, the broadest of smiles radiant on his face, a great weight lifted from his mind, raised his hand and waved to his veteran shipmates, to his valued friends, to his much esteemed and precious band of brothers.

All the musicians, similarly delighted, rose from their chairs to exchange the warmest of compliments over vigorous handshakes, with which they persisted for more minutes, every man loathe to forego that precious moment of salvation which they had found in their playing and in their companionship, a reminder of the value and the very precious nature of deep-rooted friendship throughout adversity; and still the applause persisted, until the musicians bowed to the audience, another loud 'HURRAH!' erupting.

A delighted Murphy busied about, all the while talking to himself, shifting chairs, and seizing Simon and Pat's instruments lest they fall to the deck to be damaged. Eventually, and in a great babble of happy chatter, Pat shouted out in loud voice, 'THANK YOU! THANK YOU ALL! But now we must quit this hullabaloo. Back to work... to your hammocks! Until the morrow!'

The crew gathering dissipated and the musicians retreated at Pat's invitation to the great cabin, Murphy in close attendance. The whisky tumblers were swiftly replenished and something of a more tolerable ambience was discovered, was gratefully embraced, and such persisted as all endeavoured to converse, to stimulate conversation, the most innocuous of enquiries gratefully received, every effort made to perpetuate the salvation from torment that the music had delivered.

Another comfortable hour passed in precious mental recuperation until all were visibly tiring, when Pat rose from his chair and looked to his friends, a few final words offered to bring the evening to an end, 'Gentlemen, I am embarrassed to say that I was reflecting upon my earlier, most miserable spell of puling at supper.'

'Nae matter, the day is done,' Duncan responded, 'And - *will I say* - the splendid music has set us up for the morrow.'

'I am entirely of your opinion; we will praise the good day at the close of it,' replied Pat. 'But now, I believe that sleep is nigh upon me and I must turn in. Thank you all again for your musical accompaniment this evening; it was most agreeable... and has done wonders for my own spirits. Good night, dear friends... all of you, for you are all such.'

Chapter Three

Hour after restful hour of uninterrupted, further sailing from Cephalonia throughout a peaceful day of lassitude for all aboard, and *Surprise,* despite boasting aloft a splendid array of every sail, every stitch of canvas, she still possessed, was making little more than four knots across a placid sea, propelled by the gentlest of easterly *Levanters.* The topgallants and studding sails, no more than a triumph of optimism on the part of Pat, periodically announced their ease with an occasional flutter of canvas edges under the lightest of loads. The sun, a warming friend since breakfast, was once more sinking low in its lingering descent towards the western horizon, the orange orb shimmering through the haze of the varying heat strata directly before the bow. The slowest of days was approaching its eventual end, little time remaining before the temporal finality of sorts that the sunset would soon dictate; the pleasurable consolation for weary men being that perfect tranquillity which was the soft dusk light whenever it succeeded a rare day for the crew without any event of the least note, for which all aboard were in recent times more than profoundly grateful.

Duncan Macleod, on duty, stood close to the helm as a silent, thoughtful Lieutenant Mower arrived to spell him as four bells rang out, and the shouts of 'All's well' came back from the several hands-on lookouts in relatively subdued voice, the scene before them one of exceptional quietude. No words were offered by Mower save for a brief and murmured 'Good evening, sir,' but Macleod, his curiosity piqued, asked in gentle voice, 'Mr Mower, how are *you* faring these days?'

'All is well with myself, sir, thank you. I have been in contemplation of Falmouth town... whilst enjoying the day... a most pleasant day of slow vespering; and I much delight in a sunset of such serenity as this one seems to be. And you, sir?'

'Aye, the sunset is ever the grandest of pleasures to behold, for sure it is. In fact, I am minded that were we to be gazing upon the smallest islet, the merest rock... on the bow... then I might myself even believe that I was gazing upon distant Hirta from my namesake's *MacLeod's Stone* on Harris. Harris... *my home*... aye, *home*... the precious notion that it is... at least for most of us.'

'No sir, *for all of us*,' replied Mower emphatically; 'Most certainly so. We have all indulged our thoughts of home, *our dreams of it, we have*; and I have no doubt that you have too.'

'Aye, I will admit that is the case,' Macleod conceded gracefully. 'Are you still about poetry, may I ask?'

Mower was the ship's poet. 'I am, sir. Would you care to hear my recent poem? It is about *home... going home;* and it is also inspired by my voyages aboard this vessel... with these men of Falmouth. It is my most earnest endeavour to approach the talents of William Wordsworth, that most splendid of poets. You may be acquainted with him?'

'He is not familiar to me, Mr Mower; I confess I am more accustomed to the works of Rabbie Burns; but, please, continue.'

'I have studied his works these two years gone... and I would like to believe that my own modest effort has something of a poor resemblance... is something which I hope is near akin to his wondrous ilk... *but perhaps I deceive myself?*'

'Never in life, Mr Mower; please, proceed.'

Mower retrieved a small paper from his pocket and, as the helmsmen leaned closer and Macleod nodded encouragingly, he began to read,

> *'I voyaged long amongst Falmouth's men,*
> *To distant lands, far o'er the wildest sea;*
> *Few firm friends did I hold 'til then,*
> *A great many and true, they became to me.*

Amidst the fright and fear of battles fought,
Amongst the roar of bright, flaming guns,
Ne'er more a brother was e'er found or sought,
More stalwart than Falmouth's own true sons.

Homeward bound and Biscay's perils far behind!
Yet fretful hearts will ne'er forget the bitter cost;
Amidst anxious thoughts of what we may yet find,
When we tell of precious friends that we have lost.

Into the sanctuary of the Fal! Our day is near done;
Nearing home, to warm hearths and families dear;
Bloody battles fought, and victories won;
Goodbye! Farewell! We take our leave of fear.'

The helmsmen, who had by now edged as close as close could be to Mower, the wheel near abandoned save for Barton's hand on one spoke, listened with fascination. In the quietude which was the soft light of the last minutes before the true dusk, the ship moving within a perfect tranquillity and scarcely a sound of note save for an occasional slap of the sail edges to disturb the steady, gentle wash of the stern wake, every man about the quarterdeck was captivated and listened most attentively, all nodding silently as Mower continued.

'And now, wide eyes search in twilight's fading light,
With precious hope and anxious hearts of love;
As the darkling cedes to that infinity of night,
Bright stars so splendid in the Heavens above.

At last! Behold Falmouth town, a joy to see;
A welcome vision under the soft moon light;
No more the dread and fears of what might be;
Thanks be to God, we have left behind the fight!

The anchors hold fast, the dawn is come upon us;
The tide washes upon the pebbles on the shore,
As the boats disgorge into the welcome crush,
Of the waiting throng, calling out a wondrous roar.

A host of anxious families awaiting on the quay;
Home at last, and cherished dreams are realised!
Grasping arms, joy everywhere so wonderful to see;
Tears too, for brothers lost, as together we cried.'

From a dozen men who had gathered about the helm, Wesleyans for the most part, there rose a quiet chorus, 'Amen'.

'You have been cultivating a secret talent for the poetic word, Mr Mower, and it is flowering... blooming even. You write very well and with an admirable construction; I congratulate you.' Despite the lingering warmth in the air Macleod shivered and sighed before resuming in a voice of dismay, 'But I am reminded of Captain O'Connor's words; you may recall that he spoke with praise for another of your poems, but did not greatly care for its final verse; and nor do I for this one, for it is a reminder - *an unwelcome one* - of those many men - *poor souls* - who have been lost to us these three years gone. Plainly, it is a burden on your mind... *as... as it is on mine.* Thankfully we have left behind... *that place*... and I most fervently hope ... *I hope* that no more of our wounded shipmates will be lost to us.'

'Our trust is with Dr Ferguson, sir,' declared Mower, 'and with Father Michael,' swiftly adding, 'That is to say, *with Mr Marston.*'

Macleod scratched his stubbled chin as he reflected on the young Lieutenant's words; certainly, he could not recall anyone aboard ever previously referring to Marston with such reverence as had Mower just then in referring to him as *Father Michael.* He wondered: *was everyone aboard now so greatly affrighted, so set back and praying for the wounded?*

The sun blinked out as if in reluctant farewell to leave behind a great stillness, as if time itself was left hanging in the sky, akin to an ambient presence which seemed loathe to depart; yet a dark blue dusk persisted as the ringing out of eight bells signified the end of the last dog watch. It reminded Macleod of Pat's invitation to join his two close friends later in the cabin. There was yet a precious hour to spare, and so he determined to take the opportunity to visit his wounded shipmates and his friend, Simon Ferguson, in the cockpit. With a smile and a nod to Mower, he slowly descended the companionway to the lower deck, his introspective thoughts shifting to a concern for the sick, wounded and incapacitated. The darkness below was striking, even compared with the low light of the gloaming, and Macleod stumbled forward in the gloom until, his eyes gradually adjusting, he drew back the dividing curtain to enter the cockpit where he could make out in the weak light of the lamps the surgeons, Simon Ferguson with Michael Marston, attending the wounded, an uncomfortable score of unfortunates, their discomfort instantly discernible amidst the low groans of men stoically enduring their pain.

Marston was the ship's chaplain and assistant surgeon; in both roles he had been a tower of strength during the most difficult of times in Greece; on occasion he had spoken with words of comfort to support both Pat and Simon in their spells of extreme anguish and through their many hours of bleak despond. He was sitting on a tea chest alongside the cot of a wounded man, clutching his hand and speaking to him in a low voice.

Macleod slowly stepped closer until he recognised the patient. Not wishing to interrupt the chaplain, he beckoned to Simon, and both of them stepped outside of the cockpit. 'How are you doing?' asked Duncan.

'As well as might be expected,' murmured Simon without the least enthusiasm.

'And Marston?'

'That man is the treasure of the world; I could not, myself, long endure without him... down here, in this locus of distress... *in this pit of despair*.' Simon's voice was little more than a whisper as he continued, 'He is attending Kitto; you may recall that he was struck down in the conflagration off... *off Oxia Island*... when O'Connor was waiting for you and I... and others... to escape Missolonghi.'

'Is Kitto in peril?' asked Duncan in nervous voice; 'I have sailed with that man for ten years and more. Dear God forbid we will lose him! Why, he joined *Tenedos* on the very day that I did. We came aboard in the same jolly boat... I remember it well.'

'I confess I cannot be sure of his prospects.'

'Are any others of our shipmates in... in danger?'

'Hammett is the man I most fear for,' Simon's voice and his face assumed a deep dismay.

'Hammett?' Duncan groaned, 'Another of our *Tenedos* veterans... I am mortal cast down to hear that he is... is...' but his words failed him and he could find nothing more.

A tired Macleod eventually stepped through the coach and knocked on the cabin door, entering on Pat's shout. Simon was already seated at the table as Duncan took his chair. Murphy and Freeman were busying about their charges, pouring red wine until the waiting glasses were near brim-full, a bowl of walnuts lingering beneath Murphy's covetous eyes; another and larger one was well concealed within the cabinets reserved for the musical instruments at the stern gallery. The whisperings of conversation were little more than desultory, certainly nothing of amicable discourse on any subject at all until eventually, a regrettable meld of hunger and ill-temper prompting him, supper being uncommonly late, Pat called out in a voice which scarcely concealed his rising ire, 'Murphy, do you suppose there might be something to eat this evening? We cannot long endure solely on liquor! Are you now about the supper? I recollect that there was mention of a fine steak and kidney pudding... these two hours gone, or am I much astray?'

'Well, sorr, 'tis near ready at the galley... so Wilkins says.'

'Cut along and find out! I am as hungry as a horse; no, not at all... *horses ain't in it!*' barked Pat, acerbically, before he turned to his friends; 'I confess I did not take dinner... Murphy said it was lobscouse... the damnable concoction that

49

it was when it reached my table... burned... yes, *burned it was*... and quite ruined. I tossed it over the side from my quarter-gallery.'

'What was it? May I ask?' enquired Simon, rather disinterestedly.

'Eh? *What was it?* I venture it was nothing more than rotten millers... *rats*; *yes, rats!* For such is how it looked and... *and smelt*. Sure, there was a poor disguise of pickles... or something resembling pickles... red peppers and suchlike... swimming in a sea of vinegar.' Pat grimaced, 'I wager there is not a man aboard the barky who would have eaten the execrable swill in preference to the cook's slush.'

'Not a dish commensurate with Wilkins's customary abilities, might one say?' Simon ventured tentatively.

'Anyone might be minded that Wilkins had fallen overboard after breakfast... I will say I ain't seen him since,' declared Pat.

'He remains aboard, but the man has suffered quite the tumble; he was taken to his hammock after falling over... and... and striking his head upon the stove in the kitch... *the galley*,' explained Simon.

'Falling over! Over what, tell?' enquired Pat, his curiosity piqued and overtaking his ill-temper.

'I believe he mentioned the ship's goat. Seemingly, she was tethered to the stove and awaiting milking when she discovered the meal which Wilkins had prepared for your dinner.'

'Aye,' Duncan interjected, 'it was a famous Strasburg Pie... and quite delicious; I confess I enjoyed a... will I say... *significant* portion afore the goat found it... cooling on the stove.'

'What? You ate my dinner?' exclaimed Pat, his exasperation rising to new heights. 'You mean to say, the truth is out?'

'Not at all, nae...' Duncan could hardly hold back his laughter, 'There was a great quantity left... aye, plentiful enough for six portions at least... even after my own dinner...

but Wilkins stepped away for a moment, and then Mildred espied the pie, and it was overset upon the deck... and she ate the lot... not even a crumb remained at the end... *for so Murphy said.*' Simon joined in with Duncan's laughter, both men much enjoying Pat's discomfort.

'The damnable animal!' Pat swore.

'Let us not condemn the creature that found something better than her customary ration,' spluttered Simon with difficulty between further bouts of loud laughter; 'After all, it is a commonplace conduct for all of us aboard this vessel, is it not? Indeed, I put it to you: who would refuse fresh-baked bread for aged ship's biscuit... infested with weevils...' Simon was revelling in the rare moment of humour, 'Allow me to develop the notion further and postulate: who would forsake prime, lean roast beef, steaming hot, for a bowl of greasy lobscouse... its overcooked meat more akin to fat... amidst the fried onions and failed disguise of hot pepper and spices?' Simon and Duncan laughed aloud again.

'If Wilkins was in his hammock and the goat had eaten all in sight, then... *who cooked my dinner*, the foul swill that it was?' demanded Pat, his bad temper not mollified in the least by the explanation and the laughter, which irritated him further.

'Murphy it was,' Duncan roared again with laughter, 'Aye, he rose to the occasion!' Simon laughed too, tears in his eyes.

'Murphy? Murphy!' exclaimed Pat. 'Why the man struggles to make the simplest of dishes... even the toasted cheese is oft ruined. All is now clear! The vile filth which he presented as my dinner... it was Murphy, *the knave, the accursed rogue!* I am in contemplation of the lash... twelve strokes will serve him out!'

'Pat, I need hardly suggest...' said Simon, controlling his mirth with difficulty, 'that it is ill-considered to castigate the man for his well-intentioned endeavours... for your personal interests... the timely preparation of your own comestibles; indeed, I am minded that he is no fainéant.'

'Eh? Fainéant? The man is an idling scoundrel!'

The debate on Murphy's merits or lack thereof was halted by the reappearance of the very rogue in question, the steward entering the cabin in something of an air of triumph, burdened with a large tray from which bountiful clouds of steam and scintillating aromas arose, filling the air and teasing the nose, a most delightful picture presented to the eye as it was placed on the table by the steward who endeavoured to do so with a theatrical flourish. 'Well, sorrs, here it be!' declared Pat's villain in loud voice. Freeman, following, set down the plates and cutlery.

'Praise be to Saint Patrick,' called out Pat in loud voice; 'Murphy, must we presume that Wilkins is back at the helm - *the galley?*'

'Well, he is so... this past hour, sorr.'

'Bless him! And thank the Lord, Mary and all the Saints!' declared Pat, recovering a modicum of patience and goodwill for his countryman. 'By God this looks to be a famous pudding. Here, Duncan, allow me to cut you a small portion - *a very small one!*' Pat laughed out loud for the first time. 'Doubtless you enjoyed your fill at dinner.' He laughed again. 'Simon!' added Pat, licking the gravy from his fingers as he cut again through the suet pastry crust with rising enthusiasm, 'This is uncommon delicious; here, take this, a goodly plate of pie. Oh, for a bottle or two of good London porter to wash it down, eh?'

The trio of friends tucked in with gusto, with occasional compliments about Wilkins, with praise for the pie and even for the red wine, a Greek one that had formerly attracted no more than scathing opprobrium and comparisons with vinegar, notwithstanding that the lower deck readily embraced their own seven pints per week of it. Further helpings of the pie were offered by Pat with his remark that, 'There ain't any sweet pudding to follow.' The further portions were liberally dispensed and all at the table confirmed their approval most emphatically when an attentive Murphy substituted the sour red wine with port wine. With boundless enthusiasm the tray of pie remnants was once more severely ravaged, and consequently dwindled to scarcely a mouse's serving, much to Murphy's disgust and disappointment.

'Will you tell of your plans, Duncan... your dreams perhaps?' Simon ventured the first mention of a future, one which he himself hoped would be far away from recent times and violent places.

'Aye, my plans... *my dreams...*' Macleod spoke slowly as if he could not come to terms with talking of such; 'My dreams are of my croft in Harris, with my dear wife, Kathleen...' He halted briefly, 'I hope that her consumption has relented, for I am in fear of what I may yet find upon my return...' Another momentary pause, a few seconds of introspection, and a thoughtful Macleod spoke further, 'I dream of time with her and with my precious daughter, Brodie... striding o'er the machair amidst the scent of the heather... with easel and pencils... even with paints, perhaps; aye, for the landscape is bleak... scant of the least thing, save for the stag... and the clear light of the dawn and the dusk there is quite the marvel of the world...' Duncan's face fell and his voice dropped to a whisper, '... and on a fine morning, when the sun shines... when the cloud lifts and the wind withers away to a blessed nothing, I confess the place reaches deep into my soul; it does so...'

Pat stared, mute; for nothing of such poetry had he ever heard from Duncan before; it was something of an unexpected revelation. His friend continued, perhaps sensing his dear companions were set back, and he strived for a humorous note, '... but I dinnae care to contemplate any return to sea... save... *perhaps...* in a skiff... and with the notion of catching a brace of salmon for dinner.'

'A delightful prospect, no doubt,' acknowledged Simon quietly, digesting Duncan's heartfelt sentiments; 'And yourself, Patrick O'Connor; will you describe your own intentions... *your aspirations?*'

Pat smiled, a sight his friends were pleased to see, and he spoke up in buoyant voice, 'Oh, no doubt Sinéad will see me looking to the potatoes and cutting the turf from our wet acres of peat bog!' He laughed, and his friends, their spirits rising, laughed with him. 'I have long held a particular dream... I have so... I too am fishing... with my son Fergal... at sea aboard a Galway hooker, one which I have long preserved in a shed near the Cleggan quay; and we are out on a grand summer's day... to the waters around Inishbofin and Inishark. Did I tell you my grandma hailed from 'Shark? In fact, she is buried there...' A thoughtful hesitation, 'She has been much in my dreams these recent months... a rare diversion from more pressing matters... and so too has the island.' A moment's reflection, 'I have always believed it is the most wonderful of all the places I have ever visited... indeed, I venture it is the treasure of the world. I remember... in my childhood summers... when I was a mere stripling - *younger than the youngest midshipman* - and I landed upon the island for the first time on a glorious summer day... and I enjoyed my grandma's mutton for dinner - a feast it was, or so I thought - and I believed that Heaven would be much like 'Shark... such a homely... homely...' Pat's words tailed off for a few moments as he reflected on his dream. His voice and his face fell as he spoke again, 'But I must not bless the fish until it gets to land.' Another few seconds and he resumed in a deliberately warm tone directed towards his friend, 'Simon, what of you? What of *your* plans, eh? I dare say you have been thinking of home... perhaps too *in your dreams?*'

'I am in hope that we will get home... to Tobermory... without the loss of a deal of time, such that I may strike an accommodation with my landlord; and Flora - *Mrs MacDougall* - and I will see the repair of the roof of my - *our* - home when I return. Unfortunately, of late there has been a paucity of news from home... from Mrs MacDougall, the latest being that letter which came with the packet... with the notice of eviction; and, I regret to say, Flora is in great fear, the rent so very much behind...' Simon sighed. 'Will I say, I have received not a sou of pay since December, and so I do not possess the least funds to send to Mull.'

'I am of a similar mind, old friend,' declared Pat, 'I am also awaiting such... no pay yet received this year... and neither have I ever received even a penny piece from those two damnable swindlers, Perkiss and Peddler... the scoundrels that they are... for payment of their shareholding in my mine venture.'

'I will concede, brother, that there was ever something of an indefinable aura of... *of malfeasance* about Perkiss,' murmured Simon with grudging admission.

'An infernal scrub! That is what he is!' declared Pat with a vengeance; 'You can straighten a worm, but the crook is in him, and only waiting.'

The ambience taking something of an unwelcome downturn, most particularly so after the joyous musical interlude of the prior evening, Simon stood up from his chair and nodded to his friends, 'I must return to my wounded charges, to Marston. He will, no doubt, by now be preparing them for the night, for what small comfort and respite they might find in sleep. I thank you both for your most cordial companionship this evening; it was so, and it has been a most welcome sojourn; but now... *now...* I must look to my patients. I bid you good night, dear friends.'

'Aye, good night,' replied Duncan, echoed by Pat with feeling, both men smiling.

A few more minutes passed in silent reflection when Pat sighed and looked to Duncan, 'Will you join me on the deck? I will go around the ship. Since leaving Argostoli I have had a feeling that... that I can't shake; a care, if you will.' Duncan nodded and the two friends left the cabin, an anxious Murphy staring in unspoken curiosity. Pat exited the coach to the gun deck where a hundred men and more were sitting all about the great guns, contented and chatting. The scene was one of rare tranquillity and illuminated by the faintest of moonlight, aided by a procession of oil lamps stretching down the deck. Pat stepped towards Tom Pickering and James Mower, his lieutenants, 'Gentlemen, I must ask your assistance.'

'Of course, sir,' Pickering replied and Mower nodded.

Pat resumed, 'It is two weeks since we fought that Turk frigate... off Oxia Island...' Macleod, Pickering and Mower all nodded, eyes wide and curious, a glimmer of dismay showing as reaction to the bleak reminder; '... and we have been anchored in Argostoli since then with the hands making repairs until we departed yesterday.' Pat hesitated, as if to question himself. 'I want you to speak with every gun captain. They are to draw the shot and powder charges from every gun.' The hanging lamp illuminated the alarm which flushed large on the faces of Pat's audience. 'It may be that the loaded powder has become damp since we quit Oxia Island. We will reload with dry powder... *perfectly dry*... direct from the magazines... but not before we espy a potential enemy ship.' Nods of comprehension all round could not disguise minds and faces filled with fresh anxieties. 'And now, gentlemen, I must leave you to that task because I am minded that I will visit our shipmates in the cockpit.'

Accompanied by Duncan and at the slowest of pace, Pat walked forward along the gun deck, offering the best smile he could manage, augmented with a nod of his head or a wave of his hand to many of his crew in passing, and a brief few words offered to a handful of his most stalwart veterans, shipmates aboard *Tenedos* before *Surprise*. In so doing he hoped most earnestly that neither his demeanour, which could conceivably be construed as hesitant to the most careful of scrutiny, nor his unusual orders to withdraw the powder of all the guns, would alarm his crew; and he endeavoured to persuade himself that there was nothing at all, the least thing, to be alarmed about; but in that he failed himself; his concerns remained, and an indefinable air of unsettlement pervaded his mind, a discomfort that he could not dispel. The precious sanctuary that was Cephalonia in the safe waters of the Ionian protectorate had been left behind, but Pat asked himself over and over again: *have we truly left behind the bloodshed, the turmoil and death's bloody hand? Are we really going home?*

At his side as they walked towards the bow, Duncan observed Pat's hesitancy, noted his obvious and returning air of concern, and he seized Pat's arm before he could descend the companionway steps, 'Pat... our words in the cabin... yesterday... after supper...' No reply and Duncan resumed, 'Simon and I, we... *we know* the truth of our words... it wasnae luck... nothing of the kind. No, *you* saved us, *you saved us all*, and that is the talk of the barky. I beg you will have nae doubt of that.'

Pat clasped and gripped firm Duncan's hand; his whispered words were quietly emphatic, 'Thank you; thank you, dear friend.' He turned away with nothing more said and stepped down to the lower deck.

The cockpit, that forward area of the mess deck so designated for medical matters and the treatment of wounded men, was a truly gloomy black hole; no natural light reached its depths from the gun deck and little fresh air circulated; hence, the stark locus of human suffering stank of medical detritus and human filth. The vile atmosphere was humid, sticky even; and the dim light, such that it was, came from two lamps suspended from the deckhead above. The stinking air was also thick with the wafting smoke and drifting stench of burnt lamp oil. A score and more of wounded men were accommodated in hammocks or atop low cots; and, as Pat approached the two tables where Simon and Marston laboured, he was assailed by the acrid, ammonia-like reek of laudanum, the plentiful supply of which had been restored in Argostoli from a moored English merchantman. Pat swallowed hard and bit down on his lip to avoid gagging as he stepped closer towards Simon.

The surgeon was leaning across his patient to attend a lower chest wound which was suppurating much blood into Simon's napkin as he gently wiped the flesh to re-assess the injury. The patient was very familiar to Pat, for his wound had been caused by a shower of splinters as a Turk ball smashed into the great cabin late during the battle with that Turk frigate which had subsequently exploded in a titanic detonation of her magazine; it was Hammett, the gun captain of *Shark's Bite* and one of his original *Tenedos* stalwarts, a veteran who hailed from Falmouth.

Hammett was barely conscious and plainly in great discomfort despite the soporific effects of the laudanum. 'How... how is he?' Pat murmured quietly to Simon, for in truth he did not care for the answer; it seemed perfectly obvious to his eye that the reply could hardly be reassuring.

Simon's attentions did not waver in the least, and he did not speak for some minutes until the cleansing of the wound was completed and the patient strapped with a fresh dressing. 'I hold to the hope that he will likely recover; at least, as long as the infernal infection does not set in. His wound is soaked in absinthe; the strong alcohol content of it is our best medicine for preventing an onset of the gangrene, but it surely aggravates his discomfort. I will continue to apply a trifle of bark every now and then. We may hope that he will thank us for it. Another few days will answer...' His voice dropped to a whisper, '... or not... as may be the case.'

Pat, momentarily speechless, a particularly uncomfortable frog in his throat, nodded and looked away towards Marston at the adjacent table, applying a clean dressing to the head of his patient. Pat was extremely well aware of Michael Marston's valued contribution as second surgeon, in which task he had served admirably throughout *Surprise's* time in Greek waters; indeed, he had proved to be the indomitable anchor for the morale of everyone aboard ship, including all the officers, and always so in even the most desperate of circumstances.

'Good evening, sir,' the chaplain looked up.

'We may hope so, Mr Marston. I much hope it remains so. How do you fare? How are things with you... with our people?'

'I am greatly concerned for Kitto and Hammett, sir,' Marston spoke with a world of concern in his voice, greatly alarming Pat.

'Did you know... *did you know*...' Pat's voice dropped to a whisper and he replied in a voice filled with dread and dismay, 'I have known that man - *Kitto* - since ever I came aboard *Tenedos*... all those long years ago; and now... and now... of all who serve aboard the barky... *every man*... I cannot contemplate being at sea without him... the old tar that he is become. I beg you will have the greatest care for him of all our people.'

'Most certainly I will, sir; and whilst I confess to a considerable concern in his particular case, I hold to my faith in Our Lord; and with that I am not discomfited; nor will I be, come what may.'

'I am sure of it,' murmured Pat very quietly, the strength of Marston's conviction a small reassurance in his own resurgence of dismay and truly something of a marvel in the bleak circumstances of the distress and discomfort which was all around them, evidenced by the subdued groans of many wounded men in pain.

Pat climbed the companionway steps to gain the gun deck once more, where he paused to assess the scene of activity before his eyes: a hundred men and more were labouring about those great guns that were dimly visible below the light of the new moon, augmented by the weak, yellow light of the lamps. He stepped, haltingly and with a deal of reluctance, at a snail's pace towards the coach and his cabin, loathe to sit once more at his table alone and without distraction. Discreet glances were ventured towards the presence of men working hard to attend the withdrawal of powder and shot, many hauling on wormers to extract tight-wedged wads and deep-set powder charges. Pat's command curiosity dictated an assessment of whether they resented the hard work at a time when such seemed hardly warranted, unnecessary even, the barky sailing away from the conflict, away from Greek waters; but no such resentment was evidenced in all those faces which met his gaze; rather, there was only warmth in all the eyes which locked upon his own, nothing other than respect in the friendliest fashion; and that, as much as the suppertime exchanges with his friends in the cabin, reassured him; it warmed his heart, and he gained that sanctuary which was the privacy of his cabin with something of a feeling of relief, the awareness of such beginning to register once more within his thoughts; something, some small part, of the weight of bleak burden was lifting just a very little from his anxieties, and he felt profoundly grateful for the unspoken but overt support of his men in that instant.

He looked all around him in the cabin, scrutinising his world of the past few years; he stared at the improvised repairs to the stern gallery, hardly a pane left of the glazing in the frames; and he recalled the order to smash out what had remained of them in order that the two aftmost guns, *Harpoon* and *Shark's Bite*, when turned about, could fire at the pursuing Turk frigate, the heavy guns manhandled to fire aft instead of abeam. He remembered with a sudden flush of angst the deep splinter striking Hammett even as Pat himself had rushed back to the quarterdeck to resume command of the engagement, the ship-handling, to check on his quarterdeck carronades and the crucial men at the helm; and his thoughts drifted to the conclusion of the long chase of his ship by the pursuing two remaining Turk frigates, culminating in the violent detonation of the powder magazine of one of them, off Oxia Island. His further thoughts reached deep into memory to recall, to grasp, the substance of the words which Simon and Duncan had more recently offered to reassure him that he had done all and more that any captain could have done, but his doubts lingered: *was it true?* More questions raced through his thoughts with a fresh surge of anxiety: *could he have done anything differently? Would so many true shipmates such as Hammett and Kitto have been struck down if he had acted in another fashion, perhaps sailed away to return to Oxia at a later time, perhaps at night? And if he had done so then perhaps the pursuers of the barky might not have been encountered once again?* He sat down at his table, feeling particularly lonely in his reflections and uncertainties.

Murphy's entrance after the briefest of knocks on the door broke his train of thoughts. 'Well, will 'ee care for coffee, sorr?'

'Yes please; coffee will be most welcome... will answer the case; thank you... and perhaps we will look to the whisky... and, *Murphy*, will you share a tot with me? What do you say?'

Murphy, perceiving his captain's returned despond, spoke up in good voice, declaring, 'Well, sorr, there be more friendship in a half-pint of whiskey than in a churn of buttermilk.'

'I believe you are in the right of things there,' murmured Pat gratefully, nodding in a flush of heartfelt affirmation.

'... and 'ere be the last of the marchpane biscuits, sorr; they be grand if 'ee dip 'em in the coffee... not for long, mind; a moment or two is all.'

'What? Biscuits?' Pat sat down in his chair and looked up at his steward. Murphy had been exceptionally attentive all day; indeed, he had been so for every minute since *Surprise* had departed Argostoli, notwithstanding his dismal failure in cooking; in fact, he had rarely left Pat's cabin. Pat reflected: *was his own discomfort so apparent to everyone aboard the barky?* He decided to ask his steward, and spoke in friendly voice, 'Murphy, speaking as one Galwayman to another... will you care to remark upon the... the morale... *the spirits* of the hands? I am affrighted that perhaps my own may not be... so... so...' Pat's softly spoken words were halted by his nose: Murphy's near proximity, listening, could not conceal the strong taint of whisky on his breath. Pat's swift glance at his table top revealed a greatly significant diminution in the level of the whisky bottle, still present but hardly two inches remaining.

'Well, sorr, 'tis sure that all the duty watch, the larbowlins, all be in good cheer, keeping their spirits up; there be no doubt of that...'

'It's good to hear that *some* spirits at least are preserved.'

'... and as for the starbowlins, well, since the extra grog ration was served during the music yesterday when they was all attending, they be as 'appy as pigs in...'

'Very good!' Pat interrupted his steward. 'And what of yourself, tell... in good spirits?'

'Well, I be very happy too, sorr.' Murphy frowned, perhaps suspecting Pat's discovery of his own generous libation, something of mild rebuke in Pat's phraseology.

'That is very pleasing to hear. I will take that coffee now, and perhaps you might avail yourself of a cup? They say it does wonders for the... *the spirits.*'

'Thankee, sorr; it's coming up d'reckly,' Murphy, disappeared without further ado.

A knock on the door and Duncan's face appeared, 'I beg leave to join you... if it pleases you.'

'Come in, do; it certainly does please me. I do not care to spend the last hour before my cot lamenting my lot. There! A rhyme Mr Mower would be proud of! Will you take a whisky with me? Murphy has kindly graced us by leaving a thimbleful.'

'Aye, a grand idea; I will... *the mumping scoundrel.*'

Pat poured the remnants, the tumblers having been washed by Murphy, perhaps to conceal his nefarious consumption. 'Tell me, old friend; are you here because of concern for my most sour disposition?'

'Not at all! We all share those same bleak feelings... a despair of sorts; and I include myself, I do; but my heart goes out most particularly to the surgeons. Their burden prevails upon them still. For sure, the cockpit is a place that turns my heart... *and my stomach.* I am sorely set back to say that, and I confess that I scarcely dare to leave the deck to gain my cabin... save by the *aft* companionway.'

Pat nodded, 'For Simon and Marston it is a heavy load, for sure.' A minute passed as the two friends savoured their whisky. 'Have we truly finished with that place, Duncan?'

'There isnae the least doubt, old friend... I dare say we will raise Malta by Tuesday, even with this faltering wind and slow progress; and from there it's Gibraltar for water and provisions...'

'I am much concerned since the warning from Adam...
his mention of two Turk frigates...'

'Aye, as am I; but we will soon be far from Greek waters;
and I am minded that the Ottoman navy - *that is, the Turk part
of it* - since the Greek war started has had its hands full; so
much so that I doubt they will venture very far west...'
Duncan paused, Pat did not look convinced, and so he
resumed, 'The Deys of Tunis and Algiers are no longer in the
Sultan's pocket... and they possess no ship of war of any note,
and so we might likely expect to raise the Rock without
encountering any Turk vessel.'

Pat nodded, and he tried to anchor his own thoughts upon
his friend's conviction, in hope that such might dispel his own
enduring fears. At least, he thought, the barky's cutter,
Mathew Jelbert, had sailed independently; and, being
exceptionally swift of sail, his junior Lieutenant, William
Reeve, might be expected to take her safely into Malta ahead
of *Surprise*.

Chapter Four

Monday 8th May 1826   04:30   *The south Ionian Sea*

The feeble wind of the prior day had faded away to nothing under the silvery light of the new moon during the night and had failed to recover the least zephyr since; such was noticed immediately by a fatigued and anxious Pat as he stepped out of the coach precisely as a solitary bell rang out the beginning of the morning watch. He gazed up and all around him, his eyes lingering on the familiar Arcturus, still bright despite the weak moonlight and just the first faint inklings of twilight announcing the coming dawn with a lighter shade of grey in the eastern sky. He observed with deep dissatisfaction that the sails hung slack from the yards and the braces exhibited nothing of strain. The exceedingly slight and gentle rolling of the deck also signified immediately to his mind and further confirmed his worst fears: the barky was not moving in the least. He looked down over the side and could see scarcely a ripple on a flat sea surface which resembled nothing other than a millpond. As he gained the quarterdeck the unsettled ambience about his men, visibly discernible in the glances directed towards him, registered immediately with him; the absolute calm, the general stillness, had seemingly presented itself as portentous; for so it seemed to tired minds; and then the moment was broken by the shrill whistles of the bosun's mates to awaken sleeping men.

The helmsmen all touched knuckles to foreheads as he reached the wheel. 'Good morning, sir; nothing to report,' announced Codrington, lieutenant on duty, staring with apprehension at Pat's gaunt, lined face, at his sunken temples and red eyes deep within shrouded black slits. No one on deck professed the least sign of contentment, for happiness was absent, utterly; the news of the more acutely endangered state of health of Kitto and Hammett had permeated the ship during the night; yet another two *Tenedos* and *Surprise* veterans, longstanding shipmates of numerous prior voyages and friends to many aboard, not least their fellows in their gun crews, were endangered.

'Good morning, Mr Codrington... lads,' announced Pat, taking very deep breaths in hope that the cold air might somehow help to revive his tired mind. He stared intently all about the ship, for it truly was *his ship;* it was also his home at sea and that of his veteran shipmates; he looked to the drooping canvas - *no load there in the least* - and with a ranging scrutiny he stared up to the sky. He lowered his gaze and scanned the horizon in every direction: low-hanging ribbons of cloud were beginning to be vaguely discernible in the rising light, not shifting in the least as he studied them with painfully sore eyes and the searching stare of a bewildered mind, all his thoughts shifting, coalescing, to what would be in this new day, to what might come, to what might befall them all. The persistent uncertainty, a fear and a doubt that he could not dispel, blighted his heartfelt search for comfort, for small cheer. At least, he consoled himself, the barky was heading west, away from the war; or at least she would be if only a wind would develop. A light one would suffice, the merest of breeze would be most welcome; for in truth they had not sailed as far as he had hoped; for, Pat realised, a mere half a day of sailing in a blowing westerly would put them right back into the war zone, where Turk frigates patrolled; and he could not forget Governor Adam's warning.

A half-hour passing was signalled by Clumsy Dalby ringing loud two bells as Duncan appeared at Pat's side. 'Good morning, sir; and how are you?' the Scot ventured, expecting little of cheer in reply as he assessed his friend's evident disconsolation, a pained sense of anxiety perfectly evident.

'Oh, all is well; thank you,' Pat lied without the least conviction; 'I am obliged to you for your enquiry, but allow me to say that I will be much the happier when we see something of the *Levanter* returned to its duty.'

'Aye, I am of the same mind; I will ne'er be happier than when we sight Malta and the Grand Harbour on the bow.'

A few minutes more passed by as Pat stared all about him in slow inspection, in some respects grateful for the calm ambience of the dawn after a sleepless night much disturbed by unwelcome dreams which he did not greatly care for, disturbing ones from which he had awakened several times in a muck sweat, an hour or more passing each time before he found sleep again. He was still tired, but he welcomed the appearance of Michael Marston, pacing slowly across the quarterdeck to join him; it was a welcome distraction. 'Good morning, Mr Marston; how are you?'

'I consider myself blessed to be here, sir; and good morning to you.'

'That is an admirable sentiment, it is so; and I commend you for it.'

'Thank you, sir.'

'How do you do below? How are things?'

'Would that I could cast off my concerns for several of Dr Ferguson's patients... Hammett and Kitto are a grievous worry.'

'Well, I am sure they are in the best of hands... *none better*. But... on a happier note... if it is not discordant to say so in... *in the present circumstances*... may I say how much I enjoyed our musical sojourn of Saturday. It was... it was the most glorious hour; thank you again for that.'

'I was minded that, together, we carried off a remarkable consonance, sir,' offered Marston.

'I do not know what a consonance is,' murmured Pat, 'but I am sure it is a very good thing.'

'It was the finest of musical achievements, sir.'

'Indeed, and I hope we may enjoy the pleasure again in the near future.'

'Thank you, sir; it was the most welcome respite from the cockpit for Dr Ferguson and myself.'

'No doubt... no doubt,' murmured Pat, nurturing the very same small consolation, the great relief that the music had been, albeit so very transient. At least the seed of thought, of repetition, was firmly planted.

Marston, observing his captain's hesitancy, spoke again, 'Would that we might pass more evenings in such pleasing endeavours as we make passage home; in fact, I am in hope that we will do so.'

'As am I, *Michael*... I am so.'

A tired Pat stepped away from the helm and down to the deck, from where he retreated into his cabin. He was cheered by the welcome aroma of coffee and the sight of a huge bowl of steaming porridge. He was more than delighted to see his closest friend in all the world, Simon Ferguson, already seated at his table, helping himself to the hot breakfast with evident relish and without the least reservation.

'Would you be eating your heart out... cracking on so?' declared Pat, striving for levity.

Simon looked up, 'Why, as to that, I do beg your pardon for not waiting for you, brother; but I confess that the delightful scent of porridge was the most welcome reminder of home... in happier times.'

'Could you manage a cup of coffee?' declared Pat, pleased to see the simple pleasure exhibited in his friend's demeanour.

'Upon my soul, I certainly could so.'

'I beg your forbearance... but will you tell me of the situation as it is in the cockpit? That is to say, how do our shipmates fare?'

Simon paused his eating, took a great gulp of his coffee, and spoke in a voice of greater resolution than Pat might have anticipated after the recent news of Kitto's and Hammett's decline. 'All is as well as can be expected. Sure, there is a plenty of discomfort and certainly a surfeit of flux - *the conditions downstairs are scarcely better than the filthiest pigsty* - and too a plethora of audible murmurings of pain... and a deal of unhappiness for those of my patients who are, for the most part, not sufficiently dosed to become unconscious; but the greater significance is that - *save for*

Kitto and Hammett - I do not fear for the lives of any of them; and that is a blessing that they and I have not been sure of these two weeks gone; indeed, it is a great comfort.' Simon paused for another gulp of coffee and resumed as Pat simply nodded, 'Yes, there is a future without a limb... in a dozen cases... but we may be thankful that there is *at least a future* for such men; and we must hold firm to our belief that they will be thankful for that... and I do so myself.'

'We will lose no more men... not a one?' asked Pat, seeking further reassurance and finding it difficult to shed his unease and uncertainty. 'But what of Kitto and Hammett? I spoke with Marston yesterday and... and he has concerns for them both.'

'Neither man is well... far from it... However, they both exhibit a considerable fortitude in their distress... a determination, if I may say so; but I am afraid to say, there is some small measure of deterioration in their condition these past forty-eight hours.'

'Will you tell me they will survive?' asked Pat with desperate anxiety evident.

'I believe we may only hold to hope that such is the case, but there is no certainty... I much regret to say.' Simon turned away and attacked the porridge once more with evident relish.

'I am mightily anxious to hear that,' declared Pat with a huge exhalation; 'I will look to Patrick, Mary and all the Saints.'

'I incline more to the view that it is Marston to whom we should look and, indeed, extend our thanks, for he is - as I have come to increasingly value this year gone - a most excellent surgeon.'

'I am sure of it,' murmured Pat, for he harboured not the least doubt himself. 'If you recall... when we began this... this venture... and it is near three years gone to this day... I was always minded that there was no room on a ship-of-war for a chaplain... but Marston has proved me wrong. Yes, on many an occasion he has done so. His presence as a surgeon has been a marvel... *a marvel*... aboard the barky.'

'He exhibits the most admirable steadfastness as a chaplain too, and - *I believe I break no confidence, but this is for your private ear alone* - he holds you high in his affections; indeed, he is in reverence to you, he is so. Will I tell you something?' Simon paused momentarily, waiting for Pat's cautious nod before he resumed, 'It was in that dreadful place... as matters neared the end... I speak of Missolonghi and those final few hours before we escaped... the massacres were abounding all about us... screams were everywhere in the air... and the corpses outside were piled high... no timber at all - *never the smallest of even kindling spare* - with which to burn them. I had lost a deal of patients... the most severely wounded unfortunates; there were so many... so very many... and I was brought to a halt... my hands shaking, *my mind's very equilibrium was shot...* and I knelt down... with Marston... upon the floor. We were surrounded in blood and detritus... *it was strewn all about us*, and we prayed together. *God's love, I prayed...* Do you hear me?'

Pat kept his silence, stunned, and he merely nodded.

Simon set down his coffee mug and stared, wide-eyed, at his friend for long seconds, 'Long before that... near two years ago... you will recall that I fled the cockpit in a deal of distress... after that battle to defend Samos... such a multitude of wounded... so very many... a shambles... The final straw then was the death of Yescombe... I am sure you remember him; he was another veteran shipmate of ours... with us for many years, many voyages; and when I could not save him - *his condition was immedicable* - I despaired. I was lost... Pat... *I was lost...* and I panicked and fled the cockpit. Do you recall that moment, *do you?*'

'That was but a fleeting instant of crisis, old friend... a long time ago. It was no panic; no, never in life; and we paid it no mind, none at all; be assured of that, I beg you will.' Pat flushed with alarm, for he had heard Simon's concerns in that particular matter once before, and he wondered whether, perhaps, Simon had never managed to recover any degree of personal reassurance. 'Will I say that such... *such distressing moments...* they afflict us all; and I include myself, I do. There are days when I am quite stuck in my thinking... all thrown out... like the movements of a watch that has been neglected and is in want of the sweet oil... but it is the true measure of the man to resume... *to carry on...* and you did, brother... *you did*; and we were all grateful to you, *all of us aboard the barky*; we were so.'

'Have we done with all such misery and grief, Pat? *Have we?*'

Pat could only nod, for of words of confirmation he could find none which he felt able to offer, and the sickening feeling of doubt lingered still in his own mind.

Monday 8th May 1826   13:00   *The south Ionian Sea*

Dalby and his drum on the gun deck beat out the familiar sound of *"Roast Beef of Old England"* as Pat sat within his chair in the great cabin awaiting his dinner, but he paid it no mind. He sipped coffee whilst he reflected on the disturbing sentiments which Simon had expressed earlier, on the leaving of the Greek struggle more generally, and on the further, homeward voyage to come. The familiar two bells rang out without interrupting Pat's thoughts in the least. By his reckoning *Surprise* was about halfway through her passage to Malta, but he fretted about the feeble wind strength; the earlier weak indications of an easterly *Levanter* had dwindled away during the late morning, and progress had correspondingly slowed; so much so that *Surprise* was once more near becalmed. His earlier anticipation of arriving at Valletta shortly after tomorrow's dawn had fallen by the wayside, cast away entirely as no more than wholly optimistic, given the capricious failure of the wind to blow. He had considered a dawn arrival to be quite perfect, to his way of thinking, for the harbour was always busy, being the very crossroads of the Mediterranean; in fact, it was much busier than ever since the end of the war against Bonaparte. His thoughts wandering wide, without the least brake or boundary in the quietude of his solitude, he recalled *Surprise's* first voyage to Greece

70

three years previously, her first task being to ensure that Lord Byron safely arrived for his own mission of personal support for Greek endeavours. He felt a mild flush of satisfaction in recollecting the relaxed progress of that voyage; indeed, it had been something of a reunion with his two close friends and a celebration of a return to sea together; but later came the bitter price to be paid, the fighting and the death of so many of his men, many of them longstanding veterans and shipmates of former voyages; and Lord Byron himself had also paid the ultimate price. The brief pleasure of his company in Cephalonia before the poet had crossed to the war-torn mainland was very memorable; in fact, it had made a lifelong impression on his friend, Simon Ferguson, who revered the man. Pat's mind drifted back to the present, to the approaching sanctuary of Malta, and he recalled Lord Byron commenting on his own impression of the Grand Harbour; and, although *Surprise* had not actually called at Malta when outward bound, voyaging in great haste and passing by the island, His Lordship had plainly been familiar with the great Mediterranean port and its harbour beforehand, for he had stated it as being *"remarkable for the prodigious strength of its fortifications which present from the sea an appearance of unconquerable power"*. Pat recalled well that moment when the poet had offered the words.

Pat himself was perfectly familiar with the Grand Harbour, having made many visits to Malta during the war against the Corsican tyrant, and he concurred entirely with Byron. He mused further on the fateful loss of his Lordship; indeed, Simon Ferguson often talked with a passion about the great man, whom he had befriended in the final months of his life, to the extent that, in the quiet hours of the evening in the cabin, he occasionally recounted the sad events of his death; an event that had so greatly upset Simon that he could not refrain from cursing and railing vehemently against Byron's doctors, who, so Simon swore, had bled him beyond the point of recovery, and so to his ultimate death. That particular, painful tragedy, to Pat's mind, had self-evidently much afflicted Simon.

Minutes passing, and his own thinking drifted to a closer focus upon his dear friend, a man whom he considered to be the learned man of the world, or at least as much so as anyone he had ever met. Being the ship's surgeon, Simon had, of course, seen many deaths during the last three years, all of them distressing; yet, whereas all losses that the surgeon had attended had been victims of wounds, of battle, in the case of Byron, Simon had been no more than an impotent witness to the distressing final hours of the great poet and Philhellene; and forever afterwards, whenever Byron's name had been mooted in the cabin, Simon had vowed bitterly that the great man's loss would haunt him for the rest of his days. Pat marvelled at the so greatly profound effect that one man might have on another, the loss of his life most particularly; and he wondered vacantly what more Byron might have contributed to the Greek cause, had he lived; but there was no answer that he could find, and eventually he dismissed such thinking as an indulgence; not, perhaps, an absolute waste of time, but surely fruitless; and he reconciled his frustration with the thought that such philosophical leanings were not his particular kettle of fish.

His thinking returned once more to the barky's approaching arrival in Malta, and it occurred to him that such would be the affirmation that he so fiercely sought, the definitive event which would confirm to his doubtful mind that poor Greece was really left behind, was in the past, that the barky's task was over, finished, and that they truly were going home. And yet there remained, even in the anchor of mental relief which was that precious thought, the niggling doubt that he could never quite dispel: *was it really the case? But how could it not be so?* Worse: *was he, Patrick O'Connor, clutching only for the flimsiest of straws?*

In the uncomfortable moment of Pat's uncertainty, Pickering rapped hard on the door and, discarding all protocol and without waiting to be called, he entered in a hurry and spoke up immediately, 'Sir, I beg to report that the mizzen lookout reports a sighting, a distant sail on the starboard quarter.'

'What?' Pat's heart skipped a beat as he sprung up from his chair, quickly forgetting his coffee remnants and all thoughts of his dinner in his haste to seize his telescope and leave the cabin. He hastily gained his quarterdeck and stared over the taffrail through his glass, but he could see nothing; no sails were visible.

'Was there any sighting from the main?' he asked Pickering.

'No sir, nor any shout from the fore.'

Without ado Pat seized upon the ratlines and climbed to the mizzen top, the astonished watchman shifting aside as Pat squatted down, out of breath in his haste. 'Where away?' gasped Pat.

'Over there, sir,' Green pointed to the left of the trailing mizzen boom, to starboard.

Pat stared for a minute and more before he spoke in noncommittal voice, 'I see no ship, no sail... nothing at all.'

'It comes and goes, sir,' Green had no doubts, even if his captain did. He looked again himself through his glass, another minute passing before he replied, 'It's not there now, sir, it's gone.' Sensing the importance that a perceptibly agitated Pat placed on the matter, and perhaps his own credibility at stake, Green persisted, 'I swear there was a sail, sir; distant, yes... for sure it was; but I saw it, *I did.*'

Pat stared again, more minutes passing with the telescope to his eye, unmoving, staring, his thoughts a whirling amalgam of doubt and anxiety: *was there a ship out there, astern?* Finally, still seeing nothing, he spoke once more, 'Green, you will climb to the crosstree and look again; look from up there... look hard... and shout if you see anything, *the least thing.*'

'Aye aye, sir.' Green started his ascent and Pat settled himself more comfortably to watch once more, sweeping the horizon in every direction, but he could still see nothing.

From below, the evident anxiety on deck, something of a commotion, intruded on Pat's focus, and he began to wonder if his climb had been a wild goose chase; perhaps Green's sighting had been a trick of the light, an apparition; it was certainly not an unknown phenomenon. His roving gaze with his telescope wandered from the horizon, up, up into the expanse of the southern sky where he noted with a rising sense of foreboding a darkening of the air. His eyes fixed on far distant clouds, which confirmed his worst fears: the wind had veered and was building from the south, the warmer *Scirocco* was coming. He cursed aloud in his solitude; nothing could be more unwelcome, nothing else could make passage to Malta slower; for a southerly blow, such as the *Scirocco* presented, would dictate repetitive, laborious tacking to make the least progress towards the south-west and the safe haven which was the Grand Harbour.

His rising awareness of hunger reminded him of his overdue dinner, and he wondered whether it was now cold or perhaps even baking to a crisp on the galley stove; he imagined that Murphy was watching with a degree of vexation or, possibly, glee; for his steward was a man with a great affinity for punctuality, and the absence of his captain at the precise time for his dinner would have much irked him; Pat had no doubt about that. He fidgeted with rising discomfort and decided that he was wasting his time and his dinner; he castigated himself for being unreasonably alarmed and without justification. Perhaps, he thought, he would wait a little while before descending to the deck, for he would surely be very hungry by then.

In the moment of Pat's prevarication, Green shouted from the mizzen crosstree, or rather he screamed, 'SAIL HO! STARBOARD QUARTER!'

Pat clutched tighter his telescope and cursed, a great anxiety seizing his mind and his stomach, an acid bile rising to burn his throat. He stared intently through his glass, cursed aloud, panned across the horizon from abeam to astern; yet still he saw nothing; there was no intrusion whatsoever within the glaring absence which was the great expanse of sea all around. He more slowly swung back his telescope, urging himself to patience, to caution, halting at the slightest impression of anything, the least thing; and then his eye caught the tiniest, the very faintest, possibility of a sail against the horizon, scarcely a grey smudge against a greyer canvas: *was it really a sail?* He could not be sure; his gaze froze and he fiddled with the telescope focus ring, back and forth several times, the tiniest of incremental adjustments. Yes! There it was, a sail for sure; and now, in his absolute concentration, he could make out three sails, three masts and even a hull, the thinnest, the narrowest, horizontal streak on the very horizon itself. And then it was gone, as if no more than a disappearing dream. He set down his glass on his lap and tried to think: *was he right to be concerned? After all, and as he had been thinking earlier whilst awaiting his dinner, Malta was the crossroads of all nautical traffic in the Mediterranean; and so it could not be considered unusual in the least to see other vessels; one such was neither here nor there. Or was it?* He could feel his heart pounding like a drum being beaten - *hard* - and his mind was engulfed by a rising tide of anxiety and concern. In that instant he recalled once again Governor Adam's cautious warning: *beware of Turk frigates!*

Pat looked down towards the quarterdeck and the gun deck; sure enough, a great gathering of men stared over the starboard side and also astern; a few of the crew were looking to larboard; and a great commotion had resulted, loud and excited. Gathering his thoughts, his pumping heart subsiding only slightly, Pat climbed down the ratlines, taking his time whilst thinking, and so regained his quarterdeck, where Murphy, Simon and Duncan awaited him.

'Well, begging your honour's pardon, sorr,' Murphy spoke up in a voice that was determined to be heard before all others, 'but your dinner be a'ruining... going cold... on your table.'

'Thank you, Murphy. I will attend in just one moment.' Pat turned to his friends, 'I did espy a ship... three-masted; and so, potentially a frigate; but she is far distant, perhaps twelve miles or even more.' A further minute of thought and he stepped down the companionway and to his cabin, no appetite at all for the slightest thing. He dismissed the, now cold, sea pie without a second thought. Murphy fussed about him in silence, departing after a minute, rightly discerning that his captain did not care for the least interruption nor any company. Pat tapped his fingers on the table, reached for and unrolled his chart: it was at least one hundred and fifty miles more, or thereabouts, to reach Valletta. The barky was making a miserly three knots, perhaps only two; evidently, his hopes of arrival at dawn on the morrow, his earlier estimate of that now long abandoned, had plainly been recklessly optimistic; it most certainly could not be achieved, even were the wind to begin blowing a gale. He cursed himself and turned to pick absently at the pastry top of his pie with his fork, chewing absently and swallowing slowly without tasting the least thing: *could it have been a frigate? A Turk one, perhaps?*

A discordant seven bells ringing out brought Pat's mind back with a jolt to the present, all his concerns rushing upon his mind as might a raging tide breaking upon the rocks of the shore, and imposing upon him a great anxiety. Discarding the uneaten pie, his untouched glass of wine and the cold coffee that a solicitous Murphy had deposited before him without the least acknowledgement a half hour previously, he marched out of the cabin to the steps and so up to his quarterdeck.

'Anything to report, Mr Codrington? The least thing?'

'Nothing, sir.'

Hour after hour passed by as the afternoon slipped away into the beginnings of the evening, and an anxious Pat gazed all about the horizon through his glass in every direction, searching, scrutinising the tiniest aberration, all of which he concluded were distant traces of cloud of a darker hue, always hovering just above the horizon and occasionally merging with it in a confusing meld, five miles distant; but the least imperfection in the horizontal definition sparked anxious, even repetitive, investigation with his telescope. He spoke to no avail with the descending lookouts at the end of both the afternoon and the first dog watches, maintaining his own attention without pause, unable to shed the anxiety within him, the absence of all other ships not the least comfort despite his best efforts to convince himself otherwise. 'Damn! What is happening to me?' he exclaimed to himself, setting aside his glass for the first time in an hour, the helmsmen mildly perturbed to observe his discomfit.

Duncan Macleod, returning to duty with Tom Pickering for the last dog watch and approaching the wheel, heard the utterance, and his quick eyes measured the scene in an instant; the disturbing glances from the two men at the helm and also Jeremiah Prosser, the master being present too, served as confirmation of concern for their captain. He paced slowly across the deck to stand next to his friend at the starboard rail but held his tongue for several minutes. 'May I borrow your glass, sir?' he enquired in gentle voice.

'Eh? My glass?' For the first time Pat noticed his companion; 'Sure.'

Taking the telescope, Duncan commenced to slowly scan the horizon, from the starboard bow to the starboard quarter. He stepped back to the taffrail, raised the glass once more and gazed aft for fully five minutes; and then he stepped across to the larboard rail and stood, immobile, for fully ten more minutes, sweeping his gaze from forward to aft, the most minute and incremental shifts in his stance permitting a complete picture, all of which revealed nothing, the least thing, save for the low cloud. It was all theatre, as the master eventually came to realise, a performance, deliberately *lentissimo*, and plainly intended to assuage the self-evident concerns of Captain O'Connor.

Whether Pat realised this was never revealed because Simon Ferguson came upon the deck as Duncan returned the telescope to his friend, smiling. 'There is nothing to be seen, sir.'

'Nothing at all?'

Duncan added the famous comment, 'I see no ships.'

Simon immediately perceived a strange tension in the air between his friends. 'Would that be Nelson?' he directed his comment towards Pat.

'Am I being practised upon,' declared Pat with suspicion, beginning to perceive something of the ilk.

'Never in life, soul,' replied Simon with a smile. Duncan could not hide a grin, and the master and helmsmen studiously averted their gaze. 'The light will soon be leaving us, I see,' remarked Simon, staring aft, the sun extremely low in the sky. 'Perhaps it will serve us all well to partake of an aperitif... before supper?'

'Yes, there is something in what you say,' murmured Pat in dispirited tone; 'I am afraid that the sighting of that vessel... earlier... on the starboard quarter... has quite set me back... robbed me of my wits.'

'No doubt your wits will soon recover... will be aided by a delectable tint; indeed, I am sure that one such will serve amazingly. Look, Mr Pickering is come here to take command of our estimable vessel,' Simon spoke in encouraging voice.

'Aye, and I am in the way for a wee dram,' declared Duncan emphatically.

'Perhaps Murphy will soon be about the toasted cheese?' Simon persevered, noting his friend's dejection; 'What do you say, old friend?'

'An excellent notion,' replied Pat, hesitancy and reluctance discarded as he assessed the very few minutes remaining before the sunset, and the impossibility of any hostile Turk frigate closing upon the barky, at least until the morning; the stirrings of hunger, too, were becoming difficult to ignore. 'Let us repair to the cabin and look to a welcome bite.'

A plentiful disbursement of sherry was poured by Murphy for his charges as soon as they were seated about the table; the steward also permitted - as he saw things - a generous ration of the walnuts to be consumed, a rare delicacy at the best of times and never to be served in liberal fashion; indeed, it was one of his own favourites and the least consumption of walnuts by other persons invariably offended his inclinations as a sour curmudgeon, the sourest; but Murphy too exhibited a sense of perception when it came to his master's moods, and he realised that this was one such necessary occasion, when no expense - or at least no withholding of his precious walnuts - could reasonably be spared. He hovered, ever attentive, about the table, eavesdropping for some indication of his captain's intentions, the least thing; for Murphy took great self-satisfaction in being the harbinger of all developments for the keen ears of the crew, many of them valid and others merely the instruments of his nefarious manipulations, a tot of a seaman's rum usually accepted as a fair price for some news of note for the lower deck. However, on this occasion, as Murphy set down the steaming plates of toasted cheese, he realised that such talk as was offered about the table was more of a personal nature, an exchange of aspirations for homely matters, but nothing of particular currency for him in his gossip with the crew; and so he reconciled himself to the situation with a degree of concealed disappointment.

'What news of your mine venture?' asked Simon; 'Might there yet be any prospect - *the slightest* - of revival on the... *the financial horizon...* the striking of the smallest of gold vein, perhaps?'

'I regret to say that I have heard nothing of cheer from my wife,' replied Pat in downcast voice, a vision of a charismatic Sinéad filling his mind with an uncontrollable and rising surge of emotion; 'Indeed, in the last letter she lamented the great mounds of dross strewn across the land, all of it overlaying those acres from where our customary winter peat is cut.' Pat frowned, 'Doubtless it will be a cold winter.'

'What of Peddler and Perkiss? Surely there is a... a *not insignificant* sum due to you from your investors?' Simon persevered. 'Have they paid you? I beg you will forgive my enquiry if it is in the least degree intrusive.'

'No, no payment in cash has reached Sinéad; and, as you will recall, they owe me quite the vast great pile of money, several thousands. It scarcely helps the case... our prospects... *yours and mine...* that my bank, Pole Thornton, failed... in December of last year... when so many others did.'

'Yes, and the Plymouth Dock Bank will ever be accursed in my own thoughts,' Simon's voice signified a downturn in spirits generally. 'My most meagre savings were lost to me when it closed its doors... *the grasping scoundrels!* Heaven knows how I will secure my home from Salmon's predations.' A brief interlude of reflective silence for all and Simon spoke again, 'I did receive a letter from Peddler, sent from Tobermory; it came on the packet last week. Apparently, he is now residing there. He informed me of proceedings commencing against Salmon - *my landlord* - in the Stornoway court. I am led to the conclusion that is likely why he seeks to repossess my home. Perhaps he is expecting to lose the case?'

'I am amazed that you are still inclined to believe anything that Peddler tells you! Surely you must now see that anything from that man, any statement, pledge or promise is about as valuable as a nine-bob note! It must be the case that he is looking to you for a douceur... *in order to plead your case with Salmon perhaps?* Was there any mention in his letter of the other good-for-nothing swindler - *Perkiss?* His whereabouts or intentions perhaps... *the least thing?*' enquired Pat.

'I note your firm reprobation, I do, brother; but I venture to suggest that you may yet be a trifle premature in your condemnation; for there is no evidence - *the slightest thing* - of criminal purpose on the part of either party.'

'Evidence? What! Do you dismiss the gold theft?'

'*The presumed theft!* Indeed, you are to consider, my dear, that it was the *non-existent* theft, if my memory serves me. I concede that there was a robbery of mere ballast iron... *pigs*, if I may use the nautical terminology,' declared Simon with a degree of self-satisfaction. He resumed, 'I regret to say only that Peddler apprised me of his fears for the prospects for

Perkiss's corporate interests. He mentioned P M A, which we may safely presume is Peninsular Metal Alloys. You will recall that was the selfsame foundry which cast the iron-plating about the gold ingots sent from St. Petersburg for the Greeks... which we transported to the monastery at Mount Athos.'

'I certainly do, the very same ingots which the two rogues endeavoured to steal from the Calamata quay, *the wicked dogs!'* Pat spoke with indignation.

'Which was denied by Peddler; indeed, he professed ignorance in the matter of how the thieves came to be aware of it.'

'No doubt it was the local boggarts who were responsible,' replied Pat in acerbic voice; 'Or perhaps it was Robin Hood's descendants... Was there a Greek branch of his family?'

'I have known that man, Peddler, since we both were knee-high,' Simon persisted with his defence of his friend; 'Why, I attended school with him, and in our youth we enjoyed every summer evening and weekends together exploring Mull... until I left the island for Edinburgh... for the University Medical School. I cannot conceive that he would disappoint me or stoop to the least disreputable conduct; indeed, he has given me his personal assurance that he will hold firm to that shareholding which he now possesses in your own venture, the gold mine, such that Perkiss - *who I cannot vouch for* - cannot secure the controlling interest which you fear may be lost to him.'

'Huumm...' pronounced Pat in a voice that shouted loud his scepticism. 'I will concede that any fair man might place some weight upon the word of his old school friend, one who he has known since he could but walk in short trousers; but, I regret to say, your friend Peddler has proven himself to be as sound as a three-legged chair; indeed, I would never myself have wagered tuppence ha'penny on his integrity save that you vouched for him. And as for Perkiss, I don't doubt that the next time we clap eyes on the rogue he will undoubtedly be engaged in some new fraud. I dare say - *given the moment* - the infernal projector would dare to claim a knowledge of the whereabouts of the Philosophers' Stone; indeed, I'm sure he could conceal a blush whilst peddling claimed fragments of the True Cross to his creditors. Did not King Alfred claim he presented a number of such to the Abbot of Shaftesbury?'

Simon laughed, 'To the nuns of the abbey it was, dear.'

'Perhaps the man has struck up an accommodation with the nuns. I doubt that Perkiss is particular. Perhaps Peddler will vouch for him there too?'

'Gentlemen,' Duncan interjected, noting the downturn of dialogue, 'Will we look to more comfortable matters? It is surely long past time for a welcome glass of brandy... or a wee dram; if, that is, anything of suchlike can be found.'

'Certainly, they have their soporific benefits,' murmured Simon, looking to his other friend, 'and I am ever in want of sleep; but, did you yourself receive any mail on the packet, tell? Something from home, perhaps?'

'Aye, a letter from Kathleen,' Duncan's demeanour dropped, 'It is a trial to speak of it.'

'Please, go on,' prompted Pat, his anxiety rising in an instant.

'I regret to say that the consumption has not relented.'

'Dear God, no!' exclaimed Pat with excitement, 'Sinéad is ever in fear of news of a decline in her sister's health.'

'She is so ill-disposed that she has taken to her bed, and Brodie attends her. My daughter has reported that the minister has been called... from Rodel church.'

'When we reach home... *when we reach home*...' declared Simon in low voice with a world of concern, 'I will attend dear Kathleen in the first instance... and we may yet hold to the hope of her recovery. Until then, until we are perfectly familiar with the case, I beg you will not fret unnecessarily.'

'Thank you, old friend,' mumbled Duncan as the frog reached his throat and the tears formed in his eyes.

'You are a good-hearted soul,' murmured Pat to Simon with an infinity of admiration in his voice.

Chapter Five

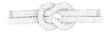

Tuesday 9th May 1826   04:30   *The south Ionian Sea*

The low morning twilight of the eastern sky, astern, was slowly ceding to the brighter, true dawn, but the scant wind and a lingering degree of rainfall, scarcely more than a drizzle, was disappointing to all aboard *Surprise*. The starbowlins and idlers were on deck and staring all about them, for hardly a man had escaped the furious speculation which had persisted since Green had alerted them yesterday to a possible frigate on the starboard quarter. That had been many hours ago, but since then the night had given no one any mental respite; for the rising sense of apprehension, even anxiety, was general amongst all on board, both officers and men alike, and could not be dispelled.

Pat himself had been on the quarterdeck in his oilskins since the end of the middle watch, his own deep-seated worries at the forefront of all his thoughts. Green was reputedly the best man atop the masts with a glass and had been designated as the principal lookout for the morning watch, and so he had been shifted to the main crosstree from the mizzen top, the small but potentially significant increment in height that it offered.

Pat cursed because the visibility was far from good in the enduring weak light of the gloaming. The intermittent and light rain showers of the night, borne on the easterly breeze, had, thankfully, near ceased; and the decks, formerly awash with a film of water, were fast drying. From above there was a steady drip of cold water droplets, falling to splash on his uncovered head from the yards. He noted with interest that the wind was discernibly beginning to strengthen and now blew from the south: the dry and dusty *Scirocco* was noticeably stronger than the gentle but hoped-for, easterly *Levanter*. Pat shivered whilst he scanned the gently rolling miles of sea in every direction, but there was little definition in distance within the overcast of the dark, low hanging clouds which hugged the horizon in a broad spectrum of grey from east through north to west, a lingering reminder of the indifferent conditions for progress which had persisted throughout much of yesterday; and all about him on the starboard side the cold ambience of the night and its rainfall lingered still in the form of long, feeble tendrils of low-lying fog, scarcely a yard above the sea surface, a grey patina of ceaseless slow movement; and everywhere was a chilly panorama of more grey, an unrelenting march of many shades of it, in both water and sky. Pat reminded himself with a sigh of sinking disappointment that Malta yet remained some considerable distance off, at least another hundred miles or even more.

Duncan and Simon appeared on deck to stand next to their friend. Codrington, on duty, greeted them with his best effort at a smile, but it made no impression, for gloom was endemic, even unease; and a silence borne of apprehension pervaded everywhere about the quarterdeck. A near half-hour passed with nothing said, the dim light gradually improving as the slowly rising sun, indistinct through the low cloud astern but most welcome nevertheless, peeked its head through the murk lying low about the horizon.

'SAIL HO!' Green's shout jarred everyone from introspection. 'LARBOARD BEAM!' Heads everywhere turned; Pat raised his glass, swiftly wiped away a residual rain spatter from the lens - water drops were still falling from the rigging - and he stared over the side with total concentration. Seconds went by, a hundred men and more were gazing into the obscure distance, the poor light and low hanging clouds shrouding everything. Within every man, unwelcome anxieties, formed by uncertainty, were rising to shape their thoughts.

'I see her,' declared Pat eventually, gritting his teeth, 'Yes, I see her, one point forward of abeam. Plainly the damnable fellow did not shorten sail during the night... *has been cracking on.*'

'DECK THERE! SAIL HO!' From the maintop Green shouted again; 'STARBOARD BEAM! *STARBOARD!*'

Pat turned about and looked across the quarterdeck and over the rail on the starboard side. 'By God, there's another one... another vessel... and I venture they are both frigates!' Pat's worst fears were confirmed in a huge surge of angst, a mental tidal wave as frightening as the real thing. 'CAN YOU MAKE OUT A PENNANT?' he screamed in full voice.

Excitement on deck rose substantially, and loud, voluble discussion abounded; to the extent that men from the larboard watch, alerted by the noise, began to come up from below, scores of them. Within minutes a great press of men gathered at both rails, some rushing from one side to the other via the foc'sle and even that foremost part of the quarterdeck, and much shouting resonated everywhere. From the main crosstree Green shouted again, 'TURKS! THEY ARE FLYING RED COLOURS! TURKS! TURKS!'

'Damn! Damn the Turks!' exclaimed Pat vehemently. He continued to stare through his glass, as did Duncan and Codrington through theirs, whilst Simon waited with a display of patience that the surgeon did not feel in the least, minutes passing in trepidation whilst he wondered what might result; and he strived without the least success to contain his rising apprehension and deep-seated fears that his surgical skills might yet be required once more.

'The starboard vessel is five miles off,' declared Pat eventually, snapping his telescope shut; 'Perhaps six; I doubt it is more.' Five minutes passed in silent thought until he walked across to the larboard rail and stared again at the unwelcome sight of the second frigate, the light improving just a little. 'The larboard fellow is six miles off; yes, I think six.' He turned to Codrington, 'Mr Codrington, we are making how many knots, would you say?'

Codrington turned to the bosun, 'Mr Sampays, kindly heave the log.'

'Dalby, the log, if you please!'

Clumsy Dalby, something of a deliberate frequenter to the quarterdeck even when not strictly on duty, for he perpetually sought to impress his captain with his limited talents, threw the line over the lee side whilst Sampays counted down the sand-glass. The line slipped languidly through Dalby's hand until the bosun shouted out, 'NIP!' Dalby reeled in as Codrington peered at his grasp. 'Six knots, sir; never a fathom more.'

'The line tells us six knots, sir,' echoed Codrington to an inquisitive Pat, 'six knots and not a fathom more.'

'Very good,' declared Pat by rote, although such was patently not to his liking. 'And the wind?' he prompted, despite knowing the answer before it was spoken.

'South... and steady on the larboard bow, sir; we have been close-hauled on the wind these two hours gone. The *Scirocco* is nigh upon us, I venture.'

'Indeed, and our course?'

'A point west of south-west, sir; as close as she will hold; that is to say, without the sails shivering. We have held her as near to the wind as near can be... all night, since the wind shifted.'

'Very good, Mr Codrington,' Pat resigned himself to a calculation of what confluence the wind and sea conditions might bring about for *Surprise* and her unwelcome neighbours. He turned to the assembly of his officers, all gathered about him, anxious curiosity plain to see in their eyes, trepidation written most particularly in Simon's gaze. 'Well, gentlemen, seemingly we are bound for Sicily's Cape Passaro... two Turk frigates likely pursuing us... *the damnable fellows.*' He tried for humour to put a different face on how he felt within, 'If only we might count on Byng coming to our assistance, eh?'

Blank incomprehension from Simon and puzzled stares of enquiry from almost everyone else told him that he had missed his mark. 'A man must make his attempt upon jest when he possesses but little else; would you not agree?' The silence endured.

Duncan whispered in Simon's ear, 'Admiral Byng took or burned sixteen Spanish prizes off Cape Passaro. It was a long time ago.' Simon, resolutely unimpressed, only frowned in reply.

'That fellow to larboard has the weather gauge, but nothing yet of great note,' Pat resumed in a voice with which he earnestly endeavoured to project a confidence that he himself did not feel in the least. No reply was returned as all present hung on their captain's next words.

Simon turned to Duncan and broke the continuing silence in nervous tone, 'How is it that those fellows have found us... and in the dark of the night? How could that be?'

'The new moon is scarcely waxing, and so I doubt *that* afforded any moonlight to help them,' replied Duncan; 'Perhaps they have been following the lamplight of the cabin and the gunroom? The night was clear, for much of it at least, and there was no rain of great note until an hour before the dawn.'

'Not at all,' declared Pat in loud voice and emphatic flat contradiction. 'More likely it is that... that when we saw one of them yesterday... they saw us too at the same time; and so they set their course for Malta... for that must be where they believed we were heading.'

'But how have they bracketed us?' pressed an anxious Simon.

'*Ships in the night*, I venture... nothing more,' said Pat in resigned voice. 'Doubtless the two of them diverged in the darkness... to their present separation.'

'Aye, that must be the case,' declared Duncan, adding, 'I wonder if they be the Turks that Adam referred to?'

'For sure,' Pat concurred gloomily, '... and now we are the meat in their sandwich.'

Simon spoke up once more in louder voice, his concerns rising, 'Surely, we are now a long way from Greek waters... from the area of interest for any Turk vessel? For Heaven's sake, why would they follow us to near Malta? Are they truly following us? Can we be sure of it?'

Pat considered briefly before replying, 'Yes, we are far removed from Greek and even Ionian waters... sixty leagues and more... and there is no sensible reason for any Turk frigate to be this far west; that is to say, there is no *purpose* for them here... *save to chase us*. I am persuaded that these ships are likely the ones we fought *before* the fall of Missolonghi... in the last days; and perhaps they bear us a grudge for the destruction of their fellow... the third vessel. You recall that it exploded at Oxia Island.'

'Such damnable malignity!' remarked Simon, shocked.

Pat gazed all about him, he looked to the sails - under no more than a moderate load - and to the yards - swung round as far as ever possible and all braced tight for close-hauling; he peered down over the stern rail to the wake - nothing of great turbulence. The barky was no longer slow, but she no longer held to the perfect course, for her bearing would ultimately put an unwanted Sicily on her bow. It was an uncomfortable conclusion that he did not care for in the least. However, and it was only the smallest of consolations, he deduced that the Turks would also be considering their own progress, and hopefully too their essential purpose; perhaps weighing the merits of it *or otherwise*. He turned his thinking to a calculation of their potential convergence. 'Five hours, I venture we have five hours if we hold to our course and they to theirs,' he pronounced to all who were listening. 'That will put us and them in range of the guns... *long range*, that is.'

The mood of all sank discernibly, a profound silence falling upon all present, and not a man added to Pat's pronouncement, not even Simon venturing further questions. The appearance of Murphy prompted Pat's thoughts in a different direction, 'Gentlemen, do you care to join me at my table for breakfast? Mr Codrington, would you do me the courtesy of extending my compliments and calling Mr Marston, Mr Pickering and Mr Mower to the cabin? With yourself, of course.'

'Certainly, sir.'

At his table, Pat sat with all his officers in something of a general air of apprehension, no one speaking, no one invited to speak, as Pat sipped his coffee, all the time thinking of the Turk frigates. The breakfast, a lukewarm gruel, seemingly appealed only to Simon, everyone else eating slowly and without the least enthusiasm. Eventually Simon spoke up to break the unwelcome silence but, seemingly, with no more than a platitude ventured, 'I am indebted to you, Pat, for recalling my desire for a proper porridge *with salt*. This is quite splendid. May I trouble you for the shaker; a trifle more of salt will serve very well.'

'Why,' Pat himself welcomed the intrusion, 'my dear grandma swore by a bowl of stirabout for breakfast.'

'Might I say that I hope there is no other signification to it?'

'Other signification? What do you mean?' Pat looked up from his own unenthusiastic eating, the porridge already congealed into a lumpy, uninviting mass, no more than lukewarm. He frowned and resolved to admonish Murphy, but for what precisely he never got to decide.

'The last meal for a condemned man, perhaps?' murmured Simon in despairing voice.

'Come, Simon, 'tis merely the routine... the regular breakfast for the men, no time before now for any other preparation... *so Murphy said.*'

'I beg your pardon, gentlemen,' murmured Simon, all at the table staring at him, their incredulity plain to see on several faces. '*I beg your pardon*, I am allowing my personal concerns to come to the fore; I will desist.' He resumed before Pat could speak, 'Forgive me, but will you indulge my curiosity?'

Pat nodded, his friend's rising apprehension plain to see, 'Please, go on.'

'Our pursuers... the two - *doubtless vengeful* - Turk battleships...'

'*Frigates*; they are frigates, Simon.'

'I beg your pardon, but surely this is no time for... for the unfamiliar - *to me at least* - minutiae of the mariner, *or even such as might be familiar*... to the... *the old salt*... such as yourself. In the matter of our two pursuers... if your thinking is... is - *will I say - running on the right lines*... is it not within our competency to... to run away? Perhaps we have the legs of them?' Simon's anxiety shone throughout his speaking.

'We may hope that is the case,' declared Pat in a voice that did not carry hope or conviction in the least; 'However, that they were broadside on... abeam of us... after a night's sailing suggests they are at least as fast as the barky. I am minded that they may have gained a mile or so since we first espied them. Perhaps they have recently been careened at Patras... and are not burdened by the accursed weed.'

The nods about the table indicated a consensus, and Simon glanced to Marston, sitting beside him, an anxious look the only response from his colleague. A brief moment and he ventured a despairing enquiry to Pat, 'I admit I am no navigator - *doubtless you have remarked that.*'

'You have *on occasion* mentioned *similar* words to that effect... though I was not entirely convinced.' Attempts were made to hide smiles around the table, a minor mirth which went wholly ignored by Simon.

'And in the presence of *bona fide* proficiency *such as yours* I have often been reminded that my duty rests... *downstairs*... and my talents lie along different lines. May I enquire: is it clear that the Turks will catch us?'

'Pretty clear,' said Pat with a degree of asperity creeping in.

Simon persisted, 'Can we not turn away?'

'Good gracious, Simon, do you care to poach upon *my* province, eh? What a fellow you are! Turn away from one and towards the other, sure,' Pat stared at his friend with something of a disapproving frown, reinforced by a scarcely discernible shake of his head; 'but which one would you see me flee from?'

'I will ask your forbearance... I only threw out the remark... *the notion*. Which one would be the more favourable choice, would you say?' Simon pressed but with small and dwindling hope.

'It's difficult to choose betwixt two blind goats... *so my grandma said*. She was always the sensible cove.' Pat cursed himself for the acerbic nature of his reply, which he recognised immediately; for he understood only too well the deep anxiety of his close friend, and he realised that his own angst was the painful root cause of his ill-conceived answer. He resumed, 'I am so sorry, Simon; nothing would please me more than to run... to show these fellows a clean pair of heels - *and allow me to say that I have never thought of myself in the least as a poltroon*; but no, I am minded that we must prepare for a... a probable engagement, conceivably as soon as...' Pat calculated, '... as soon as two bells of the afternoon watch; I doubt it will be earlier.'

'*Probable*: what an ill-sounding word that is,' an unhappy Simon spoke in tart voice, 'Even, I venture, an oft unwelcome imperfection in our oral definition... and wholly lacking in the least comfort of small certitude, so gravely disquieting as a consequence... at least in moments such as this.'

'I am sorry again, old friend, I am so; but that is our lot, as it seems to me.'

'Very well,' Simon sighed deeply; 'I am fully persuaded. With your permission, Marston and I will endeavour to make accommodation for *probable* forthcoming casualties by removing our existing patients from the *probable* perils of the cockpit... to the deeper bowels of this vessel... the bilges, would it be?'

For the first time Pat managed a weak smile, 'Not the bilges, no; you may find it reeks like a... a twenty-day egg *or worse*... and, for sure, it is disagreeably wet down there...' A round of small laughter, a gentle relief, echoed about the table. 'I venture the orlop will serve.' Pat turned to Mower, 'Mr Mower, please to set in train a dozen men to assist Dr Ferguson to shift our shipmates... *directly*.'

'Of course, sir,' Mower rose and left the cabin. Simon and Marston similarly stood up, alarm and anxiety fixed plain on their faces. They nodded politely to Pat without a word and departed.

'Mr Codrington,' declared Pat, 'please to ask Mr Timmins to attend the cabin.'

'Yes, sir,' Codrington rose and hastened away.

The gunner arrived within a few minutes, escorted in by a keenly curious Murphy. He touched his knuckle to his forehead and approached the table. 'Mr Timmins,' said Pat, 'Allow me to offer my best thanks once again for your most commendable works to create the incendiary shot with which we destroyed the Turk frigate at Oxia Island.'

'Why, thank you, sir,' Timmins spoke with caution and uncertainty in his voice, for the event was a little over two weeks in the past and his captain had thanked him profusely already on several occasions, as had everyone else in the crew, many times over.

Pat got straight to the point, 'Mr Timmins, please to explain your progress... that is to say... with making more of Mr Jelbert's infernal incendiaries.'

'Well, sir, I found a number of the *regular* explosive shells... rusting... *right rough they be*... in the bilges after the bosun opened the sweetening cock when we was in Argostoli.'

'I see. And are you now about preparing them such that they might be fired... that is to say, with the necessary *incendiary* contents... as Mr Jelbert perfected?'

'D'reckly, sir, but it is right proper slow going.'

'No doubt,' murmured Pat; 'but when will there be any at hand?'

'Well, sir, first the wet powder has to be pulled out through the hole in the shot carcass... careful like...'

'Yes.'

'... without the least prospect of a spark...'

'Of course.'

'... and so only a copper worm is to be used, sir... the handle being wooden... no danger there of a flash...'

'Indeed.' Pat strived to contain his impatience and managed to do so, at least to his own satisfaction, although the other faces around the table were also most anxious to hear of Timmins's progress, for the said shells had been *Surprise's* last-ditch saviour when fighting the Turk frigate at Oxia Island.

'When the carcass is empty, we stuff it with Mr Jelbert's proper special fire mixture; that is brimstone, pitch, quicklime and pork fat.'

'Pork fat? Pork fat!' exclaimed Pat; 'Does Wilkins know about this?'

'Oh aye, sir; we mix it all in one of his big pots... *the biggest*... not right near the stove, of course.'

'Of course, thankfully not.' Pat was relaxing just a very little, not caring to interrupt his gunner or at least deciding that such was likely to be futile, Timmins always being measured in his detailed explanations and never a man to be hurried. Pat resumed, 'I wonder if that was the pot in which Murphy cooked my dinner yesterday, the foul concoction that it was?'

'Oh no, sir, the pot is stowed in the for'ard magazine; we are mixing it all in there afore we return the gunpowder itself to the jumble... *the concoction*; and when 'tis right proper mixed all together we fill up the carcasses, full like, and next we wedge tight the hole... in the shell... with the fuse... That be a small wad doused in brimstone...'

'I see,' Pat sighed, realising in his exasperation that the gunner would not be curtailed from the detail he obviously felt was necessary.

'... and then we drape the shot wad... the one to hold tight the ball in the barrel... of the gun... with more brimstone... Mathew Jelbert himself - *bless him* - said *long ago* it was the proper finishing touch... but we ain't got to making any soused wads yet, sir.'

'Thank you for the... *the explanation*, Mr Timmins; for sure it is a most... *most complicated* procedure, no doubt; but *how many* of these shots are you able to make?'

'There ain't a deal left of the special shells, sir; no... the hollow 'uns with the drilled hole; only a few of 'em were found below.'

'I see. How many would that be... *exactly*, Mr Timmins?'

'A half-dozen of 'em, sir. I dare say there might yet be more... deep down in the filth of the bilge water... More *might* be found... but only six as yet... for want of looking again.'

'And when might we see the first of the finished shots... *the first six of them*... ready to fire?'

The gunner hesitated, thought for a few moments, chewed his lip and looked up to the deckhead, plainly thinking hard.

'Mr Timmins?' prompted Pat, the first hint of irritation in his voice; 'When exactly might that be? Pray tell, if you will?'

'Well sir, rightly saying, I can promise you...' another long pause.

'Yes?' Pat's patience had reached its very short limits, and his voice exuded only his impatience, a vexatious anxiety plain to see on his face, fast approaching anger.

Timmins smiled, the placatory gesture that he felt was necessary, 'Tomorrow morning, sir. That is, if I work all day and likely all night.'

'Your efforts will be much appreciated, Mr Timmins, but allow me to say...' Pat's rising ire subsided, the nearly abrasive edge in his voice tailed off, '... *allow me to say*... that I doubt we will be in a fit state to fire them *in the morning*. By then your shells *and the barky* will likely be at the bottom of the sea. We will need shells *today... and this morning would be most welcome*. What better - *what faster* - fabrication can you conceivably offer me... *the slightest thing?*'

'It is a half-hour gone, sir, to make each one,' declared the gunner hesitantly; 'And I would not care to trust it to anyone but myself; the mixing... the brimstone on the wads... 'tis right mighty dangerous, sir... One spark will blow us all to Kingdom Come!'

'Yes, I'm sure,' declared Pat with a long, long exhalation of frustration; 'But with... with the most sterling of endeavours... *with expedition*... could you promise me... say... *even those first half-dozen shells by noon*... or, at the latest, by one hour later, today... *today*, Mr Timmins?'

The ship's bell rang out stridently above their heads to signify one hour and a half to noon, ninety minutes. Minds raced, faces stared and tongues remained silent: *was it reasonable to ask the gunner to do in ninety minutes what he himself vouched would take twice as long?* The question hung in the air, the reply potentially crucial to the survival of the barky, as all realised with an uncomfortable and rising degree of apprehension.

'Well, sir... I mayn't vouch for noon; no, sir... with the best will... *that ain't possible*... but if you could spare me Freeman to help... he is the most careful of souls in every matter... a grand man with the... *with the lads below*... in the cockpit, sir... then I venture... I think... maybe I can... prepare them within an hour and a half later, sir.' Timmins realised that every man in the cabin, all gazing at him expectantly, hung their most earnest hopes on his own endeavours; and so he quickly added, 'Yes, sir, I can!'

'Very good; you shall have Freeman. I hope I may count on you for those half-dozen precious shells by three bells... and one hour later *at the very latest*; I venture we may be uncommonly hard-pressed by then.'

The gunner had come to terms with what was desperately needed and didn't hesitate, 'A half-dozen of Mr Jelbert's shot before four bells, sir; I believe you can count on me for that.'

'Thank you, Mr Timmins; I am much obliged to you... *much obliged*.' Pat felt a huge surge of relief, akin to the door of Hades itself opening - perhaps only slightly, no more than ajar - to allow his escape from the most desperate of predicaments. 'Please, make haste; you may yet be the saviour of the barky for a second time. God speed!' Timmins hastened away and Pat turned to his last lieutenant remaining at his table, 'Mr Pickering, look to the cockpit and find Freeman, I venture he is likely there; and send him to the for'ard magazine to aid Mr Timmins - *and without the loss of a moment.*' Pickering nodded and rushed away.

Only Macleod remained in the cabin with Pat as he reflected on the prospects for the barky and his men, 'Are we ready, Duncan?'

'Aye, nae doubt of it, old friend. If we have to fight, so be it; the lads will serve the Turks out... there isnae a frigate that will stand against us.'

'But two?'

'You are forgetting that we have the captain of the world.'

Pat smiled, 'I am obliged to you, old friend. However, this *surely coming* engagement will not be a trifling matter; no, not by a long chalk. I am minded... *I am sure...* that we cannot expose the barky to firing from *two* frigates; and - *for your private ear alone* - let me say *I would rather run...* as fast as the wind will carry us and without firing a single shot; but, I venture, that ain't about to happen, no such luck; for these Turk captains must be determined men... to follow us this far. No, I cannot see them according with our flight; there's a bloody day before us... *no doubt of that.*'

'Do you have any plan formed, at all?' asked Duncan, perceiving a small indication of confusion in his friend's mind, or at least an indecision.

'Oh, only a general notion... sure. If Mr Timmins can deliver the incendiary shot, that may yet save the day... *save the barky*; but with so few shells... *so very few...* we cannot allow our gunners to miss with ne'er a one; and so we will have to get close... *uncomfortably close*, and that may yet be our undoing... it much pains me to say.'

There came a knock on the door and Murphy entered accompanied by one of the crew, a scruffy, diminutive individual, looking a little anxious, perhaps nervous to be in the great cabin, a place not usually frequented by the mere mortals of the lower deck, save for those occasions when the cabin's great guns were employed. 'Well, sorr, will 'ee care to hear out Séamus Plunket? He be a friend of mine,' declared Murphy in the brazen voice which he reserved for his orders to his captain, customarily in the matter of his master's clothing.

Pat stared in curious scrutiny of his visitor, well known to him as one of a score of Irish hands in the crew. Perhaps because of that, and perhaps too because of Murphy's inflection, which he recognised perfectly well, he spoke in neutral voice, 'At ease, Plunket. What is your purpose? Why are you here, tell?'

Plunket, plainly very ill at ease despite Pat's command, merely spluttered, 'Sorr... I... that is... begging your honour's pardon... sorr...'

Murphy, aware that his captain's patience was sure to be very rapidly tested, and the present circumstances being never less favourable for the least delay in the slightest matter, quickly interjected, 'Well, sorr; the bosun it was... he found a rifle in Plunket's dunnage.'

'A rifle? A rifle!' exclaimed Pat, his patience dispelled in a flash, his ire swiftly rising, 'What in God's name are you doing with a rifle, Plunket? Explain yourself! Be quick about it!'

'It was a prize, sorr... a hand of cards it was... with a marine. He was escorting General Adam, sorr...'

'I see.' Pat stared, astounded and gathering a confusion of thoughts: bringing a rifle aboard was most irregular, perhaps even a flogging offence. His floundering mind dimly wondered whether Murphy had some nefarious involvement with his countryman.

Duncan intervened, 'Plunket, what do you say to this? Please to explain your interest in a rifle... your possession of it... *aboard the barky.*'

'Begging your pardon, sorr; but I be a grand shot with the rifle... since ever before being pressed these twelve years gone... though I ain't used one these three years... there being only muskets aboard, sorr.'

'Plunket... Plunket...' Pat mused, 'You are a Wexford man, are you not? I am minded that your family name is familiar to me... I have something of a... *will I say... indistinct* recollection from the past.'

'That be my cousin, sorr,' Plunket had gathered a little confidence and spoke up, 'Cousin Thomas, it was.'

'Please to go on,' prompted Pat more gently, the most vague of memories, a curiosity, stirring in his mind: *perhaps there was something worthwhile to hear from Plunket after all?*

'Thomas Plunket was my cousin, sorr; he showed me how to shoot when he came home from Spain; in the year 'fifteen it was. He served with the Rifles... with General Moore... at Corunna, where he shot down a French general at nigh on four hundred yards distance... *four hundred yards!* For so my cousin said... and his Colonel could scarcely credit it.'

'That's right,' muttered Murphy.

'What! You jest, surely?' exclaimed Duncan in a voice of derision; 'Four hundred yards? Bah! No man could achieve such shooting, never in life.'

'On the contrary,' an astonished Pat spoke up; 'it's the very truth. I recall that his feat was famous with all the Jollies in Deal... to the extent that every one of them without exception... *every man jack*... when I first served aboard *HMS Starling*... endeavoured to replicate it... with the Baker rifle, but without the least success. Surely you remember that? It was not long after you and I first met, and it was always the great challenge whenever we were thwarted by lack of wind; that is, when the captain allowed it.'

'Aye, it does ring a bell,' murmured Duncan somewhat doubtfully.

'And, sorr, my cousin... Thomas,' Plunket, much encouraged, resumed, '... he shot the General's aide right next... d'reckly; he did so,' Plunket was smiling now, plainly revelling in the telling of the tale of his famous cousin; 'At four hundred yards; it was so, sorr.'

'That's right,' muttered Murphy with more emphasis.

'Well,' declared Pat, 'if you can shoot as well as your cousin then we have need of you. A rifle, you say? Do you possess of ammunition?'

'Aye, sorr, a plentiful satchel of it; the Jollie lost right plenty... two guineas... and six shillings more... he owed me.'

'And had you lost the hand... *the cards*... how did you expect to pay your debt... of such a grand magnitude?' asked Pat with sarcasm and undisguised condemnation plain in his voice, knowing full well that there was not a man aboard the barky who possessed anything like such a sum at hand, including the officers.

'I... that is... is...' Plunket stuttered but could find nothing to say. Within moments Murphy interceded, 'Well, sorr, it was the... *the special deck*... the pack of *my* cards which... that is to say...'

'Stop! I do not care to hear more,' announced Pat angrily; '*It's not a secret if three know it*... and you, Murphy - *of all people* - will be familiar with that particular old saying from home.' Pat was positively glaring at his two countrymen. 'It is plain that you are both scoundrels of the first order, knaves, picaroons! Plunket, you too are an Irishman; do *you* not recall that other sage wisdom of the old country... *do not scald your lips with another man's porridge?* I speak of Murphy's marked cards!'

Plunket remained silent, admonished and much taken aback. Murphy interjected, hoping to recover the situation before his captain threw them both out, or worse, 'Well, sorr, Plunket 'ere, he can shoot that rifle... right proper.'

'Very well,' Pat's ire was slightly mollified, his interest somewhat restored; 'Plunket, you will hold yourself ready for my call, when you will go to the mizzen top - *nowhere else* - and you will look to the Turk ships' quarterdecks for any officers you might espy to shoot. Am I plain?'

'Aye aye, sir; to the mizzen top on your shout.'

'If you can knock down a captain then perhaps that may make that small difference - *a precious difference* - which conceivably might create a distraction in the Turk vessel's command... in that brief and dangerous moment when the scales of battle are about to tip one way or the other; for these affairs are usually a damn close run thing. Do you follow?'

'I reckon I do, sorr, aye.'

'Very good. Then I hope we may both congratulate each other when the bloody work is done. The *mizzen* top; don't forget that... and shoot only at officers... *officers only!*'

Plunket positively beamed from ear to ear as Murphy hustled him out.

'Pat,' Duncan spoke up, seeking to quash such fanciful and desperate aspirations, to bring matters firmly down to earth, 'Four hundred yards indeed! Two cables! Surely such is a very long way - *too far* - for firing a rifle with the least hope of accuracy. I venture the tale has surely matured in the telling. Why, that is scarcely less than the range when even the great guns will open for the sure result... *but a rifle?* What of windage? What of the movements of our vessel... and the target?'

'At the risk of coming it the philosopher... *thankfully, Simon ain't here to hear me out...* it is ever the case that the most exceptional men *do* come along in every sphere... not many, not often... for how could we then think of them as exceptional? But it is true that Plunkett shot down two Frenchies... *two... and at a grand distance* - else the story would never have rated the telling. Why else would a hundred and more of Jollies aboard all those vessels waiting for wind in the Downs roadstead spend all day trying the shot? That they never succeeded hardly supports the case... *that is true...* save that it confirms the exceptional skill of the shooter, *the very legend himself*, Thomas Plunkett of the Rifles. We may accept that the fact that as his colonel congratulated him personally such is all that *we* need for our sure belief in the tale's veracity. I venture that if *our* Plunket is even half the shooter that his cousin was then we are surely favoured by his presence... for plainly our muskets, inaccurate that they are, will serve little purpose save that we are about to board the

Turk... or *vice versa.*' Pat grimaced and paused briefly before adding as if in supplication, prayer even, 'Duncan, old friend, if we are to engage *two* Turk frigates in a very few hours then I will be mightily pleased for even the smallest of mercies.'

'Aye,' Duncan nodded, resigning himself to what would be.

The bosun appeared at the door, plainly in a state of mild agitation. He touched his knuckle to his forehead before his enquiry, 'I beg your pardon, sir. Are you ready to permit the usual preparations... striking down the walls?'

'I am, Mr Sampays; do carry on. Clear for action, and please to ask your mates to pipe the hands to dinner. I venture there is time enough for a bite.'

'Aye aye, sir.'

Within a minute a half-dozen men arrived and began to swiftly dismantle the flimsy wooden partitions between the cabin and the coach, and the forward one which abutted the gun deck. From his table Pat could now look forward along the length of the ship, all the great guns in his sight and near two hundred men standing ready all about them. From his exposed chair, Pat listened to the bustle all about the gun deck; after a few minutes he heard the familiar strains of *"Nancy Dawson"* played by the piper.

Time slipped by in unsettled thoughts of possible eventualities until the sound of a single bell, announcing the end of the first half-hour of the afternoon watch, wrenched Pat's anxieties to new heights, a familiar old feeling, and he instantly abandoned all thoughts of his own imminent dinner. With a silent nod to Duncan he stood up immediately, leaving the cabin to gain the quarterdeck via the steps whilst consciously trying hard to avoid displaying the least indication of his rising fear and uncertainty to his men as he paced slowly towards the helm, Macleod one step behind him. Pat nodded to Pickering, the officer of the watch, but he was already pondering Timmins's promise of the incendiary ammunition even before he gazed through his telescope as slowly as could be across the starboard rail towards the

101

horizon. Sure enough, the first Turk frigate, still holding to her near parallel course, had gradually closed the separation to less than half a league. Her sails under load, her guns run out, she presented a grand sight to the military mariner that Pat was as he gazed with professional admiration at her lines. He wondered with an uncomfortable curiosity about the depth of her captain's determination, about his obvious intent to pursue his quarry, and so very far from the Ionians. He stared in careful scrutiny for what seemed an age through his glass; it would not be very much longer before firing would open, perhaps one hour more. He turned about to look to larboard; the second Turk had similarly closed, but perhaps a little less; she was, Pat estimated, two miles off the beam. Plainly the Turk strategy was to close up on their prey so slowly that they would gain their broadside firing positions concurrently; hence, neither seemed to wish to close more directly and before the other. Pat concluded that their captains must be the most patient of men, or perhaps they were simply cautious. His own mind raced: *would it be possible to deal a blow to the starboard pursuer before the other, more distant frigate could catch up and intervene?* He looked to his lieutenant, 'Mr Pickering, what do you care to report of the Gunner's progress?'

'I attended the magazine just a very few minutes ago, sir; Pickering nodded, as if in reinforcement of a favourable reply; 'and Mr Timmins has near completed the promised six shells. Perhaps another fifteen minutes and he swore he would send them to the deck. Dalby and five men are standing by to shift them.'

Pat nodded, 'Very good. Perhaps we are blessed with a trifle more time than I had first thought before the firing opens.' He continued to stare through his telescope, carefully scrutinising the oncoming two frigates, but the distance was still too great to identify either as those that *Surprise* had engaged sixteen days previously. He looked up once more to his sails; certainly, they were under load, but not as much as he might have hoped; the barky was likely making near eight knots in the southerly *Scirocco*, both the wind and *Surprise's* speed building significantly within the past hour. There was for the first time a modest lee heel to the deck, but scarcely anything of the least note to trouble his gunners. He looked high to the skies; no longer were there any clouds of significance in sight. It was already an uncomfortably hot day, and that was before the fire and heat which the great guns would soon unleash. He felt the perspiration around the rim of his hat and under his arms, and - not for the first time - he silently asked himself whether he was frightened, and admitted to himself that he was; he pondered why his feelings differed so much from the prior engagements he had fought, when his emotions had been more measured, more controlled; but to his great frustration he could find not the least of answers.

A distant and solitary flash of orange-yellow light to starboard caught his attention, dispelling his reflections; it was immediately followed by an expanding cloud of white smoke issuing from the side of the Turk frigate, billowing up and swiftly drifting beyond her in the wind.

'He is gauging the range, sir,' said Duncan, at Pat's side.

'An optimist, for sure,' murmured Pat, carefully counting; 'Well, we must presume that the Turk has made his number.'

One, two, three, four, five, six... the dull boom of the distant explosion was heard by all on deck, everyone counting the seconds since the flash, and eyes everywhere searched for some indication of the fall of the shot; but amidst the white flecks of low wave tops, stretching over an infinite expanse of blue-grey water as far as the eye could see, no splash was sighted.

'Ten cables distant... I venture,' declared Pat; 'We have yet another hour, perhaps even two at this rate, before the Turk will be in *effective* range. Mr Codrington, we will reduce canvas to topsails and fore course only, save that the main course will be close-reefed; I would not wish that particular canvas to be set afire; and we will likely need something of a contribution from it if we are to escape a Turk which, I venture, has likely been careened.'

'Aye aye, sir,' the lieutenant nodded and hastened away.

'Mr Macleod,' Pat resumed, 'ready the guns. We will prepare the great guns to fire solid shot when we open. If I am knocked down, you are to direct the smashers - *loaded with grape* - to fire aloft upon the Turk mizzen. We may hope to damage rigging, perhaps even to shred her mizzen, so as push her downwind if her master cannot counter the swing of the foresail; the better to make our escape.'

'Yes, sir,' Macleod nodded his understanding. 'I will send Dalby to see if he can find anything of langridge to complement the grape; such metal will inflict a dreadful damage upon canvas. Mr Mower, to the fore; Mr Pickering, to the waist. Tom, I fear you will have great need of your humour before very long, aye. Gentlemen, to your stations and ready your guns, solid shot to open.'

The lieutenants departed, minds focused on their duties; the former apprehension that all had felt for the most part was now subsumed within the flurry of necessary preparation; for all were exceedingly experienced officers, wholly accustomed to their duties under fire. Their sense of anxiety whilst waiting was controlled, the fear that all felt was deliberately suppressed, as far as that was possible; and all looked to their fellows to find that mutual reassurance which was the valuable comfort so vital to every man in such extreme, life-threatening circumstances; indeed, it was long recognised that for the majority of men it was the primary influence which held them to their station, to their guns, acutely so when the shot and grape were flying.

From the waist below, all on the quarterdeck heard Pickering's shouts as he began the customary procedure for readying the great guns, 'SILENCE! SILENCE THERE!' The hubbub of speculation, of universal conversation amongst the crew, died away, and Pickering resumed with a resonant shout, amplified by his speaking trumpet, 'CAST LOOSE YOUR GUN!' This was echoed by each gun captain to teams all along the deck. Loaders and spongers standing ready about every gun hastened to cast off the rope which hung from above and looped around their gun muzzle, swiftly followed by the unhooking of the side tackles which held the gun firm to the side of the ship. The fire engine had been employed to soak the deck such that hot sparks from unburnt powder would not set afire highly receptive oakum, tar and pitch between the planks, or ignite spilt powder. Great swathes of sand together with black ashes from the cook's stove were already strewn all over the deck to save the gunners from slipping and sliding when the blood began to flow. The water-filled scuttle-butts were lined up all along the centre of the deck as if in procession, awaiting the call of throats afire with choking powder smoke. A swift but unhurried routine followed, every man well versed in it: the loaders and spongers opened up the gun ports, and every gun on its truck, fore and aft, was flooded with additional and welcome light. Crews all along the ship's side stared out inquisitively, a better view available, to see what could be seen of their expected adversaries. The handspike men, in businesslike fashion, laid out their tools on the deck alongside their guns, and every gun captain attached their gunlock, bolting it tight at the touch hole. Standing back but close by every gun, one of the idlers stood ready with Pat's long-held backup for a faulty gunlock failure, holding a smouldering linstock ready to fire the priming powder charge. Further back, alongside the gratings and hatchways, round shot was stacked in ready racks, four of the cast iron balls awaiting each gun; and the powder-boys sat back four paces behind them, in anxious silence as they awaited the frenzy that they knew was coming.

Pat paced forward; he leaned down over the waist rail and stared along the length of the gun deck. Men stood ready all about their guns; in the main, all of them remained mute, shirtless, cloth wrapped around their heads and around their waists; a few remarks were offered here and there to cheer their tie-mates and members of their mess; and oddly, to Pat's experienced eye, the activity seemed no more than abstract, the customary firing drill that all were so well-versed in; even now at this late hour, the crisis near upon his ship, upon his friends and shipmates, his mind struggled to accept the cruel reality that *Surprise* had not yet finished with her bloody purpose. Bitter waves of regret and anxiety coursed powerfully through his thoughts, and he wondered, momentarily, whether his hero, Nelson, had experienced such frightening hesitations before a battle. 'God between us and all harm,' he muttered to himself quietly, adding, 'Perhaps I am become too damnably old for this?' He felt his pulse racing and he brought his mind back to an uncomfortable focus with a determined wrench. His gaze noticed not the least thing conducted in haste, a sure recipe to his mind for accidents; a shot carelessly dropped and rolling away would hinder the gun crew and potentially distract others nearby from their fast attendance to every step in the firing process, and such a loss of time might be catastrophic for the ship. He knew very well from past engagements that best prospects were afforded to that ship which could strike faster and more accurately; an effective broadside might quickly secure the decisive advantage. However, an untimely snap of the gunlock by a nervous gunner and a premature discharge was a great danger to the sponger and loader, even a potentially mortal one; but Pat had no such worries, his men were supremely competent after frequent training at sea and after the many battles that *Surprise* had fought. No, he had no fears of failure on the part of his men, and that was a comfort to him in his own, ever-present anxieties, the uncomfortable strain that it was; one which seemed to live with him, even to haunt him, all of the time these days.

His eyes caught the flashes of a dozen and more eruptions from that Turk frigate to starboard, quickly obscured by smoke, more flashes penetrating the expanding great murk rising all along her hull in incessant repetition, the sight prompting his conviction that her captain must be keen to get firing and battle underway, maybe even without waiting for his compatriot: *perhaps he really did have a grudge against the barky?* Seconds later, over the booming roar of the distant Turk guns, Pat heard the shouts from all three of the lieutenants, their speaking trumpets still clear in the gusting wind, all the gunners standing ready and patiently awaiting the next order, 'TAKE OUT YOUR TOMPION!' It was echoed by every gun captain, 'CAST OUT THE TOMPKIN!' The tomkins, as the seamen referred to them, were prised out and left to hang on their lanyard below the muzzle. Every captain hastened to strap his gun to its train tackle at the back of the gun and to the deck ring amidships, making the gun immobile and ready for loading the powder charge, wad and shot.

Pat's flickering gaze alternated rapidly between the great white cloud of powder discharge which had wholly enveloped the Turk frigate and the sight of rapid activity below him on his gun deck. For a brief moment he thought he caught sight of the splash of shot falling into the sea, but it was at least two hundred yards short. 'I venture they are warming their guns, Mr Macleod,' he remarked in measured voice.

'LEVEL YOUR GUN!' Pickering's trumpeted order was plain to every man on deck, echoed again by all the gun captains. The handspike men heaved and the captain hammered tight his wooden quoin wedge until the barrel was level and the gun could be loaded.

In that moment Murphy appeared on the quarterdeck in evident agitation, 'Well, beg pardon, sorr,' he exclaimed in loud voice, but Pat was wholly engaged in observing the Turk frigate. More gun flashes were visible after the two minutes which her captain had plainly allowed for the obscuring gun smoke from her first discharges to blow away.

'Not now, Murphy,' Pat constrained his own voice with difficulty and reined in another rush of rising anxiety.

Murphy persisted, 'Well, Mr Timmins sends his compliments, sorr, and begs to report that the... *Mr Jelbert's special shot...* all be nearly ready.'

Pat started: *nearly ready, only nearly; what did that signify?* Notwithstanding, Pat smiled, for it was welcome news. He reflected on Murphy's words; Mathew Jelbert, who had died in Pat's arms on the quarterdeck one year previously, plainly, remained revered aboard the barky; for all aboard still referred to him even now as *Mister* Jelbert. 'Thank you, Murphy. Please to tell Mr Timmins that when finished they are to remain in the for'ard magazine... and held to my order. Wait! When you have passed the message, light along to the galley; I am in the way for coffee. See what can be found; a hot mug of the black nectar would be the treasure of the world.'

'D'reckly, sorr,' Murphy hastened away.

'LOAD CARTRIDGE!' Pickering's strident voice boomed out and was echoed all down the deck. Pat returned his gaze to those guns visible below in the waist. At every gun, the man designated as the powder carrier stood ready with his salt box, within which the first two powder charges were preserved, the salt ensuring that they remained dry. A burst of activity erupted as loaders all along the deck stuffed the first cartridge down the barrel, followed by a wad; and then the sponger shoved them deep within with his ramrod, as far as it was possible to go. Gun captains hastened to prick the powder charges with a copper wire thrust deep into the vent.

Pat noted with satisfaction that all seemed well with his gun crews, those that he could see from the rail. Duncan interrupted his thoughts, 'I see splashes, sir, from the fall of shot; the balls are falling but a cable short.'

'Yes, thank you, Mr MacLeod.' Pat considered that the firing of *Surprise's* great guns could not long be delayed. He stared over the lee side; that Turk frigate to starboard had closed to probably a mile distant, no more. He swallowed, unsuccessfully, his throat drying in an instant, a flush of alarm rising which passed in mere seconds but which left his mind racing, a flood of repetitive thoughts rushing to fill his planning, his anticipatory thinking: *how would this all go? What tactics might he best choose? Was there the slightest alternative to a slugging confrontation?*

'LOAD SHOT AND WAD!' Pickering's voice, loud through his speaking trumpet, broke the train of Pat's thoughts once more and restored his awareness of the visibly ever-closer incoming Turk shot, the booming noise of distant guns noticeably louder when they followed the bright orange-yellow flashes which roared out from all along the side of the Turk frigate. Pat's close attention returned to those discharges and he counted the seconds between one full broadside and the next, concluding that it was a long three minutes, more like three and a half. That was slow, very slow, and such would never satisfy him. He expected three shots in five minutes, nothing less; at least for the first thirty minutes before his men tired; thereafter, he doubted that many men would have the least energy left after the hell that was firing the great guns; and that also assumed that his men remained alive and capable of continuing, for a great deal of damage and casualties would surely be inflicted in a half-hour. He shuddered and his mind recoiled from the terrible image that flashed into his imagination, a familiar scene from prior engagements. At least the slow rate of the Turk firing was something of a small but satisfying relief. His racing mind paused to dwell briefly on the thought that the Turk captain was about to find out, if he had not seen it before in the prior engagement near Oxia Island, that his adversary, albeit fundamentally a creature of wood and iron, was akin to the most aggressive of bulldogs, one that would certainly bite, would bite hard, and would bite extremely fast when provoked.

All along both sides, loaders inserted and rolled into the twenty-eight gun barrels the heavy iron shot, eighteen pounds in weight, the solid balls five inches in diameter. Pat understood the capabilities of his guns and gunners very well; he knew that with a one-third charge - six pounds of powder compared with the eighteen pounds of the shot - the ball would fly from the muzzle, elevated at four degrees, at seventeen hundred feet per second and reach the target, one mile distant, after just three seconds and with its speed scarcely reduced. He knew too that such a ball would not penetrate the thick oak or fir hull of the enemy at that relatively long range, and so he preferred to open fire at no greater distance than half a mile, when the shot would assuredly break through any part of a ship's hull, slowing as it did so; and in so doing the shot would smash out from the hole dozens of long, sharp and vicious splinters of wood, with energy enough to maim and even kill any unfortunate man within ten feet and even further from the ball strike. All these calculations passed rapidly by rote through his mind and he shuddered, for he remembered the appalling wounds inflicted on his own men in many previous battles of the Greek war, and he recalled that a dozen and more of his men so afflicted, even now, remained below in the care of the surgeons.

'Gun captains, watch for the falling of your first shot!' Pat heard his lieutenants' loud shouts resonate along the deck, but no reply from anyone was offered or heard, for the tension of the moment had intensely gripped every man; this was no practice.

Pat knew that his guns could fire accurately out to far beyond a mile, even to a maximum range of over two miles; but such was, to Pat's thinking, a folly, a waste of powder and shot. It was fine for the interception of a vessel akin to a blockade runner, for the fright of being fired on would invariably bring her to a swift halt, her braces slackened and her canvas flapping; but such was not the case now. No, these were opponents of a very different ilk; hence, he would hold fire until the range was very much less. *Surprise's* opening broadside, fired at perhaps six hundred yards, three cables, a range that many captains would consider to be point blank, would be swiftly followed by a reduction in the weight of her powder charges, and slower shot would result, a change which would assuredly smash out far more deadly wooden splinters and inflict consequently more casualties upon his enemy's crew. One quarter charge, four and a half pounds of powder, was his preferred choice for closer firing; but he worried that, perhaps, such might prove to be a luxury beyond him; for conceivably both Turks, not one, would then be close and firing upon him. His angst was rising and took the form of a burning acid bile in his throat. He tried once more to swallow, to cast it down, but without the least success.

He took further small comfort in the knowledge that *Surprise's* guns would be not be firing old and rotten damp grain, long-expired in barrels which had likely crossed the Atlantic several times; no, thankfully, she was provisioned with the best red Dutch gunpowder, for it offered twenty-five percent more explosive force than any powder that could be found elsewhere, most particularly the customary white letter make-do which was the norm in any Admiralty store. He had been delighted when Melville had authorised its relatively expensive purchase for the barky, the cost being two shillings per pound weight, which would be considered exorbitant by any respectable captain. Certainly, the Turks would not possess anything like it. He speculated: *perhaps that might solve his conundrum? Perhaps he should open fire at a greater range? Perhaps the Dutch powder would offer him the key advantage?* He tried again to spit out the discomfort within his mouth but failed; his throat had seemingly constricted, the unwelcome discomfort that it was, and his mouth seemed drier than ever.

'Well, sorr, 'ere be the coffee,' Murphy's voice, as grating as it usually was, interrupted Pat's thoughts, for which he found himself most grateful; it offered a momentary descent to Earth, for his heart was pounding so fast and so strong that he felt that Murphy must hear it. It was something of a fluctuating relationship which he enjoyed with his long-term steward and countryman; on occasion it even brought Pat to consider which of them was actually in charge within the cabin, at least in domestic matters, as far as anything could be described as such when at sea and in wartime. He remonstrated frequently with Murphy, but his steward had long ago become accustomed to it; indeed, he rarely seemed to take the least notice. The strange and unexpected thought struck Pat in a fleeting instant that perhaps the accord with Murphy, long refined by both parties, was not too dissimilar to his own relationship with his wife, the cherished companion that she was; and that particular rumination prompted a sudden and deep flush of emotion, for he cherished his wife a great deal; he missed her very much, his children too: *if only he had enjoyed more time with them!* But he knew only too well that such was not a luxury afforded to an enterprising sea captain; it was certainly one he had never enjoyed throughout seemingly all of his career; naval employment had seized him firmly from the earliest age at sea. He wondered in that so profound instant of reflection what his children thought of his absences, and from what seemed to be in that moment a far distant Connemara home. A cough from his steward and a tray with a solitary mug upon it was proffered, a decidedly steaming aroma detected even within the blowing wind over the quarterdeck, and Pat eagerly grasped his return to the present with something of gratitude in his mind and in his voice, 'Thank you, Murphy. That is a delight for the eyes... *and the nose*. A flower upon your head!' A suspicious Murphy nodded. Pat resumed, 'Now look to Wilkins and tell him that his stove is not to be extinguished when our firing opens; rather, tell him to run it hot, as hot as hot can be, so that we may heat red hot shot... *and not to spare the coal!*'

The realisation that the barky's great guns would soon be firing, expected though it was, registered with Murphy as a most unwelcome and sudden reminder; and this was despite the Turk frigate having been firing for some time. He nodded and stepped back to stare and take in everything happening all about the quarterdeck. Carronade crews were standing ready but inactive, the range still much too great for the shorter-range weapons to register upon the Turk frigates. Murphy was rarely on deck when firing opened, but he well understood the effectiveness of all the guns including the carronades. The latter were particularly destructive at short range: they could fire either a far heavier projectile than the long guns, one which was a true ship destroyer, and could be so in double quick time; but for that advantage a captain had to place his own command under a similar close range hail of destruction; hence, for Pat, it was one weapon for which he held the most careful of considerations before use; it was certainly not his primary one. Alternatively, the carronades could fire grape and attack either the sails of the enemy vessel or the fragile bodies of its men. Pat had decided upon firing aloft at sail canvas, the mizzen sail particularly; because he knew that, if the mizzen sail became severely damaged or destroyed, the opponent captain had far less ability to influence any turning motion of his ship, had nothing to counterbalance the foresail; and the result would be an inevitable turn downwind which could not easily be resisted. He took a gulp from his coffee mug and revelled in the familiar and satisfying pleasure of it and the relief it offered to his dry throat. 'Murphy,' Pat spoke again, his steward standing as if stunned, 'Look to the galley.' His steward nodded but could find no words; he simply hastened away.

'RUN OUT YOUR GUNS!' bawled Pickering through his speaking trumpet. Gun captains all along the deck cried out, 'HEAVE!' The gun crews unhooked the holding train tackle ropes restraining the heavy guns and hauled hard on those tackles; the carriages were tugged forward until their front wheels were stopped by the low cill of the gun port on the hull side, the barrels projecting far ahead of where dangerous flames might spark fire within the oakum of the hull planking.

'PRIME!' Pickering's voice had become a scream, perhaps a strain on his throat or even a tint of fear creeping in; for the first Turk shot had actually reached the barky, several thuds audible on the hull side; but no damage had yet resulted, as far as anyone could see. Anxious gun captains pressed the pricker down the vent at the back of the barrel to rip a hole in their gun's powder cartridge, immediately followed by insertion of the quill which was the fuse, concluding with a sprinkle of gunpowder from a powder horn into the flashpan of the gunlock. Activity stopped; the guns all along the deck were ready and their captains awaited Pat's command. Men paused from their physical exertions to take stock, to hold frightening emotions and raging fears in check, to look to their fellows for mutual encouragement; many a man resorted to a covert and swift swig from his own small flask, a welcome slug of rum most particularly much enjoyed; but such was not appreciated by any of the gun captains, and loud shouts of abuse quickly followed, a few flasks severely ripped away with violence, to fall upon the deck to be kicked out of the gun ports.

'Such a waste of powder!' declared Duncan to Pat as another broadside exploded from the Turk; 'Why does he persevere so? Does he expect to set a host of splinters flying at this range?'

'That is the case, sure, at long range; but I dare say he expects his guns to warm further... hotter, the shot to fly higher; perhaps he hopes to strike a mast or even the wheel... a disabling strike,' Pat replied absently, for the firing, beyond effective range, did not yet much concern him; rather, he was calculating how long it would be before both Turk frigates achieved an effective range: only a very few minutes remained; no longer was it hours; not a deal of time was left if Pat was to conceive a winning strategy, but he fretted and remonstrated with himself in silence because he had not yet been able to think of the perfect one; and to his great angst, his thinking returned every time to that same frightening question to which he had no answer: *how long could the barky endure if she was bracketed by both Turks?*

Chapter Six

Tuesday 9th May 1826   13:00   *The south Ionian Sea*

In the cockpit, Simon Ferguson spoke with Michael Marston and Abel Jason. The latter man was ostensibly engaged as ship's purser, but in fact he was much more than that; he was a most valuable man, one of considerable talents, and had assumed the role of assistant surgeon to help Simon and Marston during the severest of all battles, the great conflagration several years previously which had been the protracted defence of Samos island near the Turkish coast. That had been the most dreadful experience of all time for the men of the barky, for many of their shipmates had been killed and wounded during two protracted and very tiring battles over successive days. Jason had also served as interpreter in meetings with Greeks, with their admirals particularly; and had even conversed on one fraught occasion with a boarding party of Turks demanding to see the barky's official papers, a tense event as Pat possessed none such. Jason had been exceedingly fortunate to preserve his own life in the flight from the Egyptian invaders of Vasiladi, an outlying island fort near to Missolonghi; a prolonged and most desperate escape through the neck-high salt waters of the lagoon between the island and the temporary sanctuary which was the town had chilled his body to near death. A distressed Simon had nursed him constantly until he had recovered; yet even now, weeks later, it was clear to the surgeons that he remained weak. To Simon's mind it seemed plain that a still fragile Jason would require much more time to fully recover, perhaps several more months.

'Jason,' Simon spoke to his respected colleague in encouraging voice, 'I venture that our wounded shipmates... below us... upon the... *the orlop*... will require attending throughout the forthcoming encounter. I am thinking of Kitto and Hammett most particularly. Will you do me a great kindness and attend them?'

'My dear Ferguson,' replied Jason without hesitation and suspecting Simon's motives, rightly perceiving the request to be motivated by Simon's concerns for the safety of a much-esteemed friend, 'I will not.' He resumed quickly, 'I am of a mind that one of the hands, the excellent nurses that they have become these three weeks gone, can attend our *present* patients. I believe that I can be of greater facility and service here... *with you*... and with Marston in attending any *future* unfortunates. Hence, I beg you not to seek to gull me with what are plainly generous but - *will I say* - *obscure* reasons.'

Simon considered this briefly before replying, 'Very well, *you smoked it*, as O'Connor might say; however, you are to consider that I am also your physician, and were it to become plain to my eye that you are in the least physical distress then... *and I trust that you will reciprocate my good faith*... I will be infinitely obliged were you to retire from the cockpit and look to a place of recuperation... *downstairs*... a station where you may usefully continue to attend our present charges resting there. Am I plain?'

'Perfectly, Ferguson; then we are in accord.'

'Very well; will you look to our bandage and medicine stocks in preparation?' Simon smiled, his friend's accession to his precautions a small relief in a rising sense of dread and foreboding. 'I am minded that I will go upstairs and consult with O'Connor... to see the situation and gain some notion of when we may be called upon to... to... *well, you will grasp the general notion.*'

On the quarterdeck Pat continued to wrack his brain for the best tactics to fight the two Turk frigates; that one to larboard had closed to within a mile and a half; the nearer one, to starboard, was little more than a mile off the beam, and her firing was consistent, becoming dangerous, her shot skipping across the sea surface to smash against *Surprise's* hull; as yet

116

with little residual force and no obvious damage to the barky, or at least nothing which anyone had reported.

'A wee bit closer, sir, and those shots will damage our timbers,' ventured Duncan eventually in quiet voice, whilst scrutinising Pat carefully, but without such becoming obvious in the least.

Pat nodded but did not reply. He dimly suspected his friend's comment to be a gentle prod, a nudge towards a focus upon the present, the immediacy of the situation. He turned and trained his telescope on the more distant and larboard Turk to windward. 'She has opened her gun ports,' he declared in sombre tone. 'Another half-hour, I doubt it will be longer, and she will also open fire.'

Duncan looked discreetly to his friend's face, to his composure, searching for that resolute leader in whom he had always placed his complete confidence, never before doubting Pat's decision-making; for the barky had survived the most dreadful of engagements, a great deal of them, and often against superior odds in the bloody Greek war, a conflict which he had long come to hate with a vengeance. Questions raced through his mind: *was O'Connor still the same man? Was there an intimation of hesitation, even of indecision, afflicting his captain? How long could it be before even the very strongest of men faltered?* Macleod could not suppress such disquietude, but he hoped with every vestige of his being that such uncertainties had not afflicted his dear friend, for he reckoned that the life of every man aboard the barky depended on it; their very survival relied on Patrick O'Connor, on his decision-making, and now more than ever before. Duncan shivered as he realised that the despised feeling of fear was creeping up upon himself.

In that instant a shot from the nearer Turk frigate on the starboard beam skipped up from the water surface and smashed into the bulwark, breaking through in a shower of splinters and rolling in slow fashion across the deck planks, it's force utterly spent. Every man on deck stared at it, all present fortunately uninjured, before every eye turned to look towards Pat, standing between the helm and the gratings. A long sigh and Pat turned to face Duncan; seemingly his plan was decided, 'I am minded that we must look to the wind, such that it is, to assist us; and so... *and so* I believe that it will serve us better to attack that fellow to leeward... on the starboard beam.'

Duncan stared carefully at his friend, assessing the declaration and the man. Pat did not seem nervous, for he had somehow shaken off his former, tired air of gloom and apprehension, and he held himself erect and was speaking with a rekindled authority. Duncan nodded to Pat with encouraging confirmation, for he found himself hoping with a desperation that he had never formerly felt that his friend had found the resolution that would preserve all precious souls aboard the barky. The personal feeling of care for all of his shipmates resonated; it had never before become more firmly lodged within his thoughts; for it described perfectly how every man felt about his comrades-in-arms after three years of sailing and fighting together in the bloody Greek venture. Macleod continued to study his friend more closely and as discreetly as could be, and in his gaze his own most profound conviction was restored once again: here before him was a truly remarkable man, a captain that everyone aboard the barky knew would seek to preserve their lives, would not hazard them unnecessarily; and it was sure that they would follow him through the veritable Gates of Hell itself, if so ordered; and that thought cheered Duncan in his own sinking feelings of dismay, the odds against them so great, the situation so dangerous, so threatening.

'We are presently close-hauled... keeping the wind...' declared Pat; 'Our sails are as near as near can be to shivering... which might be the case were not Barton at the helm.' Pat's thinking developed aloud as he looked to his two friends, Duncan and Simon - the latter had also appeared at his side - for any indication of their understanding and endorsement. He addressed himself pointedly to Simon as if to try to assuage his friend's visible anxieties with explanation,

'The ship is on a larboard tack... close hauled...' The surgeon merely blinked and stared, not caring to reveal his incomprehension of the least nautical terminology, although that was long known to every man aboard. 'If we fall off to starboard... ' Pat continued, '... if we come off the wind to sail free... and then further... such that we will go large with a quartering wind...' Pat pressed on, '... then we may likely gain another knot or even two...'

No response from Simon, who could not comprehend a word, but Duncan nodded emphatically even as he held his silence; he sensed the emerging essence of the plan, although his comprehension was far from complete.

'We will shift our course to engage that Turk on our starboard beam,' Pat continued. 'We will strike her hard... very hard... and her fellow may yet turn away... as one of them did at Oxia Island; perhaps it was that fellow?' Pat nodded towards the larboard frigate. 'Indeed, we may pray he will heave-to... to assist the other... *the first Turk*; if, that is, we do serve him out... in proper Bristol fashion. Either way, we will make best use of every knot... and run as fast as the barky can carry us... before the wind. We may have the legs of the *second* Turk...' This latter element was stated with as much conviction that Pat could find, for he could not find much, and whether anyone believed him he could not tell, '... and we may show him our clean heels. That is our purpose, Duncan... *Simon.*' Pat smiled at his friend, a small pleasure found in his mind being made up, his prior confusion cast aside.

Simon, recognising Pat's intentions as being to avoid as much of a fighting confrontation as far as it was possible to do so, nodded for the first time but held his tongue. Pat resumed, speaking to Duncan, 'We are prepared on deck... ready for battle, Mr Macleod?'

'We are, sir.'

'The preventer stays are all snaked to the lower mast stays... and including the mizzen? We will take no chances.'

'Aye, they all are, sir.'

Pat nodded before continuing, 'Let us haul up a second clew of the mains'l. We may look to gain a swifter turn and perhaps another half-knot with the wind more directly on the fore.'

'Aye aye, sir!' Macleod busied along the starboard side gangway with something of a sense of relief, shouting instructions as he went by to those men who were not attending the guns but awaiting orders for the sail handling, and bawling loud to the idlers standing ready at the braces.

Pat, closely followed by Simon, shifted to stand near Barton at the helm, where the master, Prosser, was also awaiting his own orders. For many men aboard *Surprise* Jeremiah Prosser was an inspiration, even an icon; and, more than respect him, they revered him. He was a lay preacher of the Methodist chapel in Falmouth, an imposing figure, a steadfast who the younger hands looked to when in those frightening moments of personal doubt and danger. He was relatively old to serve aboard a ship, but had volunteered alongside sixty other Wesleyans for the first voyage of *Surprise* after she had been returned to service after refitting at Plymouth Dock after a long post-war spell laid up in Milford Haven. She had been the most suitable ship to fulfil the covert purpose of aiding Greece, no longer officially on the Royal Navy's in-service roster. Prosser had never left the ship's crew since, not even after she had twice returned to Falmouth, notably after she had suffered appalling losses fighting to defend the Greek island of Samos from Turk invasion two years earlier. Together with Pat he had served aboard *Tenedos* many years previously, remaining at sea ever since, such that his body was everywhere a deep brown colour; wrinkles covered every visible area of his skin including his face, which looked wizened as a result. His hands were large and muscular, and unkempt sideburns hung low on his face; his eyes shone with an energy, a spirit, one which exuded a complete confidence and offered an inspiration to all his shipmates. Pat, too, revered the man. 'We have quite the challenge, Mr Prosser,' said Pat in matter-of-fact voice.

'Aye, sir, but I beg leave to speak for all of us.'

'Please, do go on,' murmured Pat, the brief moment of exchange a most welcome diversion from his taxing ruminations.

'We have all given thanks that you will bring us through, sir... and with the aid of Our Lord there can be not the least doubt of it.'

From all the hands in earshot, at the helm, at the carronades, came nods and subdued murmurs, 'Hear! Hear!'

'I most heartily commend you, Mr Prosser,' said Simon, interjecting and turning to the master; 'Those are fine words, most commendable words; ones which I shall, myself, much take to heart.'

'Thankee, sir,' replied Prosser, 'but they be only what every man aboard the barky is a'thinking.'

Pat, much taken by the sentiments expressed, and finding them a most welcome reassurance in his own moment of doubt, could find no suitable words of reply. He wrenched his thoughts to a deliberate focus in his planning, his course of action, and he pulled his body to a perfectly erect posture, ignoring the enduring pain in his right leg, and he looked to his trusted companions at the helm. 'Stand ready to fall off the wind, Mr Prosser... Barton. Prepare to act swiftly on my command,' he declared in resolute voice.

'Aye aye, sir,' Prosser and Barton acknowledged and touched their foreheads.

Pat glanced briefly about the quarterdeck; he looked forward to see those of his men standing ready at the braces; he nodded to an approaching Duncan MacLeod, who was returning once more to the group clustered about the helm; he stared momentarily to the north, to starboard and that Turk frigate a mere five cables abeam, from which flame and smoke continued to erupt from her guns, an occasional shot now whistling by through the air within alarming proximity. He looked once more at his helmsmen: Barton, the senior man, had an exceptional touch on the wheel, a skill that Pat had marvelled at on many an occasion. Pat took a deep breath:

time was up. 'Helm up! Let her go off!' Pat's emphatic commands left not the least doubt of the urgency he required. One minute passed like an age; the anticipation everywhere was tangible; men hastened to take up the slack on the braces; two minutes more and the frigate's turn was perceptible, but hardly to Pat's satisfaction. 'Give her more helm! Hard over!' he shouted aloud, and both helmsmen hauled harder on the wheel. Another two minutes gone and the men at the braces were holding firm against the pull of the sails on the yards and looking to their officers for orders, and Pat shouted again, 'Keep her so!' The wheel turn was stopped; the helmsmen were sweating profusely, their grim faces dripping streams, their concentration absolute. The braces were strapped tight, the yards were held rigid once again under their load from the sail canvas, and *Surprise* steadied on her new bearing, only a little west of north-west, her new course assuring an oblique convergence with the leeward Turk. 'Helm amidships!' Pat barked the command in more normal voice; 'Steady!'

Pat shifted his focus from the helm and the bow; he looked all along the waist once more where men were still holding firm to the braces, all tied off; but still they waited for orders for further course changes as the lieutenants bawled out 'WAIT!' Everywhere about the guns was a hive of quiet discussion, of nervous anticipation; men held ramrods, stood ready with shot, clutched quoins for making gun elevations, and nearby slow matches burned ready to back up the gun-locks.

For the first time Simon ventured a tentative enquiry, 'Brother, will you enlighten me? I would value your appreciation of our prospects... the general position. What are your intentions, your purpose... with this... *this significant* change in navigation... *this racing convergence*... upon the Turk? Would it not be considered precipitate? The inveterate landsman might even consider it *reckless*.'

'Not in the least, Simon; we are lasking down.'

'Oh, I was not aware. I do beg your pardon, perhaps it is my own words that are precipitate.'

'It is the appropriate tactic, oblique not direct; for we may maintain the bombardment of the barky's guns during our approach.' Pat, perceiving his friend's considerable apprehension, placed his hand on his dear friend's shoulder, 'Oh, I possess of no better notion than that of the most esteemed of all of England's sailors...' Simon stared, open mouthed, and Pat continued, *'Never mind manoeuvres, go straight at 'em!* I have long taken that to heart; indeed, I may have mentioned it before... on occasion.'

'Doubtless there will be circumstances appropriate to such... such a... *an incautious* stratagem. You do not fear the... *the perils* of such a proximate approach?'

'Enough of such quibbling, Simon, *the die is cast,*' offered Pat, adding, 'That was Old Jarvie, *speaking at Trafalgar;* and so is the matter here and now.'

'But, tell me: is there a significant prospect of this... of our... estimable vessel being... *being lost*?'

'Oh, I will never admit to anything as unlucky as that, no; *but you'll never plough a field by turning it over in your mind,*' declared Pat to a blank stare from Simon, adding, 'My grandma.'

'Such a fount of sagacity.' Simon could scarcely believe his ears. Pat glared, unsure whether his friend was speaking sarcastically or not as Simon continued, 'And the *esteemed* advocate of... of... *the direct...* gambit?'

'Nelson, it was; the great man himself.' Pat managed a ghost of a smile, *'Desperate affairs require desperate measures;* that too was his Lordship.'

Mutual stares filled the momentary hiatus whilst an anxious Simon reflected in silence, eventually offering, *'More haste and less speed* is the maxim oft advocated by *my neighbours* - the common people of the Isles... and, I dare say, elsewhere; but for now I have the greatest concern for our wounded shipmates - *here.*'

Momentarily nonplussed, Pat resumed in encouraging voice, 'I greatly regret that we have lost so many of our people, I do so; but we have yet ten score men and more of such stalwarts aboard the barky... not a single scrovie amongst them, and I doubt the Turk possesses of one such of their ilk.'

'It is said that time flies when men wait for the most extreme of moments,' murmured Simon in great anxiety; 'I suppose that Macbeth was in accord... had the true measure of it. Perhaps one might nowadays call it the Nelsonian tradition.'

'Macbeth?'

'Yes; *'twere well it were done quickly.*'

Pat stared, bereft of the least reply for a few moments, until he lowered his voice, 'Simon, this is no place for you; the shot will soon be flying all about us, likely grape too; it will be a murderous, hot affair... The men... the unfortunates... will look to you, below... in the cockpit. Will you do me a kindness and go now to that place... and without the least delay?'

Simon, bowing to the inevitable, as dreadful as it seemed, seized Pat's hand, his emotions rising to an uncontrollable pitch, his voice trembling as he replied, 'God shield you from all harm, brother. I beg you will take great care... *the utmost.*' He turned about and hastened away, much to Pat's heartfelt relief.

Pat turned his attention to pressing matters; by now the incoming shot was striking *Surprise* hard; plainly, the Turk gunners had thoroughly warmed their guns, and holes began to appear in the sails, rents in the standing rigging, cut rope ends flapping in the wind and attracting the inquisitive eye, as well as splinter shards being strewn over the deck from shattered bulwark penetrations, from shot rising up from ricochets off the water. At least, Pat consoled himself, not a one of his men, his shipmates, had yet been struck down; but that could not last; no, within mere minutes the hurricane of fire would be building all about them, smashing the barky with destruction and violently striking the flimsy bodies of his men, hurling them back about the decks of his ship; and some of them would be pulped. He knew it; the horrible image was so familiar, so deeply engrained within his mind and memory, and so acutely painful. He stared again to starboard; the distance to the Turk had closed to little more than a quarter-mile in the past few minutes whilst he had been speaking with Simon; it was alarming, the separation scarcely two to three cables! He rushed forward and looked down over the waist rail once again; on the gun deck it seemed that most of his two hundred men were staring up at him expectantly, their eyes wide and inquiring; for they hated standing idle when the shot began flying, hated it with a vengeance; the sense of impatient impotence was all-consuming. He lifted his right arm high and he brought it down with a swift, scything motion as he screamed out with every ounce of breath in his lungs, 'FIRE!'

The words were echoed by his lieutenants on the gun deck, and by all the anxious gun captains, and it was followed in an instant by the eruption of thunder and the shooting jets of fiery orange-yellow flame which poured from all along the barky's side, powerfully cataclysmic, an outpouring of physical rage as might be directed by the Gods themselves, the power and violence of the concurrent explosions registering upon the senses as if akin to a gigantic hammer blow. Pat marvelled momentarily that even after so many years of witnessing the so-shocking spectacle it still registered so powerfully with him, seizing him to the extent that, even now, it took his breath away. The colossal noise was louder than the loudest thunderclap, the roar of the guns deafening to every man in an instant, and the whole of the ship shuddered so very violently, the collective recoil of all the starboard battery throwing the barky herself in a brutal uplift and roll from the leeward, firing side. Two tons of every gun were hurled back on their trucks as if akin to toys, the deck planking itself trembled, the sail canvas in its entirety shivered despite the strain it was under; and then came the outpouring of gun smoke, great noxious clouds of it, billowing up, up, out and swiftly away in the south wind, but leaving the Turk frigate shrouded from all sight.

On the gun deck all seemed a desperate pandemonium, the men attending the starboard guns busied in a frenzy of haste, swabbing barrels with their wet sponges, furiously ramming home fresh wads, powder cartridges, shot and more wads; vents were pricked, gunlocks primed, and every man did his utmost to speed his gun's readiness for firing; for all knew of Pat's essential instruction, drilled into them on every conceivable occasion to practice it: *fire three shots in five minutes and there is not a ship that would stand against them.*

'HEAVE! HEAVE! HEAVE!' screamed the gun captains to men hauling hard to pull forward their guns once more for firing.

'FIRE! FIRE! FIRE!' The shouts from officers and gun captains resounded all along the gun deck, but on the quarterdeck, where the carronades stood ready, their gunners patiently exercised the patience of Job whilst awaiting their order, holding their fire; for the range for the smashers was even now still too great for Pat's liking. The *Scirocco* at least blessed the men on the gun deck, for the smoke did not blow back to fill their eyes and racing lungs with its choking, blinding miasma of unpleasant and burning gunpowder particles. Too bad for the Turk, the Surprises figured, for her gunners would be suffering much from it: *perhaps it might obscure the barky from their aim?*

Pat pounded his quarterdeck, the Turk invisible for those precious first few moments of inspection: *had his gunners' broadside hit home? Where had the barky's shot struck upon the Turk? How much damage had been inflicted?* These and many more questions raced through his frantic mind. From the rail he looked down with anxiety into the waist and as far forward as he could see: the first casualties appeared in his vision; on the gun deck men had been struck down. He hoped it was by splinters and not by direct hits from shot, for the wounds from such were simply not survivable; the massive strike force of a ball would simply take off any limb it struck, and woe betide such an unfortunate; woe betide too the companions of anyone struck in the head, for it would be taken clean off, and the great spray of blood and gore was such that men were shocked and dismayed to such an extent that on occasions it rendered them physically disabled and motionless, either struck dumb or screaming in shock; whichever one it might be had rendered in the past such horrified victims useless for all further purposes, and serving their gun became utterly beyond them, their mind so brutally scarred. His mind turned to a recollection of the gunner's promise: *where were the incendiary shells that Timmins had said were nearly ready? For how much longer would he have to wait?*

In the cockpit the surgeons, Simon and Marston with Jason assisting, were busy attending a half-dozen casualties, splinter wounds for the most part but also concussions. Simon's ear caught the sound of a commotion on the forward companionway steps, a hubbub of shouting, anxious and angry words exchanged. The curtain tied back, his eyes, diverting from his patient with extreme dissatisfaction, fixed on two panic-stricken men carrying down a third in extreme haste, several others halted from ascending the steps as the bearers pushed and shoved and shouted with abandon, 'GET AWAY! STAND CLEAR!' until they presented themselves in a state of desperate anxiety before the surgeons' tables.

Marston was focused on his immediate patient and scarcely spared them a momentary glance despite the excited hubbub, but he spoke in a commanding voice, 'Silence! Silence there! Have respect for this man I am attending... Silence, I say! A slip of the knife may likely prove fatal!'

Simon, having treated his own patient, looked closely to the new arrival; 'Quickly! Lose not a moment! *On my table this living minute!*' Given his own rising sense of acute anxiety, his voice was as restrained as it could possibly be, for the unfortunate, moaning in his extreme agonies, was visibly very seriously wounded; the blood loss from his shoulder and chest was copious, a red flow streaming without let or hindrance, his shirt wholly sodden. 'Here, set him down. *Have a care!* Freeman, quickly now; look to cut away all of his vestments. Jason, I have need of your *immediate* attentions - and a wad of bandage.'

At the steps, Teague and his companions resumed their ascent to the gun deck in a subdued silence, each man clutching a heavy shot to be heated in the galley stove.

Near the helm, Pat's gaze focused on the nearest Turk on the starboard bow; less than a quarter-mile separated her from *Surprise*, perhaps little more than three hundred yards. Streaks of orange-yellow flame continued to erupt from her side, the strengthening wind rapidly lifting and sweeping clouds of grey-white smoke up and away forward of the enemy frigate. The booming sound of the explosions now followed within a second and the whistle of shot flying over the deck was plainly audible. To Pat's further consternation, he could see more holes ripped through the hammocks along *Surprise's* side, and through the standing rigging and the foresail; many such damages were already starkly visible. At least, for so he thought, there had not been a strike upon a mast or a yard, and he was grateful for even the smallest of mercies; for the barky needed all the speed she could manage if she was to survive with the least of casualties and damage; indeed, if she lost a yard and its sail then the pursuing Turk to larboard would surely catch her; when, he swallowed hard, the odds against his ship and men would be extremely severe. He cursed and turned his mind away from that distressing thought.

His attention turned to his own guns; the opening, the thunderously loud and simultaneous broadside which had violently shook the ship, had dissolved into continuous and individual firing, such that there was scarcely a second between the ear-splitting eruption of one gun and the next. Great jets of bright, flashing flame were spitting forth along the starboard side of the hull to some ten yards out, and the air had become suffused with stinking, hot gun smoke, the lesser part of it billowing back over the gun deck where men all along it were breathing in hot powder particles and reduced to coughing violently as, to Pat's gaze, they hauled with every ounce of strength they possessed their heavy guns forward once more until the muzzle and barrel projected and the forward wheels of the carriage thudded to a halt once more on the cill of the port, when the gun was ready to fire once more.

'FIRE!' Gun crews leaped backwards and sideways, ever careful not to collide with their fellows at the next gun. Gun captains pulled on lanyards, and then came the bright flash, visible even in the pervading acrid fog which began to fill the whole void of the deck, as the spark exploded its ire through the vent to ignite the powder charge. In an instant, a mere fraction of a second, the two tons of gun kicked back to be held on its stays, the violence of the recoil so powerful that men marvelled every time that it actually stopped before hurling itself all across the gun deck to crash into its fellow gun opposite or even to knock it aside and throw itself out of the open larboard gun port. The briefest moment of hiatus was upon the gunners each time as the gun presented itself once again for reloading, and the frantic fury of racing men all about the gun resumed: the sponge into the barrel to wet any smouldering particles of hot powder, the wad rammed in, the powder cartridge pushed deep, the heavy shot heaved in by the strongest of men in the crew, another wad rammed down to hold it in place, the gun captain's wild shout, 'HEAVE!', the desperate haul of manic, sweating, coughing men pulling out the gun once more through its port, until: 'STAND READY!' the gun captain screamed, and 'FIRE!', when the deafening, frightening cycle was repeated, only the gun captain spared the briefest of seconds to look to any necessary aiming adjustments before maniacal movements of eight men intruded into his momentary calculation. Sometimes a hasty hammer upon the quoin was deemed essential, a mere two seconds lost in doing so, urgings to haste shouted loud and with a passion.

Incoming Turk shot was striking hard on the ship's side, one breaking through the dense timbers to strike upon *Bull Horns*, its crew scattering as if blown by a tempest as splinters flew and struck feeble flesh, six men simply swept back and falling to the deck like cut flowers blown away in a hurricane. Shipmates rushed to drag them back, away from the gun which had broken one of its preventer-stays and swung round to crash into neighbouring *Mighty Fine*, its crew also thrown into disarray, hastily leaping to avoid the crushing force of the pushed gun, two men failing to escape the hot barrel and receiving swathes of burns on hands, arms and chests. Several more unfortunates were knocked down with broken legs and crushed feet. More men from the standby idlers rushed to help, to drag wounded, wailing men away, to haul back both guns into place, hasty repairs frantically made to their stays, more sand cast down to absorb fresh blood so as to prevent slipping. Manic gun captains looked all about them, assessing the scene, shouting orders: 'CARTRIDGE! RUN OUT YOUR GUN! HEAVE! HEAVE THERE! STAND READY!' until 'FIRE!' On and on the apparent pandemonium raged, but it was not really such, for every man serving his gun knew well what was expected of him; indeed, if he was even a mere split-second too slow in his task the vile and angry abuse showered upon him by all his fellows was loud and coruscating.

'Mr Macleod,' shouted Pat over the cacophony, 'Open fire with the smashers, aim aloft at her mizzen. You have the command; I am going to the gun deck to look to what we may do with Mr Timmins's incendiaries.' Duncan nodded and Pat hastened to the companionway.

On the gun deck all was a scene of manic, frenetic activity, a scene of absolute bedlam to the untutored eye; in fact, it was a riotous scene of Hell, of manic desperation. The eleven foremost guns on the starboard side were firing without let up; the air was a sulphurous miasma of superheated and burnt powder particles, filthy, choking and poisonous; near every man was coughing fit to retching, and all were bathed in sweat whilst racing, hauling, and leaping away in unceasing and frantic haste; but to Pat's eye, oblivious to the overbearing sensations which might lead a newcomer to overawed madness within a very few seconds, he looked, he watched and he studied, exceedingly rapidly; and he understood without the least confusion, seeing through the fog of smoke, that his men, his shipmates, were handling the great guns with extreme proficiency; nothing in the least which might warrant rebuke attached to his eye; rather, his gunners were moving about their duties with a dedication which was almost detached from the stinking, frenetic, vile scenes of wounded men, of blood and guts, strewn all about them. Gun captains were shouting out to their crews, 'CLOSE UP!' Amidst the flailing tornado and fury of incoming iron, so brutally destructive to the fragile bodies of men, larbowlins hastened about to drag the wounded back from the starboard guns, swiftly removing them to the lower deck to await their turn in the cockpit, and standby replacements were rushed immediately to work. Pat noted with satisfaction that both *Bull Horns* and *Mighty Fine* were both firing once more, and as he progressed forward, he shouted at the top of his voice all the time to his gun captains, 'LOAD QUARTER CHARGES! D'YE HEAR ME? ONLY QUARTER! QUARTER CHARGES!'

The guns had become hot, supercharged by the fiery heat of one explosion after another, so much so that they recoiled with a ferocity which strained their stays. It was time to slow the barky's shot, to slow their smashing breakthrough of the Turk's wooden hull so that the balls would penetrate with less of a clean break, and in so doing they would throw more jagged splinters into the flimsy, insubstantial bodies of the crew aboard the Turk frigate. He nodded briefly whenever an anxious eye caught his attention until, stepping through the filth upon the deck, a foul miasma of sand, blood, gore and flesh, which he did not care to scrutinise for even a moment, he came upon Clumsy Dalby and his five helpers, standing amidships, the incendiary shells at their feet, all of them plainly awaiting orders.

Another Turk shot broke through the starboard side hull, the explosion of inbound splinters flying wide and fast to strike down with considerable force six men serving *The Nailer* and *James Figg*. The same shot passed on, scarcely slowing, all across the width of the gun deck to smash again with thunderous, brutal force into the larboard hull side, breaking through that too with the most jagged of holes left behind.

Everywhere men were shouting and screaming, the stricken moaning in pain, the dying wailing in their last moments of acute agonies. Many men everywhere cursed with loud vehemence: the Turks, the war, even their comrades if they seemed in the least bit tardy in their tasks; others prayed quietly whilst busying about in their own dedicated role within their gun team; and all the while the gun captains barked orders, shouted warnings and exclaimed loud curses with the crudest of expletives. The cacophony of noise was extreme, even now and to men near totally deafened by the prolonged eruptions from the great guns; the filthy air was unbearable, acutely painful to breathe into lungs already racing for precious air, scorching the overtaxed bodies of frenetic men; and the violence of incoming shot smashing through the hull to wreak devastating destruction upon wood and flesh was terrifying, near overwhelming the senses and minds of men who considered themselves to have arrived in Hell.

'Mr Mower,' amidst the frenzied atmosphere all him, Pat shouted loud over the crashing explosions of firing, 'You are to give these shot, one each, to the captains of *Axeman* and *Nemesis.* All haste, and tell the captains plain: fire when ready with a quarter charge, *only a quarter charge...* and aim low... *low!* By now I venture our people will have their eye in and their guns warmed.'

'Aye aye, sir!' Mower acknowledged; Dalby and Hawkins seized their shot, and the three men hurried forward.

Pat looked to the four remaining men, 'Pick up your shots and follow me, aft; we will pass them along to the four guns beginning with *Salt 'n' Bile. Are you ready?*'

A chorus of 'Aye aye, sir,' with nods followed. Nankivel, Damerell, Haskell and Knapman seized up the heavy incendiaries to follow Pat as he hastened aft, passing by the bloody chaos all about those two crews who had been struck down with splinters, bloodied and wounded men already in the grip of larbowlins hastily hauling them away without the least pause.

The captain of *Salt 'n' Bile* looked round as Pat caught his eye after his tug on the lanyard, the explosion and smoke suffusion filling the air, the gun hurled back until held by its traces, everyone leaping aside and all present coughing hard. 'Here, Jenner,' shouted Pat, 'Here is Mr Timmins's special shot. Load directly and look carefully to your aim; there is not a single one more - *not a one!* - and so it must not be wasted... *it must not be wasted!* Load only a quarter charge - *a quarter!* - and aim for a spot below her guns... and as near the waterline as can be; we must hope to see her burn.'

Pat waited for a half-second only for the nod of understanding; simply hearing words unless they were shouted loud had become a tribulation, speaking them even more so in the sulphurous air and with a parched, sore throat. Gathering Pickering with him, he stepped with great caution through the violence of fiery eruptions and vicious recoils further aft along the starboard battery of guns, picking his way without haste through the scene of frenetic activity, explaining his instructions as he went to Pickering, 'A quarter charge only - *a quarter!* - and aim low - *low!* Good luck, Tom, but I must attend the quarterdeck without delay.'

In that instant another shot crashed through the hull with brutal violence near *Revenge*. The gun captain, Manico, was felled by a large splinter striking him on the head. Pat, aghast and shocked in the fleeting instant of the sheer violence of the penetrating hull breach, was slammed flat to the deck by a flying decapitated head which was flung hard against his own. He landed on his chest and was knocked breathless. Wiping blood from his eyes and gore from his face, he stared to his side where Vallack, the sponger, was struck down like a rag doll, a long splinter impaling him in the chest; Tarraway, the loader, had also been struck down by a fragment of wood broken away from the gun carriage; he too had been hurled way back beyond the gun to fall prone on the deck on the other side of Pat. Both Vallack and Tarraway were staring with wide eyes from no more than a yard of separation from Pat. Vallack, plainly, was dead. An unmoving Tarrant was either unconscious or dead; Pat could not tell in that moment. Beyond Tarrant was the headless body of a third man; Pat could not discern who it was. A bloodied head, much pulped, was involuntarily kicked aside by Collins, staggering backwards before tumbling back to fall upon the deck; his arm had been ripped off at the shoulder and his ribs crushed, some of them projecting through the flesh of his naked torso, shattered, his life running quickly away from his chest in a red torrent of blood. Pat's gaze flicked back from Collins to the decapitated head, and his horrified eyes locked upon it.'

From amidst the gore-splattered deck, Cooksey, captain of the adjacent gun, *Blood 'n' Guts*, hauled Pat to his feet without ceremony, 'Pay no mind to Reilly, sir, he's copped it.' Pat, dumbstruck, scarcely nodded but continued to stare even as an anxious Cooksey spoke once more, more stridently, 'Beg pardon, sir, but this place must be cleared for the gun. Is 'ee struck?'

Regaining his senses and his breath to some small degree, a shocked Pat looked to the man who had helped him up, and he croaked with all the words he could manage, his sore throat afire, 'No... I think not.' The pain in his chest was excruciating as he spoke once more, 'Thank you most heartedly, Cooksey, I am in your debt.' But Cooksey was already turning away to attend his gun, shouting loud to larbowlins to hasten them forward as replacements for his fallen men, to attend their stations, bawling more orders in loud voice once more even as the dead and wounded were hauled back and away from the furious recoil of the great guns. Pat, still gasping painfully for breath and much winded, stared momentarily at the scene of horror assailing his eyes before staggering aft towards the companionway steps, only dimly aware of an exceptionally great pain in his leg, upon which he could scarcely place his weight; and so he hobbled, limping, near hopping, to spare his right leg and scarcely daring to glance down to scrutinise the wet, spreading red stain over the right leg of his breeches.

Below in the cockpit Simon, Marston and Jason, assisted by Freeman, laboured with frantic haste, overwhelmed; for the wounded were being carried in thick and fast. About them on the deck two bloody corpses lay in the brutal finality which was death; silent, motionless, awaiting the helpers to carry them away, no time for even the brief courtesy of a thrown shroud. A running puddle of blood was creeping away from them in dark rivulets towards and under the drawn-back curtain, red-sodden where the canvas touched the planks.

Simon paused for the briefest of moments and stared at his table, another body laid upon it, motionless, eyes wide open and staring but all life extinguished. He was mentally thunderstruck, his frantic mind was racing, his thoughts a raging tumult of several priorities, searching for the trigger of which one would be the recall to close attendance to his task; but his body would not, could not, respond; all body control was involuntarily frozen, in shock. From three yards away, a much-concerned Marston, his friend's rigidity having caught his eye, looked across to his colleague and called out, 'Hold fast, Ferguson; pray do not shrink from your duty for even a minute. Hold fast! I beg you will, for Our Lord is with us!'

Simon, much shaken by the celerity of the stream of patients and the death of his last one, near dead even before he reached the surgeon's table and then expiring before his eyes, only nodded but said nothing; but his concentration was jolted out from the trauma with which he was labouring and he waved to the two men approaching with the next wounded man, the unfortunate quickly lifted to his table, shrieking from the pain of a huge splinter, stuck deep into his thigh a handsbreadth above the knee. Simon reacted instantly and the blood-soaked breeches were sliced away in great haste. Freeman seized the patient's hand and spoke into the his ear with kindly words, the casualty staring, wide-eyed and frantic as Jason poured the laudanum into his gasping mouth, a copious quantity of it, whilst Simon wiped around the splinter with his cloth, looking closely and searching in assessment for indications of the severity of the wound. 'Hold down our patient! Hold him tight!' He spoke loud to Tremayne and Hocking in a voice of great anxiety, 'Hold fast, for this will be painful, and I fear he may escape the table in his agony. Jason, look now to tying the stick about his mouth.' Simon wrapped a leather strap about the high leg near the groin. 'Freeman, haul this tourniquet as tight as can be... else I fear we will lose him within minutes when the blood flows.'

Seizing in both hands the splinter, the size of a hammer handle split in half along its length, Simon began to pull it out, slowly, much blood spurting around it. The hesitation of a single second, not longer, and Simon tugged once more, a forceful eruption of blood following in a stream. The agonised patient screamed and immediately passed out. Simon teased open the wound with his thumbs upon the skin, and he stared intently as the flow diminished from its prior torrent, and he shouted out aloud to his helpers with a flood of relief akin to euphoria, 'I believe that the femoral is not pierced! We may hope that he will keep the leg!' He swiftly wrapped bandage about the wound, pulling and tying it tight even as the first red blots appeared, a trickle and then a flow spreading quickly through the bandage. 'I am minded that we will let it bleed - *healthily* - for that may wash out the infection before it is stitched. Set this man aside and let us look to the next.'

Scarcely a half-minute passed before another casualty was laid upon his chest on the table, writhing and whimpering in a semi-conscious state, aware of pain but beyond all powers of thought save for his agonies. The copious outflow of blood from splinters embedded in his back had long soaked his shirt and his trousers, so much so that they resembled nothing more than the bloody cloth with which Simon swabbed his table after every patient.

Freeman cut through the shirt and folded it back even as Simon gazed in close inspection. Gently, he pressed upon the skin athwart the largest of the three projecting splinters, teasing the flesh aside. 'Freeman, hold our man as still as still can be. Put your hands here, about his shoulders.' Delicately, he prised the largest of the wooden invaders out, a sudden flurry of red following as the patient screamed and struggled to shift. Freeman held him firm. Simon peered closer through eyes which burned as if afire, his head held mere inches above the wound. He looked, watched and hoped with a grim passion for a half-minute before he stirred to speak, 'Jason, pray pass me the needle; I believe the lung has been spared... thankfully, for there is no froth of air.'

Standing on legs which protested the slightest shift of the deck as the frigate's bow rose and fell upon mere wavelets, his ears having long given up all hearing save for loud and proximate shouts, Simon stitched with dogged application. The patient, fortunately, had passed into unconsciousness, which eased the regularity and rapidity of the sewing up of the ragged gash. Two minutes more and the stitches were tied off. The remaining two splinters were smaller, representing nothing of danger in Simon's assessment, and a similar remedy was quickly concluded, the patient immediately swept off the table. Simon stared momentarily at his helpers, Jason and Freeman, their faces radiating a grim but stoic determination to persist, to carry on. Silent nods were exchanged, dismay temporarily set aside, commitment was rekindled, even as an exhausted Simon blinked to clear his eyes and regretted that he had no such remedy for his rising despair, and briefly wondering for how much longer the bloody mayhem might continue.

Pat, much bruised by the violence of being thrown to the deck and his heavy, face-down fall upon it, strived to cast aside the severe pains in his chest, his leg and his head. Plainly, it was, to his racing thoughts, a most severe bruising of his head; but he paid it little mind. Accustomed as he had been for some weeks to struggling on his right leg, he also tried to ignore the excruciating pain emanating from that as he gathered his senses. He stumbled, groggily, along the gun deck, all the time looking to his gun captains as he struggled to gain the steps and so to the quarterdeck. He hastened with laboured breathing and stiff legs, his prior wound - for so he thought - paining him considerably once more, to join Duncan near the helm. Ignoring his friend's anxious face and alarmed, wide eyes, both being unspoken solicitations of his health, and discarding from all thought the red stain which covered the entirety of his vestments below his waist, he seized MacLeod's glass to stare at the alarming scene of convergence before his wide eyes; for the leeward Turk was looming large, much less than two cables off the starboard bow! An alarmed Pat wondered for how much longer the two frigates would be able to fire as they closed upon each other without each setting the other afire from the close proximity of roaring gun flames; but he most certainly did not care to contemplate a boarding either way; not with the second, pursuing Turk frigate a scant half mile on the larboard quarter and inexorably closing.

Pat decided that the vital moment of his strategy had arrived: he could not allow any further convergence; and so the barky must shy away, must hold to the wind on her larboard quarter, in order to maintain nothing closer than a parallel course, even a slightly diverging one, but to hold to a separation which would allow his experienced gunners to maintain fire upon the starboard Turk with accuracy. Recollection of the bloody carnage below on the gun deck had already slipped to the back of his anxious, racing mind; all focus of thought was firmly on the present, the immediate. He stared over the bulwark and looked with racing breath - his chest was a great discomfort - for the first discharge of incendiary shot from his guns. In choosing to make the course change, a sweeping curve and turn away from the starboard Turk, he knew very well that it would favour the windward pursuer, that Turk closing from the larboard quarter and visibly gaining. *So be it*, Pat thought grimly, *she would have to await her turn to feel Surprise's bite!*

'Six shots, six shots... six...' he stopped his own spoken repetition as Macleod, concerned by Pat's increasingly stumbling gait and the evidence of a bloody wound, stuck close to his side, staring at him without speaking; for he saw plain that his captain would not welcome interruption, nor even any expression of care for his welfare; for his concentration was absolute, inviolable in the acute moment. Duncan simply prayed that the wound was less severe than it looked, and he resolved to watch Pat intensely.

Pat, ignoring his wound, shouted to Duncan, 'GRAPE! LOAD GRAPE, Mr Macleod!' Duncan hastened to the taffrail and echoed the order to Pickering below.

Those gunners with Jelbert's incendiary shots had been asked for the utmost accuracy, tasked with low shots which would penetrate the Turk hull at close range, but with lesser powder charges such that they would not exit the other side of the hull but burn within, ultimately setting the ship on fire. Pat wondered whether his express request for such a precise aim and tactic had held his gunners back, for he had emphasised the finite number of the incendiaries: six only, and just one for each of the chosen guns; indeed, he had laboured loud his instruction not to waste them with careless aim; and now he berated himself for not staying below, in close attendance, offering guidance and visible support to his gunners; but then he reminded himself that such was not his role; nor was it necessary, for his gunners were all as good as good could ever be. The painful seconds were ticking by slowly and he asked himself again why there seemed to be a lessening of the firing from below his feet, from his great guns: *what was going on?*

He looked to his side at Macleod, he stared at Prosser; the master was also standing ready at the helm. Finally, he decided that matters could wait no longer. 'Hands to the braces, Mr MacLeod.' He turned back to the attentive faces staring at him from the helm. 'Starboard the helm, Mr Prosser.' Barton, at the wheel, reacted immediately and without waiting for the master to reiterate the order.

'Give her more helm!' Pat could no more conceal the anxiety in his voice than stop the trembling which now afflicted his legs; in that instant he could feel that his wounded leg was shaking severely; so much so that he feared it might be visible and discouraging to his men; certainly the sight of so much blood, *his blood*, might well be. He clutched the back of his right thigh and squeezed hard, but to no avail; the pain in his leg was much worse than ever before. He bit down on his tongue to pre-empt the surge of pain which might prompt anguished exclamation, and he shouted aloud, 'Hard over!' before he whispered to himself through gritted teeth, 'May Saint Patrick protect us! God between us and all harm!'

Slowly, the bow began to swing perceptibly away from the encroaching Turk frigate as the shots from her, so extremely dangerous at this relatively short range, continued to smash their brutal way through *Surprise's* wooden bulwarks, as they thudded loud against and undoubtedly broke through her hull on the lower deck. Other shots whistled through the air, further tearing the already much-ripped sails. The incoming barrage had become so prevalent, so intense, that Pat wondered in a rising tide of anxiety whether *Surprise* would really escape from the conflict this time; for she truly had become the meat in the sandwich and, if nothing rapidly changed in her favour, would swiftly be devoured.

In that instant Pat perceived the heel of the deck shifting very slightly; *Surprise* was, as Pat looked towards her starboard side, on the slightest of up roll; and then came the thunder and fire of the barky's broadside; the bright flashes were blinding to his staring, sore eyes before fiery flames jetted out for thirty feet and more, the retina burn lingering in his vision for seconds. The immediate boom of the explosions was, even now, still painful to his ears, already near deafened after his excursion to the gun deck. The eruptions were followed in an instant by clouds of billowing powder smoke, white with millions of black particles swirling within the overall grey miasma, some of them still burning red-bright, before the wind swiftly carried away the choking, poisonous filth towards the Turk. Plainly, the gun captains with their incendiaries had waited patiently for their moment; no shot would be lost into the sea falling short of the Turk on the down roll. Pat hoped with all his heart that all six would strike

140

her hard, on the up roll as it had been, to smash through her hull on the chosen points of target. No moment in any conflict before had ever seemed more desperate than now.

Pat and every man on the quarterdeck all about him stared with fixation at their adversary as *Surprise* continued her diverging turn away, the Turk captain seemingly not yet having responded to the barky's change of course. Pat peered through his glass with a burning, painful eye at his enemy, no more than a cable off, *a scant two hundred yards!* He scanned the Turk's quarterdeck but could see no captain nor any other officer. He wondered whether that was why the Turk had not initiated a turn of his own ship to continue the convergence with *Surprise*. Pat scrutinised the length of the Turk hull; there were certainly three holes below her gun ports at her waist, and he was sure that his glance had caught a fleeting glimpse of bright flames, small that they were. They swiftly became more visibly distinct, instantly engaging his eye, as an angry fire always did; and it was increasingly plain to see within a few seconds the rising flames on her gun deck through two of her ports. He became convinced that the incendiaries had struck home, or at least several of them had; and then came the eruption, the explosion, a great outpouring of bright orange-red fire from out of a midships gun port: one powder charge and possibly more had surely exploded outside of its gun; there could be no other explanation.

Pat turned his glass to look again at the Turk's quarterdeck; all was pandemonium there, but still he could not see any obvious officer. Furthermore, her guns had fallen silent except for final shots from the two aftmost ones, those within her captain's cabin. Perhaps, Pat wondered, a lieutenant was still striving there to encourage his gunners to keep firing. He scanned again all along her sides; yes, her guns had ceased fire. Behind the bulwarks all along her waist, on the forecastle and on her quarterdeck, everywhere was filling up with men, and the rising flames had plainly taken hold in at least three places, for visible fire was erupting from the two gun ports he had already studied, climbing her hull side, licking and burning tinder-dry oakum between hull planking; and yet a third fire was jetting out through one of the holes in her lower hull, below her gun deck. The Turk was aflame, for sure; and the incendiaries, practically impossible to extinguish, had set alight tar-soaked deck planking, such that Pat had no doubt that the Turk frigate was doomed and would soon be consumed entirely by the already rampant flames; indeed, it seemed as if her crew believed so too, for now all way had come off her, her braces had been slackened, her sails hung limp and flapping from her yards, and men were plainly striving to put her boats into the water, several booms already run out. She was no longer an adversary, merely a vulnerable target, were Pat minded to stay and fire upon her until she was smashed by great weight of shot to splinters and detritus, and encumbered by the bodies of dead men; but Pat was not so inclined, for the weight of necessity, of haste, pressed hard upon him; for the second Turk frigate was fast approaching, closing; another rapid convergence was nigh on imminently upon the desperate men of the barky, and he had no more of Jelbert's special shot with which to play a winning card: no, *Surprise* would soon be in dire straits, and his men were surely tired, likely already exhausted. He looked more closely through his glass at the burning Turk, a sad sight; he focused upon her quarterdeck; for the first time in five or more minutes he could see her captain, his head and left arm both wrapped with bloody bandage, standing immobile and supported by two of his men, presumably contemplating the end of his purpose, his command finished, his ship presently sure to sink; that is, if she did not explode beforehand when the fire reached the powder in her magazines. Pat wondered: *had Plunket and his rifle wounded the Turk captain in the crucial moment of decision, when the barky's course change had not been followed by the Turk as Surprise turned away?* His own feelings were mixed; he held a certain sympathy for a fellow captain in the moment of an absolute loss, fire and destruction about to consume his vessel and likely many of his men; but he was grateful with an overwhelming wave of thankfulness that there was no longer any threat from that particular enemy; her time was short, and his racing anxieties receded a very little.

'Cease fire, Mr MacLeod, she is finished,' declared Pat with a long, long exhalation, the great wash of relief flooding his mind and body, his absolute concentration of thought on the fight at least temporarily swept away, the abatement of tension so sudden that both his legs began to shake uncontrollably. He leaned forward to grip the mizzen mast and he seized it with both hands.

'AVAST FIRING!' Duncan bawled to the carronade crews; AVAST FIRING!' he screamed again over the waist rail, and slowly, fitfully, almost with reluctance, the great guns spluttered to a halt all along the starboard side, the great clouds of gun smoke drifting away to leave an uncanny silence save for the clearly audible shouting and screaming of terrified men aboard the stricken Turk frigate, so close. Three of her boats were already in the water and rapidly filling with men who, if not in panic, were certainly well aware that there could only be one future for their ship, a short one, one which they wished to be as far away from as possible when it happened; for every mariner aboard a warship feared most a magazine explosion. Perhaps some of their fellows were even now drowning the magazines, but they were not waiting to find out.

For the first time in fifteen minutes of absolute concentration on his first adversary Pat turned his gaze aft, towards the second Turk frigate. She had approached to not much further than a quarter of a mile away, and *Surprise's* earlier course change, turning away from the starboard Turk frigate and several minutes passing as she did so, had allowed the larboard Turk to close faster, for she was sailing large, the *Scirocco* for her a most favourable quartering wind. Once more Pat determined on his tactics, much more quickly this time; for the barky's fore course had taken tremendous damage from the first Turk and displayed a dozen holes and several long tears, near ripped through from top to bottom under the strain of sailing large. He bellowed his orders to the

helm, 'Mr Prosser, put her before the wind! Steer north...
NORTH! Larboard the helm!'

Prosser spoke loud to his helmsmen, but such was
redundant, for Barton and his shipmate were already heaving
hard to pull *Surprise* away from her westerly course to turn
north, to run. Duncan shouted out Pat's orders, and two score
of men hastened to haul on the braces.

A minute later and Duncan once more stood at his
friend's side, Pat's intentions becoming clear. 'We are running
from this second fellow?' he asked of Pat. He was neither
seeking something of an assurance nor any confirmation that
such really was his friend's intention, for such was perfectly
obvious; indeed, it seemed eminently sensible to himself, for
there was really no choice in the matter, *Surprise* being so
badly damaged. His actual intention was to bring Pat to a
dialogue such that he might enquire of his increasingly
obvious and bloody wound.

'Yes, we will run... like the hare before the hounds, and
we will see which of us has the legs of the other,' replied Pat
with difficulty, for his chest pain was excruciating and his
breathing laboured. He added with an attempt at a smile, *'It's
better to return from the centre of the ford than to drown in
the flood.'* A brief flush of relief, the first for some time,
succeeded his spoken maxim; 'Not Nelson... *my grandma it
was.'*

Duncan merely grinned wide, much relieved to see the
momentary lift of spirits within his friend.

Within minutes *Surprise* was running fast before the
wind, but the second Turk was close, less than two cables and
still gaining. Plainly, her captain had not deigned to heave-to
to save the survivors of that sister ship which was burning
bright.

Pat, his chest heaving as he painfully gasped for breath,
wondered what he himself would have chosen to do in such
circumstances; *perhaps,* he mused, *the Turk captain's blood
was up; perhaps he was the man who had shied away from
tackling Surprise off Oxia Island when his then fellow frigate*

144

had exploded in a catastrophic magazine explosion? Pat glanced back across the starboard quarter; the first frigate was aflame and at a stand, but she had not yet blown up. *Perhaps,* he speculated, *the crew had successfully drowned the magazines before the fires could reach them?* Fire was rapidly consuming her, flames were roaring up the resin-soaked rigging, the tinder dry canvas burning bright, no longer the least prospect of being extinguished; and the spreading fire was plain to see all along her gun deck, erupting outwith all the gun ports along the length of her side. A hundred men were in the water, appealing for help at the sides of over-filled boats, six of them filled to capacity with desperate men.

Pat, leaning back against the mizzen mast, his shaking right leg a fiery agony, stared through his telescope; he could see that some of the men aboard the boats were striking the clutching hands of men in the water with fists to prevent any more of their shipmates climbing aboard and so swamping their boat: *God forbid he would ever find himself in similar circumstances.* At least, Pat noted, her magazines had not exploded, and he silently thanked Saint Patrick for small mercies; for it was an end he would never wish on any mariner, even an enemy. He shrugged and reconciled himself to disregarding the sad, dismaying spectacle; he had more pressing matters to attend.

Murphy, since the cessation of firing, had appeared near the wheel. He was clutching a tin mug which he passed towards Pat, 'Well, beg pardon, sorr; is 'ee in the way for coffee with a whet of brandy?'

It occurred to Pat that his throat, long exposed to hot gun smoke, assailed by drifting, burning powder particles, and strained by a great deal of shouting, was as dry as the proverbial bone, a particularly dusty bone; and he looked favourably upon his steward in that moment, more favourably upon the coffee. 'Why, thank you, Murphy; you are quite the decent cully - *at times.*' Murphy frowned. 'My throat is as dry as a bear with a mad head... a sore head... *You will grasp the general notion.*' Pat downed the whole of the divine liquid, lukewarm but most welcome nevertheless, in one. He addressed his waiting steward, 'We must turn our attention to the other fellow. You are to look to Wilkins and the galley; take Dalby and three men with you; they will lift the shot from the oven *when Mr Macleod calls for it in the cabin* and when Mr Codrington - *he will attend the galley directly* - vouches it is glowing red hot... *red hot*,' adding as an afterthought, 'There *is* shot in the oven... heating, Murphy?'

'Well, sure there is, sorr; eight of 'em be roasting right hot... and Wilkins is burning his last bag of coal.'

'Very good; we will have need of them before this day is done, and likely soon. I dare say a cold supper will serve... and hunger is a great sauce... *the greatest.*'

Pat coughed painfully and cursed the extreme discomfort all about his leg once more; for the first time he became fully focused on his wet clothing, soaked in blood, a generous spread of it over all his breeches' leg to just about everywhere, even a small puddle of it on the deck; and the pain in his leg was utterly excruciating; but, gritting his teeth, he forced his mind away from it to stare at the compass: *Surprise* was at last running directly north, away from the onrushing second Turk frigate, but in so doing she was bearing away from the planned haven which was Malta; but that did not seem the least bit important in his racing anxieties. He looked aft over the taffrail; the pursuing Turk was directly astern, her bow rising and falling gently in the vestiges of *Surprise's* fading wake, and now no more distant than a cable. 'Her captain is a determined fellow,' Pat declared to all about him near the helm, all his lieutenants having returned to the quarterdeck. 'Mr Prosser,' he called out, 'cast the log line, if you please.'

Prosser called to the man standing ready with the line, 'Cast the line, Verrant.'

'Eight knots and two fathoms, sir!' Verrant shouted out after some minutes.

'Mr Macleod, Mr Codrington,' Pat declared, 'Will you both accompany me? I am going to my cabin to look to the two guns there. The gunners have them braced and ready to

146

fire aft, as we did before at Oxia Island. We may not have the legs of this other fellow and I do not care to consider for how long he intends to keep the chase. Mr Mower, you have the deck.'

'Aye aye, sir,' replied Duncan; Codrington nodded; Mower, his eyes ranging all about him in grim assessment, nodded too.

An excruciating struggle down the steps to the cabin and Pat looked to the pair of guns turned about and pointing directly aft, ready to open fire through the stern gallery upon the second Turk frigate. At least they would be when Pat ordered the window panes, many of them repaired of late in Argostoli, smashed out once again. The gunners made short shrift of it, the glass all falling away astern until the pursuing Turk was in plain view, so very close and greatly alarming.

The Turk frigate was looming large, her vast press of sail spread wide below her extended studding-sail yards; evidently, every stitch of canvas she possessed was all run out, and the entirety of it displayed the sense of purpose that she was about, which could only be revenge. The majesty of her bulk and presence filled the vision of all in the cabin with a frightening awareness of her closing proximity, for she was pursuing at point blank range and gaining; her prominent bow, rising and falling, was cutting the very froth of *Surprise's* wake in an alarming announcement that presaged imminent death and destruction.

In the cabin, the waiting gun captains, Chegwin and Pascoe, old tars both, were undaunted and itching to open fire. 'Stand ready at Mr Macleod's command.' Pat's instructions were scarcely now more than a whisper, for shouting was long beyond him and severely aggravated his acute chest pain; 'Hold fire and wait for his order.'

'Aye aye, sir.'

'Mr Macleod, fire these guns to clear the cold shot within and then reload with quarter charges, but wait until Mr Codrington brings the red-hot shot from the galley.'

'Aye, sir,' Duncan nodded.

Pat resumed, 'Mr Codrington, make haste to the galley and send Dalby and his men here to the cabin with the first four of the heated shot at the earliest moment. Leave four shot in the stove to stay hot *and to await Mr Macleod's call.*'

'Very good, sir,' Codrington nodded his understanding and hastened away

Pat, struggling with increasing difficulty to stay on his legs, climbed the steps once more to return to his quarterdeck and the helm, where he turned to study the pursuing Turk frigate. She was still gaining, slowly but surely; and Pat wondered to what extent the great spread of Turk sail might be shrouding *Surprise's* own, for they were both running directly before the wind. Flame flashes and puffs of white smoke erupted from the Turk frigate's bow as Pat watched; her chasers had opened fire, and the boom of the shots arrived within less than a second. And then the two guns in *Surprise's* great cabin roared in reply, long fiery flames flashing bright, and a cloud of smoke poured out and up, drifting back to envelope the quarterdeck. Pat coughed for a minute, in pain and with difficulty, his lungs seemingly on fire, his chest protesting the abuse.

The helmsmen turned round to look, to gaze with keen anticipation at the Turk frigate; for they knew, they understood very well, the destructive power of the eighteen-pounder guns in the hands of their experienced shipmates; and they were confident in their expectations that the Turk would very swiftly be served out and with a most unwelcome ration. It was rare to the extent of being virtually unknown for a frigate to fire more than modest stern chasers at her pursuers, and those only from the visible quarterdeck; but the barky's great guns would be far and away much more destructive than the relatively lightweight six-pounders when they were turned about to fire aft; and, such firing being entirely unexpected, the Turk captain would surely get the unwelcome shock of his life.

Pat, now leaning back against the mizzen mast and grateful for its support, silently developed his thinking: *the cabin guns, firing red hot shot and with a quarter charge of powder, would inflict enormous damage upon the Turk at that close range, the target an easy one. Perhaps such shot would fly all the way down her gun deck, ricocheting to do dreadful harm to her men until, it's force spent, it lodged within timber somewhere aboard the frigate, setting fire to flame-susceptible caulking, steeped in flammable pitch.*

More shots whistled by through the air from the Turk's chasers. Pat looked forward: two more holes had appeared in the fore course. *The Turk was firing high,* Pat mused, *her bow chasers aimed so as to rip through the barky's topsails or the rigging; perhaps the objective was to damage yards in order to slow the barky down; but perhaps not, perhaps the Turks were simply firing late on the uplift of the wave crest. If the latter was the case, her captain would surely be by now vehemently remonstrating with his gun crews; more likely one of his officers would be. It would not be long before they got their eye in. The quarterdeck was about to become a very dangerous place.* Pat could plainly see the heads of the Turk gunners about their chasers, one gun each side of the bowsprit, an officer with bicorne hat standing behind them.

And then, from above his head, from the mizzen top, came the crack of a rifle shot, and when Pat looked again, he could no longer see anything of that officer on the Turk foc'sle. He wondered: *could that be Plunket firing? Two hundred yards... two hundred yards.* Pat's thoughts raced: *Plunket had been convinced that his cousin, Thomas, had knocked down two Frenchmen at four hundred yards, but that was on land. Séamus Plunket was firing from a precarious platform atop a moving ship and at a shifting target; was it conceivable that a rifleman could down a man aboard another moving ship at two hundred yards distance?*

The twin jets of fiery, orange-red flame shooting out astern from the great cabin and the simultaneous, thunderous boom of the two guns within it cast out all such considerations from Pat's tired mind, still absorbed in a great flurry of frantic thinking: *MacLeod had fired the first of the red hot shots!*

At the helm, Barton and Green grinned at each other and shouted out indistinct curses as they turned back to the wheel. From his position at the side of the mizzen mast Pat heard this, more loud curses shouted by his carronade crews, and he allowed himself the tiniest of wry smiles despite the ever-increasing pain in his right leg and the profuse, greater spread of blood all about his breeches, a red flow visibly running over his boots. More significant, to his way of thinking, was that for the first time in the day he had glimpsed the prospect of survival for his ship and his men - *even the known rogues amongst them were very precious to him* - and amidst the most desperate of many and varied concerns which continued to race, alarmingly, through his mind, in that moment he felt something of a warming flush of pride in all his veterans, and a tiny glimmer of hope.

Chapter Seven

Tuesday 9th May 1826   16:00   *The south Ionian Sea*

In the dimly-lit cockpit any thoughts of a smile were far from the frantic minds of the surgeons and their helpers, all of whom were bathed in flowing swathes of perspiration as they worked with frenetic haste under an overburden of loud and struggling patients, the most unfortunate of them fast-fading. The atmosphere was hot, steamy, foetid and utterly vile; the humid, still air was filled with the nauseating stench of decay, of human soil and the coppery smell of blood, a lot of it; and the ears of every man were assailed by desperate cries for water, by shrieks of pain, and - so very excruciating to the ears - shrill screams of agony as dreadfully wounded legs and arms were severed rapidly and without hesitation from the bodies of maimed men who would never be whole again. Amputated limbs were tossed away to fall into - or miss - the nearby bloody buckets. The frenetic burden was so great that neither Simon nor Marston scarcely looked up as one patient succeeded another across their blood-swept tables, which offered the most disgusting spectacle, scarcely less than the deck itself, which was covered in a residue of blood, guts, flesh, brains and gore, a deeply offensive meld which scarcely merited the time to sweep it away before the next man was laid flat before their sore, tired eyes; eyes which burned excruciatingly in their sockets amidst the acrid smoke of the oil lamps. Their aprons were sodden and similarly soiled with the detritus of flesh, of fragments of clothing and splinters extracted from wounds before the most rudimentary cleansing; their arms were bloody past their elbows, and red streaks ran across their faces as they wiped away the constant stream of sweat which dripped upon everything below their immediate concentration. A thin film of diluted blood ran red all across the deck below the surgeons' tables, despite the sand strewn all about and the efforts of Chegwin with a constant wash of saltwater and a broom to expel it beyond the cockpit; a failed effort, the red tide returning every time the bow of the barky lifted on successive waves.

The fearful catastrophe within their cramped, tiny room utterly enveloped the minds of all the desperate men working quickly between the claustrophobic wooden walls, and nothing, nothing at all, offered the least influence in any respect towards a mitigation of the horror all about them. There was no opportunity to pause, the briefest moment of rest quite impossible to countenance by Simon and Marston as they endured, as they cut with saws and knives, and as they sewed flesh folds over bloody stumps. Hell was here before their fearful eyes and they knew it; the chilling reaction gripped every man like a vice, seizing minds which were hovering near the threshold of panic, rendering them incapable of anything more than the manic task in hand, one rapid operation performed immediately after another.

'Jason, the bone saw... lose not an instant!' shouted Simon; 'Freeman, the tourniquet; swiftly now, as tight as can be!'

The surgeons worked with an anguished haste, without sparing even a moment to slake parched throats; for the mere few minutes of their frantic attentions made the difference for many a man hovering between life and death; there was no time to contemplate protracted surgery of any kind: a wound to an arm or a leg and the limb came off, swiftly, the patient screaming as the bone saw worked for little more than a minute and with a maniacal intensity before the limb was cast away, the rump rapidly stitched with such crude application that would have brought condemnation in any hospital in the world; the world, that is, where the surgeon possessed more than five minutes of time before his wide, horrified eyes were presented with the next distressed casualty.

'Calm yourself, I beg you will!' shouted Marston, stooping over his patient, who was staring with wide, crazed, manic eyes in his agony, much of his leg below the knee missing, the shattered bone and bloody stump a horrible sight, more lacerations evident in his thigh. 'I assure you that the severe pain will not afflict you for many minutes more. Here, drink this down... quickly now... drink it!' The laudanum was swiftly administered, the mouth strapped with a tied wooden spoon so the patient would not bite off his tongue in the acute pain when the bone saw bit deep, the experience excruciating if the saw had not, for want of time, been restored in great haste to a sharp hone after several operations.

For the most fleeting of moments between such procedures, one surgeon briefly looked towards the other, as if seeking a mutual reinforcement; but a meeting of the eyes was rare, the brief interval for each seemingly never coinciding with the other; and so they resorted to the only mechanism they could find with which to offer mutual support: they shouted loud to each other over the wailing cacophony of groaning men in extremely painful distress all about them, briefly and with words which they hoped would be heard over the din and which might offer encouragement: 'Hold fast, Ferguson, for Our Lord stands with you!' from Marston every once in a while; 'I am in awe of your endeavours, Marston!' shouted by Simon.

The patients were usually conscious unless a head had been struck by a splinter or a fall, or if too much blood had already been lost. Wideawake men screamed, whilst the unconscious, blessed in their unawareness, lay comatose; and the semi-conscious murmured prayers or, in some cases, pleadings to precious kin who they feared, in their despairing hearts, they likely might never see again.

All contemplation of the nature and concept of triage was forgotten in the alacrity demonstrated over the two operating tables; a man with a severe wound to the lower body, the stomach particularly, the least sign of any part of his guts ripped out and torn, brought a heartfelt sigh, a distressed frown, and a reluctant shake of the head; for there was no prospect of successful surgery and recovery. When the unfortunate was shifted away, a large dose of laudanum was offered with consoling words of false hope if he was conscious; the doomed man was then set aside on the deck amidst the human detritus which was the rivulets of blood and fragments of gore, for the prognosis was hopeless; and the next casualty was immediately presented upon the table, the surgeon increasingly despairing.

Wounded observers laying on the deck were reduced to weeping at such sights, and terrified men strived to hold their tongue, to keep their screams and pain in abeyance, sometimes aware of the dreadful burden before the surgeons, the extreme load placed upon them being obvious to the terrified eye in a mere instant of scrutiny as the scene of horror that the cockpit presented swiftly registered upon their fearful minds. Other casualties were quickly prepared by the assisting attendants with encouraging words, spoken with reassurance and compassion.

Simon swabbed a particularly bloody head wound and shaved away the mop of bloodied hair all about it to gain a clearer look; the gash in the flesh atop the skull was initially horrifying, but he persevered; he wiped away another flush of blood with his cloth, scrutinised it closely, and to his great relief there was nothing of brain, no particles of such, mixed within the copious red flow. He nodded to Freeman, standing ready, and murmured in a voice filled, even shaking, with relief, 'Strap him up.' He nodded to Johnson and Taft, attending, and they lifted the patient away from the table, Freeman urging care.

Marston too had completed his own operation in that same moment, and the two surgeons looked up and towards each other in a momentary halt, a pause for breath, for a recovery of resolve; 'Marston, my strength is fast fading, and I am in dread of beginning yet another operation when, for want of energy, I may sink to my very knees before I might tie off the severed blood vessels.'

'Have no such concern, colleague, for I shall attend in but an instant, were that to be the case; *which I am sure it will not!*'

The next casualty, wounded in the upper torso, was hoisted up from the deck where he had been lying since being brought in five minutes previously. Simon peered at his unmoving body, leaned over his face with rising dismay, and felt for a pulse at his wrist, but to no avail; he set his ear against the bloodied chest, cupped both hands around it and listened for an age, his mind reluctant to accept his conclusion, subconsciously refusing to acknowledge it; 'This man is dead,' he whispered eventually, much set back. Jason gasped and Freeman stared in abject dismay. Recovering himself, Simon beckoned the two helpers, both standing ready at his call; and he waved them forward to the table. He shook his head, could find no further words, and the body was removed.

A frenzied two hours, and suddenly it was all over; the surgeons raised their heads as if caught by surprise in the flash of realisation that there were no more patients and their tables no longer exhibited the worst of what one man would do to another in the cruel collision of great wheels turning within the political firmament. Yet, even as they sighed with what little of relief was gleaned, for the momentary ending of their burden was a severe shock in itself, they themselves remained overwhelmingly traumatised; and they struggled to escape that stupefaction of shock, to wrench their brutally stricken minds to a more conscious process, to an emerging awareness that the lives of many men had been damaged and destroyed; and the utter futility of the conflict in the longer, temporal sense registered with both surgeons as deeply dismaying.

Simon, traumatised by the magnitude of the shock and with the slow realisation of relief dawning upon him, a blessed respite from the bloody burden, looked to his shaking hands; he felt his legs trembling, which was not unexpected after so long standing at his table. He gratefully seized the proffered tin cup filled with rum from Johnson, swiftly drank it down in one, coughing as he did so, and he stepped outside the curtain and shifted to the base of the steps below the higher gun deck, hoping with a fierce determination for a breath of fresh air, cool air, anything, the merest gentle zephyr, as long as it was not tainted with the coppery smell of blood. Stumbling outside of even the dim light of the lamps and his eyes reduced to sore, red slits, he slowly slumped down to sit on the bare deck, the final, flimsy remnant of his physical strength utterly gone and an absolute exhaustion swiftly overtaking him. His mental energy was also wholly expended and he leaned back against the hull in silent distress, his eyes closing, his legs and his chest shaking with uncontrollable tremulations. In the relief and sanctuary of sorts which was the darkness the streaming flow of his tears had begun and was unrelenting.

On the gun deck, a desperate Duncan Macleod paced up and down, from the mizzen to the foremast and back again, assessing the damage and the casualties. He spoke momentarily with Mower and with a half-dozen gun captains, those that spared him a moment of acknowledgment in their haste to ready once more their guns for firing. The wounded had all been removed to the cockpit to await the surgeons, but the dead, a half-dozen at least, still lay on the deck before his powder-reddened eyes; for they had been hauled away from the guns and checked in grim fashion for life by their tie mates; but haste precluded care, and they sprawled in their own blood in contorted positions adopted in the final flickering moments of life, with glassy stares and frozen expressions of fear, agony and torment. Macleod swallowed hard but found no relief in his dry mouth; he wrenched his gaze away and struggled to speak with an enquiring gun captain, before he hastened away from the terrible scene of dreadful carnage as fast as seemed decent in his rush for the nearest gun port, where he leaned out and vomited, retching for several minutes until his throat felt red raw and throbbed painfully.

On his quarterdeck a mentally tired and dog-weary Pat, trying hard to keep his feet, stared aft once more at the oncoming Turk pursuer. Handicapped to a small degree by the scrap of sailcloth that the master had insisted upon tightly strapping around his wounded leg - Pat would accept nothing more, nor would he leave the deck - he was much less mobile. He realised that the barky's salvation now rested with his gunners in the cabin, for he himself could do no more. The first red hot shots from the two great guns had struck home, for in plain sight he could see broken holes within the frigate's bow. Once more the bright orange-yellow flames and bilious smoke jetted out from the cabin below, a near instantaneous roar of thunder with them, and stinking clouds of hot powder rose high to blow back over the taffrail and flood the quarterdeck air, the deck planking of which tremored. Pat coughed painfully for a minute in a futile effort to escape the burning sensation in his raw lungs. The extremely proximate roar of the guns still oppressed his ears, so very loud that it had been for such a long time. He steadied himself from falling, the pain in his leg now more excruciating than ever, and he looked again in careful study of the enemy. Surely, he thought, no captain, no sensible officer and certainly no man with the least caution, would hold to such a pursuit, for the Turk was effectively a sitting duck; his chasers, small bore guns of six-pound shot, did not alarm Pat in the least, for they held only small prospect of damage from only the luckiest of shots; however, the eighteen-pound balls from *Surprise*, red hot ones, would guarantee infliction of huge destruction upon the Turk frigate, unquestionably so; and, for sure, her captain would quickly realise that the barky was about to wipe his eye. Indeed, it was likely that he was being apprised of it in that moment, for the impact of the damage was the least of his problems: the fire that would result was of a far greater magnitude in the rising scale of destruction sure to be inflicted upon his vessel. 'That really will not do, sir,' murmured Pat to himself, thinking aloud; 'It cannot serve you well to persist.'

And so it proved to be; whilst Pat stared the Turk let go her braces, freeing her yards from their tight grip; and her canvas, relieved of all pressure, was reduced to flapping. Pat continued to stare as her crew hauled hard on the braces to swing her yards round as far as could be; her wheel, too, was plainly swung hard over to bring her rudder round, to bring her hull broadside on to the south wind. Plainly, as Pat realised in an instant, all was intended to end the chase quickly and so preserve the Turk frigate. Even so, momentarily Pat's heart leaped into his mouth, for he feared that the Turk was perhaps endeavouring to fire her broadside in raking discharge the length of the barky; but no, he quickly realised that such was not the case, for all way was falling off her, seemingly no urgency applied to maintaining the pursuit, even for the few minutes it would take to fire one final broadside. Why that was the case Pat did not know, and nor in his exhaustion did he much care to consider, save for the thought that perhaps the Turk had become affrighted by the strike from red hot shot and feared another one; however, the race was run, the fight was finished, the bloody conflagration was finally all over at last. Pat, in his professional wisdom, commended his adversary; for the Turk captain had plainly accepted that his chance was gone. At least, Pat reflected, there was some prospect of rescue for some of the men of the first frigate, visibly doomed. He stared at it once again: flames were roaring atop her yards and masts, her crew were all either in her boats or, by now, likely drowned. He could not dispel the horrible thought that matters could easily have gone the other way; it could have been *Surprise* sinking. He recalled his words of a few hours ago to Plunket: *every victory was usually a close run thing*. This one had been closer than he cared to contemplate, and he wondered whether Plunket had been successful with his rifle; certainly, there had been a brief delay before the first Turk frigate had reacted to *Surprise's* turn away. *Had that been significant?* He did not know. His head was extremely painful and throbbing as if being beaten by a hammer, his excruciatingly sore leg was shaking like never before within blood-soaked breeches, and his mind was swimming with a multitude of thoughts, an analysis of events, and - for so he himself recognised - he was still feeling something near panic; a great confusion seemed to be taking over in his head, and he wrenched his thinking away from it to stare once more all about him.

The bitter engagement was over, it was finished; his eyes reaffirmed the truth of it; about the carronades on the quarterdeck exhausted men stood in limp posture gazing astern at the Turk frigate, all sense of urgency gone, all physical energy dissipated; and a rising relief strived to make its seemingly reluctant path to Pat's severely over-taxed mind. His own physical strength, as was plain to him too, was also gone, utterly; and he shifted slowly with faltering steps, struggling with his trembling right leg, much bloodied once more through the makeshift dressing, hobbling with difficulty to the capstan between the mizzen and main masts, where he promptly sat down, nearing collapse. The master quickly appeared at his side. 'Mr Prosser, make fast your guns,' Pat ordered. A half-dozen of his men, anxiously noting his incapacity, hastened to offer assistance. His head swirled with the arriving floodtide of thoughts: *the barky had escaped, against all the odds;* but within moments a concurrent grip of gloom wholly overtook that relief, overpowered it totally, as his mind filled with the bloody consequences of the day and the hugely distressing question: *what would be the butcher's bill?* He felt his head throbbing wildly, as if the hammer was beating down harder than ever before upon it, and a wet trickle was running down his forehead into his eye; he blinked and wiped it away with his hand: blood! His eyes were rapidly losing focus as he looked to his blood-soaked breeches; the sodden canvas bandage strapped about his leg had slid down and fallen away; and for the first time he saw the wood splinter which protruded and was embedded within his leg. He dimly heard the shouts of Barton racing towards him, 'Hold fast, sir! Clap on to my arms!' And then he slowly toppled forward into the hands of his helpers as blessed unconsciousness overtook all of his anxieties.

The dim light of the Argand lamp registered as a distant blur in the darkness as Pat blinked repeatedly, trying to clear his vision; to no avail, all his surroundings remaining indistinct, blurred. He could feel a rhythmical swaying of his body, and his hearing still served him after a fashion as he adjusted to the subdued sounds all about him. The familiar creak of timbers and indistinct noises from above enabled his slow deduction that he was in his cot, the lowest of washing noises from the stern wake bringing him at last to his conclusion. Another minute and he could discern the mechanical thud of the pumps working, the familiar, rhythmical sound that it was. Grasping for a greater awareness of his situation and the least thing which might come to mind in his confusion, he recalled, indistinctly, a prior agony of something seemingly beating upon his head, even as his leg felt as if it was afire in his last moments on deck, and then came a more acute recollection of gasping for breath and never gaining enough of it, as something - another memory, he could not recall what, save that it was most unwelcome - was obstructing the great gasps with which he fought for air, something tied across his mouth, holding it open as he bit down upon it in the most excruciating pain. Even now, in his confusion, he was sure he could feel the flow of tears which had washed his face as he tried desperately, but failed, to scream out aloud. And then a greater clarity, a rising consciousness, arose within the obscurities of his tired mind, and he endeavoured to sit up, struggled momentarily, but failed. The extreme pain in his leg and the pulsating discomfort all about his head told him in no uncertain terms to lay still, and he slumped back with a groan. His mouth strongly protested its dryness and he wondered how he might find a glass of water; he tried to turn his head to gauge a better understanding of what was happening about him, but to no avail.

'Rest, brother,' the voice uttering the low words of comfort seemed familiar: *was it Simon? Could it be?* He could not make out any definition above him, merely a blurred perception of a figure above his cot.

'Simon... Simon? Is it you?' Pat croaked out the words in little more than a whisper, his throat so raw and dry, and his mouth feeling so parched.

''Sure, it is. I have been sitting with you this last half-hour. Here, drink this down.' The water trickled from the glass held just above his lips; his head near prone, much liquid spilled as he glugged it down gratefully. 'Thankfully, we have been sailing away from the fray these past eight hours... beyond the sunset and into a welcome darkness. MacLeod is in command of our dear *Surprise* and all is well.'

'Simon... what... what happened to me? My eyes are all astray.' Pat's confusion and anxiety filled his voice, but his vision was clearing, something of a focus gained as he noticed the plethora of dried blood spatters covering his friend's shirt.

'You were struck in the leg by a considerable splinter; it was deep and an accursed difficult one to remove. In fact, despite a plentiful dose of the poppy...'

'Eh? The poppy?'

'The opiate - *the laudanum*. Despite the most generous dispensation of it - *thankfully, you may recall, our stocks were replenished in Argostoli* - the surgery inflicted much blood loss and great pain upon you as Marston drew out the wicked culprit - *and a most admirable excision it was*. Indeed, I could not but hear your screams from my own table three yards away. You may consider that Marston - *the diligent fellow* - preserved your leg. I venture you may be in need of both of them if you are to die as an Admiral.'

'I am obliged to you for your humour, brother, but I fear I have missed my tide... to become an admiral, indeed!... and here in this backwater of... *of irregular service*... as a letter-of-marque... and in the service of foreigners... *foreigners, Simon! A letter-of-marque, indeed!* Such is scarcely more reputable than a damnable, blackguard pirate.'

Simon reverted to the voice of necessary caution which he employed whenever he sought to impress his urgent view upon his dear friend, 'It was a close run thing... the saving of your leg, and quite the careful surgical procedure; hence, it was necessarily slow, for the splinter had lodged a mere whisker from the femoral artery. I am sure I could not have done better than Marston myself. Doubtless you felt a considerable pain when it snapped, the residual point lingering deep for a further two minutes until removed.'

'I have some small recollection of that moment,' murmured Pat, drowsiness coming upon him despite being shocked to hear the gravity of his injury and its remedy. 'Indeed, I feel quite knocked up, even now.'

'You were also *knocked down...* near the time of the final Turk shots - *for so I was told.* The barrage dislodged a - *I forget the culprit* - an iron boom... a... *a boom iron...* or some such weighty device which is normally employed in the higher regions of the... the masts - *the yards...* I have always considered that a strange descriptor; would you not agree?'

'A trifle more of water, if you please.'

'Allow me to add that you are the fortunate man of the world... that the object was collected by a sail and so slid down most slowly within the great fill - *the expanse* - of the canvas... as slow as such falls can be slow... but unfortunately it passed through the... the splinter net... *netting...* which was torn away, to strike your head. Barton recounted the event to me and showed me the... *the item.*'

'Lord, Simon, my head is devilish sore... hurts like hell!'

Simon frowned, 'I venture that had it *fallen free* from... from such a great height... then you would no longer be with us... or, *at least*, not entirely in possession of your intellects... or even the full measure of your head.'

'I dare say it has scraped off a little of my copper.'

'Please to describe any imperfections of sight or hearing, the slightest thing.'

'The second Turk, what happened?' Pat disregarded Simon's question and his own painful discomfort, and he raced to express his anxious curiosity.

'A sensible man, apparently he was so. Mr Prosser described to me his turn away and towards the scene of his fellow... that ship in distress. The light from that burning vessel was visible for many hours as we sailed away from the conflict.'

'Will you tell me about the men? Did we lose a great many of them? I confess I am greatly affrighted even in asking the question.'

Simon sought to leave his answer in abeyance, not wishing to further burden his friend, and so he prevaricated, 'Our losses were not of a magnitude that... that might have been... *so MacLeod declared.* We will look to what can be done there, to what might be said... *in the morning;* for I am sure you will then be feeling much the better; but now... *now,* brother, I must away to... to... *downstairs...* and you will oblige me by doing nothing, the least thing, save to stay here in your cot. In such instances, the injured body must be afforded a sufficiency of time for the natural humours to recover, and neither must you fret your spirit. I beg you will rest; Murphy is attending for every necessity, to any want.'

'Help me up, will you; I must gain my quarterdeck,' Pat gasped the words, tried to sit up but failed once more, his energy so weak and his pains so very great. He sighed in despond.

'I will not,' Simon spoke with grave concern in his voice; 'Lie back, brother; you must rest.' But no answer was returned, for Pat was already asleep.

Wednesday 10th May 1826   18:00   100 miles N.E. of Malta

The indistinct sound of four bells ringing out brought a drowsy Pat to full wakefulness. His head still throbbed, but less so; his eyes remained painfully sore, but at least he could see clearly. The swirling, burnt powder particles had served out a particularly unpleasant consequence to many aboard the barky, and it would be days before hundreds of eyes might recover without the painful smarting which prompted men to the water tub to wash their eyes every hour. Pat's leg pained him to the extent that he rubbed it hard and harder, wincing and withdrawing his hand as it caught upon the stitches. There was also something of a numbness about his leg, but he was grateful at least to find it was still there. Thankfully, his strength had recovered such that he could at least haul himself up to a sitting position, and he swung his legs out and to the deck, but he remained sitting on his cot. Despite that modicum of success in movement, he felt that he still did not yet possess the strength to stand, and so he contented himself with a tentative calling out for his steward, 'Murphy... Murphy there.'

'Well, sorr... 'tis the long sleep 'ee has had.' The familiar sight, even the smallest of smiles on his face as he appeared from the coach, was never more welcome. 'How is 'ee?'

'Like a bear with a sore head... *two* sore heads... and off its legs. Coffee would be the most welcome pleasure of the world right now... if you please.'

'Well, it's a'coming up right d'reckly, sorr; a minute or two is all; it be awaiting your honour's call... on the galley stove this last hour.'

'My compliments to Mr Macleod and Dr Ferguson, and perhaps they will join me when... when they are at leisure - *that is to say, when they are not at a stand.*' Murphy nodded and hastened away.

When Murphy returned, he was accompanied by Duncan who hastened to sit in one of the chairs adjacent to Pat's cot. 'It is a relief to see you sitting up. How are you feeling?'

'I would like to say never better, but I think you would smoke it. How many men did we lose?'

'I regret to say there were nine killed... they... they went over the side this morning. Marston insisted upon a service... thankfully brief; and we have a score and ten or thereabouts who are wounded. I regret that Simon is minded that one or two may not survive.' A momentary hesitation and Duncan resumed, 'Codrington, Pickering and Mower... all of them... were wounded.'

Pat groaned, 'How are they? How do they fare?'

'They are as comfortable as can be; their wounds are light. Codrington and Mower were struck by splinters, into the shoulder and arm respectively; and Pickering took a musket ball into the flesh of the leg. The surgeons have removed the splinters and ball.'

It was several minutes before Pat spoke again, the loss of so many of his men so painful to acknowledge. 'And the damage to the barky?'

'Much of the starboard hull about the gun deck is greatly damaged, several gun port lids entirely fallen away; the bulwark is also much smashed all along the length of it... two of the boats are broken beyond repair...' Duncan's litany reduced him to a gloomy voice, 'The carpenter has plugged a score of holes between wind and water... and there are a deal of repairs necessary for the rigging... a great deal... and as for the sails, I fear that the sailmaker is quite despairing; he has not ceased puling his lot all day.'

Pat's face registered his deep dismay but he held his silence as Murphy handed out the coffee, a generous measure of brandy instilled within it, 'Well, Dr Ferguson insists on a regular drop for 'ee, sorr; a proper strong measure. Drink it down; it will do you good... serve you well, right proper.'

Pat had his doubts about that, but he recognised his steward's benevolent concern, and so he did not reply other than with a nod of thanks. He sipped the coffee, immensely grateful for its small gesture to a normality that he did not feel in the least, and he welcomed its comforting, roborative influence, not least upon his sore throat, whilst he gathered his thoughts. 'How is Simon?' he ventured after a further minute, 'And Marston? How are they faring?'

'Very well,' Duncan lied; for in truth both men were at their wits end, the calls upon them so many and so extreme. Marston was most particularly anxious for his dear colleague's welfare, having found him sitting on the deck outside the cockpit, unmoving in a silent rigidity, a state which had much disturbed him; and he had sought Duncan's help to coax Simon out of a profound state of shock; but Simon had since recovered well, so much so that he had been able to attend Pat in the cabin on many fleeting occasions during the night, much concerned for his dearest friend. Duncan tried for something more, something of help, for Pat in his evident dismay, 'It could have been far, *far* worse, Pat. There isnae a man aboard of a different persuasion. Your decision to attack one and flee from the other... well, there wasnae any other choice; we all see that... nae other choice at all; and I beg you will consider the matter in that light.'

Pat sighed and despaired, but could find no words. Murphy, seeing his captain's abject dejection, spoke up, 'Well, sorr, beg leave to report... Séamus Plunket... he reckons he shot down the Turk captain... wounded him, like.'

'Did he indeed?' Pat's interest was captured. He reflected for a moment, recalling the brief absence from deck of the captain of the first Turk frigate before the flames began to consume her masts and sails. 'I do recall that there was a... *an absence*... on her quarterdeck... for some minutes just as the barky made her turn... and before the gunners fired our broadside of Jelbert's shot; yes, I believe that was the case. And Plunket reckons he shot him... from at least a cable away?'

'Well, sorr, he be telling every man who will listen that he did; he swears he did so,' replied Murphy in a voice that declared that he held not the least doubt about it himself; 'And every man has been listening... and Séamus... he be the hero of the barky, sorr.' Murphy nodded emphatically and then brief reflection prompted his addition, 'Well, that is to say, sorr... saving your honour's presence... every man be minded that 'ee, sorr, be the right proper hero... that 'ee saved the ship. The lads all be talking about it. Mighty close it was... *mighty close*... No hare ever escaped a Galway lurcher with a smaller lead; no, for sure.'

Duncan interjected with something of relief in his voice, looking to cheer his friend, 'It's a fact, aye; I have heard it myself from many a man about the decks.'

'Perhaps I will take a trifle more of brandy, Murphy,' declared Pat. As he drank it down, he felt the rising return of fatigue overwhelming him, and he lay back in his cot, falling asleep within moments despite the pulsating pains in his head and his leg as Duncan and Murphy anxiously looked on.

Surprise swung at double-anchor in the flat calm waters of the Grand Harbour, Fort Ricasoli on her starboard beam, the buff grand structures all about her conveying an undeniable perception of majestic permanence and invulnerability, in glaring contrast with the severely damaged barky, which registered with all souls aboard and did nothing to lift anyone from their dismay.

Mathew Jelbert was tied alongside the barky, the cutter's safe arrival having been reported to Pat whilst he rested within his cot in the cabin, recuperating from his head knock, and forbidden - as far as such was possible to dictate - by Simon from venturing from it, much to his friend's extreme dissatisfaction. Yet, for the present at least and in the perceived safety of the Grand Harbour, Pat acceded to his doctor's instruction, growing more irritable as every hour passed, until his concerns were mollified by reassurances that his friend, Duncan, had safely brought the shattered barky into the sanctuary of Valletta during the half-light before the dawn proper, after an approach in the enduring southerly *Sirocco* for the final hundred miles and without encountering any further Turk hostility. After such reassurances, Pat had slipped in and out of fitful sleep, his anxieties conflicting with his exhaustion to enforce an alternation every few hours and a resultant exasperation each time he awakened, Murphy usually receiving the sharp edge of his tongue.

Neither was Malta a sanctuary from which Simon and Marston had much benefitted from, the two being wholly absorbed below deck attending the wounded. Nine men had been most hastily interred to a watery grave during the prior day, Pat being absent and sleeping in his cot. Their brief funeral, cursory even in comparison to prior hasty ceremonies, had been a miserable affair, so many more valued shipmates dead and near two score wounded to a greater and lesser extent. The bloody battle with the, ultimately burned, Turk frigate had been as costly as any for the Surprises, and morale was consequently much cast down.

Despite the calm of her surroundings, the fit men of the barky, although exhausted, were working with as much haste as they could muster, driven in all things by Duncan and the bosun; for her damages were extensive: much of her starboard side had been shattered and the bulwarks broken away; the hull about the gun deck was smashed through with many shot holes; three of the great guns had been wrested from their broken trucks; and the sailmaker was in despair, for the fore course and much of the topsails were greatly rent and torn, holed and ripped, the standing rigging similarly so. Indeed, the bosun was as dismayed as much as anyone had ever seen him, for all but the cutter of the frigate's boats had been nigh on destroyed or, in the least, were wholly unseaworthy. Mr Sampays was not a happy man, and all persons about the barky, both officers and men, went to great lengths to avoid his irascibility, unusual that it was, but which seemed ever worse by the hour.

Pat too, in his cot, felt his ire rising as his enquiries as to the state of his ship and his people were met with little more than platitudes, his anger scarcely deflected by his friends' reference to the necessity for him to rest, to seek recovery in sleep; but as his strength slowly recovered and the dressing around his head was removed, he vowed to embark upon a personal inspection, much to Simon's dismay; for the surgeon was sitting in silence at the side of his cot. Pat stared with tired eyes, he felt acute pain in his leg, and his head seemed to be being beaten upon by a stick; but amidst his own discomforts he scrutinised his companion carefully, for the surgeon scarcely resembled the man who he had known for so many years; rather, before Pat's gaze there seemed to be a physically shattered remnant of the former man, more nearly resembling a cadaver in the shock of close scrutiny; for he was unshaven, unwashed, and dried blood was very evident upon his old shirt, which was scarcely better than a pauper's rags; yet, even so, his deeply sunken and reddened eyes, set amidst shrouds of black within a gaunt, whitened face, one which appeared visibly aged more than Pat had ever noticed before, gazed back with an infinite concern for his friend.

'Brother, I most assiduously beg you to keep your cot,' pleaded Simon; 'You are unwell... you have been wounded, not once but twice; and you must not consider yourself in the least ambulant... most certainly not. MacLeod has every matter in hand, I do assure you.'

'To hell with my cot!' exclaimed Pat with unusual vehemence.

Simon tried his last shot, 'If you hold to this present irascibility... insist on rising, on exertions which are ill-considered... *at best*... and...' the smallest of hesitations before the largest of exaggerations, '... imposing such a strain upon your leg, injured again as it is, then it is with regret that I must caution you that... that such a *vigorous* perambulation...' Simon swallowed and held to a straight face, '... may lead to... *to complications*... and *conceivably* an unavoidable... *procedure*.'

'What do you mean, *a procedure?*'

'One which will require a deal of fortitude... *an amputation of the wounded leg*.' Simon stared at his friend with a malicious pleasure, for he knew that all urgings towards caution would surely fall upon stony ground, would not be entertained.

A sharp intake of breath, and Pat spoke in enervated voice, 'God's my life, Simon! *Amputation indeed!* I beg you will spare me the hocus pocus in the medical line. Do you take me for some country spalpeen who is just come down from the Maumturk mountain... a buffoon fresh from the Carrownagappul bog, perhaps?'

'I merely stated that excessive exertion *may* lead to the necessity for a surgical procedure.'

'For shame! I am only in contemplation of gaining the fresh air... the merest breath will serve!'

'The air herein is as fresh as that upstairs... *upon the deck*; there is no credible contradictory perspective. Look about you; you possess of not a single pane of glass at the back of this cabin... *the stern* would it be?'

'And what are our people to think, eh? Their captain laying up in his cot, languishing; *yes, languishing...* and doing nothing, *nothing at all...* while they, doubtless, are hard at work.'

'I can assure you that all the men hold to the view that your conduct, your decisive actions, your sound direction... saved this fine vessel and every soul aboard from a complete destruction at the hands of the Turk. Hence, not a single man would care a jot were you to remain bed-bound all the way home to Falmouth. That is to say, *of course they would be concerned*, but only for your health. Patrick O'Connor, do not believe for one moment the least thing to the contrary. You must keep your cot and hold to the long rest, the longer the better; and not another word will I hear about the matter.'

'Well, if you insist; but it is a damnably wearying place when a man is awake for hour upon interminable hour, scarcely the least thing to occupy his time. Why, another day and I will go stark mad.' A momentary pause, 'Are you sure that... that our people pay it no mind?'

Pat appearing to be somewhat mollified, Simon pressed on, 'Will I say that despite the most dreadful - *that is to say, the several* - setbacks which we have incurred, I am of the same mind myself as the men, as is every officer aboard, all of whom I have spoken to in this matter. And now... *and now*, I must beg leave to return to my charges *downstairs...* for several exhibit grave cause for... *for concern*. If it pleases you, I can tarry here no longer, *for not a minute more.*'

A crestfallen Pat could only nod, even as he slumped back into his cot, defeated, staring with infinite concern as Simon shuffled with a slow, stooped gait across the cabin to the door. He imagination stirring, he contemplated the likely situation below in the cockpit, and he was sure it was the most ghastly of scenes. He remembered well the desperate minutes of close firing, the incoming shot; and in an instant his natural aversion to the sight of distress, of blood and gore, rose in a strongly unpleasant wave of nausea which conflicted most painfully with his overriding wish to see and, as far as he could, to comfort his wounded shipmates; for he had observed over the years that a warm few words would exert the most benevolent effect upon the sick and dispirited in their extreme discomfort; and so he chafed with a deep dissatisfaction at his delay in doing so. He cursed his leg and he cursed more the still-painful throbbing within his temples. He lay back in abject frustration, and within a few minutes he had fallen asleep again.

A very much muted seven bells rang out as Pat stirred from his slumber, Dalby being under instruction to refrain from anything louder; but the absence of all physical obstruction, the least thing, facilitated the resonant peal everywhere about the barky's decks; even the faintest of sounds registered with the wounded and the surgeons below in the cockpit, where a weary Simon and Marston were still toiling, assisted by Jason.

'I do believe, my dear Ferguson,' opined Michael Marston, 'that we have done all that we can for our patients for the present moment; would you not agree?' Marston stared hard at the ashen face of his deeply fatigued friend and colleague, for his great concern was that Simon might to some degree revert to the immobilising state of shock in which he had found him outside the cockpit after the bloody battle. 'Will we look to Wilkins, to the galley... for some comestibles? Perhaps a tint of port wine or a madeira might offer a modicum of restoration for the... *the essential morale?*'

'Thank you, but no,' mumbled Simon, failing to turn his gaze from the panorama of physically violated human beings, some in cots and others about the deck on blankets atop straw. The surgeon fretted silently, for doubtless some of them, immobile, unconscious, cleansed as best they could be in the recent hours by Freeman, would already be lying in a renewal of their own soil. At least - Simon strived for the merest scintilla of consolation - they had eaten nothing solid for twenty-four hours, their only nutrient being grog infused with sugar, a copious quantity of it. A very few, the lesser wounded, were in hammocks, the least injured of them talking to adjacent shipmates. Freeman, even now after so many hours attending, moved slowly about them all, offering water, grog, even rum, the small comfort that it was. Simon stared, wondering, speculating; many of the distressed men in great pain would also be mentally desecrated; perhaps all of them to a greater or lesser extent; and he recognised in that acute moment of returning angst his own mental violation; he recalled his deep and profound shock, so debilitating, so powerful, that it had struck him into physical immobility after the recent battle. His desperate hours of exertions to save the lives of the catastrophically wounded, working without pause in such frantic haste, dictated that for not a single minute had he halted, manically engaged for over two hours. His physical energy had all been dissipated, but the frenetic haste in operating on one man so swiftly after another had also shattered his nerves, utterly.

'Colleague,' Marston persevered, 'my eyes do not deceive me; plainly you are in want of a necessary recuperation, a rest... at least a brief one... a few hours of sleep. You have scarcely left the cockpit... and our charges... since the end of the conflict, and that was two days ago. You must embrace a respite. I beg you will. Please reconsider.'

Simon dimly recalled that he had stumbled from the cockpit, his hands shaking, tremors in his arms and legs, when the stream of casualties had ceased; he remembered with dismay that he had been wholly gripped by the shock in the moment of halting, which arrived in a swift and all-consuming tide of crushing mental and physical inability. It had not been the first time that such had happened to him; he well remembered the earlier incidence too, and he felt a deeply coruscating self-condemnation. A similar incapacitation had struck him after the battles to defend the island of Samos from invasion. Recovering somewhat, he spoke to Marston without turning his head from his scrutiny of the wounded, 'I am sensible of your attentions, Marston, and you have my best thanks; however, I am unable to sleep, even were I minded to try for such.'

'I am sure that a very few drops of laudanum will assist you; perhaps fifty.'

'No, Marston, I think not... for such is a dangerous path.'

'Perhaps an Almoravian draught will serve? I recall you mentioned once that the esteemed Dr Maturin swore by its efficacy? Do you possess of such a medicine?'

'I do not. In any event, I believe that it was an opinion from which Maturin later recanted. Let us hear no more of it.'

'Very well. I dare say you - *and Maturin* - are in the right of things about that. But surely we have something of an alternative remedy... the least thing?'

'Marston, will I say that your concern is admirable, and I honour you for it; but for the moment I will hold to my station, here... amidst the unfortunates. The Dear knows I have a deal of consternation for Hammett most particularly.'

Marston spoke up with conviction, 'My dear Ferguson, I beg to differ. It is plain to see that a respite is necessary... the briefest of which will allow a modicum of benevolent recuperation.' No response and Marston pressed on, 'Allow me to say, colleague, that it is clear to me that you are not fit to stand longer on your legs... but our patients are deserving of your most considered opinion, and in your present state of fatigue that can no longer be sure.'

'Really, colleague, it does not become you to exaggerate!'

'Will I remind you that even Our Lord felt obliged to rest... on the Seventh Day; and we... *mere mortals that we are*... we also cannot do better than halt when that necessity is come upon us, and plainly it is so. Come with me, let us take to the deck, to the fresh air; let us look up to the blue skies, to the Heavens above... where Our Lord is surely looking down upon us... is with us... in this hour of our great distress. Come with me... Ferguson... *please*... I beg you will; I am with you. Will you take my hand?'

Marston's heartfelt pleadings registered, finally capturing Simon's attention, and after a brief, dissatisfied silence and recognising the truth of his friend's words he turned to look to

173

the chaplain at his side. He was, to Marston's eye, in a moment of difficult reflection; and then he nodded, and he grasped the chaplain's extended hand, held it firm and shook it, something of a reassurance, a reinforcement, held firm in the physical bond. 'Marston, I am most sensible of this kind gesture of friendship.' A mutual nod and the two surgeons stepped back from their tables, from their charges, the wounded, and passed through the curtain. Marston briefly looked back to exchange nods with Jason who was staring with evident concern.

'Will we look to Captain O'Connor in the cabin?' Marston suggested. 'Perhaps Murphy might furnish a most welcome pot of coffee... that precious standby. What do you say?'

'Yes,' murmured Simon at last with a sigh of resignation, 'On reflection, that is an excellent suggestion. Thank you.' Together they walked the length of the lower deck to the aft companionway, Marston trailing and anxiously studying his friend as Simon climbed the steps, until they passed through the coach and, with a brief knock which was answered to their great pleasure by Pat, stepped into the cabin.

Pat had dragged himself from his cot, ignoring Murphy's remonstrations, and he sat at his table, a great pile of unopened letters upon it. He was plainly enjoying the escape from lassitude; he was enjoying the coffee more, the pleasant aroma of which permeated the air. His wide smile as he saw Simon was beatific, 'Simon, old friend, come in, come in! Marston, please, join me, be seated. Murphy... Murphy there! Light along to the galley and fetch another pot of coffee for our shipmates.' Pat bawled, 'Make haste!' as Murphy hesitated. The steward was staring with great dismay at Simon's blanched face, so very gaunt, his eyes mere reddened slits, his demeanour one of absolute resignation, which was something of a belated personal acceptance of his own exhaustion.

'You will excuse me, I'm sure, but I am mortified for not rising to greet you,' declared Pat, his feelings a mixture of pleasure in meeting Simon for the first time since many hours languishing in his cot and his anxiety in seeing the surgeon in such abject depression, as seemed the case; 'The leg ain't yet up to a deal of standing about.'

'It is no matter; your seating, that is. And I am minded that the second wound to your leg is healing admirably,' Simon replied; 'I believe it is true to say that you possess of the luckiest leg of the world; for, in the bedlam which has been the cockpit during these recent hours, I will say that I have amputated legs with lesser wounds... and you are to consider that your own has been wounded not once but twice. However, I believe we may cast aside my prior fears of amputation.' The surgeon decided enough was enough as Marston stared pointedly at him in searching scrutiny and disbelief. At least the story, preposterous that it was to the chaplain's ears, had ensured that Pat had kept his bed for the crucial first few days; in fact, his head injury had been the major influence, and the bandages had been removed by Jason only a few hours earlier; for the purser was a man of many talents, a gifted linguist, a polymath even; for, whatever he turned his hand to, his success seemed assured; he had acted as third surgeon, assisting Simon and Marston on many occasions. He was also something of a trusted confidant to Pat, who shared with him his thoughts and concerns during spells after the dusk when they gazed at the celestial heavens with Pat's telescope, their shared astronomical interest forming the foundation of a most cordial dialogue, one which oft allowed for debate beyond the customary reservations and protocols of rank.

Pat stared, not quite able to decide on the sincerity or otherwise of Simon's diagnosis, present or past. 'I am mightily pleased to hear it,' he pronounced eventually, ostensibly discarding his suspicions but harbouring a lingering intent to investigate at a later time. 'Wilkins has promised a magnificent feast,' Pat announced, 'for we are honoured by the Governor himself, Lord Hastings, who will be attending; he has sent his personal cook, a native Maltese of reputedly

175

considerable talents, and with a deal of fine provisions...'
Pat's voice dropped to within a shade of dissatisfaction, '...
and his aide with this grand pile of letters... to which I will not
attend until the morrow. They came only this morning aboard
the Malta packet. His Lordship was alerted to our presence by
the postmaster when several letters of a seemingly official
nature were remarked, they being addressed to us in
Cephalonia. I do not care to blight my day with such... *as
those*... for the present moment. You will join me later for
dinner, gentlemen?'

'Most certainly, sir!' Marston seized the moment with
great emphasis, not caring to allow Simon the least latitude in
the matter.

'Excellent!' Pat brightened. 'Macleod will also be
attending, it much pleases me to say; and I am minded to
invite Jason too; if, that is, he can be spared from the cockpit
for an hour. Aahh, here is Murphy. Let us look to the coffee.'

The steward deposited the tray and stared at his master as
a pleased Pat poured without delay. A first sip and Pat smiled,
'Murphy, did you ever taste such delectable nectar back home
in Galway?'

'Well, sorr, all we could afford was tea... *on Sundays
after church*. Sure, there was a coffee shop in Galway town,
sorr... *for the rich gentlemen, that is... merchants and the like*;
but we had *Scotch* coffee. I remember my mother would bleed
the cow and mix the blood - *boiling* - with butter and salt... *we
had no sugar in them days*... before adding the burnt bread
crumbs.' Murphy grimaced, 'Well, it was never to my taste
until my father added moonshine.' Murphy offered a rare
smile, 'He kept it in the jakes... in secret, like; but the whiskey
was ever much the better without the coffee, sorr.'

'No doubt... no doubt,' murmured Pat, nodding with sage
recollection and regretting his question. Murphy's
reminiscence of an unpalatable and rural Irish practice had
brought something of a setback to the mood at the table.
'Thankfully, we may pay that recipe no mind now, eh? Will
you look to Mr Sampays... *my compliments, of course*. He is

176

to preddy the deck before Lord Hastings arrives... and to ready a welcome party of the hands, all clean and tidy, all slops pressed right clean, *and every man with his hat!* Thank you. Carry on.'

Chapter Eight

With impeccable punctuality, General Francis Rawdon, Lord Hastings, came aboard, opting for the larboard side after being apprised in advance of Pat's immobility. The welcoming party, expecting him on the traditional starboard side, turned about to greet him anyway with pipe and salute, excusing the diversion; for he was, after all, only a soldier; and hence the hands reckoned that he likely would not be accustomed to the old traditions. He was announced at the cabin door by Murphy. MacLeod, who had been on deck to greet him, hurried to show him into the cabin where Pat tried hard but failed to gain his legs. From the assembly at the table, all save Pat standing as Hastings entered, the focus was upon an aged-looking man with grey, much-receded hair, slightly full of lower face, yet still retaining a perceptible aura of purpose, of authority, but without the least air of arrogance. Pat, with evident difficulty, tried again and hauled himself with the aid of the table top to his feet, standing on one leg but striving not to show it, but he could go no further. Hastings, observing his host's discomfort and cognisant of its probable cause, having studied the many and varied frigate's damages as he came aboard, stepped quickly to stand directly before Pat, and the two men shook hands.

'Welcome aboard, sir,' Pat spoke with noticeable warmth, 'Upon my word and honour it is a pleasure to make the acquaintance of such a renowned soldier and, if I may say so, a most celebrated Irishman.'

'I am obliged, Captain O'Connor, for your gracious opinion of me... obliged, sir; but allow me to say that the pleasure is all mine, I assure you. It is I who is delighted to meet such an accomplished Irish seafarer.'

'Sir, allow me to introduce my officers; my First, Captain Duncan Macleod.'

'A great honour, sir,' declared Duncan, shaking hands.

'And my most particular friend and ship's surgeon, Dr Simon Ferguson,' Pat continued.

'Your most humble servant, sir,' murmured Simon, who bowed his head from the far side of the table. Pat introduced everyone else present, and all took their seats.

'May I say, Captain O'Connor,' declared Hastings, that I have these two years gone been fascinated to hear what little news has reached Malta - *none via official channels, of course* - of the sterling efforts of your vessel and your men in, *will I say*, those... *politically disputed...* waters to the east.'

Pat's anxiety surged once more as he endeavoured to think of a diversion from such an unwelcome subject, 'Sir, I will beg your forbearance when I say that aboard the barky... *this vessel...* we have long held to a practice of there being no mention of politics in the cabin, for we have oft found that such is generally the end of all comfortable talk.'

'I see. Yes, I do perceive that in the... *the enclosure...* the small world of... *of containment...* at sea for long spells, such talk as politics, on which men rarely if ever find that chimera of perfect accord... might well promote a disagreeable air... a contumelious brabble; even, perhaps, a minor antipathy... betwixt colleagues.'

'Exactly, sir; that is always a... a considerable concern. The very same remark was in my own mind until you uttered it. No ship can sustain success if there is the least ill-will amongst its officers, and we are all much mindful of that, and it behoves us not to venture into such dangerous waters.'

'I suppose that is an admirable notion; indeed, it is... *if a tad idealistic*, but do you not find that such a lack of political debate is something of a... *a fundamental contradiction...* ' Hastings ignored Pat's reservations, '... when your principal purpose in these parts has been an engagement in that most brutal extreme of politics itself? I speak of the Greek conflict.'

Pat's alarmed mind raced towards finding a subject which, whilst contradicting his stated avoidance of politics, might secure a firm cerebral focus for His Lordship before his thoughts returned in the least towards the Greek conflict. 'There are certainly occasions suited to political debate, sir, no doubt,' declared Pat with discernible doubt, 'and allow me to say - *and with the utmost brevity* - that I am in perfect accord with your own most honourable and well-known aspirations for *Irish* causes... your benevolent and most laudable interest in electoral reform and... and emancipation for our Catholic brethren.'

Simon stared, speechless and astonished, for a political statement from his friend was about as rare as hen's teeth; but Hastings beamed, plainly delighted. Pat hastily beckoned all to take their chairs, and everyone sat down to engage in a diverse exchange across the table, led by Hastings with more innocuous enquiries. Within a few minutes a most cordial ambience was achieved and, thankfully, to Pat's mind, there was no return to the subject of the barky's Greek service.

'Captain,' Hastings eventually interjected with a degree of authority, halting the congenial conversation, 'I recall that there is one matter which I must bring to your attention. You may not yet have remarked it, but my aide... he brought a great bundle of letters to you this morning. All of those of a conceivably military or naval bent were deposited in my office by an officer of the packet from Falmouth... and it did not escape my own attention that there was a most particular letter which is closed with an Admiralty seal, one which may therefore be of some significance to you. Accordingly, I deemed it necessary to deliver it myself; hence, my visit today; and here it is, sir.'

'Thank you for your most kind attentions, sir, in that respect,' replied Pat, 'I confess that until your arrival I was obliged to keep my cot. I have something of a leg wound... which, I am pleased to say, is healing well - will recover fully - *with the blessing*; but... what with the barky being quite unfit to depart for a day... *or longer*... and sleep, blessed sleep, coming very easily this past day, I was minded to look to the post on the morrow.'

'That is perfectly understandable in the circumstances,' said Hastings with audible sympathy, 'Indeed, I cannot conceive that there could be anything of sufficient importance to intercede in your recuperations.'

In the background Murphy busied about the table, pouring sherry in bountiful measures, even distributing the last of the walnuts, which was the most generous of donations, as he saw things. Within twenty minutes, convivial conversation tentatively developing towards more expansive dialogue, all talk was suspended upon a general registration of the tantalising aromas and the sight of the trays delivered by Wilkins and His Lordship's cook. 'With your permission, sirs,' declared the cook, 'For your pleasure and for your first dish, I present to you... *octopus stew*.' Ignoring without the least hesitancy any potential breach of protocol, the cook proceeded to ladle generous quantities into the bowls that Murphy had set down.

'Octopus! Octopus? Did I hear it right?' Pat asked of his guest with a notable degree of reserve. 'How does it eat, sir?'

Hastings, observing a hesitation about the table for a dish that had never before appeared in the great cabin, spoke up with conviction, 'It is a famed local delicacy, and I do assure you that the creatures were all caught fresh this morning... from the waters off Gozo.'

Pat nodded and, though salivating - for the prospect certainly smelled divine - he interjected before the eating began, 'Gentlemen, a brief toast, if you will.' Heads and glasses everywhere were raised. A momentary pause on Pat's part as he instantly discarded the traditional Thursday toast, "to a bloody war", and switched to a more palatable one in the circumstances, 'Our native land, King and country!' The resounding accord echoed all around the table, and the feast began. Murphy deposited trays piled high with divine, fresh-baked bread and shifted to pouring voluminous quantities of white wine, a local one brought aboard with Hastings.

'By all which is holy, this is a mighty fine dish!' exclaimed Pat, chewing with determination on a thumb-sized piece of gristle but not caring to extract it with risk of the least embarrassment to himself or Hastings. Swallowing hard, he dunked a large slice of bread, the largest he could seize from the tray, into the blessed liquid. 'I have always sworn by a fish for the most tasty of all ingredients for a stew... and plainly an octopus will serve very well.'

'The octopus is no fish,' Simon spoke up for the first time, 'It is a cephalopod.'

'That was my very same thought,' declared Pat, staring at his friend with a careful eye, *'though I did not care to elaborate.'*

'It is related to the squid and the cuttlefish, a branch of the molluscs,' declared Simon with all the authority of the naturalist that he was, ignoring Pat's hint entirely.

'Well, I never ate one in Connemara, the plenty that there was of the cod, the pollack and the salmon,' Pat strived to move on, wondering what the discernible inflection, something of a raw edge, in Simon's voice might signify.

'An excellent white, your Lordship,' came an unexpected and saving contribution from Jason, hitherto mute, the purser delighting in the simple but profound relief of his own rare absence of late from the cockpit.

'Indeed, Mr... *Jason*. A glass with you, sir! It hails from a small village in the hinterland, Girgenti, where people of good sense have resisted the lamentable official policy of rooting up all their vines so as to plant wheat.... Wheat indeed! What Philistines the state oft seems to deliver in its service!' Cautious nods about the table indicated at least a willingness to concur.

'Indeed, sir; and scarcely a one - once they are sitting comfortably within the largesse of His Majesty's purse and their small realm - *scarcely a one* exhibits the least leaning towards the betterment of his fellows,' declared Pat in emphatic voice, but he regretted his words immediately, something of politics about them: *what had he himself come*

182

to, to vouch such an opinion in the cabin, and with a distinguished visitor present of all things?'

'Perhaps we expect too much of them?' Simon interjected in loud voice, to the astonishment of his friends and before Pat might expand significantly or even in the least; for Pat's political opinions, infrequently expressed that they were, oft seemed to exhibit a necessary call for a deeper consideration; at least to Simon they usually did. 'Is it not reasonable to be sceptical of, even to discard, all hopeful expectations of such as panaceas, of ill-conceived, albeit conceivably benevolent, state interventions; for to believe otherwise - *that is to say, without inductive reasoning* - leads to the tyrant, the dictator... and who of sane mind would welcome such polities? Who would - *I put it to you* - vouch for even the least of Bonaparte's endeavours? Note, I do not say his achievements.'

A stunned table paused, unsure of what Simon was about. 'Certainly not,' murmured Hastings eventually, somewhat taken aback himself by Simon's intervention, and possessing not the least sympathy for the Corsican.

Scarcely heeding His Lordship's comment, Simon resumed in full flow, in louder voice, a discernible conviction visible and rising from within, 'Whilst we may commend those of great minds and of an academic persuasion who expound upon their considered philosophies, ones which might conceivably lead to an improved society for all... unfortunately, their writings... *I will mention those of Thomas Paine, for example...* are invariably received by the establishment not as enlightening but as seditious... and their expounding of all such diverging opinions are rebuffed as treasonous... which is greatly offensive to my own conscience and, I regret, much to our enduring and collective loss.'

All present stared at Simon, fascinated; for never before had he spoken with such evident vehemence, for he was a man of a retiring disposition generally and customarily avoided all subjects with the least propensity for friction; furthermore, such political discourse was invariably frowned upon within

183

the cabin. No one could fathom his present passion for the subject in the least, save that perhaps it may have been sparked by his earliest exchange with Pat: *perhaps the octopus had much to answer for?* But more likely, as rational minds came to consider, perhaps it was the respite from his duties and concerns within the cockpit, something of a welcome diversion found, a blessed alternative to the unrelenting pressure upon the conscientious surgeon that he was.

'Dr Ferguson,' Hastings stared pointedly at Simon but not in the least in any hostile fashion, 'Might one extrapolate from your discourse that you favour the Republic over the Monarchy?'

'Sir, do not suppose that I am espousing a political opinion,' Simon moderated his voice, much to the relief of his friends; 'I am an academician, a natural philosopher and a student not only of medicine but of history... and of such perceptive luminaries as have graced our knowledge over many centuries with wisdom; and who are we to despise the genius? Aristotle, *for example*, proposed that the collective decision of the many - *a democracy* - will likely be better, or at least safer, than that of the sagest individual, the most virtuous of men, even though the thinking of the many... *when considered individually...* may be inferior.' The Surprises simply stared in stunned stupefaction as Simon continued, 'I once debated this with a much esteemed and learned colleague, Dr Stephen Maturin. He admitted to me that he held republican sentiments, and he placed great credence upon the veracity of Aristotle's conclusion. Indeed, at the time of the Civil Wars the essentials of such thinking became the basis of beliefs for the Levellers; however, Cromwell... *not, perhaps, a man we might consider to be a moral philosopher...* did not incline to their view and locked up their leaders. I recall that even before then the Knipperdollings - *that is with a K* - held to a similar perspective.'

'The k... knipper... dollings?' gasped a horrified Pat, the subject not in the least to his liking and the debate rapidly sliding away from his grasp and certainly his comfort.

'Sure, it is spelt with a preceding letter K, which might make for an awkward pronunciation to those of an English tongue,' declared Simon with a discernible testiness in his voice, not welcoming his friend's interruption; '*or an Irish one...* were they not aware that it is, in fact, a silent K.'

Pat simply stared, a rising awareness of his friend's distress registering, but he did not reply.

'And I believe that they favoured a man taking more than one wife!' Jason, hitherto largely silent, rose to the occasion in offering his own contribution, for he was plainly enjoying the political drift, the rare moment in the cabin that it was; and he smiled beatifically. Marston frowned, Duncan stifled a guffaw, Pat scowled at everyone, and Hastings stared with something like amazement, wondering why his innocuous conversation had unleashed such strong sentiments within Dr Ferguson.

A silent Marston was much taken aback by Simon's demeanour, most particularly shocked by his testy rebuke to Pat. He concluded within moments that it must be an indication of a release from tension of a man who had been under the most extreme strain for a very long time, the near vehemence of his words perhaps something akin to the bottle discharging a particularly energetic cork.

'Humbug!' blurted out Simon, 'That is mere humbug, Jason.' But before he could say more Duncan choked him off with a fierce stand on his toes under the table.

'My dear Ferguson, you yourself are quite the learned gentleman... and you have the advantage of me,' murmured Hastings, taken aback but speaking in gentle voice and striving to slow the rising tempo, 'I am not familiar with the latter... the Knipperdollings.'

'They promoted their own interpretation of a political agenda, sir,' Simon had taken the hint and spoke in more moderate voice; 'although, ultimately, one of their triumvirate of leaders appointed himself King of Münster and declared it to be New Jerusalem. Such did not serve them well in the end;

indeed, *their end* - of the three leaders, that is - was exceptionally unpleasant.'

'How so?' An astounded Pat hardly dared ask his learned friend, and he regretted the question as soon as it had slipped his lips.

'They were burned at the stake, their bodies ripped by tongs as they squirmed, their tongues torn out to silence their agonies, and eventually their hearts were pierced with a red-hot knife.'

'My God!' Pat gasped; the discussion was taking the most unpleasant turn he could conceive of, and he wondered: *what on earth was Simon about?*

Simon, ignoring all aghast stares about the table, seized the moment, the silent vacancy, and resumed in emphatic voice, 'In more recent times, and in all good conscience, I believe that the essence of Aristotle's... *enduring...* opinion was the very foundation of the works of the aforementioned Tom Paine.'

Pat directed a particularly severe glare at his friend but still said nothing.

'Did not Benjamin Franklin hear him out... give him credence?' Jason interjected again in light-hearted voice; 'Indeed, did not George Washington actually *act* upon his writings... in the Colonies? It was even - *I heard this on good authority* - mooted in London that he participated in the drafting of the Declaration of Independence in the Americas.'

'Was that not, therefore, seditious... treasonous even, *for all love?*' exclaimed Pat at last and with a discernible hint of outrage. He paused as if to take stock, the trend of conversation not in the least to his liking, but found himself in the moment of his indignation bereft of the least thing to say, to suggest.

'Perhaps it might be judged so... to the illiberal mind,' Simon resumed, 'but to all men of reason, I ask you: is the pursuit of a happiness founded upon universal enfranchisement to be considered absurd... *not to be countenanced?*' Simon directly addressed Pat, 'Did you not

186

yourself venture endorsement just now for his Lordship's advocation of Catholic emancipation? Might that not that be considered in Westminster to be a trifle seditious?'

Pat stared in silence, aghast, as Simon continued, 'Would you consider it sound if the government were to deny even the Pope a vote? That is, were he to be living in Westminster.' Simon spoke with conviction, with still a degree of ardour; and plainly, to the ears of all present, he was stating his case, his previously unspoken beliefs.

'Simon, I beg of you, that is coming it pretty high and it ain't quite civil,' Pat replied with a most indignant glare verging on malignant, and he spoke in an utterly exasperated voice, all customary table etiquette fast fading within a rising anger, 'Gentlemen, I am not in the way to persevere here. I beg to suggest that we have heard enough of... of the Levellers... and the... *the nippers... nipperdolls* and other such wild zealots with fancy notions... no doubt wicked coves, sinners, all of them... damnable enthusiasts even. Let us revert directly to our humble station as honest, God-fearing seafarers... *and soldiers, your honour.*'

'Would you be acquainted with any such enthusiasts... Dr Ferguson?' Hastings interjected, ignoring Pat.

'On the contrary, sir, I assure you that I am not in the least acquainted with any enthusiasts, not a one,' retorted Simon with an audible degree of indignance; but then, perhaps realising that he was being overtaken by his own passions, and mindful of Pat's appeal, he checked himself and relented, adding, 'Save that I will concede that Murphy has quite the fascination for the bottle... and scant concern for his liver.'

'Eh? Murphy?' Pat seized the moment, 'Simon, you are in quite the fervour; but I suggest that we desist, for we have run foul of politics. Plainly, that is now come upon us, and it is become disagreeable; indeed, I am myself become vexed. We have near found in the subject of the... *the Americas, the so-called revolution...* a discord... *our own contumelious brabble!*'

All eyes turned anxiously to Hastings, for His Lordship was famous for his exceptional and sustained military career fighting against that particular rebellion; but the great man, surprisingly, did not react save to offer a smile and a few words in gentle voice, 'I confess that I, myself, have something of an affinity for the bottle... for a good wine, Doctor Ferguson; it is, after all, quite the custom in the Mediterranean, and a man can scarcely be condemned for his adherence to conventions immemorial; would you not agree?'

'Indeed, sir; you have the truth of it, no doubt,' Simon spoke on the mollified side of a neutral tone, recognising Hasting's contribution as an attempt to secure a more amicable accord about the table; and no one else introduced any further challenge to the customary and rekindled protocol which was the absence of politics; and so a general pause for reflection settled about the cabin, Simon's friend's still much taken aback by and evaluating his diatribe.

By now the stew had all been consumed, but the wine was much to everyone's taste and still flowed in abundance. The stewards, both of them shocked still, for even Freeman had grasped the essential subject. Such as the prior exchanges had never before been heard by Murphy in the cabin, and so he hovered close by, listening, keen to hear everything and anything; but then Wilkins appeared to ask the steward's service, and they left the cabin. Hastings, reflecting, appeared visibly nonplussed, perhaps re-evaluating the strength of feeling as had been expressed, reflecting on the adverse change in the ambience, the dangers in the perpetuation of what had become a heated debate; and so he discarded his own further interest in all matters political and philosophical. Stirring, he turned to Pat and ventured his own greatly more innocuous enquiry, 'Will you tell me of your intentions, Captain O'Connor?'

'We are most pleased to be homeward bound, sir,' replied Pat with relief, 'once we have effected the most modest of repairs. That is to say, once we have watered and provisioned... of a sufficiency to fetch home without any need to call at the Rock.' Pat did not elaborate on his inclination to avoid further Royal Navy ports, for he was perfectly convinced that Hastings was in the right in his criticism of the inelasticity of the official mind, and he did not care to expose his ship and its recent purpose in the least to further official scrutiny.

'I share your aspirations for reaching home, I do so,' declared Hastings with a sigh; 'I have scarcely seen the old country in a lifetime of public service... and not at all these past thirteen years.' A frown of regret on his face and he continued, 'Seven years fighting the rebellion in the Colonies... eleven years in India... At least Malta can offer an old man a temperate climate... and the most commendable cuisine. Are you still hungry, Captain O'Connor?'

'I am amazing short-set, sir... *amazing*.'

'Very good! I believe you may be *amazing delighted* too with the sterling efforts of my cook... the exemplary talent that he is.'

The cook reappeared that very moment, with Freeman, Murphy and Wilkins, all four men burdened with steaming trays; and Hastings paused his melancholic introspection.

'Bragioli!' announced the cook with evident fanfare.

'I am not familiar with the dish,' declared Pat, looking to his guest.

Hastings brightened, 'It is another of Malta's culinary marvels, to be sure; rolled beef slices - *no mollusc!*' He laughed and the table laughed with him; the mood lightened. 'Stuffed with egg, bacon, bread crumbs, garlic and parsley, and slow cooked in a red wine sauce. Aahhh, here come the potatoes, and I espy carrots... and onions too; my cook has excelled himself.'

As the cook and Wilkins busied themselves with food distribution, Murphy poured a red wine of Malta, all the time staring with desperate anticipation at the divine vista of wonderful food, which certainly surpassed everything that Wilkins had ever cooked. The diners certainly seemed to think so too, for all gorged with serious intent and scant diversion, mere pleasantries and only a few of them offered about the table. 'On my life, this beef certainly eats very well, sir; much the tastier than our customary salt pork!' Pat spoke up as his eyes wandered towards the first of empty plates, Allow me to help you to another portion, your Lordship.' Murphy's instant alarm was visible to a few persons in close inspection as eyes everywhere ranged around the table, a deal of attention paid to the remaining vestiges of the food, a lingering salivation present.

'I am obliged to you, Captain.' Hastings looked all about him as all other persons were pondering whether to cease or to further indulge far beyond all reasonable satiation, for the beef was of such a quality as had not been enjoyed for very many months, if ever. However, the merest instant of hesitation proved fatal, for Murphy whipped the tray of leavings away with scarcely a glance towards a gesture from anyone for more, pronouncing the imminence of a hot pudding, one to be much desired, and the absolute necessity, as he saw things, to leave an essential space for it, albeit his language did not quite observe the customary proprieties to any desirable extent, 'Well, begging your pardon, sorrs, the grand pudding of the world is a'coming... right d'reckly; and best not wait 'til 'tis gone cold.' The beef roll remainders were gone in a flash, to the deep dissatisfaction of several persons further considering their inclinations, which Murphy ignored; and then he was gone, no one protesting the blatant display of greed in the presence of His Lordship, for fear that such might indicate a general lack of manners within the cabin and about the dining table.

Eventually, the pudding seemingly delayed but the port wine having been served, Hastings spoke with evident satisfaction as he looked up towards Pat, 'I thank you most sincerely, Captain O'Connor, for your hospitality this day; for it is the rare day when I may make the acquaintance of a fellow Irishman in a senior position such as yourself. Allow me to ask: is there anything, the least thing, that I can do to facilitate your voyage?'

Pat brightened and cast off a little of his inherent caution, 'We are, sir, a trifle short of provisions. Our *personal* stores in particular - *those of mine and my officers* - are exhausted, but we are similarly entirely out of funds. The Admiralty has not paid any of us even a penny piece these six months.' Simon grimaced and nodded in emphatic accord, which did not escape Pat's notice. Thankfully - for such occurred to Pat for the first time - his surgeon was not wearing his greasy old coat, much blood-stained and, to Pat's mind, fit only for the milking goat's bedding.

'Then you will have no concerns for the accursed income tax, Captain?' Hastings smiled but then added hastily, 'I do beg your pardon... a most feeble jest.'

Pat ignored the incongruous joke entirely, 'I regret to say that my own bank has failed, as has that of my surgeon, Dr Ferguson. Neither will my credit here - *which is reduced to the fag end or even beyond* - extend to as much as a loaf of bread. We are entirely broke, sir, *broke*; and I am quite put to the blush to say it. Therefore, I have no means of purchasing provisions for all the men aboard, let alone for my own table.'

'Bah! Banks!' Hastings spoke with vehement disdain. 'Banks! They are the province of the unscrupulous... of scoundrels... indeed, of swindlers!' The table was much taken aback and all hesitated, their attention seized as Hastings continued, 'I had the great misfortune to suffer the attentions and improprieties of such rogues in India; indeed, I did, and to my great cost. Can you conceive of any man of intelligence borrowing at an interest rate of twenty-four percent per annum? *Twenty-four percent!* Can you? It is the action of an imbecile, is it not? But then the borrower in question was reputedly one such.'

Observing both Pat and Simon nodding in the most emphatic accord, Hastings halted, perhaps reflecting; and Pat spoke up, 'I have, myself, had the great misfortune to deal with banks and their officers, much to my regret; in fact, my dear friend here, Ferguson, has also lost all of his money as a consequence of their... seemingly... *ill-conceived* speculations.'

'I endeavoured to protect his interests, I did so...' Hastings resumed, seemingly oblivious to Pat's interjection, '... the Maharajah... and then... and then the charlatans, the promoters of the rank and foetid schemes which they created... those who had perpetrated such great corruption... they endeavoured to conceal that a loan on the books... one recorded in the records... *did not actually exist!*... as was revealed later to the most careful of scrutiny. Indeed, a fraud on the grandest scale had been perpetrated! And Metcalfe discovered it...' Hastings hesitated, noticing the staring faces and the abject fascination of his audience, 'But perhaps I should say no more, gentlemen, save that there lingers a taint about the whole vile scheme... and my own name is not entirely free from it... such that... *such that* I scarcely dare contemplate returning home... to suffer the taunts and opprobrium which will certainly follow from those selfish and vicious gossips who cling to abuse in their efforts to promote their own self-aggrandisement... often when claiming that they are acting in the interests of their fellows by serving on such as committees. You will not be unfamiliar, I'm sure... Captain... with persons of that small-minded ilk, so contemptible in the estimation of every honourable mind.'

'I am not... *not unacquainted* with suchlike, sir,' murmured Pat carefully and with apprehension, the table conversation taking another unexpected and, to his mind, unwelcome turn.

'Did I not bring the clean water of the Yamuna River to filthy and polluted Delhi? Did I not suppress the Red Sea pirates? How is a principled man expected to respond to such nefarious, self-serving malcontents? Tell me, gentlemen; I beg you will.'

Pat stared, open-mouthed, as Murphy and Wilkins returned in that revelatory moment and broke the spell. Lord Hastings sighed deeply and descended from his excited diatribe in a halt borne of frustration as a shocked and spellbound table awaited with the keenest anticipation what more might be revealed.

'Well 'ere be the pudding!' Murphy's gleeful pronouncement in grand style perhaps reflected his own enjoyment of the surplus beef rolls, eaten swiftly in the galley.

'Sir,' Pat, looking for safe waters, spoke in warm voice and with a world of generosity in its inflection, 'I am not entirely unacquainted with the dubious practitioners in banking circles; no, I am not; much to my own loss, I regret to say; but if it be of the slightest interest to you... your Lordship... *the slightest*, it would occasion me the greatest of pleasure was you to accompany me... *my officers and I...* to return home... and to any port of your pleasure; indeed, I am in the way, myself, to return to Ireland on my return... and a call at Dublin is neither here nor there.'

'Captain O'Connor,' Hastings spoke in mild tone, an audible gratitude in his voice, yet tinged with regret, 'I thank you for your kind offer, and nothing at all would please me more than to see fair Dublin once more... *nothing*... but I doubt that, at my age... an old man... *I doubt* that I will ever see Ireland... or England... again in my lifetime. I thank you most sincerely for your kind words... and I beg you will avail yourself of whatever necessities that your ship may require... *on my purse...* before your departure. If you are also in want of new slops to clothe your men, be assured that the Malta storekeeper for the fleet will honour all calls upon my account.'

Murphy halted, unsure of what was happening, for plainly something unusual was. Everyone else at the table stared with undisguised fascination at Lord Hastings, a little unsure, even unbelieving, of what they had just heard from their captain and his visitor, and also its significance; for here before them was one of Britain's most celebrated soldiers, and a self-confessed reluctance to return home was utterly beyond their ken.

'Thank you most kindly, sir,' Pat replied, 'for your most generous gesture; we are, all of us, much obliged to you...

infinitely obliged for your benevolence, and I am sure that the most modest of expenditures for small provisions will suffice to carry us home.'

A glaring silence persisted until Murphy tentatively repeated his announcement, 'Well, sorrs... will 'ee care for a portion... the pudding... while 'tis warm?' A collective sigh, a deflation, was signified; Pat nodded, Murphy served; and eyes and noses seized upon the further delight before them. 'Sweet bread pudding!' announced the cook in triumphant voice, 'Baked with orange and lemon peel, with sultanas and currants and spices!'

The dessert was too enticing to neglect, despite the keen interest in what more Hastings might offer, and all set to with a passion, devouring the succulent sweet with evident pleasure.

'Sir,' Pat broke the contented silence, 'Should your cook ever express a desire for alternative service, I beg you will endeavour to notify me without the least delay!' The laughter from all present, including Hastings, lifted the mood from earlier hesitations.

'When do you look to depart, may I ask?' Hastings spoke with a genuine concern, the pudding all devoured.

Pat sighed, 'I confess that in our present incapacity... *I speak of the barky...* we could scarcely think of even shifting about the harbour if Lord Melville *or even the King himself* ordered such.'

'The significant damages to your vessel did not escape my attention, Captain; and if there is anything I may do to assist, the least thing, please do not hesitate to ask. But now... I much regret... now I must take my leave.'

'You are very good, sir, too kind entirely. I too much regret that the circumstances, such that they are, do not afford me the time to make better our personal acquaintance. Perhaps... on a future occasion... I may look forward to cultivating that with much joy and satisfaction.'

'I will be uncommonly delighted if that proves to be the case,' replied Hastings in a voice which carried a meld of both pleasure and regret, so obvious to the ear of all present.

Pat struggled once more to his feet as Hastings rose to depart, and there was much handshaking all about the table, the tired and war-weary officers of *Surprise* volubly bidding farewell to perhaps the most celebrated visitor ever to the cabin, all of them much taken by his benevolent goodwill. After the cabin had been vacated by all, Pat slumped back into his chair with a bewildering mix of confusion and fatigue filling his mind and body; and he closed his eyes and tried to make sense of what he had witnessed, of what he had heard, that which had shocked him like never before from his close friend, Simon: *politics!*

Friday 12th May 1826   11:00   *Valletta, Malta*

In the mid-morning of the new day, a recuperating Pat sipped coffee with Duncan and Simon, the three companions sitting at the table and enjoying a most welcome sojourn from their duties, relaxing in the simple pleasure of longstanding friendship, few words offered through a quiet hour save for those interruptions which were the occasional reports of progress from the lieutenants, all three of whom were busying themselves with supervision of repairs about the ship and appearing intermittently in the cabin with their reports. Thankfully, to Pat's mind, Simon had descended from his fervour of the prior day and exhibited a little more of his more customary air of amenability.

Pat gazed at Simon for some minutes before he dared venture an enquiry in gentle voice, 'May I ask, old friend, of the... *the foundation* of your - will I say - *exasperations* yesterday, when Lord Hastings attended the cabin?'

'My exasperations?' Simon stirred.

'You spoke with feeling of Aristotle, Tom Paine... of universal emancipation... the kipper codlings... and suchlike,

195

yet you have never before mentioned that such things lie so close to your heart; for it was evident that they do.'

'You are a Member of Parliament, are you not?'

'Sure, but I am scarcely ever there, as you know; and it is an Irish seat, without the least influence.'

'That is my point; there is no influence, not in the least, for the mass of the disenfranchised populace, and any inkling of reform is but swiftly snuffed out, its proponents imprisoned - *or worse.*'

'Of what do you speak?' asked Pat, taken aback.

'The Blanketeers, for one.'

'Eh? The Blanketeers?'

'In the year 'seventeen the textile workers of Manchester marched towards London to protest their dismal lot. They carried no more than a blanket to keep themselves warm; hence, *the Blanketeers.* Yet they were dispersed by the King's Dragoons and their leaders hanged. In the year 'nineteen the Hussars charged a gathering of citizens protesting in St. Peter's Fields, in Manchester, indiscriminately cutting down women and children with a slash of the sabre; eighteen were killed and - so it is said - seven hundred were injured; *seven hundred!*'

'I was unaware,' murmured Pat, shocked; 'Indeed, I recall I was at sea for near all that year, and I never there beheld a newspaper.'

'I remember well the risings in Glasgow in the year 'twenty,' declared Duncan with an inflection of undisguised anger in his voice; 'I was in Greenock, attending the port. The Hussars killed an eight-year old boy and a woman of sixty-five years, and the militia shot dead another nine fellows protesting outside of Greenock prison. Wilson, Hardie and Baird were hanged and beheaded for that protest.'

'But surely such retribution was never in His Majesty's personal purview?' whispered Pat, as uncomfortable as ever he had felt at his table on any occasion before and his anxieties rising.

'You may consider that the King - *I speak of when he was Regent* - benefited by near two millions of pounds a year from the Treasury's benefice - *two millions from the public purse!* Yet a common man can be hanged for taking a rabbit from a warren!' retorted Simon, immediately becoming angrier by the minute. 'Indeed, a child may be hanged for stealing a handkerchief or - if the magistrate were to take pity upon him - transported to Van Diemen's Land, never likely to return. And now the execrable wastrel, George, is King! A more unfeeling, cowardly, selfish and voluptuary dog does not exist!'

'Simon, you must never say such things!' exclaimed Pat with a rising fear for his friend; 'Indeed, were such sentiment to be heard outside of this cabin, why, I venture you might be hanged yourself!'

'Is the right to a vote too much to ask of a civilised society? If it is so then what have we been fighting for, and in a foreign land where the national maxim is *Freedom or Death?*' demanded Simon, taking not the least notice of Pat's concern. 'Was that not the popular call in Paris in the year 'ninety-five, *Liberty or Death?*'

'I recall that was the case in Glasgow,' declared Duncan, '*Liberty or Death*; aye, that was the motto there.'

'What have we come to again in the cabin?' exclaimed a despairing Pat before a huge sigh expressing his reticence; 'You are to consider that were I to hear such tales from the lower deck then I would be obliged to inflict a flogging, perhaps even to hang at least a brace of men from the yardarm; and were I not to do so then Melville, upon hearing of it, would likely hang *me!* Gentlemen, I beg of you, let us hear no more of such talk.'

'The last of the shot holes along the starboard side have been plugged, sir,' announced Codrington with a welcome intervention, stepping in from around the door. His left arm hung limp at his side, which did not escape Pat's attention.

'Thank you, Mr Codrington,' replied Pat, 'Pray tell, how is your wound?'

'The shoulder is sore and stiff, sir; however, it is healing well.' Codrington looked to Simon, 'Thanks be to Dr Ferguson.'

'Yes, thanks be to him,' murmured Pat, glancing at his close friend who sat in silence; 'He has ever been our salvation these three years gone. Indeed, I could scarcely contemplate any future voyage without his presence. Carry on, Mr Codrington, but - *please* - with great care.'

'The three boats promised by Lord Hastings have been brought alongside, sir,' declared Pickering twenty minutes later, venturing a single step into the cabin but halting to lean against the door in obvious discomfort whilst clutching the crudest of walking sticks.

'Thank you, Mr Pickering,' Pat strived to speak in supportive voice; 'Perhaps you should take to your cot? At least for the next few days.'

'Oh no, sir, there is too much to do... a deal of matters to attend.'

'I am in awe of your dedication, Mr Pickering,' declared Pat, 'but this is neither the time nor the place for it; why, it is plain to see that your leg gives you a deal of pain.'

'Not at all, sir... not at all,' Pickering lied, unconvincingly.

'Thomas Pickering, did I not insist upon you keeping your cabin and your cot?' Simon spoke up for the first time and in remonstrative voice.

'I have, sir... until this last hour... when I rose merely to take the air... to... to attend the seat of ease... *the head.*'

Simon sniffed, 'Very well, but you are to return to your cot without the least delay... *else*... else I cannot vouch for the stitches in your leg. You are to consider that were your wound to open then there are no safeguards against the entry of a foul miasma and consequent infection; and I can do little against the gangrene save to contemplate amputation.'

'Oh, there is scarcely the least pain, sir... and not the least blood; in fact, none at all.'

'Mr Pickering, I am afraid that will not do; perhaps my instructions missed the mark? In any event, pray do not - I repeat, *do not* - endeavour to usurp my medical authority in the least aboard this vessel; do you hear me? Your wound is a severe one, and if you care to keep your leg then you will bend to my direction - *without fail or the smallest of deviation.* Am I plain?'

Pickering swallowed and Pat spoke in kindly voice from behind his table, 'Tom, I think you are brought by the lee. Dr Ferguson has made the matter plain. Will you please take to your cot... *directly*? Perhaps we might speak again later, before supper? I will look in on you, if I may.'

'Of course, sir. Thank you.' Pickering nodded his reluctant acceptance and hobbled out through the door, a solicitous Murphy standing ready to catch any stumble.

'How severe is his wound, Simon,' ventured Pat in a low voice.

'Two score of stitches... and a deal of pain is assured for many weeks to come; however, *and thankfully*, the projectile tore through only the flesh of his thigh, tearing the muscle but sparing those precious and fragile joints which are the hip and the knee. He will make a full recovery... no doubt, but perhaps a limp may remain... as well as twelve inches of scar.'

Pat swallowed hard, his sympathy for his lieutenant considerable, his feelings for him reinforced by the throbbing pain he felt in his own leg. 'Thanks be to Saint Patrick,' he murmured to himself.

Scarcely a quarter-hour had passed before the last of his lieutenants presented himself. 'The sailmaker has stitched the rents in the fore course, sir,' proclaimed Mower with visibly affirmative pleasure, from three paces before the table.

'Thank you, Mr Mower. How do you fare?'

'Ship shape and in fine fettle, sir,' Mower swallowed hard as he lied, as was obvious to all; for it could hardly be the case as his arm was strapped to his chest.

'I rejoice to hear it,' remarked Pat, struck dumb and much impressed by the latest of so many demonstrations of personal fortitude in the face of uncomfortable physical adversity amongst his crew.

To all such further reports presented to Pat as the morning developed, he murmured thanks and brief expressions of satisfaction to all bearers; for all of them were plainly anxious to see his own recuperations for themselves; indeed, they were pressed to do so by dozens of the hands; and, ultimately, Pat realised that all such attendances, unceasing and reporting the most minor of matters, reflected the concern and the affection of his crew for him; but he stuck resolutely to his chair and his coffee, calling upon Murphy for periodic replenishment when the pot near emptied, and clinging with a fervour to the preservation of the precious moment of quietude, to the sublime and enduring feeling of blessed relief, to a welcome cessation, however brief it might be, of the racing concerns which had long filled his mind to the exclusion of the least sense of normality. He was deeply grateful that his momentary mental frissons of panic, always concealed from his shipmates, had faded away at last, but a sense of emptiness drifted in and out of his thoughts, ill-defined and so greatly perplexing to him. Eventually, he stirred from his introspection, perhaps becoming aware of his somnolence in the presence of his returned friends, to direct his enquiry, spoken with a deal of reluctance and anxiety, to Simon, 'Will you care to tell of our wounded shipmates? How do they fare?'

'My principal concern is for Hammett, for he exhibits a considerable fever. I had thought his wound was healing well, and there is no evidence of the infernal gangrene... but I am much affrighted that there is... *is something amiss* which is beyond my ken. Kitto, too, exhibits something of a delirium.'

'I see,' murmured Pat, his prior feelings of small contentment sinking rapidly; 'And the others of our people?'

'Marston and Jason attend them... with only the briefest of pause... Freeman too. He is now directing his every waking hour to serve the more recently wounded. I have less fears for near all those men, they are in good heart. However, I must away... I must return to the cockpit to spell either Marston or Jason, for we are... all of us... nigh on asleep on our feet; indeed, I believe I would be so were it not for the invigorative influence of this coffee, most welcome that it is.'

'Will you stay for another cup, old friend? Murphy has gone to the galley for another pot.' Pat looked at his friend's demeanour with a deal of concern, for Simon seemed to be more careworn than ever.

'I should like it of all things, I would so... but no, I will not; however, I thank you for the kind thought.'

'You do not look quite happy... indeed, you look desolated. How are you feeling... yourself... tell?' Pat ventured a final enquiry in tentative voice; for the truth of the matter was revealed in the least scrutiny of his friend: an unshaven Simon looked utterly exhausted, more so than any man that Pat had ever seen, and his inability to help his friend distressed him.

'Tolerably well...' A pause and momentary reflection, 'But I must not be dishonest with you. Actually, disagreeable... damnably snappish... out of kilter; *there, I am being honest*. In all sincerity and with the utmost reluctance, I will admit to a recognisable diminution in my body strength these recent days,' Simon spoke in a low voice, scarcely more than a whisper, '... but the tired part of me is *inside*... beyond all physical refreshment, and to some degree... *to a significant extent*... I feel the growing fatigue of my mental faculties... excessive fatigue, *excessive beyond all measure*. These brutal and bloody experiences have much affected me...' His voice tailed off.

Duncan and Pat held their silence; they sensed that something, some matter of great importance, of deep significance but hitherto unspoken, was about to be revealed.

'The loss of so many of our valued people has much set me back, men who I have most earnestly valued... *I will call them friends... yes, friends;* for no longer will I ever encounter them *on earth*... and now they exist *only within me*... in my recall... in those moments when, in rare quietude, they return...

at least in my thoughts. All of this... all of such... has brought me... *reduced me*... to the verge of despair... So much grief, so many men lost... and so my spirits have truly become as low as ever they might be... and such is... *is extremely disagreeable to me*. Yet in my dreams... *in those dreams of blessed home*... which seems all that is left to me, I cling to the belief that therein I will find that recovery, the blessed restitution of soul... that I crave with a fervour... such that I may deal with all future eventualities...' Simon fell silent at last, plainly much disturbed; and in the shocked hush, he looked to his two friends, their wide-eyed faces aghast.

Pat and Duncan could only stare, could find no words; for here was a Simon that they had never seen; certainly, he had never before been so outspoken on the subject of his personal feelings, and it explained with brutal revelation his acerbic manner of the prior day.

Simon strived to resume with at least some small lift in his voice, 'I will add that without the benevolent attentions of Michael Marston - *he is deserving of the highest meed of praise* - I am minded that I would be... would be...' Simon's thoughts and words tailed off again, and then he stood up; 'But enough of my mind, now... *now*, I must look to my patients.' With that, he departed, his friends held to a stunned silence.

A long and thoughtful few minutes later, Pat, a deep gloom descending upon him after hearing Simon's so shocking statement, turned to his other bosom friend, 'Duncan, what are we coming to in the cabin? Simon has never before come out with all this revolutionary talk - *never!*'

'The man of intelligence, the principled man, must always be concerned for the less fortunate of his fellows; indeed, I dare say that very purpose must be the essential foundation for any man in the medical line, the surgeon most particularly. Will he be looking for an extra guinea or two from the man upon his table during his endeavours?' Duncan sighed, 'No, he will not; for such isnae the thinking of those most admirable of our number, and Simon is surely one such.

These estimable men - *for they are capable of marvels* - are doubtless ever mindful of their wider world... and, I'm sure, its numerous injustices; so much so that I venture that the complete inability to introduce *political* change - *the slightest thing* - must surely be as insurmountable a frustration as it is for the common man, the oppressed, the weaver who has lost his job to the new-fangled loom. Aye, that's as may be, but I must myself also cease this blathering, for I make no claims in the political line. I will be greatly content when I fetch home at last to the Isles... to Harris and my family.'

Pat stared, open-mouthed, but decided to leave all further such debate well alone, 'Will you look to that infernal pile of letters, if you please? I must at the least attend to the one with the Admiralty seal... yes, that one.'

'I am sure that all such missives may safely await another day,' remarked Duncan, for he saw clearly his friend's fatigue; for Pat had not roused himself from a brief nap much more than an hour ago. 'Please dinnae forget that the bandages were removed from your head only yesterday... and I wilnae mention your leg.'

Pat nodded but slit the letter below the seal. The red wax fragments scattered across his table. Extracting the letter, he peered closely as if his eyes were struggling to focus or his mind failing to grasp the written word. A minute of silence, sixty seconds and more of absolute concentration, all passed by without a word until Duncan, staring at Pat's face, blank, mute, incomprehension writ large upon it, spoke up in gentle voice, 'Pat, is there something of particular significance, pray tell?'

'As God's my life,' exclaimed Pat in shocked voice, 'what is this? How am I to believe it? How?'

'Will you care to explain?'

'Melville... the First Lord... you know well the man?'

'Sure, I have made his acquaintance... in London before we embarked upon this damnable venture, but nae since.'

'Allow me to read to you his essential instruction, if you will. We need not concern ourselves with the customary pleasantries... *Dear Captain O'Connor*... he goes on... *it is with grave concern and considerable dismay that His Majesty's Government hears through those customary channels of diplomatic intercourse of the fall of Missolonghi; and, similarly, other regrettable setbacks for Greek military fortunes throughout the Morea and more generally other parts of the Ottoman Greek territories. Most particularly, the Prime Minister laments that such developments might conceivably diminish such disincentives as may still endure to potential Ottoman expansionist ambitions throughout the region and further afield, to the extent of conceivably effecting an increased interest by the Porte in the Ionian possessions of His Majesty.'*

'There cannae be any doubt of that!' remarked Duncan in loud voice; 'And we dinnae need *diplomatic* intercourse to tell us... for every man who has spent a night indulging himself in the several pleasures available within Argostoli town... *intercourse or nae*... will know of the same fears!' Duncan laughed, but not the merest scintilla of a smile crossed Pat's stern face.

'Listen, will you?' The tension in Pat's voice was back without the least doubt, plain to Duncan's ear; and he sensed with a rising dismay a portent of bad news in Pat's tone of voice, a visible exasperation swiftly rising within his friend. He looked hard and saw it in Pat's face, in his eyes, narrowed, a frown plain to see, and in his lips, pursed. Pat resumed in angry voice, 'Melville continues... *In the circumstances prevailing within the eastern Mediterranean, and most particularly in those waters about the many and various Greek islands, the locations of severe and substantial naval encounters...* Encounters indeed!' Pat exclaimed with vehemence.

'Aye, *bloody battles* they were to my mind,' Duncan felt his own heart rate rising, pounding even, and his body temperature soaring too. The sense of anxiety was palpable, exhibited by the patina of sweat that had quickly formed on his brow and all down his back, uncomfortable, unwelcome;

something bad was imminently about to assail his ears and his mind; he sensed it, and he inwardly cursed.

'... His Majesty's Government is minded that the Royal Navy must ensure the presence... of a ship of war... as a visible deterrent to Ottoman interest.'

Duncan groaned, the gist of the Admiralty message was plain, and he liked it not one little bit. Pat continued, 'In the circumstances, the officers and men of His Majesty's Ship SURPRISE, acquainted as they are... and with a considerable familiarity with... the waters in question, will offer the most favourable instrument for the execution of said undertaking...' Pat's anger was visibly rising, his voice too as he concluded his unwelcome recitation, 'Accordingly, you are hereby required and directed to repair to Corfu with the utmost expedition where you will report to the Governor, General Sir Frederick Adam, who will furnish you with such further instructions as may be necessary. It is ordered that HMS SURPRISE will henceforth hoist Royal Navy colours whilst remaining on hand within the eastern Mediterranean... such that the officers of said vessel will hold themselves readily available for such official purposes as shall be so ordered by His Majesty's representatives within the aforesaid Ionian Islands.' Pat lowered the letter to his table top and stared with incredulity writ large at Duncan. 'On my life!' he exclaimed. 'What are we to do?' Anger mixed with despair, all of it loud in his outburst. 'Until now I had scarcely ever thought of the Admiralty as idiots... idiots, Duncan! I suppose that such a damnably stupid notion could only be the product of a politician - yes, a politician! For sure, Melville is no sailor!'

'Aye, and if we turn about for that place... for Greece once again... if we speak the least word of such a damnable notion... to the people...' Duncan exhaled a long sigh but spoke with great anger, '... then - there isnae doubt - there will be ructions; aye, perhaps even a mutiny, one which will make Bligh's look like a tea party!'

'Have a care!' shrieked Pat, much taken aback; 'I do not greatly care to hear that word - mutiny - uttered aboard the barky, nor even whispered.' A protracted silence endured for several minutes, both friends shocked to the core by Melville's order, turning over its implications - all bad and potentially disastrous - within their minds. Eventually Pat spoke, 'It is plain that Melville knows nothing of our recent... encounter - *encounter indeed!* - with the two Turk frigates, nor even does he know that we have departed Cephalonia.'

'Aye, and the barky cannae fight again without she has a deal of repairs... *proper repairs*, not the makeshifts which were all that was possible at Argostoli and Malta... even were the men to be agreeable to doing so... which isnae likely. We cannae do this, old friend, nae.'

Pat sighed, a long, long exhalation, and he spoke in decided voice, 'I do not see the least prospect of a change of mind in London, even were we able to explain our present circumstances and to seek one... *which we are not.* Melville is a man who exudes a sense of purpose, a determination; I doubt he will brook any view contrary to his own. He will insist upon us holding to his order... will not countenance going back on it... nor will he tolerate a refusal... I think we may be assured of that... *I have met the man.*'

A long silence followed, the bleak prospect of a return to Greece, to the bloody war, plainly absorbing the thoughts of both friends to the exclusion of all else. Eventually, Pat spoke again, 'I am minded that there is not a single man aboard the barky who is willing to return to Greece; indeed, there are nigh on three score of men below who are wounded... and so we are perilously short-handed... even were we to be in contemplation of a return. No, that won't do!'

'Aye, I am sure you are in the right of it,' murmured Duncan, his face a grim picture which reflected his deeply troubled mind.

'What to do?' Pat resumed speaking his thoughts aloud, 'I cannot contemplate a return... and I certainly could never countenance anything, the least thing, which might present any prospect of a mutiny.'

'And if you refuse Melville's order? Surely you are not wholly without influence... without respect... in London, being a Member of the House?'

'No, I regret that is not the case... not in the least. There is no standing which attaches to any Irishman, sadly. No, I regret to say that we are all regarded as second-class citizens of the Kingdom, and certainly so at Westminster where the word of an Irishman counts for about as much as a Brummagem brass farthing. And the measure of their respect - *the lack of it, that is* - for any sea captain was demonstrated when they put old Jack Aubrey in the stocks. *That was an outrage!* Do you recall that? I was there and it was quite the scene. At least all present accorded him the respect which he deserved... not a single stone was thrown, *not a one.*' Pat sighed. 'The memory of all the crowd - *seamen all* - cheering Aubrey will live with me for ever.'

A long pause with no reply from Duncan; the dire implications of Melville's order were sinking in. Pat retrieved the much-depleted whisky bottle concealed within his desk from Murphy's predations, and he poured out near all of it into two tumblers. He drank his own down slowly even as Duncan downed his in one. The two men stared at each other with nothing said until Pat uttered what seemed to be the most incongruous of requests, 'Will you pass me that ink bottle?'

'The ink bottle... what? Are you now about writing a reply to His Lordship, for all love?'

'Eh? A reply? No, I never have had a handle on the tactful... or set up for the sweet style of the shyster... such was never my line of country. The ink bottle, if you please!' The unusual vehemence of Pat's reply startled Duncan, and he quickly pushed the ink bottle towards Pat, who was still visibly much incapacitated, the slightest of movements plainly an exertion for him. Duncan stared with blank incomprehension as Pat slowly unscrewed the bottle top; a momentary hesitation followed, scarcely a second, before he poured the whole of the ink bottle contents all over the letter on the table, the dark blue flood swiftly obscuring the written word, obliterating the essential message.

'Damn! Damn Murphy! The careless curmudgeon! The scoundrel son of a Galway beggar!' Pat shouted aloud; 'Look at what he has done now... *the mumping villain*... and before I had the least opportunity to read the letter!' He turned to an astonished, speechless Duncan and spoke in low voice, 'Listen now, we must be out of this place... gone from Malta... before ever we see another Royal Navy vessel or even a packet ship... I do not care to be presented with a duplicate order or hailed by any captain until we are far away from this place... *far, far away*... even the furies of Biscay will be welcome.'

Duncan, still astounded, could find no words as Pat went on, 'I do not care to hear from anyone aboard of more repairs needed before we depart... *the least thing*, from neither officer nor our people. I will not entertain any concern of the carpenter, nor of the bosun... not even the sailmaker; no, we will haul our anchor at... *let me see...* at eight bells of the afternoon watch... whilst we still have plentiful light enough to leave the harbour and the island... and not a single minute longer is to be lost, *not a one!* Is that plain?'

'Plain? Aye, perfectly! But that is scarcely more than four hours away... it is noon already now. There will surely be a deal of confusion... discontent even... and many a question.'

'We will pay that no mind... *none at all!* At eight bells, please to ensure that the men are ready to depart. There will be no waiting if any man be left ashore, and no more of our boats are to leave for the quay, save for one which is to bring back those of our men who are ashore and expected to be returning. We will accept no more deliveries from the town - *nothing, nothing at all, the slightest thing!* We will hoist the Blue Peter immediately and fire the recall signal gun now and at every turn of the glass.'

Duncan nodded, his own thoughts racing; for he was astonished by what he had just witnessed, more so by the tone of desperation in his friend's voice. He hurriedly mopped up the still spreading ink tide with his handkerchief, and he stared at the sodden letter, a pulpy, blue mess and utterly indecipherable; and he rejoiced once more in the remarkable man that his dear friend truly was. 'Will you excuse me?' he asked in a strange meld of shock and awe, 'I will take my leave to organise the barky's departure.'

'Have a care, Duncan; not a word of explanation must reach the ears of any man... else I will be cashiered... hanged even... and that after being flogged around the fleet... *perhaps even shot on my quarterdeck!*' Pat laughed, finding a release from the grip of tension in his swift resolution, not the least delay for a tremulous argument even within his own mind. He found that his laugh had, much to his own surprise, quieted his former dismay and anger. Duncan, who could not dispel his own astonishment, simply smiled and nodded as he rose from his chair.

The unexpected knock on the door wasn't a returning Murphy with the anticipated coffee pot but Simon, and Pat's somewhat recovered heart plummeted in a horrible instant, a rush of hot bile rising from the very pit of his anxious, churning stomach, his heart pounding wildly once more; for Simon's face revealed perfectly his own dismay. His dear friend could find no words as he stumbled across the cabin to the table and slumped into a chair, mute and visibly destroyed. 'What's afoot?' Pat ventured gently.

Several painful seconds passed; 'What are you drinking?' Simon's voice was scarcely discernible through his distress.

'Whisky,' Pat's brief answer was no more than a whisper, for he was deeply shocked to see his friend's demeanour, crushed so. 'There is but a small drop of it left; do you care for it?'

'Pray let me have it.'

Pat and a still present Duncan waited patiently, looking closely to their friend, both men very much feeling that any words from them would be an unwelcome imposition upon a visibly much distressed soul. Pat poured the scant remnant from the whisky bottle; he offered it with a cautious nod of encouragement. Careful scrutiny revealed Simon's cheeks wet with tears.

Simon downed the small tot of whisky in one. His eventual but feeble voice wavered, 'I have lost a deal of men upon my table these three months gone... and every one was so greatly painful a loss... certainly it was. I have become accustomed to the screams of the wounded, even now as they lie in their agonies... incapable - *if they are in cots* - of adjusting to the swinging and general shifting about of the floor... but Marston and I... we had hoped... *we had very much hoped*... that in quitting Missolonghi that would be the last of the deaths...' Simon was reduced to mumbling, in rising difficulty and struggling hard to find his words; he swallowed hard, 'I regret to say... *I very much regret to say*... that... that our much-venerated shipmate... *my patient*... Hammett, wounded at Oxia... is lost to us... *has died*. I could not save him.'

The bad news was not unexpected, Pat being aware of the poor prospects for his veteran shipmate, but the fierce shock of the unwelcome news struck hard, like a physical blow, and he felt all of his composure desert him in an instant; his body strength surged away as if borne upon a wave, broken and swiftly retreating from the shore. He slumped backwards in his chair, his hands falling to his sides; he closed his eyes and, once again, he silently despaired.

Chapter Nine

In the few hours after leaving Valletta's Grand Harbour and notwithstanding her many and varied damages, *Surprise* had made good progress. The initial protest of the sailmaker had been most brusquely overruled, ignored even, for so it seemed to a puzzled crew who were mystified by their unexpected departure, something of a considerable shock and prompting much speculation, most particularly so after the body of their shipmate, Hammett, had been hastily carried ashore and buried with small ceremony at the Msida Bastion Cemetery, expedited by an obliging Governor Hastings. *Surprise* had then swiftly hauled up her anchors and promptly sailed. Despite the mystery of such celerity and the dismaying setback of a funeral with scarcely a shipmate in attendance, save for the pallbearers, the crew had accepted that some good reason must have dictated their leaving of Malta in such rapid haste; indeed, the exceptional nature of the brief burial ceremony proclaimed such, shouted it loud. And so, in some small confusion, the crew had reconciled themselves to necessities and applied themselves with enthusiasm to their tasks of ship-handling; and the mood aboard, despite the painful loss of Hammett, old tarpaulin that he was, was maintained as one of subdued rejoicing; for every man believed that it could only be the benevolent intention of their revered captain to bring them home as soon as could possibly be which had prompted a resumption without the necessary repairs, all of which were very visible and some of great consternation to the bosun, the carpenter and more so the sailmaker. Yet even now, and despite the good cheer of being homeward bound, all three of those non-commissioned officers could not constrain their most audible expressions of concern for the state of their ship, most particularly her hull and her canvas, as they busied about the decks, foraging for the least scrap of materials with which to make good; at least, to make good with what vestiges might be applied to plainly serious defects; and so their happiness was constrained, moderated, and they pressed the lieutenants for an explanation for the greatly premature leaving of Malta, as they considered it to be, at every opportunity.

However, no clarification was ever forthcoming, for the officers too were in the dark, no reason ever offered from the cabin and none requested; for, in the customary formality of the Royal Navy, such enquiries were not appropriate, were not likely to be well received; and so the battered frigate sailed on, away from Malta, further away from Greece, from Turk warships; and every precious mile, in the thinking of the men, was one more valuable mile less in the long voyage home. Concerns for the many and varied leaks, the pumps constantly attended, and for the tears which threatened in every gust to shred the sails from top to bottom, were all put out of mind by the men of the crew; for they were sure that the barky would endure; they knew that the barky had endured much worse. It was the common sentiment, and that was enough; it sufficed for weary men with tired minds and bodies; they had made sail once more, they were homeward bound; and that essential thought was a marvel, one which surpassed any and all concerns.

Pat, still struggling with painful difficulty with his leg wound, had occupied a chair on his quarterdeck in all the hours since leaving Malta, taking his scant meals and coffee *in situ* as he studied everything all about him, the least thing, including all physical minutiae and the greater movements of the heavens in the form of clouds driven by the welcome return of the *Levanter*, a quite moderate strength one in which he rejoiced; for such placed no great strain on his canvas yet propelled the barky at near eight knots; a most estimable velocity to his way of thinking. He stared with regularity through his glass in every direction, silently praying not to see anything, the least thing, save for the expected Pantelleria on the bow; but that was not now, could not be; for he knew that the island could not possibly appear before the dawn of the morrow.

At a discrete distance about him his officers had gathered in the diminishing light, the sun seemingly hovering on the horizon on the larboard bow. Keenly, they still waited in anticipation of some eventual revelation which would explain the hasty departure; but, as the hours had passed by, they had reluctantly concluded that none such would be forthcoming, at least not in the immediate future; and so they contented themselves within the general ambience on deck, which was a relaxing one; a tranquillity had been found in the approaching dusk light, a cordiality in conversation observed, even between officers and crew; and that sufficed, was all that was required; for that is where three years of strife had brought them to, lowering expectations and reducing them at times to mere spectators, as if swept along like mere flotsam on their world's fast flowing tide which was time. However, they were no longer in prospect of fighting, and the weather, good or bad, was of little concern; certainly nothing could disturb the moment, the quietude, and within that sense of small comfort they silently rejoiced.

It was not, however, an ambience which prevailed below deck, for the surgeons remained on edge, enervated despite a profound weariness; in the cockpit the mood was as desperate as ever. Amidst the wounded, the trio of Simon, Marston and Jason endeavoured to ameliorate the pain of the casualties, at least as far as such was possible with what little they possessed in medicines. The laudanum stocks were much called upon, the supply of bandages also heavily taxed; and the unfortunates, near sixty men, were spreading a considerable way aft, out of the tiny space which was the cockpit and along the mess deck, accommodated in makeshift cots such that they could not fail to make their uncomfortable presence felt by the rest of the crew at mess times and when striving for sleep amidst a sustained backcloth of groans of pain. The spartan meals of salt pork and ship's biscuit which was all that remained for the crew were serenaded by the moans of greatly discomfited men; however, for the fit, for their more fortunate shipmates, that was no matter; indeed, near every wounded man was visited by his tiemate or members of his mess, and many of their off-duty hours were spent sitting on the deck planks attending with words of comfort, a mug of grog and an illicit whet of stolen rum. For all of these small consolations for their charges the surgeons themselves were grateful, and they responded with words of encouragement to the nurses, to be reiterated to the wounded; and the consequences were welcome to all; for, as time passed, the great anxieties subsided, slowly but surely; and the surgeons came to the view that, if only the discomfit could be endured until gaining Falmouth, not another man would be lost to them; but they could not be certain, and so the worry continued, their anxiety persisted. The hours slowly passed by in the relatively unventilated fug which was the air below deck; tensions eased, and men became acclimatised to their lot, the more fortunate more than reconciled to their heartfelt duty of care for their wounded shipmates in the meld of comradeship which was the very essence of the lower deck. A stability of sorts had been found, a straw of relief had been grasped, and for that every man aboard, officers and men, found themselves exceedingly grateful.

Near the taffrail, Pat watched in silence from the comfort of his chair as the sun blinked out its farewell. Ten more minutes slipped by in peaceful reflection in the weak light of the gloaming, Pat struggling with reflections on the events of the day, the shock of Melville's letter, his own protest with the ink flow, the dismaying death of Hammett - so acutely distressing to Simon - and the hasty flight from Malta. *What was his life coming to?* His mind wandered without reaching any conclusion. Ultimately, the final, fading residue of the sun itself on the western horizon all gone, he took small refuge in the familiarity of his ship; he looked forward from his chair, his eyes ranging over a reassuring full press of the sails, the pale expanse of the canvas plain to see in the soft dusk light, and he reckoned the barky must be making at least seven knots, perhaps eight; and that was a comfort, for Gibraltar would be reached in three days and perhaps even Falmouth within two weeks. *Falmouth!* It was surely a home of sorts, certainly so for almost all of his crew, who were Falmouth men save for a small retinue of Irishmen, a few Scots and even one Welshman; those were the few exceptions to the Cornishmen; and then he remembered Sampays, the bosun, who was a Portuguese, and Freeman, an African of unknown origin. *Such an amalgam*, he considered, *and all were volunteers, not a pressed man aboard. The press; it had long been gone*; and so his thoughts meandered in his welcome solitude.

An absence of cloud enabled the soft light of the moon, approaching its first quarter, to cast the weakest of illumination all over the ship, augmenting the last few minutes of fading twilight, and the quietude was broken only by the gentle wash alongside the hull and the persistent creak of the rigging; all of which brought a most muted ambience to everyone present on the quarterdeck, all proprieties and formality about who could legitimately attend the hallowed space entirely cast aside in a cherished sense of companionship; even, it might be said, given the extent of mutual support between every man aboard, of something near family. A low conversation endured in the background, Pat only half hearing but not listening to the exchanges between his helmsmen and the master, another four men of the crew as well as all his officers in attendance. In that so very pacific moment as Pat's thoughts rambled, Marston stepped up from the companionway and approached his chair, where he stood in diplomatic silence, awaiting words from his captain.

Pat nodded and managed a weak smile, for he could not comfortably rise, but he extended his hand in welcome. 'Good evening, Mr Marston; I hope I see you well.'

'You do, sir; a trifle tired... that is all; but who would not be so after our recent tribulations?'

'Yes, you are in the right of things there, most certainly. May I say that it is a great pleasure to see you on deck. Indeed, I cannot recall the last occasion. Perhaps it was our

famous musical sojourn? What a grand pleasure that was, eh?'
A pause, a frown flickered across Pat's face and he added, 'I
am in hope that your presence does not portend further bad
news? For my own fortitude has been sorely tried these recent
weeks.'

'Not in the least, sir; I am pleased to report that the
wounded are washed and fresh-bandaged, and they are as
comfortable as can be. Dr Ferguson is minded that - with
God's good grace - we will lose no more men.'

'That is a considerable relief, it is so.'

'But I must confess, sir, that I do myself hold to
reservations in the case of Kitto. He is increasingly frail.'

'I am uncommonly sorry to hear that; I have a particular
regard for that man, I do.' A thoughtful minute of silence and
Pat spoke again, 'May I offer you a whet? It is something of a
consolation in these troubled times. There is yet the final
bottle of my whisky hidden in the cabin, if Murphy ain't yet
found it.'

'Thank you, sir, but I respectfully decline. You may recall
that I abstain from all strong liquor.'

'Of course, please excuse me; that is a virtue afforded to
so few of us in these difficult times, but - *if my memory serves
me* - the great man himself - *Nelson* - was quite abstemious.'

'Most admirable,' ventured Marston absently; 'How are
you faring - *yourself* - may I ask?'

'Allow me to say that I am mightily relieved that we find
ourselves at last in the *western* Mediterranean. For myself, I
have no concerns; doubtless this damnable - *excuse me* - *this
wounded* leg will be much healed before we fetch home to
Falmouth. If it is in the least degree feasible and if it pleases
you, perhaps you, with Dr Ferguson and Mr Jason too, might
favour me with your company in the cabin for a glass of wine?
Perhaps too a bite of supper? There is a prodigious grand
stock of salted fish in the hold since we tied up in Malta... it is
a cousin of the herring and a considerable delicacy in those
parts; and, as has ever been known to be the case, the herring
is good for the strength, at least of the body. I collect that

Wilkins has promised a sweet, rich figgy-dowdy for pudding... with proper ripe figs... and a grand plum sauce. Will that answer?'

'I rather think it will, sir, and I will be delighted to join you; thank you. I will relay your invitation to my colleagues. There is at last a... a modicum of... *of less acute concern...* below... in these recent hours... and a cordial sojourn for an hour or so will be greatly beneficial for the humours.'

'I am much gratified to hear it, I am... very much so. Do you care to pass a little while, *some few minutes*, with me before I quit the deck, here in the air, *in the fresh air...* the relief that it must be after the long ordeal below... no doubt? We will enjoy these precious final moments of the darkling, as beautiful an evening as ever I saw in dear Connemara... and... and I hope it will restore our... *our vexation of spirit...* will answer the case.'

'Most kind, sir; a most estimable notion.'

The tranquil minutes passed by in a silence born of personal introspection by both men as the twilight faded away completely, leaving the deck bathed by the weak glow of moonlight. In the background nothing disturbed the peaceful tranquillity, near silence, broken only by the gentle wash of the wake and the muted sounds of the sails and rigging. Hardly a word was spoken on the quarterdeck save for brief utterings between the master and the helmsmen, until Dalby rang out what seemed a clamorous eight bells at the end of the watch. Seemingly it served as a prompt of sorts, for Pat spoke his own musings aloud, quietly and in little more than a whisper, but to no one in particular; for so it seemed to the careful listeners closely attending all about him including Marston, the helmsmen and the master, 'I have fought... in many hard fights, but that last one was... was the bloodiest of them all. Would that it had not been necessary.'

Neither Michael Marston nor anyone else present about the wheel could find the least thing to say; their captain's privacy was to be respected, and for several men the most unpleasant comparisons came to mind, most particularly those earlier, bloody battles fought to defend Samos island; for all recollection of such would never be expunged, as all men who had fought there had long ago realised; but that particular event was most certainly not a subject that anyone wished in the least to ever mention again, and so they turned their faces away and kept their silence.

Thursday 18th May 1826   15:00   Cadiz on the beam

The sun was bright and still high in the sky as the backcloth to a steady day of progress, Gibraltar left far astern without the barky pausing even to water. All haste for Falmouth was the common thought aboard, and such water and provisions that *Surprise* still possessed, although running low, would suffice, or perhaps almost so; but not a man cared to delay the barky on her homeward voyage by even a minute. Home, blessed home was getting nearer as every hour passed by, and no diversions could be countenanced in the least; the precious thought had quite gripped everyone.

Pat sat in his chair upon the quarterdeck, revelling in the cheerful mood of his shipmates, enjoying the warmth of the afternoon, the enduring strength of the wind, and the placidity of the sea generally. He was talking with Duncan and Simon. 'I dare say we will fetch home within a week,' he ventured with a small smile.

'Aye, and for that we will ever be thankful,' declared Macleod emphatically; 'Aye, more so than ever before.'

'How are our people... below, Simon?' ventured Pat cautiously; for, in truth, he did not care to hear the least thing which might blemish his own rare feeling of contentment.

'All are as well as might be expected, and the prospect of reaching home is more efficacious for their well-being than any remedy that I possess... but I regret to say that I hold but dwindling hope for Kitto; Marston attends him constantly.'

'I beg leave to speak with Marston,' declared Duncan, 'and with Kitto too; I would see how he is coming along.' Kitto was a *Surprise* veteran, a *Tenedos* one before that, and a much-respected larbowlin and gun captain of the *Tempest* gun crew.

'Coming along is scarcely appropriate to the case... *sadly,*' Simon spoke in dejected voice. 'I regret to say that Kitto is no longer entirely in his intellects.'

'I was not aware,' murmured Duncan.

'We fear for him,' whispered Simon quietly and with reluctance. 'He is the bravest man I can recall in my care, for his injury, so severe, must inflict the greatest of pain and, no doubt, the utmost mental confusion.'

'It will be the world's pity if we lose *him*... I have served with that man for more than ten years...' Duncan spoke in a voice of the utmost despond, 'Aye... and what a flat I would consider myself to be were I not to speak with him... in his hour of great distress.'

'Very well,' replied Simon cautiously, 'but a very few minutes must serve; *and please,* have a care; do not presume upon his strength.'

Macleod nodded, departed the quarterdeck and descended to the sickbay. Head down, he crouched low and nodded to Marston who responded with a brief nod of his own. An anxious Macleod turned his gaze immediately towards Kitto, and he knelt down upon the deck at the side of Kitto's low cot. The gunner was unmoving, his breathing faint; it was plain to see that he was weak and perhaps only scarcely conscious. His sallow, shrunken face, his cheeks hollowed, exhibited the most disconcerting prognosis. He could not move his head, which was heavily bandaged and which covered his right ear where it was much bloodstained, but his eyes flickered as he seemed to recognise Macleod, and then he blinked rapidly, several times, the faintest of whispers, inaudible, escaping his blue, puckered lips.

'I regret he is... this past hour... unable to converse,' murmured Marston, crouching alongside Duncan. The chaplain gently took Kitto's hand.

'Is there... is there the least hope?' ventured Duncan in a halting whisper.

'I regret that I am not sufficiently proficient to know. Dr Ferguson is... *is not* in hope of a recovery... but... but this morning he remarked to me... *and I believe he endeavoured to succour my own spirits*... that after Trafalgar one poor soul, *believed dead*, aboard *Swiftsure*... a mortal wound to his head...' Marston whispered very quietly in Macleod's ear, '...he was about to be consigned to the deep... when he was heard to breathe once more...' Duncan gasped as Marston continued, 'He was carried back to the cockpit and, later, after a week in hospital... that ball which had entered his temple... came out through his mouth.'

'Dear God Almighty!' exclaimed Duncan, quickly adding, 'I do beg your pardon.'

'Dr Ferguson has considered the possibilities for trepanation,' Marston resumed, 'but is minded that it will be too invasive and will not answer; a greater pain would surely be inflicted and to no end; and so we are keeping him as comfortable as can be with a plentiful dose of laudanum.'

Macleod took Kitto's immobile hand, relinquished by Marston; it was cold, but he squeezed it gently and spoke in quiet voice, 'Jonathan Kitto, 'tis Duncan Macleod here before you. Hold fast... stay with us... I beg you will... for your friends are here with you.' Kitto's eyes blinked several times, the merest trembling movement of his lips just discernible. Duncan continued, 'We are all here... all about you... every man of the barky stands with you... at your side.' Kitto blinked twice more and then his eyes closed.

'We must leave him be... to rest,' declared Marston; 'I will attend him... I will pray for him... until...'

Macleod nodded but remained on his knees alongside the cot as Marston rose; and as he looked to his veteran shipmate, and much to his own great surprise, he himself began to pray, silently; until within a very few minutes he was entirely gripped by the severest feelings of dismay, by a confusion of anger and guilt, for which he could not account, when he switched to silently cursing himself with a passion as the increasing rivulets of salt tears became a steady flow down his cheeks.

Several more minutes slipped by until Marston knelt down once more beside Macleod. He put his arm over his shoulder but said nothing until Duncan, with a painful infinity of regret, slowly rose to his feet, Marston rising with him, kindly words offered in a whisper, 'Here; if it pleases you, take my handkerchief; I beg you will.'

'Thank you; I find I am... am...'

'As are we all... much set back,' murmured Marston, holding firm to Duncan's shoulder; 'Hold fast, Mr Macleod, for Our Lord is surely with us in our difficulties.'

'Thank you again, Mr Marston... *Father*...' whispered Duncan; 'I will away... to the deck; Captain O'Connor awaits me. I will be obliged if you would inform me of... of Kitto... of any... any changes.'

'Of course, you may rest assured of that.'

In stumbling gait, an anguished and overwhelmed Duncan left the cockpit and haltingly climbed the steps to the gun deck. Avoiding all curious glances from the men present nearby lest they observe that distress which he could not shake off, he stepped up to gain the foc'sle and, seeking privacy, he crossed to the foremast, against which he gratefully leaned back in his torment to absently stare aft in the darkness, seeing nothing distinct save for a general awareness of the sails above, a little of light cast by the near full moon. The constant and gentle salt breeze on his face was subliminally welcome and so greatly in contrast to the vile stench of the cockpit, the smell of which seemed to linger about him, at least within his mind. He stood there for some time, his brain seemingly slowed and refusing to think clearly, an unwelcome mental fog clouding all his attempts at constructive thought until, time slipping slowly by in his immobility, the sound of the wash breaking at the bow and surging alongside the hull dimly registered with him, and he embraced it as the small and gentle reminder of normality that it was, until gradually a calm returned to settle upon him, a recovery of sorts, and his disquietude diminished, for which he felt, more than ever before, profoundly grateful.

Monday 22nd May 1826   14:00   Lisbon on the beam

'How is Kitto?' a deeply worried Pat could manage only a whisper as he nodded towards the man on Marston's table, the new bandage about his head already showing signs of blood.

'I regret to say that I am now very much in fear for his life, sir,' Marston struggled with his words; 'Dr Ferguson and I... we... we have determined that a small splinter, perhaps only a fragment of one... or even a spent musket ball... the object pierced his ear and is lodged within the skull. He bleeds... but not greatly. I am sorry to say that neither I nor Ferguson are competent to treat his injury; hence, we are both much affrighted that it is only a matter of time... *a very little of time*... before... before he crosses life's final great river... to... to shelter under the shade of the trees with Our Lord in Heaven.'

'We will lose him today?' gasped Pat, shocked.

'He lingers still and we endeavour to comfort him as best we can... but we will persevere... *until the end*, and I will pray for him.'

'As will I, *Father Michael... as will I*,' Pat struggled hard to find his words, uttered eventually in a whisper which was scarcely louder than silence, 'May Saint Patrick, Mary and all the Saints preserve his precious soul.' He turned away from the scene before his rising distress could become evident, for he could find nothing more to say; and without wishing to appear in haste he left the cockpit without further ado. His earlier small pleasure in his day was gone, swept away entirely in a breaking wave of anguish.

Tuesday 23rd May 1826 05:00 off the coast of north Portugal

Approaching the helm as the true dawn light appeared, a weak, low sun offering itself as little more than a watery haze through the low-hanging cloud strata, Pat yawned wide and sighed as he strived for further wakefulness. A night of little sleep had been his experience, mere brief catnaps of rest gained despite the soporific effect of plentiful brandy consumed with Simon and Duncan in the cabin after supper. All hopes and expectations of a respite from enduring anxieties in the bleak hours of darkness had been cruelly broken by the discomfort of unwanted dreams, nightmares even.

He cast his mind back to the final hour of the prior late evening, when a final bottle of brandy offered by Murphy from his own supply - *as he saw things* - had been consumed in a last ditch but futile effort to console Simon, who had sunk into an absolute despair consequent to the death of Kitto during the late afternoon. Unfortunately, the brandy failed; it had achieved nothing at all for mutual aspirations of gaining small relief from huge dismay; and so it had been long past midnight before Duncan and Simon had finally left the cabin. Murphy, in rising dismay himself, had fretted all about them for the whole of the time, all three friends ultimately becoming subsumed within a deep despond, even a distress, all attempts at mutual consolation having foundered on the sharp rocks of angst and despair.

Looking up from personal reflection and casting his gaze all about him, Pat endeavoured to greet an approaching Marston with welcoming words, the chaplain's demeanour a visibly unhappy one, 'Mr Marston - *Michael* - I am much pleased to see you this morning.' His voice dropped, 'I beg you will allow me to say how very much I am dismayed by the loss of Kitto, which I am sure... *have not the least doubt*... was *inevitable*... his wound being so... so greatly severe, and despite your best endeavours.'

'Thank you, sir. Dr Ferguson and I were much set back.'

'I am sure of it,' murmured Pat, a brief recollection of the prior afternoon flashing through his mind. 'How are you this morning? How are you faring... Kitto's funeral before us?'

'I will remain mindful of Psalm thirty-four, sir: *The Lord is near to the broken-hearted and saves the crushed in spirit.* I fear that we are all a trifle crushed in spirit.'

'Indeed, we all are,' declared Pat with audible angst, 'Yes, to tell you the truth, I am... *I am*... and it is a tragedy that it should be so on a voyage where our intentions were only to deliver food to aid the starving in that damnable - *excuse me* - that *ill-ventured* place... and such... such materiel as might comfort those poor souls in their struggle.'

'It was surely the most benevolent of intentions.'

'Yes, it was a mission of mercy... and we had hopes that it might offer something of a lifeline... even a brief one... that it would make a difference... at least offer a little *hope... that precious standby.*'

'I am sure that it did, sir... at least in that brief moment.'

'But now... *now*... it is we who are reduced to a want of comfort as we mourn the loss of yet another of our shipmates, Kitto.'

'I beg you will allow me to reiterate the words of Matthew, sir, for they may be a comfort: *Blessed are they that mourn: for they shall be comforted.*' Pat looking discernibly unimpressed by Matthew, Marston resumed, 'And so shall we be comforted by our faith in God, sir, as we... as we *hold together* and mourn Jonathan Kitto.'

'Michael, are you prepared?' asked Pat striving hard to avoid allowing even a hint of his own despair to enter his voice.

'I am, sir, but I beg you will allow me to accord our respects to our former friend and valued shipmate *with a proper service*... with customary and *appropriate* words... before we bury him this morning?' Marston's particular unhappiness was revealed without the least of further pleasantries. 'Dr Ferguson and I are minded that only in so doing might we bring to an end the acute focus of all thinking aboard on these... these distressing losses of... of...' Marston, customarily a man of infinite resilience in the worst of circumstances, could say no more, and his face betrayed a deep dismay, a profound sadness.

'Of course; a shipboard funeral, when all exigencies do not preclude such... that is to say, when the occasion can be managed... is the immemorial custom of our service.' Pat seized both the chaplain's clasped hands within his own grasp and spoke softly, finding something, some small residue of a deep and personal reserve, one most rarely called upon, from which to draw with his fulsome reply, 'Michael, *dear friend*, I am most mindful... in this hour of *our* sorrow... of your own most valuable and enduring support for all of us aboard this vessel, I am so; and I include myself as a grateful beneficiary, I do. Indeed, I recall very well your words to me when I was so greatly affrighted that Simon was lost to us... It was two years ago *or more*, but in fact... *in fact*, I will never forget *your words*... for in that particular moment they answered amazingly: *hold fast... hold fast to hope... to hope! For such can never be lost whilst we keep our faith in the Lord.*'

'Thank you, sir; I will endeavour to keep that precious maxim in mind myself as... as we... as we hold to our uncomfortable duty this day and its... *its necessities.*'

'It it pleases you, may I venture the smallest of suggestions?'

'Of course, sir.'

'Your service... it is not my intention that we will read the Articles.... for I am minded that we will... all of us... we will be in - *will I say* - a deal of despond, and I hope you will not consider this in the least impertinent... perhaps you might care to consider omitting anything of a... *a penitential nature?*'

'That is perfectly appropriate, sir. I am, myself, already aware of a considerable disconsolation amongst our people; Kitto was a much-valued shipmate.'

'Thank you, Michael.' declared Pat before turning towards the helm, 'Mr Codrington, please be so good as to speak with Mr Tizard to prepare our shipmate for burial.'

'Aye aye, sir.'

'We will call the hands to divisions at seven bells for Mr Marston's - *Father Michael's* - service,' declared Pat.

'Very well, sir;' Codrington acknowledged with a salute and hastened away to the companionway steps.

Murphy appeared and hastened to Pat's side, ever solicitous of his captain's needs, 'Well, sorr... the stirabout and coffee be ready; your first breakfast be awaiting your honour's presence... in the cabin.'

'Five minutes, Murphy, and I will be there... *my best thanks*. Will you look to Dr Ferguson to see if he would care to join me in the cabin? Compliments, of course. Is there enough of the porridge?'

'Well, there be a right plenty of it, sorr. I will ask Dr Ferguson d'reckly.' Murphy hesitated only briefly before adding, 'Sorr, begging your pardon... will 'ee remember to shave... afore the service? The master has called *clean to muster* at seven bells.'

Pat rubbed his hand over his chin; the prickly stubble had progressed to its softer length; Murphy was in the right of things, as usual. 'Of course,' and he nodded, a sinking feeling of resignation coming upon him, a melancholia rising as his thoughts drifted to Kitto's imminent funeral.

Five minutes passed and the swiftest of shaves accomplished, Pat emerged from his quarter-gallery clean-shaven to sit at his table, waiting for his friend and contemplating with disfavour his cooling porridge. In truth he could scarcely contemplate eating a thing, for his stomach was all awhirl, much discomfited with those same anxieties which had long flooded his thoughts since his awakening and which had seemingly migrated south. He mused in silence on his discomfort: *could such... such intimations actually migrate from the mental to the physical?* Nonplussed, he resolved to ask Simon at some future date. And so he contented himself solely with the coffee, which he fortified with a generous measure of whisky from the small bottle which he had, miraculously, long preserved from Murphy's predations whilst secreted within his map chest.

In that moment his closest friend in all the world entered after the briefest of knocks on the door. Murphy was close on his heels. 'Pat, I am come to take breakfast with you, if it pleases you.'

'Of course; sit down, old Simon, please. Here, allow me to help you to a bowl of this splendid porridge before it goes cold. Murphy will pour you some coffee.' A keenly attendant Murphy poured, when Pat nodded discretely to him and waved his head in a signal to leave the cabin. Alone with Simon, Pat waited for a minute whilst his friend began eating until he could contain himself no longer, 'Will I tell you that I am mightily relieved that we will fetch home in but a very few more days... and although Falmouth town ain't exactly home... for you and me... it is for near all of our shipmates, and that is a very good thing... given the... the setbacks... the deaths... of so many of our people. I confess I am mortally set back myself... I am so. I scarcely dare consider boarding my cutter... and stepping on to the quay... so many widows to tell... to speak with... so much grief as there will surely be. Yet, even so, I cannot bring myself to speak with Marston... in his... *his capacity*; that is to say, *as a minister*... about that... *my* feeling of... of foreboding... about that necessary event. Indeed, I am quite in dread of it. I dare say it is surely the spoon with which I must yet sup a deal of sorrow.'

'I had supposed for some time that such was so... *was the case*,' replied Simon, pausing with his own spoon and taking a generous gulp of the welcome coffee. 'I have never given strict credence to the Church and its teachings, brother, as you know; yet I am come to the view that there is certainly something... the definition of which I have never managed to attain... something, *some foundation* to the... the pious strictures which is... still indefinably... of great value... is significant, and that is plain to the meanest intelligence. Marston has surely grasped that... and he is ever a confidant of the utmost value. You cannot refute that in the least. I urge you to open your own thoughts to him, to engage with him...

and without the least reserve... on any matter of which you have the least doubt. *Of course, I do not speak of navigation.*'

'Well perhaps there is something in what you say, though I am much affrighted that I might be reduced to weeping - *yes, weeping* - in his presence; that is the measure of what I find I am come to.'

Simon stared for a minute with nothing said; it was plain that Pat was disconsolate. 'Will I tell you something now, my dear?' Pat, silent and thoughtful, nodded, and Simon resumed, 'In Missolonghi... in the final few days of the siege, Marston and I... we were in Lord Byron's house; you will remember that it was our makeshift hospital. *I am sure* I had reached my personal nadir in spirits... as, I believe, had Marston... and... ultimately... we were brought to our knees on the floor... *to our knees, Pat*... in despair *together*... amidst the detritus of our surgical endeavours... all about us the soaked bandages, the bloody bucket... severed flesh... limbs even... for we had been operating for interminable hours... and always with the utmost haste, so many wounded pressed upon us... and we prayed. That is to say, *I prayed*. I could not... in that bleak moment... countenance continuing in my task, in my duty and obligation... as a surgeon. I was quite... quite... *finished*. I prayed, Pat, I did, and... *and it was a comfort.*' Simon set down his spoon, sat back and sighed deeply.

Pat could find nothing with which to reply, for he was mortified; he knew from long experience that Simon's accord with religious matters, both words and ritual, was little more than a wish to observe the proprieties in a world where faith was usually perceived as more important than material possessions; not that his shipboard fellows ever possessed even the smallest token of wealth, for a paucity of such was invariably the case; albeit all of them aspired to gain something, some degree of financial improvement, from their endeavours; and the talk of taking a great prize, one with bountiful treasure to be apportioned amongst the crew, often recurred on the mess deck; but then Pat recalled that it had been a very long time since he had heard any mention of such a popular dream.

Murphy, listening attentively from the door, was similarly set back, for Simon was the surety, the anchor, the comfort to all of the crew, all of them holding firm to the resolute conviction that - were they to be wounded - Simon would assuredly take care of them. It was therefore substantially discomfiting to him to think, even for a moment, that their safeguard might be, himself, in the least difficulty. His mind flailed in a furious flurry of anxious thought: *what could he, Murphy, do?*

No words were ever found, neither by Murphy nor Pat, for in that moment Lieutenant Codrington knocked on the door and entered upon Pat's shout, 'My best compliments and duty, sir. Mr Marston stands ready on the deck to receive you... that is to say, the church pennant is flying.'

'Very good. My compliments to him and I will be there in but a very few minutes,' replied Pat, a long sigh following. 'Simon, will we go out now?'

A loud cough from the door prompted Pat and Simon to stare at Murphy, who was standing there with Pat's full-dress uniform draped over his arm.

'Of course,' mumbled Pat; 'How could I be so forgetful? I do beg your pardon; you have my best thanks, Murphy. Simon, would you care to attend Marston? I will be there without the loss of a moment.' Simon nodded and departed the cabin. The enduring silence was absolute as Murphy helped Pat to change his clothes, neither man uttering a word, the overwhelming sense of the occasion settling upon them both as if a heavy weight.

Ten more minutes passed until Pat, dressed in his finest attire, stepped out to the gun deck, the most sombre of occasions dictating the slowest of steps, his mind awhirl with glum memories of similar past funerals at sea. Before him as he halted alongside Marston stood almost two hundred men, all of them in obviously downcast mood.

'Silence, fore and aft,' a subdued Codrington spoke only in normal voice, for he had no need to shout as an absolute silence already reigned, save for the ubiquitous gull, a dozen of which called out from the yards, seemingly in rude ignorance of the moment.

Pat turned all about in inspection once more of his ship; he looked up to the sky, to the dawdling clouds - still no real movement there - and finally he scrutinised his crew on the quarterdeck; he looked closely at the faces of men he had known for a decade or more, and to his great satisfaction he saw only the customary stoic stance of his veterans. He knew that Kitto's death had hit everyone hard, for the majority of the crew were Falmouth men, and everyone thought of every such town compatriot as his neighbour; in fact, many of them considered themselves to be more than that, to be family; and, aboard the barky, such bonding was actually a fundamental perception that was extended much more widely than solely to Falmouth men, born and bred, or even to those who were merely resident in the small Cornish port. Freeman, an African, had long been thought of as family too; for the common experiences and hard life, the injuries and the deaths, all exerted that considerable familial influence upon shipmates, whatever their origin, nationality or colour. Freeman, ebony black as he was, was as much a comrade, a friend, a shipmate, as all those born in Falmouth town; and Pat momentarily rejoiced in that brief reflection, for when those events of acute danger had presented themselves, as they so often had, or might do so again, he knew, he reminded himself - *he was assured* - that every man would do his utmost to serve the interests of his shipmates, his brothers-in-arms; and that thought was something of a small comfort in the rising sensation of his distress.

Some six score of devout Wesleyans amongst the crew were dressed in washed shirts of various colours and shades, the newer cotton brighter and the older much faded. All presented themselves in bleached, white duck trousers, starched to a demonstrable rigidity and plainly their best attire, washed and prepared overnight. A significant number of men still possessed faded, Royal Navy-issue, blue jackets, although for some men these had long worn to rags and been discarded in the heat of the Mediterranean. Yet all such that remained of brass jacket buttons were highly polished. Every man of Falmouth was adorned with a purple scarf about his neck, a particular custom for all funerals for those of their particular Methodist persuasion; and all men wore a broad-brimmed sennit hat, set straight on their head. All present had also combed out and fresh-tied their pigtails and shaved, and there was no evidence of excessively unruly beards, for many of the Wesleyans boasted such, usually accompanied by extravagant sideburns.

Behind Pat, who cursed the pain in his leg silently, his officers waited, also in silence, staring patiently at the ship's company. Above Pat on the quarterdeck, Clumsy Dalby rang the bell as softly as softly could be for seven bells. The bosun's loud tap of a fid upon the capstan was redundant, for no man had uttered so much as a whisper; but all came to an attentive stand, unmoving, gripped by the solemn nature of the sad occasion. The master, a lay preacher himself in Falmouth, barked, 'HATS OFF!' and every man, save for a distracted Pat, accorded instantly, tucking their hat under their arm.

Pat, still lost in thought, stared for several minutes in silent contemplation at his crew, his valued veterans, his precious band of brothers; his eyes picked out the nearer faces, men whom he remembered from his earliest times at sea; for nearly all in the front rows were old *Tenedos* hands, and not a one was rated less than able. He collected his thoughts as best he could, a confusion besetting him, as it often did, as he wondered, bleakly, where to begin. Despite the loss through many years of a great number of his shipmates, he was always hugely dismayed by funerals at sea, but this latest one, one which had followed so many on a voyage which had begun with aspirations of being solely of an essentially humanitarian nature, had seemed so very inequitable; and that struck hard at his mind's equilibrium; for the bleak and brutal reality of the loss of another of his men deeply oppressed him more than ever. At last, he bit hard on his lip and recovered his essential sense of purpose; his moment was upon him and it could not further be delayed; he removed his own hat, tucked it under his arm, and he began to speak in a low voice, 'Good morning, Mr Marston.' He raised his voice and, near shouting, addressed the whole crew, 'GOOD MORNING, LADS.' A hearty swell of reply followed from all present. 'I will say a few words before Mr Marston... *Father Michael*... will conduct the service.'

Pat looked again to his audience, to the second and third rows; he recognised more faces, he knew every one, seasoned veterans of many voyages, men who had sailed with him for a decade and longer; there was certainly no one who could be called a vagabond, a criminal or even a landsman *aboard his ship*. He blinked hard, took a deep breath and began to speak, 'When I first came aboard *Tenedos*... a goodly number of years ago, Jonathan Kitto was a young lad, a runner for one of the guns... as he himself learned to become a prime gunner... Indeed, I remember those days very well, for nothing was the least trouble for him... nothing at all...'

'Hear hear,' a quietly spoken low murmur of chorus from the assembly echoed an emphatic accord in the halting pause as Pat gathered his next words, ultimately spoken in a voice of profound humility tinged with distress, and greatly moving to the ears and minds of his men, 'A long-serving shipmate he was... one of Falmouth's own... and a most amiable man.... and I am most heartily set back that he has lost the number of his mess.'

'Hear hear,' came the endorsement again from two hundred men.

'In those years when we first served together, I remarked, even then... that Jonathan Kitto always worked with the utmost patience when it came to teaching his fellow gunners... and he always exhibited a deal of partiality and good temper to every man... and that was the case later... to all of us present here today... *officers and men alike*... I admired his dedication... I took that very well; in fact, I believe that I learned a deal from him... I did so. In fact... *in fact,* there were... *there were times* when I was humbled, *myself...* I was so... *yes, I was humbled...* by his gracious conduct, and in those years since...' Pat spoke very slowly, his recollections forming the slowest of flow into his faltering words, and he reflected briefly on how much his personal fortitude had seemingly diminished,'... in all those years since... and here most particularly aboard the barky... when we have seen battle and been through much distress... *together...*' Pat consciously raised his voice, '... *I was ever pleased to call him shipmate!'*

'HEAR! HEAR!' the chorus was louder, greatly emphatic.

Pat halted; visibly and increasingly discomfited, he could find no more words in the rising grip of distress which he could no longer hold at bay; indeed, his eyes were watering profusely and he bit hard on his lower lip. A few seconds passing, he turned his head to the bosun and whispered with all the voice he could find, 'Mr Sampays, please to confirm that... that all is ready, if you will.'

'Yes, sir; Kitto has been all washed on the carpenter's bench this very morning, and he is dressed up right fine and tidy in his best clothes. The canvas shroud is all sewn up tight, two shot at his feet... and he awaits your command for burial... ready on the board, sir.'

Pat nodded, 'Very well.' He turned to the chaplain at hs side, 'Mr Marston, please to continue.'

Marston began in firm voice, 'We are gathered here today to pay our respects to Jonathan Kitto, long revered as our shipmate... and beloved as our brother... for whom we grieve with infinite sorrow in our thoughts and with all our hearts.'

'Hear hear,' the soft chorus resounded through the assembly.

'We are met here to hail a brave man who gave his life that others might be free. At sea that we are, he will not be buried in consecrated ground, but he will for evermore be hallowed in our memories...'

'Hear hear,' the louder acknowledgement came from two hundred voices with unfaltering resolution.

'... never to be forgotten by us... for we are, all of us... on this sad day... his brothers; and from this day forth... we will remember him.'

'Hear hear!' Pat found himself near shouting, along with every other man within his gaze.

'But now... *now* it falls to us only to bury him... and we therefore commit his body to the deep, to be turned into corruption, looking for the resurrection of the body... when the sea shall give up her dead... and the life of the world to come...' Marston halted, in a most considerable degree of difficulty himself, for he still despaired at his own failure to save his patient, Kitto; and for a fleeting few seconds he lifted his eyes and allowed his gaze to fall upon the silent multitude standing patiently before him, all awaiting his next words; and it registered with him for the first time that every single man had donned his best clothing, to the extent that it could be described as such; and it struck him most acutely in that moment of realisation just how much Kitto truly had been such a greatly esteemed member of the ship's crew. He sighed, and recovering his composure and remembering his words, he resumed, '... through our Lord Jesus Christ... who at his coming shall change our vile body... that it may be like his glorious body, according to the mighty working, whereby he is able to subdue all things to himself. Amen.'

'Amen,' two hundred voices replied in loud accord.

The traditional words delivered, Marston paused once again in an absolute rigidity; the gravity of the solemn occasion and the emotive words of his sermon had brought a halt to whispers and all bodily movement within his congregation, and an absolute silence reigned. Pat, recognising Marston's difficulty and his own composure a little recovered, intervened, 'Lads! Lads... afore we bury our shipmate... we will hold our station... stand in silence... to remember... and give our respects to Jonathan Kitto... for his loss is a great loss to us all.'

'Hear, hear,' The crew's low, quiet endorsement, murmured by all, was followed by the requested silence as every man, old tarpaulins all, gathered his personal thoughts, vivid recollections of Kitto coming to the fore, memories of a cherished companion coming to mind, images of a smiling, cheerful man, a friend to many aboard the barky.

During the silent interlude and for the first time since coming on deck, Pat's senses were alerted to the normalities of shipboard observation; his ears detected the sound of a low wash alongside the hull, nothing of substance but certainly present; his quickly glancing eyes caught the greater press of the sails, the former idle crack of canvas edges lost to a light air, but hardly a wind; for so he thought; more of a strengthening breeze, a cat's-paw; but for all the little that it was he was grateful, and that most modest of a return to the smallest velocity of ship's movement was the tiniest inkling of comfort in his painful dismay, in his enduring personal distress, and he gave silent thanks for it even as he once again hung his head.

Another minute passed in silence before Pat, recovering his train of thought, looked up once more to see the many expectant faces of his men all staring at him. His own personal discomfort was perfectly evident to everyone, for in all of his body demeanour, in his sad face, in his recessed, tired eyes, he looked careworn as never before; his best uniform had failed to disguise it. He realised that it was time to resume, to finish with the unhappy affair, to demonstrate resolution to his men; and so, his own emotions raging, his sentiments on fire, he called out aloud, 'THANK YOU, SHIPMATES!'

There was a collective exhalation as if of relief as Marston stepped one pace to the fore, also grasping the necessity to progress. He took a deep breath and resumed in loud voice, 'I will speak but a very few words more... *customary words...* before we conclude our service and our respects to our lost shipmate. *Those that go down to the sea in ships... and occupy their business in great waters... these men see the works of the Lord... and his wonders in the deep.'*

Marston hesitated briefly, as if to remind himself that the final moment really was upon him, 'We bid our farewell to our friend, our brother... Jonathan Kitto. May he rest in peace. Amen.'

All the Wesleyans throughout the gathering spoke louder than ever as the ship's complement shouted out as one, 'AMEN.'

Pat looked all about him once more; he observed the profound dismay on scores of faces, and he nodded his head to the bosun, standing at the open gun port where Kitto lay on the wooden board, supported by four shipmates from his own gun crew. Sampays nodded his acknowledgment, the board was tilted up, and Jonathan Kitto slid down, down to his watery grave, an audible splash unavoidably noted in mind and memory by all present, another disturbing and unforgettable memento of tragedy.

On the quarterdeck the glass was turned and Pickering nodded to Clumsy Dalby who rang the eight bells out with loud emphasis, with vigour and emphatic intent, for his own intention was not merely to signify the end of the morning watch but to bring to a close the funeral and the rigidity of two hundred men standing in dismay and lost in their personal thoughts. Pickering shouted aloud to the bosun, 'Pipe to breakfast!'

On the gun deck the gathering dispersed, the starbowlins going forward to the galley to await their servings of gruel, the idlers and larbowlins talking amongst themselves as the officers moved amongst them with gentle words, with soft reminders to duty, with a hand on an arm or shoulder here and there, and a wan smile with a few words of gentle encouragement for the more obviously distressed among them, many lips being bitten hard.

Marston approached Pat, standing, unmoving, from where he had spoken, 'You spoke very well, sir... if I may say so.'

'Why, thank you, Mr Marston... *Michael,*' murmured Pat.

'I beg you will forgive me, sir, for... for remarking that you look to be... to be - *will I say* - tolerably set back.'

236

'Eh? Set back? Yes, I suppose I am... I am so... indeed, I fear I am not wholly in my intellects. My fortitude is also much diminished, and I am sorry that it should be so... so readily... *apparent.*'

'Oh, there is nothing to be sorry about, sir, not the least thing. I was *myself* much dismayed, as were all before me; and yet I looked at the demeanour of many a man... and, yes, I observed their distress... not a one of them unaffected... but, sir, I also looked most closely into their eyes... as I did too in looking to you.'

'I see,' replied Pat, a rising great confusion precluding any further clarity of thought.

Marston resumed, 'And in that instant... I believe that Our Lord spoke to me... and I saw... *I saw* in every man... *most particularly in you... in your eyes...* I saw *fortitude...* I saw *courage*; and in that particular moment... *in that moment...* it was a great help to myself; it was so.'

'God and Mary bless you,' whispered Pat, distraught and near overwhelmed in the moment, his throat tight constricted and utterly dry.

Chapter Ten

Friday 26th May 1826   12:00   *Bay of Biscay*

The warm sun at its noon zenith blazed down with seeming benevolence upon the quarterdeck and the gathering of *Surprise's* officers, every one of them taking the air and grateful for the welcome consensus of small comfort gained by being together, preserved even; whilst all around the frigate the Bay displayed its customary presentation of white horses atop an unceasing stream of low, blue-grey rollers, seemingly akin to an aqueous progression towards infinity; or, at least, towards a distant Cornish peninsula, a precious place where home increasingly beckoned to the tired spirits and minds of exhausted men. Home! The much nearer proximity to that blessed sanctuary was a greatly cheering thought, and it buoyed the spirits of all; perhaps more so for the wounded, many of whom had been brought up to the gun deck to take in the air, the fresh air; so very welcome after the foetid miasma which was the cockpit and the orlop, the latter place still the locus of rest for the more severely wounded unfortunates.

Pat, still much troubled by his leg, sat in his chair as he prepared to take the noon sighting with his sextant, oblivious to the occasional tiny shower of salt spray landing all about him. Indeed, a blessed feeling of relief, even of stasis, had settled upon his thoughts since his awakening in the dawn light; for his perilous work was near done and no more of his men would be lost, for so Simon had assured him; and what Melville would make of his failure to obey the order to return to Greece scarcely presented the least concern. And so he had sat, for hour after blessed hour of the morning, glorying in the warmth, his hair increasingly wet and flicked by the wind, his breakfast brought to his chair by Murphy. The pleasing anticipation of his dinner was already firming in his thoughts, and that it was such an innocuous focus was, in itself, most welcome.

Simon, near the starboard rail, gazed with unsatiated interest through Pat's borrowed glass, hoping for a sighting of a whale; but his attention was always diverted by swooping seabirds, always the gull and never any avian of note or even of the least interest. Not that he minded at all, for his enduring assurances to Pat had been a comfort even to himself; and - *for so he found* - in that brief moment when he had uttered the valuable words, they had been a profound but welcome beginning to the small relief which had penetrated his own black cloud of bleak concern. And so he clung to that rising renaissance in his spirits, and for it he was exceedingly grateful. A half-hour passing and not the least thing sighted in the water, he turned to Pat, 'I am in hope of sighting something of the marine life and the native avians that cling to these coasts.'

'I venture we will see Ushant on the morrow as we approach in the darkling light; indeed, I wish it were sooner, for there are a deal of outlying rocks all about that place... an uncommon great danger to all vessels.'

'I am with child to see it.' Simon's face had, to Pat's great pleasure, shed the recently perpetual lines of worry, of strain, and for the first time in many months he saw the old Simon, the face of the naturalist; and his friend positively glowed with delight as he continued, 'For the waters abounding the island are reputedly a locus for Cuvier's Beaked Whale - *Ziphius cavirostris* - an uncommon rare species; it has been remarked in these waters by Artedi himself, the great man of ichthyology.'

'Itchy ology? It sounds fair like a painful rash. Something in the medical line perhaps?'

'Not at all; it is the study of marine creatures, fish most particularly. Artedi has long been the acknowledged expert in all aqueous species.'

'Was he so? Did you meet the great man?'

'Unfortunately, no; he fell into a canal in Amsterdam and drowned.'

'That is... *unfortunate*; water is ever the peril,' murmured Pat; 'But as to avians in these parts, I am not familiar with other than the gull, the guillemot and the cormorant; scarcely rare birds, any of them.'

On the gun deck the ports were all fixed open, and great draughts of moist air, leavened with salt spray when the bow crashed down into the sea, washed as if with the breath of Heaven the white-pallor of the faces of wounded men on deck, men who had festered below for weeks but who were profoundly thankful to be alive and recovering. Between them all Freeman moved about in unceasing attention, offering greatly-diluted, five-part grog and stirabout, the porridge sweetened with the pulped remnants of the Cephalonia grapes.

Marston conversed with Jason near the taffrail. He frequently glanced below, his eyes ranging over his wounded charges sitting and laying all about the deck upon various measures of small comfort.

'Will I say, I have been in awe of your unceasing attention and unfailing service to those unfortunates of our shipmates who have been struck down these past five months, Marston,' offered Jason quietly, 'Note, I do not speak solely of your medical endeavours, but also of your liturgical ones, which have been much appreciated. I honour your devotion to our people, I do so.'

'It has been no more than that which any other man of God would have provided, my dear Jason.'

'I respectfully beg to differ, colleague; indeed, it has not escaped my notice that there is a deal more interest in the scriptures since we departed Falmouth, and not only that but I am minded that there is not a man aboard - *and I include myself* - who would hesitate to seek guidance and solace from your good self when beset by the least confusion.'

'Come, I am sure you exaggerate so.'

'Not at all, not in the least. Those of our people of the Wesleyan persuasion most particularly hold you in great respect, the utmost, and - *I break no confidences here* - even reverence.'

'Do they now? Jason, tell me: are you sure you are not temporising... with these... *these flattering conceptions*... such that they are. Do you have something to say... to ask of me?'

'What will you do, may I ask, when we make home? Our ship, the dear *Surprise*, is most parlously damaged, as you know; and there must be a considerable doubt about her future... *our future... serving together*... as we are... *have been*. I confess to a degree of... of uncertainty.'

'Oh, I do not know what will befall us - all of us, but we must place our trust in God and be not afraid. James tells us that *we must believe and not doubt, because the one who doubts is like a wave of the sea, blown and tossed by the wind,* and that is where we have been, dear Jason; but we have left that place behind, we have. Isiah tells us to *fear not, for when you pass through the waters I will be with you, the rivers will not overwhelm you, and when you walk through the fire you shall not be burned, the flame shall not consume you.*' Marston seized Jason's hand, 'We have crossed those rivers *together*; we have walked through those fires - *in Greece* - and we were not consumed, and nor shall we be, *whatever might be our future.*'

Jason squeezed Marston's hand tight, 'Thank you, dear friend, I am much obliged to you for your kindly words.'

Duncan had engaged with the three lieutenants for some hours, seeking to solicit accurate reporting of their recovery from the wounds they had suffered, but such replies were always spoken with reluctance, describing a scarcely credible diminution of their lingering discomfort and disability; and so he resigned himself to the approaching haven which was Falmouth, where the three stalwarts would have precious little to do and no responsibilities at all. Mower stood with him near the helm.

'Sir,' Mower spoke up unexpectedly, 'I have been considering your thoughts on that last verse of my poem.'

'Have you now, Mr Mower, and what is your conclusion?'

'I have rewritten it. Would you care to hear the substitute?'

'I would so.'

Mower found his scrap of paper and, as all the nearby gathering of *Surprise's* people inched closer to listen, he began to read,

'A host of cheering Falmouth families await us on the quay;
Home at last, and our cherished dreams are realised!
Grasping arms everywhere, so wonderful to see;
An abundance of joy, of love, from all whom we prized.'

'Aye,' declared Duncan with satisfaction, 'I find a deal more favour for that version. It answers amazingly well.'

'Hear, hear,' declared the audience emphatically.

To Pat's roving eyes, the sail canvas displayed a welcome fill, the standing rigging was creaking and groaning under only the most normal of strain, the yards were braced firm to hold steady the barky's gait, going large and making nine knots on the prevailing south-westerly, which was the welcome weather that Biscay had seemingly conceded, and he rejoiced in it.

At the helm, the supremely cheerful master, Jeremiah Prosser, observed the lightest of touch in the company of Barton and Green, holding the wheel. 'A hundred and twenty leagues to home!' declared Prosser with conviction.

'Home, blessed home, on Sunday!' echoed the helmsmen in cheerful voice. At the stern rail six men attended long lines, streaming through the white wake and baited with sardines to catch any interested tunny fish or, as became ever more likely, bass as the barky progressed ever further north. Pat much doubted that any fish could take the hook, the barky dashing along so well, and he was sure his anglers would know that too, but no one gave it any mind.

An exuberant Dalby rang out a strident eight bells for the end of the last dog watch, but scarcely a man paid the loud clanging the least heed; for all of the crew, both officers and men, were on deck, thronging the sides, filling every inch of the foc'sle and venturing even on that forward part of the quarterdeck where they might escape reproof; not that such had occurred for many a day and mile as the barky ploughed her wake ever closer to Falmouth, to home. The mood aboard was, since the Bay crossing, ever more contented, a rising sense of happiness abounding, although still constrained by minds which had been subjected to too great a strain, to horror and terror; yet, even so, a great discussion abounded everywhere about the decks, much talk about the imminence of arrival; and although every man was aware that Ushant, the familiar milestone that it was, was not quite home, nevertheless, it was a precious signal that home was near before them, that they would assuredly arrive in the coming day. Home and family was nigh upon them and they rejoiced in a profound sense of relief.

Pat decided upon a tour of inspection and, accompanied by Duncan, he walked slowly and with difficulty along the starboard gangway, few words exchanged, both men acutely aware that the end of the voyage, the finishing of their service was imminent; and so they ambled at the slowest of gait whilst staring all about them, somewhat vacantly absorbing the scene of tranquillity, taking in the sense of happiness radiated by the faces of men who acknowledged their passing with a smile and a knuckle to the forehead, a scant few words of greeting exchanged with familiar old salts, faithful stalwarts who had served for ten years and more with them aboard *Tenedos* before *Surprise*. On the foc'sle the two friends paused to stare at the low sun nearing the horizon to larboard, a very few minutes remaining before the sunset. Pat's ear caught the sound of the bow splash as it fell on successive wave crests; he looked back to cast his gaze all along the ship and his eyes briefly registered the firm fill of canvas aloft and the gentle lee heel of the deck, scarcely the least thing, all elements melding within his subliminal grasp of the barky's course, sailing large on the customary south-westerly; until his slow, ranging mind returned to more proximate attention as his ears caught the sound of musical instruments from below.

With rising interest Pat stepped down to the gun deck where he came upon a large gathering of men sitting on the deck around four musicians. Lieutenant Mower with his guitar was accompanied by three of the crew: Beer with a fiddle, and Knightley and MacLean both with guitars. As Pat and Duncan halted so did the music, and fifty faces stared at their captain.

'Please, do not pause for me; I beg you will not; do continue,' announced Pat with a broad smile on his own face; for, in truth, the music was a most welcome discovery amidst the general quietude, a reminder of a more normal life, and the rush which was the recognition of that essential feeling was more welcome to him in that moment than ever before. 'Please, pay me no mind; another song, if you will. I beg your indulgence and may I join you?'

The outpouring of welcome left no doubt about the response, and so Pat and Duncan sat down upon the deck planks, rubbing shoulders with familiar old tarpaulins. The musicians began again, a symbiotic blend of contrasting strings, the violin overlaying the softer guitars with a higher backcloth, but entirely in harmony as MacLean began to sing, very softly,

'Oh Dear you are... *the one I love*,
You are the one... *I'm thinking of*,
You know it's still... a *long... long way*,
But I'll be home... *at the end of the day*.'

In the momentary interlude between verses, Beer brought his fiddle to the fore, overshadowing for that brief few seconds the gentler and more melodic guitars to bring an introduction to the second verse as Maclean resumed,

'I'll sing my songs... *just for you*,
And I'll bring my love... *home to you*,

244

I can hardly wait... *to see your face... again,*
But I'll be home... *at the end of the day.'*

Pat sat in absolute thrall to the mood, the music and the singing, surrounded by his fascinated shipmates and entranced by the marvel presented to him. The musicians, plainly, were much enjoying the moment as MacLean began the next verse,

'Just miles and miles... *of rosy sky,*
I'll fall asleep... *by and by,*
I'm crying now... *'cos you're so far away,*
But I'll be home... *at the end of the day.'*

The sublime sense of relief which struck Pat in that instant, the words of the song so greatly moving, was simply overwhelming, and he felt himself weeping, great rivers of tears flowing down his cheeks which he could no longer hold back, for his fortitude had finally failed him in that moment, utterly; and then came a rising fear of allowing his shipmates to see him so visibly distressed; but as he stared at others all about him he observed the general reaction to the song was uniformly the same: men everywhere, every one of them, were similarly taken aback; and his anxieties receded, his fear faded, and he sat, in silence, dumbstruck as the musicians entered upon the final verse,

'Oh Dear you are... *the one I love,*
You are the one... *I'm thinking of,*
So many words... *I need to say,*
You'll hear them all... *at the end of the day;*
I'll be home... *at the end of the day.'*

The musicians stood up to take their bow, the registration of a powerful triumph plain to see in their faces, which was echoed in the loud flurry of applause: clapping, whistling and the calling out of many and varied complimentary words, with all of which Pat was in complete accord. He rose from the deck to shake hands with all the musicians, warmly and with great feeling, a great happiness consuming him, but he could find no words adequate to the moment.

The Chops of the Channel had exhibited nothing of its anticipated discomfiting turbulence; rather, that particular locus, as if extending a welcome, had deigned an exceptional benevolence in the sea state and had been left astern shortly after the dawn. The barky, served by the customary south-westerly of those parts, had made good progress, racing past the Scillies in good visibility, ever onwards as if the scent of home, like the dogs pursuing the fox, had been taken. The Lizard promontory had been passed on the larboard beam shortly after breakfast, the treacherous rocks of the Manacles and Shark's Fin Reef left safely astern mid-morning in excellent visibility, their dangerous presence plain to see in the white foam erupting all about them. The noon sighting had been completed and Pat, in leisurely anticipation of entering the Carrick Roads, was sitting in his chair on deck in warm sunshine near the stern rail and in contemplation of his dinner whilst weighing the mere possibility, however remote, of his favourite sweet pudding, frumenty, to follow; albeit he was reconciled to Wilkins using the final scrapings of the grape remnants as a poor substitute for the customary currants. Nevertheless, it was still something of a pleasing prospect, however innocuous, and certainly more appealing to contemplate than the promised dinner of dried peas with lumps of pork, salted pork; for the barky's provisions were so greatly depleted, near nothing left save for the oldest casks of salt pork and boxes of mouldering biscuit, and so the officers shared the primitive food of the lower deck. At least, for so Pat contented himself, that promised beef steak at the Royal was near close at hand: *beef! Fresh beef, roasted and perhaps served with a Yorkshire pudding!* The very thought was a treasure to contemplate after the salt pork of the past few days, and Pat licked his dry lips.

Barton was at the helm and the master in command, for Jeremiah Prosser was extremely familiar with the local waters, being a veteran Falmouth sailor. 'I will be uncommon pleased to fetch home, sir,' Prosser stepped back towards the rail and interrupted a silent Pat's musings, for his captain had scarcely shifted or spoken since the sighting and - much concerning for his men - seemed to be slumped into almost a stupor. 'This voyage has been a most severe tribulation... quite the trial of endurance. How are you, sir? How do you fare?'

The interruption registered with Pat and he looked up and stared closely into the wizened face of the master; the lines and myriad wrinkles covering the deeply sunburned skin of his face served only to emphasise a perception of intelligence radiating from his bright, blue eyes, and the warmth of a palpable concern in his voice struck a raw nerve in Pat's mind. 'Oh, it scarcely answers to say that I confess I have been much set back in recent times... the humours have been somewhat overset, and something of a melancholia has descended upon me, I regret to say. It will be a great relief to see the barky safely home at anchor.'

'That will answer for all of us, sir; for sure, it will,' Prosser spoke with the unquestionable authority which was the foundation of the respect held by all for him. 'It is the same feeling for all of our people.'

'Thank you, I am much obliged for your solicitude.' A momentary pause, Pat was feeling obliged, indeed wanting, to perpetuate the connection with his stalwart veteran, 'Upon my word, Mr Prosser, I am sitting here like a pig who has found and gorged upon the winter store of potatoes and is become beset by a lethargy! What a precious, puling soul I am become.'

'Never in life, sir; we are all much put out, every man jack aboard.'

'Indeed, and it is a tragedy that it should be so, and with home so near... nigh on the bow. Why, would you believe I was just now in contemplation... *dreaming*... of roast beef... served rare and with a rich gravy and a Yorkshire pudding... *or two!* And washed down with a proper pint of good honest stingo... *or two!* Ain't that the grand thought, eh?'

Prosser brightened, 'Tom Selley serves the best roasts in the town, sir, at the King's Arms on the Greenbank Quay; and the Royal boasts the finest of all beefsteaks in Falmouth town... but it is the rare day when I can afford one. The mackerel and the pilchard are more my line.'

'We can but dream, Mr Prosser,' replied Pat wistfully, remembering the glaring vacancy which was his purse. 'I dare say we will be on short commons for dinner... and likely supper too... and as for breakfast...' Pat laughed, Prosser was pleased to see, 'Why, even the millers of the hold will exhibit an appeal I never before felt for them!'

'No, sir,' Prosser gulped, 'that will never be the case; my home and my table - *whatever little it may offer, there is usually a fish* - will ever hold a welcome for you in Falmouth.'

'Thank you, Mr Prosser... *Jeremiah*; I am most uncommon gratified to hear that... I am... I take that very well... more so than ever I can say. Here; take my hand; I beg you will.' A firm handshake confirmed the mutual and heartfelt bond.

Simon was also at the stern rail, accompanied by both Marston and Jason, the trio feeling truly relaxed for the first time in many months and engrossed in watching for the least sign of marine life through the glass which Simon had borrowed from Pat. Simon stared with abject fascination and small delight at the abounding plethora of seals and dolphins which were seemingly trailing in the barky's wake, their avian counterparts being gannets and cormorants, rising numbers of them wheeling about the masts and perching upon the rigging, seemingly in a vocal sympathy with the mood of the crew, a loud excitement, all calling out in a shrill cacophony. Occasionally the sun was briefly occluded by a cloud which presaged the thin shower which drizzled lightly upon the congregation at the stern rail, a discernible drop in air temperature also felt by all, but no one paid it any mind.

'I cannot recall ever before feeling such a gratitude for the damp sea air... the *cold* sea air, the pleasurous breeze that it is upon a tired soul,' remarked Marston, striving to lift the mood from a seemingly subdued withdrawal into solitary but disagreeable reflections, however intrusive his friends might find the least interruption to be.

'I am minded to agree, colleague,' murmured Simon weakly, fastening his coat; 'I never before held to the least appreciation of the cold... much accustomed that I am to it, living in the bleak northern parts... nor indeed the forceful billows, and certainly not the wet... which is seeping in.'

'It is the rare pleasure to find a modicum of normality returning,' concurred Jason with feeling.

'Will I venture that our world - *our particular world* - such that it is and what we may desire that it will be,' Simon spoke up at last in more than a murmur, 'may offer us something of that precious normalcy, a foundation even for the restitution of our personal ataraxis; at least we may hope so; but I ask myself, I do: can we conceive that such is really the case?'

A nearby Pat, who had overheard the conversation at the rail from his chair and was somewhat perturbed, stared up and at his friend, 'Will I presume that ataraxis, *which I am unfamiliar with*, is a good thing?'

'I venture *we are all* unfamiliar with ataraxis these three years, brother,' replied Simon in a low voice of resignation; 'All quietude of the mind, every vestige, has surely left us all... fled... like swallows before the hawk; our minds have become distorted, leaving us bereft of the least remnant of mental repose.'

A shocked Marston, looking careworn himself, interjected and spoke directly to Simon with a voice which, whilst it implied that it would brook no rebuttal, not even the least expression of doubt, was gentle, consolatory, 'Allow me, dear friend, to remind you of the words of John, *In the world you will have tribulation. But take heart; I have overcome the world.* Ferguson, we have been subjected to a deal of tribulation; we certainly have; and yet *we will* overcome our incertitude. You are to consider that our personal catharsis will surely be found in our friends, for we have many such within this estimable vessel, the dear *Surprise*. I know myself that it is so, and so do you, when you reflect upon that. *To our friends* is where we must look to recover that foundation of our serenity, and it is truly here to be grasped; for they are here, all of our friends are present before our very eyes.'

'There ain't the least doubt of that,' declared Pat with heartfelt emphasis, 'and your words were uncommon edifying too, Mr Marston, if I may say so.' There was a subdued murmur of accord from a small and fascinated gathering of the crew, eavesdroppers who had ventured ever closer from the wheel, Pat not much caring to shoo them from his presence, the customary and regulatory distinctions of rank and hierarchy much eroded of late. 'Come on, old Simon, here we are, near Falmouth town; the sun is shining and there ain't no fog in the air; we will be tiding it into the Roads with scarcely the need for even a topsail to carry her until the barky makes her turn, and I dare say the King's Road anchorage awaits us within an hour or two, not longer... a true delight to behold, you must admit; there's joy for you.'

'Thank you, Michael,' mumbled Simon still staring at the chaplain, for Marston had become something of a mentor and had discretely taken his hand. 'As ever, I dare say you are in the right of things.' He turned his head towards Pat, 'Thank you too, brother. Gentlemen, I most humbly beg your pardon for my lamentable air of discontent; this is neither the time nor the place to repine. I am indebted to you both for reminding me.'

As the forenoon watch had ended, more of the waking, off-duty crew had emerged from below until near every man of the barky was on deck, at the larboard rail, on the foc'sle and even intruding upon the sacred quarterdeck, for strict formality had long quitted the barky. Every man was in anticipation of reaching home in the afternoon and anxious to do so; even a glimpse of such familiarities as the recognisable coastline presented a joy to the eyes and the minds of homesick men. The long day of sunlight assured them that making home was perfectly feasible, to be expected, the thought to be revelled in; for there were just a very few more miles remaining. A great discussion, ribald, noisy, vigorous, near everyone participating, reverberated around the deck, scores debating what would be done first on setting foot upon the precious quay.

Pat was much enjoying his own relaxing day thus far when the shout came down from the man at the main top, 'SAIL HO! LARBOARD BOW!' Rising from his chair with a degree of discomfort, his leg wound still paining him, he stepped across to the taffrail on the larboard side and, retrieving his glass from Simon, he raised it and stared forward. On hearing the shout, all the great gathering of men on deck similarly stared into the distance, a great hubbub of speculation swiftly consuming everyone. Within a half-hour, *Surprise,* scarcely making five knots before the weaker wind of the afternoon, closed on the sighted vessel and all became clear: it was an unusual vessel, boasting both sails and a smokestack, and was accompanied by a small schooner. Yet, to Pat's eye, albeit sailing close-hauled against the prevailing south-westerly wind, the duo were making exceedingly slow progress; indeed, as he scanned the set of their sails it occurred to him that their movement could only be deliberately slow, a veritable snail's pace, for the steamer's sails were reefed and only her topsails offered the least benefit. *What was the intention of her master?* he wondered.

His gaze focused more closely on the steamer; at her visible, larboard side an odd structure had been built on, attaching to her hull; but whilst it enclosed her paddle wheel it seemed to be something of an extravagance of construction. Pat stared further: both the steamer and the schooner were very close to each other, and Pat surmised that some form of conference of her officers must be in progress; in fact, his eyes caught sight of a cutter rowing its wet passage through the chop of the sea between them. He stared more closely but could see no Royal Navy ensign at the masts of either, nor any other flag. It was something of a mystery and it lodged firmly in his mind: *who on earth could they be?* At least, he felt assured, they could not be Turks, for such was inconceivable, being so very close to home.

Duncan, at Pat's side, announced his own discovery aloud, 'I can see the name on the bow of the schooner, sir, and she is called *Unicorn*.' *Surprise* ploughed on and within an hour she came near alongside the approaching vessels, their progress no more than a crawl. 'The steamer is *Perseverance*,' declared Duncan.

'Why, I do believe that vessel - *the steamer* - may be familiar to me!' exclaimed Pat. 'Indeed, I remember meeting with Mr Daniel Brent, a shipbuilder with a Rotherhithe yard, in London three years ago. Do you recall the meeting of the London Greek Committee which we attended with my cousin, Canning?'

'Aye,' replied Duncan, 'Was there some mention of a ship being built for Greece... and Cochrane to become involved?'

'Indeed, there was; yet I had thought that Cochrane was serving in the Brazils since some years... certainly still in South America.'

In that moment the schooner fired her signal gun, and all attention aboard *Surprise* was immediately captured, all eyes staring across the intervening gap, scarcely a hundred yards or less.

'What does that signify?' asked Simon, a little nervous with the unwelcome sound of the shot as he appeared at Pat's side.

'It is a salute, the custom, one ship to another; nothing more.' Pat turned his telescope to her deck and stared with absolute fascination for several minutes. 'By God, Duncan; there he is! It is the great man himself, Cochrane! Do my eyes deceive me? Here, take my glass and take a look.'

'Aye, you are in the right of things, 'tis Cochrane for sure!'

All along the deck as the word spread that Lord Cochrane had saluted the barky, the already high spirits rose further and became a wild enthusiasm. Cochrane, the seafaring legend of the Royal Navy had saluted them! Never in their wildest dreams had they imagined such an event; it was unbelievable! Not even the King himself could have struck a more significant chord; it seemed prophetic, being so close to home.

Pat, much delighted himself, turned to his assembly of lieutenants, all closely following his discourse from a yard removed, 'Mr Pickering, you may find this a trifle irregular, Cochrane not considered to be - *will I say* - *in favour* at the Admiralty - but he is certainly a man of shining parts in the navy line; indeed, he has liberated Chile and Peru, and I honour him for that. I am minded that we will fire a proper salute, as befits the case. As we may hold to the belief that he is in command of those vessels - *admittedly something of a most minor flotilla* - I believe it is perfectly appropriate... that is to say, *we are obliged* to fire a salute such as befits a commodore; and so we will fire eleven guns from the larboard battery. Carry on, Mr Pickering, if you please.'

'Aye aye, sir.' Pickering hastened to the steps, Mower and Codrington at his back as he gained the gun deck. 'Open the gun ports!' he barked. A manic two minutes followed, 'Draw the shot!' Men hastened all about the deck to do so, ten minutes passing. 'Run out your guns!' The gun crews had got wind that the barky was about to salute Cochrane and responded with alacrity, all of the larboard battery swiftly hauled out. 'Ready!' shouted Pickering; 'Fire One!' Mower, near the foc'sle echoed the order, 'Fire!' and *Venom* erupted. Five seconds later, Mower had shifted to *Dutch Sam* and shouted again, 'Fire Two!' At five second intervals, with the three lieutenants and every man of the gunners all in great excitement, the rolling broadside swept all along the side, from *Tempest*, *Crucifixio*n and *Hell's Mouth*, all the way to *Billy Warr* in the great cabin.

On the deck of *Unicorn*, arms were raised and hands waved in acknowledgement. Pat and all his officers reciprocated with great enthusiasm, as did the men of the barky all along her side. every man delighted with the prospect of a great tale to tell for years to come: *Cochrane, the great man, had exchanged salutes with the barky!*

Slowly the steamer and the schooner were left astern, and *Surprise* made her turn past the Black Rock and into the Carrick Roads, another half-hour of making short boards in a very feeble wind bringing her ever closer towards the master's planned anchorage, as near to the town as the depth of water at low tide would allow.

'Mr Macleod, please to take in all sail,' declared Pat.

All way swiftly dropped off the slow-moving frigate until she finally stopped at the place of her intended mooring. For Pat it was a personally very moving moment; in strange fashion it seemed almost that his world itself had stopped or at least paused, and he shook his head as if to awaken from the strange, cerebral halt.

'Mr Macleod, ready the boats; let go fore and aft,' Pat spoke in a voice which carried a world of audible relief, which did not go unnoticed on the quarterdeck.

'Mr Sampays,' Duncan turned to the bosun, 'Let go stock and fluke!'

'Aye aye, sir!' Willing hands awaited the order that every man had dreamed of for weeks, certainly so during the final days of the homeward voyage. The bosun bawled out to the aft anchor crew, standing ready, 'One, two, three; let go!' before turning forward to repeat the call, both anchors splashing into the water and a loud shout of 'Hurrah!' rising from the crew generally, to which Pat paid no mind; indeed, he felt much like shouting himself.

All along the many quays and opes of the town small throngs of people were gathering and growing in number as time passed by. The barky's remaining boats - those that remained in good fettle - were swiftly lowered and were soon joined alongside by local fishing vessels that came out from the quays.

Surprise was at last at anchor, in her home port, and a quiet feeling of relief settled upon all aboard; enthusiasm was moderated and shouting died away; they were truly home at last, and the profound realisation was allowed to take hold, to sink in; for, in truth, it was something of a sobering moment as well as a joyful one. Some few minutes passed before Pat spoke again in subdued voice, 'Please to lower the ensign to half mast, Mr Macleod. Our people may go over the side as soon as they please. Let us look to our wounded shipmates first.'

Sunday 28th May   15:00   Kings Road anchorage, Falmouth

A weary but much cheered Pat gazed everywhere all about the quarterdeck from his chair - his leg still a burden - as the men of *Surprise* departed for the town. Moored since an hour in the King's Road anchorage, the visibly ravaged frigate had swiftly been surrounded by all manner of small boats, almost all of them fishing vessels come out from the several landing places all along the Falmouth waterfront; so many of them that it seemed as if there would never be the least let up from the shouted greetings and calls, from anxious enquiries of all kinds, all of which were made in loud voice from a hundred men and more come out to greet the barky, *Falmouth's own*, as she was considered to be. Her own boats had been supplanted by dozens of local ones, and the unloading of her crew was progressing well; for three score of Falmouth men, many of them Royal Navy veterans, had come aboard to assist in the carrying of the wounded from their cots on the mess deck; and those unfortunates, of all people, brightened a great deal as they gained the fresh air and saw, for the first glance in a very long time, the welcome roofs and smoking chimneys of home, blessed home. For many in their discomfort and distress it was a sight that they had feared they might never see again, and their spirits were much uplifted.

In the diffuse light of the cloudy mid-afternoon, one thankfully without the least rain, even more gulls had appeared as if in welcome, diving and swooping to settle upon the yards and to watch with loud, calling interest at the men busying about the decks.

Near Pat's chair his officers gathered as the crew numbers dwindled away. It was a strange mood, one that all struggled to come to terms with; for the heartfelt Falmouth homecoming, for all present, delivered more than the physical arrival; it offered too an arrival of sorts in the minds of men who had long been deeply oppressed, spiritually homeless even, halted in the trough of bleak despond and uncertainty which had been the war; and yet, although bodily salvation had seemingly arrived, the mélange of deep-seated, frightening memories, so firmly rooted that they seemed unlikely to ever fade, much coloured the spirits of the present, and not in the least in any comfortable fashion; and little was said, conversations were brief, exchanges subdued, even hesitant.

'Will we go ashore now, Pat?' ventured Simon Ferguson quietly and looking at his friend, seemingly absorbed that he was in introspection. Of all persons aboard, Simon was much the most relieved, for his patients would be accorded far greater comfort and the most careful attention ashore, within their own homes and with their families all about them, a plethora of willing nurses which far surpassed the barky's meagre resources.

'Eh? Ashore?' Pat, distracted at last from his thoughtful reflections, turned his head and slowly became aware of his audience all about him on the quarterdeck, still a considerable number of men present, the wounded having been given priority. He looked up to see many familiar faces gathered about and gazing at him, all with a projection of infinite benevolence; for so it seemed to him, and in that moment, he was much moved by it. He looked more closely at Simon, Duncan, Marston and Jason, and his gaze ranged further, to Pickering, Codrington and Mower, to the master, Jeremiah Prosser, who was yet to go ashore, to Sampays, the bosun, and Tizard, the carpenter; he looked wider still to see more of the old stalwarts of his crew, Barton, Clumsy Dalby and Murphy too. His eyes rested briefly on Freeman, the former slave and certainly a man who had become a stalwart, a veteran, a true shipmate; and he wondered what the black man would do, for he had no home in Falmouth; no home anywhere, save for what perilous place might yet remain in Africa; if, that is, any of his family remained after many years of the brutal depredations of slave traders. Pat wondered whether he would see many of the familiar faces again after they had departed for the sanctuary of the shore, to their homes; and he wished, more than ever before, to reach his own home in still distant Connemara; and in that moment he could find nothing to say, no reply could he conceive of, for the gulf between his rising emotions and his dry mouth seemed utterly unbridgeable, and so he simply stared, words beyond him.

'Do you care to go ashore, brother?' Simon reiterated gently, for his friend was surely disconcerted; that was plain to see, and every man present was hanging on Pat's eventual reply. No words still forthcoming and Simon persisted, 'I recall you promised me a fine beef steak at the Royal when we fetched home. Allow me to say that I am calling in your pledge.'

Pat gazed up, up to the mast tops, up to the bright sky, not a cloud now in sight in the clear spring afternoon. He felt the gentlest of breeze ruffle his hair and, striving to dispel the confusion which had beset him, he looked to his friend and considered how he could best reply; indeed, how he should reply. A few moments passed and a calm settled upon him, something of a clarity had returned to his thinking, a considered value had been placed anew upon his surroundings, upon his men most particularly; and with some difficulty and quickly aided by Murphy he dragged himself from his chair to stand upright, still supported by his left arm on the helm. He nodded to Simon as if in reply but turned to the master, 'Mr Prosser, will you kindly call all hands aft? Thank you.'

The master reiterated the words to Clumsy Dalby who bawled them out loud, 'ALL HANDS AFT!' and the crew shuffled towards the helm, fifty men and more of the barky's men remaining. The Falmouth helpers held back behind them, mindful of their status as visitors but watching with great interest.

A raising of Pat's arm and the attention of his audience was captured, the quiet hubbub all about the quarterdeck dying away until everyone was staring at him in expectation. 'Gentlemen, allow me to say...' This was spoken in a whisper. 'If it pleases you... ' Pat raised his voice, 'Allow me to say that I would like to buy you all...' and louder still, 'I would like to buy you all - *every man jack of you* - a fine beef steak at the Royal; indeed, I will be honoured if you will accept.' Pat, in the grip of a fiery emotion, one which entirely possessed him and which was unlike anything before, had forgotten the vacancy that was his purse, and he was shouting now, 'COME WITH ME... ALL OF YOU... COME WITH ME!' A momentary hesitation, a recollection, 'That is to say, if I do not find I am arrested as soon as I set foot upon the Customs House quay!' Pat laughed out loud, a release of sorts, the profound sense of relief rising within him. His laugh was echoed by Duncan as everyone else stared in puzzlement, for the reason had remained a secret. 'But first,' Pat found a firmer voice and steadied his thoughts amidst a raging sea of passion, which he recognised was rising quickly and which would soon overcome him, would bring him to speechless tears, unless he could quickly get his words out, 'But first... *first...* I will shake the hand of every man here, every one of you, and - *I will say it plain* - may you all please accept my most heartfelt thanks for your endeavours... for your valued presence as... *as my shipmates.*' Pat's voice had fallen away, was faltering, was near reduced to little more than a whisper, '... as my true brothers-in-arms... aboard the barky.' He raised his voice once more, 'THANK YOU! I THANK YOU WITH ALL MY HEART!'

The near riot of noise, of thanks, of loud congratulations, of frenzied handshakes, persisted in an uncontrolled outpouring of bedlam for fully five minutes during which the local Falmouth men who had come aboard to offer their help stood amidst the barky's veterans on the quarterdeck, more of them gathering about the helm each minute, until - *at last* - the handshakes had seemingly ended; but then, from all those of the crew still aboard, and augmented by the Falmouth helpers, there came a resounding clapping of hands and a most determined, loud stamping of boots upon the deck, immediately followed by the heartiest three cheers ever heard by every man present.

Monday 29th May 1826 08:30   *Falmouth*

All the officers of *Surprise* save for the three lieutenants, who had been sent ashore with the wounded, had gathered in the great cabin to discuss with Pat the immediate future for the barky and the pressing necessities bearing upon them all. It was a strange atmosphere; superficially all were at ease, yet the absence of almost all the crew had brought about what seemed an unnatural quietude, almost a complete silence, which was somewhat unsettling; for there was nothing of the customary bustle of activity and the single vestige of customary life was the ringing out of the bell every half-hour, which sounded dolorous, mournful even; but that nothing else was happening was hard to accept, to come to terms with. The peaceful repose registered as strange to the mind, even something of a mystery which could not be comprehended; and so they sat, deep in thought, the last of the grog dispensed to the remaining handful of the barky's men. Near all the crew were ashore and every man remaining, including all the officers still present, was mindful that they had been invited to a service of Thanksgiving to mark the return home, to be held in the Methodist chapel in the early evening.

Murphy and Freeman busied about the table, pouring liberal draughts of fresh coffee, brought ashore that morning and the most considerable improvement on the last scrapings of recent weeks, the doubtful vestiges of which Pat had suspected were adulterated with the excrement of invading rats in the hold, a likelihood he had determined not to comment on for fear of further upsetting a still frail Simon in his enduring personal distress. Wilkins ran back and forth to and from the galley, bringing a veritable feast of heavily laden trays of bacon, eggs and sausages, with larger trays upon which were overlaid with dishes of black pudding, pig's kidneys and fresh bread with butter, the latter two of which seemed to everyone present to be quite the delicacy after the dry biscuit, much infested with weevils, which they had been reduced to whilst crossing the great Bay which was Biscay. The fresh comestibles, donated by many of the families of the barky's veterans, were greatly appreciated, savoured with a relish and much remarked upon.

The mood of all had lifted with the coming of the new day, with the firming realisation that they truly had left poor, wretched Greece far behind, and at last they had reached the precious sanctuary of home which was Falmouth; minds slowed and tensions melted in the treasured thought that here was something of a beginning of a normalcy, one which would not be broken by the deafening assault of the exploding great guns and the frightening sights of shot flying and sulphurous smoke rising all about them; they would no longer be subjected to the screams and shrieks of bloodied, wounded and dying men, would not be burying any more unfortunates overboard. However, the process of accepting the new reality was slow, as if it could not quite be believed, and the table dialogue as every man gorged with satisfaction on the breakfast banquet remained cautious to a great degree, no man wishing to utter the wrong word, to say the least thing that might break the dawning ambience of such profound relief.

'Allow me to help you to another brace of sausages, Mr Marston - *I beg your pardon - Michael,*' ventured Pat, the chaplain sitting next to him, his food all eaten up.

'Thank you, sir; I will take just the one sausage.'

'And another egg perhaps?' Marston nodded without the least sign of reluctance. Pat served and then resumed, 'There is a great plenty of fresh provisions come aboard, the likes of which I ain't seen since we departed Falmouth three years ago. The townsfolk have been sending laden boats since the dawn. Plainly the news of my empty purse has reached them all!' Pat laughed and all present laughed with him. 'Are you minded to speak at the chapel this evening, Michael, may I ask?'

'If I am invited, I would like to do so, sir. Doubtless Mr Prosser will inform me if that is the case; he is an elder of the chapel, as you may know.'

'Yes, of course.' A pause, 'I recall that... at the service... the one to commemorate Mathew Jelbert, the chapel was filled to capacity, not an empty seat within... such a great multitude attending; indeed, I venture there was scarcely a soul in Falmouth who was not there.'

'The Christian belief is strong in the town; sir, particularly so with those of the Methodist persuasion. May I ask you something, sir... with your permission, of course?'

'Please do; anything, the least thing.'

'I am minded that the congregation might likely welcome some few words of yours, sir; not anything of a great speech... merely the essentials... that is to say, at the least some few words which might be taken as a comfort by those who have lost loved ones... those who we have left behind... those unfortunates of our people whom we buried at sea.'

Pat's heart rate soared in an unwelcome instant, and he wondered whether Simon had mentioned to Marston his hesitations in that matter. His throat constricted and his mouth dried immediately; his short breathing accelerated as he recalled his faltering, brief speech on the last such occasion in Falmouth, when he had announced the name of the new cutter, *Mathew Jelbert*, to celebrate and commemorate the name of the much-esteemed master gunner of the same name, a man who had been revered as the father figure of the barky, a man who had been lost in the battle with Turk vessels when *Surprise* had escaped the blockade of the great anchorage and bay which was Navarino. That was a place which Pat hoped he would never see again. In that moment he felt overwhelmed by the memories, by the stark vision of the dreadful scene; all of which came flooding back in a tide of grief, and he faltered, 'To tell you the truth I am no great speaker... no orator... Sure, I can read the Articles... something in the official line... but I am not much given to speeches.'

Marston interjected in kindly voice, 'Perhaps I may be of some small assistance, sir... to draft with you a short piece... a very few words... ones appropriate to the occasion? In case you may be called upon for such... and, that is, if you feel obliged to speak to the congregation... the community.'

'A most admirable suggestion,' Simon spoke up with resolution, with an emphasis which affirmed his accord with the essential proposition.

'Very well,' pronounced Pat with discernible reluctance as he stared with searching scrutiny at his close friend, opposite; 'Just a very few words... for a minute or so... not longer. We will look to that matter after breakfast, after I have read the post... Some letters have come aboard this morning, sent from the Packet Office.'

'I will go ashore to look to our wounded shipmates,' declared Simon.

'As will I,' echoed Jason. Nothing further said by anyone, a mere nod offered by Pat, and the two left the cabin together.

A final gulp and Pat set down his coffee cup as the stewards busied about to clear the table. When all was done Pat reached for the pile of letters, grasping first the official one with the Royal Navy seal. He sighed before breaking away the red wax, wondering what might merit such a letter rather than the customary routine of a telegraph to Plymouth, transcribed and passed on by a messenger to the ship and officer in question when anchored in the Hamoaze or the Sound. Surely such as this could have been brought to Falmouth by a Royal Navy schooner, as had happened before. It seemed odd to receive what must be a missive of some significance whilst in a relative backwater via the Packet Office. Setting the puzzle aside and extracting the letter from the envelope he began to read aloud in a voice which was scarcely more than a murmur:

'16th May 1826. To Captain Patrick O'Connor, commanding His Majesty's Ship Surprise, in anticipation of said vessel's arrival at either Falmouth or Plymouth.'

So that was the explanation, Pat realised; the letter had likely been delivered to Falmouth some time previously. He read on, still aloud:

'Sir, in the event that your ship has reached either of the above-mentioned ports and cognisant that you may not have received our earlier missive instructing the return of the aforementioned ship to the Ionians, you are hereby required and requested to report in person to the First Lord of the Admiralty at your earliest convenience upon receipt of this letter.'

Pat, somewhat shocked, paused as the immediacy of his instruction registered. Marston blinked, similarly astounded, but remained silent, and Duncan groaned. Pat resumed reading:

'You are summoned to advise on the prospects for a new vessel, a steamship, the Perseverance...'

'We saw her yesterday!' declared Duncan, astonished.

Pat only nodded before resuming:

'... the Perseverance, which was ordered and since constructed in Mr Daniel Brent's shipyard, ostensibly to serve as a Malta-bound packet or merchantman. However, for such is the opinion of the Admiralty, her true purpose is to serve the interests of the Greek rebellion in the present conflict with Ottoman authority...'

A sharp intake of breath from Pat before Duncan exclaimed, 'The Greek *rebellion* indeed! The poor buggers!'

Pat grimaced and nodded again:

'Such service would be a criminal activity, contrary to the Foreign Enlistment Act...'

Duncan was outraged, 'They paid that no mind in our case!'

'... however, that would not be the case unless and until said vessel was equipped with armament at a place within His Majesty's diverse realm. It is our further conclusion that she

will likely be so equipped upon arrival at a foreign port. Said steam vessel, having been completed in the early weeks of May at the aforementioned gentleman's East Country yard at South Dock, Rotherhithe, she is about to commence North Sea proving trials before departing for Greece...'

'Departing... departing? Why, she has plainly fled the nest!' Duncan could not contain his ire.

'... Their Lordships are aware that Lord Cochrane has taken an interest in said vessel to the extent of personally and covertly inspecting her...'

'There can be nae doubt of that,' declared Duncan, 'Personal interest indeed!'

'... on the 13th of this month with a view to taking command...'

'Aye, so that was the explanation of his presence yesterday.'

Pat continued reading aloud, ignoring his friend's interruptions, for he could scarcely believe the amazing coincidence of the Admiralty letter and the encounter with Cochrane:

'The aspirations of said individual would scarcely be compatible with the declared purpose of said vessel being to engage in the maritime trade between London and Malta.'

'Cochrane, a merchant captain!' scoffed Duncan in derisory voice; 'Aye, I venture he will be perfectly happy with five pounds a month... *five pounds!* Is there a Stock Exchange in Malta, tell?'

'Come now, Duncan; there are plenty of people - *a prodigious number* - who swear by the man... claim he is a capital fellow, and - as we know only too well, *at least I do* - a deal of matters in the financial line lie far beyond the intellects of many - *certainly many a humble seafarer* - and I include myself, I do.'

'Aye, and in Scotland we call a spade a spade.'

Pat, his head down once more, his eyes focused and his mind alarmed and all awhirl, resumed:

'Their Lordships are particularly minded that it would serve His Majesty's interests were you and your officers to scrutinise the aforementioned ship at all times from the neutrality (from the perspective of the Ottoman naval authorities) of a Royal Navy vessel in order that the activities of said ship might be reported to London by a competent authority conversant with the waters of and the military situation extant in the Ottoman Greek provinces.

'Therefore, you are hereby requested and required to notify your arrival at any English port, and with the utmost express to report to the Admiralty in London with your advice on the present condition of HMS Surprise and her suitability thereof for an immediate return to Greece... signed by Melville etc.'

'WHAT?' shouted Duncan in full voice, 'RETURN TO GREECE!'

'On my life! What am I to do?' exclaimed Pat. '*Her suitability for an immediate return to Greece indeed!* The infernal lubbers! Nigh on three score and more of our people are wounded, I have no lieutenants fit for sea, much of her starboard bulwarks are shot away, the hull is breached and plugged in a dozen places... and her canvas is scarcely more than rags... *yes, rags...* ones which would disgrace even a stinking, Liffey garbage scow!'

'Aye, and I cannae see a single man signing up for such a... *a fantasy*,' Duncan spoke with vehement anger. 'Aye, for a fantasy it is, nae more than that.'

'Sir, if I may be of assistance, the slightest thing?' Marston, who had been listening in incredulous silence, spoke up in more moderate voice, 'Is it conceivable that their Lordships are unaware of that engagement - *so greatly injurious to our shipmates and to this vessel* - which was fought after our departure from Cephalonia?'

Pat stared, wide-eyed and open-mouthed, at the chaplain as his brain endeavoured to calculate the possibility, a near minute passing without reply. Duncan, regaining something of his composure, was the first to speak, 'Aye, that may be the case; we were but twenty-four hours at Valletta, and there isnae any Mediterranean packet yet arrived at the quay, and so I think it could be so.'

Marston continued, 'Sir, in my capacity as a man of medicine, I could not countenance you undertaking any other course other than rest, for the severity of your injuries dictates such; and I have not the least doubt that my estimable colleague, Dr Ferguson, will hold to the same opinion. You are quite unfit to travel, sir... *quite unfit.*'

'Thank you, Mr Marston,' remarked Pat, 'But am I now to conclude that I find myself beholden to a committee? I grant you it is a well-intentioned one.'

'I do beg your pardon, sir, I intended no such inference. The opinion and concerns of the medical practitioner for his patient must never be subservient to rank and standing, for such is a dereliction of duty, a casting out of our sacred Hippocratic oath; and without the utmost adherence to that oath we are mere pretenders, impostors... *quacks, if you will*; hence, I believe that neither Dr Ferguson nor I could accommodate your wish to take to the coach.'

Pat came down to earth quickly, a sigh of despond succeeding outrage and protest, 'I see. I dare say you are in the right of things; but let me tell you that when the First Lord commands, it is for us mere mortals to obey... and that is whatever inconvenience might result.'

'Sir, I speak not of inconvenience but of mortal danger, were any infection to afflict your leg. Dr Ferguson was concerned for the possibility... *the possibility*, sir... of amputation; and, whilst we have shelved such concerns for the present, an uncomfortable - *indeed, arduous* - journey such that the coach invariably offers would present inestimable dangers... *inestimable ones*, sir. No, it is quite impossible; neither I nor Dr Ferguson could conceivably countenance such... *we will not.*'

'Very well,' murmured Pat, though in truth he gave such concerns little weight. 'Perhaps we will send Reeve and *Mathew Jelbert* to Devonport to send news with the telegraph...' A pause, 'On reflection, I cannot credit that Melville will be satisfied with that. Doubtless he will perceive of me sitting down here... far from his province... and with my hands tucked square in my pockets and my feet upon a chair... and likely clutching a glass of grog! No, that will not do.'

'Will I say, Pat, that Simon and myself have a greatly pressing urgency to return to the Isles.' Duncan interrupted Pat's train of thought. 'You will recall that my wife is afflicted by the consumption... and Simon is much concerned about the loss of his home and what will happen to... *to his intended... to Mrs MacDougall... and her bairns*. I venture those are truly his and my concerns, *ones of the utmost express*. I will also venture that I cannae see Simon ever stepping aboard a ship-of-war ever again, for I havnae ever seen him so greatly reduced.'

The statement struck the strongest of chords, 'I am not... *not unaware* of his... the diminution of his energies...' Pat's voice tailed off. 'It is a sorry state of affairs, is it not? We are all mightily set back... I am, myself, mortally cast down.'

'Sir, not wishing to be in the least considered to be presumptuous, may I make a suggestion... if it is of interest? Perhaps it may be of some small practical value?' Marston seized the moment, perceiving an absence of clarity, a void, in the thinking of his friends.

'Please,' Pat, utterly deflated and bereft of the least notion, nodded.

'Plainly, there is scarcely a man amongst us who is fit in body or - *will I say, and speaking frankly - even in mind* to take to the coach... to the roads for London at the behest of their Lordships. It is clear to me, sir - *perfectly clear* - that Mr Macleod and Dr Ferguson *must take to the sea...* to gain their homes in the Isles and at the earliest opportunity; for their personal circumstances dictate such a course without question - *without the least question*. But how to get there? I suggest, sir, with your kind forbearance, that they make passage aboard our consort vessel, *Mathew Jelbert*. I further suggest - *indeed, I must insist* - that *you yourself* do accompany them, for you are not the man who will sit idle in Falmouth with such a concern for your friends weighing heavy upon your mind.'

'What? Will I ignore the First Lord's call... his order, a most explicit one? Come, Mr Marston, that is nigh on mutiny. I grant you we are not at sea, but that will be how Melville will take it.'

'Sir, I learned a long time ago that Captain Patrick O'Connor would solve the most protracted quandary... would resolve the most dangerous dilemma... *would always find his way*. I have observed that process on many an occasion, and that is what we must now do... with all our shoulders put to the wheel and guided by Our Lord. I do not say there is a perfect answer, no; for I have long ago also learned that such rarely exists, but an answer can be found, I'm sure of it.'

'Well, perhaps there is something in what you say,' replied Pat, 'and I confess that my intellects may not be shining as bright as might be. You may have remarked upon it...' And then came a stirring of thoughts amidst the confusion, offering a little light upon the matter, scarcely an inkling and little more, but it was enough; it swung Pat's mind to a state more receptive of Marston's efforts, 'However, I will reflect upon your statement... *Michael*; yes, I will consider of it.'

Duncan, who had been following Marston's suggestions with a fascination which was absolute, for the chaplain had never before ventured on to the hallowed ground which was his captain's decision-making, felt a great flush of warmth rising within him for the man, for he had never sought his advice on a personal basis, as both his close friends had on several occasions; and the explanation of why they had felt able to do so was here before him, and he understood, perfectly: Marston was far more than solely the ship's chaplain, far more too than the assistant surgeon; he was a friend, a sage even, and a man who could be turned to in the most dire spells of distress, indecision and quandary. 'Pat,' he felt obliged to contribute, for the moment was now and could not be postponed or the prospect of a solution set aside, 'I am minded that Marston... *Michael*... is in the right of things.'

Murphy, previously hovering just outside the door with determined curiosity, had listened to all of the conversation, and he hastened in with the much-cooled coffee pot to set it down upon the table. Pat, absently, waved him away, but the steward ignored the dismissal and simply stood, a yard back, until Pat looked at him with a disgruntled awareness of his presence. 'Murphy, what are you about? Do you have nothing more to do? Is there a want of clothes for washing? Speak up, man!'

'Well, sorr, *my* old grandma always said to me... *do not keep your tongue under your belt.*'

Duncan and Marston, astonished, both smiled wide, which Pat could not fail to notice. 'What are we coming to in the cabin? The accursed committee is upon us?' he pronounced eventually in mild voice, though in the poor light of the cabin, nothing of the morning light reaching the shattered stern gallery, his audience were unsure of whether he spoke in anger or in jest. 'Have we arrived at some infernal democracy?' he continued, 'Are we come to a shipboard republic?'

Murphy knew well his captain's temperament of old, understood perfectly how far he might speak to him with a controlled air of indignance, with an injured or even a put-upon inflection of voice, one always pitched no further than the limit which he knew Pat would countenance before angry remonstration would result, and he spoke in a voice held at that perfect boundary, 'Well, begging your honour's pardon, sorr; Mr Marston has said it right... *Get down on your knees and thank God you're still on your feet...* my grandma again, it was.'

Pat gaped at his steward for a mere moment of reflection, angry rebuke on the very tip of his tongue, before his charged demeanour visibly subsided and he replied in more gentle voice, 'I am sure your grandma and mine would have made the best of friends. Is there any more of your wisdom this morning, Murphy? Is there anything else which might answer the case?'

'Well, sorr, you should never stop the plough to kill a mouse.'

At this both Duncan and Marston burst into loud laughter, and even Pat managed a smile; for the former spell of despond, angst and morose exasperation was broken, much to the relief of all at the table. 'Murphy, I thank you for such pearls... and we must hope that they are not cast before swine; indeed, I think not. In fact, I believe that you may have changed the current of my thinking. Will you do me a great favour? Light along to the galley and fetch a *hot* pot of coffee - to aid our considerations, this one is now cold - *for we must turn our attention to your advice!* Perhaps we might next hear you grace our table with a few words of the Latin, eh?' Another burst of laughter followed and Murphy grinned wide before leaving in haste before his captain might add condemnation with a scolding.

Duncan spoke first, 'Pat, I believe that Michael has made the bones of a plan. Were you minded to agree, then you, Simon and I will sail to the Isles aboard *Mathew Jelbert*. Mr Reeve will take the barky to Devonport - I dare say Mr Prosser will accompany him - where her damages may be assessed and her repairs countenanced; at least we may hope that such will be the case. Mr Marston will remain here in Falmouth to attend the sick and wounded of our people, and so it must fall to Mr Jason to take the coach to London with such tidings as you may care to impart to their Lordships. What do you say to that?'

'It is a rum venture, no doubt,' murmured Pat doubtfully; 'Perhaps the morning will bring a clearer view.'

'Sir,' Marston followed a long pause, 'may I suggest that we turn our endeavours towards writing the most modest of speeches in preparation for our attendance at the chapel this evening... in case you should be called upon?'

Pat and all his officers arrived outside the Methodist Chapel to an exuberant welcome from those of *Surprise's* crew who were not confined to their beds with sickness or wounds. A great host of local people, including the families of both present and former crew members, were waiting too; and so the mutual greetings were effusive, an all-enveloping ambience of warmth between all persons present promoting the most cordial of exchanges between everyone. The officers' standing and rank was not wholly forgotten but observed in the gentlest of fashion, and presented no bar to many a discussion, all hesitations quickly subsumed within mere minutes by warm greetings and mutual wishes of infinite goodwill, all words expressed with the utmost benevolence, from which Pat found a degree of comfort; for his own heartfelt anxieties were enduring still.

For all present it was a reassurance, a confirmation, that, despite the casualties, both wounded and dead, that familial bond which was the longstanding and enduring cohesion between all the people of the small seafaring community yet held firm, the tenure of something so very precious was perpetuated; and for that, as the sense of it registered within the mind, everyone was profoundly grateful, Pat more so than many; for, in truth, he had dreaded encountering the families of those of his men who had not returned. The feelings of loss had long haunted him, tormented him even, and he could not cast off the black spell; it oppressed him and it had reduced him to nervous apprehension as he stood, largely silent, gazing all about him at scores of his people and the hundreds more who were their families; and at every small group upon which his eyes fell and where there was not a one of his men present, his spirits fell lower and lower as a despairing sensation of guilt slowly crept up upon him, until he felt it was akin to the great weight of the world, and his own spirits became much diminished.

Mower appeared from within the crowd to stand before Pat, a stooped, elderly lady at his side, somewhat wizened in her lined face, 'Sir, I am sure you will recall Mrs Jelbert.'

'Why, of course. How do you do, Mrs Jelbert?'

'Emblyn, sir, *'tis Emblyn*; for we are friends,' Mrs Jelbert spoke up in warm voice, smiling as she took Pat's hand.

'Of course, we are; I beg your pardon, I do,' declared Pat. 'I trust you are keeping well?'

'Certainly, I am, sir. I am come this evening in hope of seeing you. I wish to thank you for bringing back young Jago safely to his family... bringing him home. I thank you from the bottom of my heart.'

Pat was utterly overwhelmed in a mere instant, bowled over by the surge of emotion which enveloped him totally; Mrs Jelbert had lost her husband, Mathew, and her son, Annan, aboard the barky in the fighting of previous years; and yet she was here and with only warmth exhibited towards him for bringing back her grandson. He could find no words, could not say the least thing in that intense moment of profound shock; and he floundered, completely taken aback.

Mower, sensing his captain's dismay, interjected, 'Sir, Mrs Jelbert has asked if she may sit with you during the service.'

'What?' mumbled Pat; 'Yes; yes, of course.' He looked to Mrs Jelbert with a profound sense of admiration, 'Emblyn, it would be an honour... it would be so... was you to sit with me... and I thank you for the precious notion, I do; thank you.'

'May I thank you again, sir, for your kind help this past year? The pension that you established for me has been a Godsend, it has so.'

'No thanks are necessary... not at all, not a word... I do assure you.'

In that moment there was a loud call from the chapel door to call in the congregation, and the crowd began to enter. Pat, with Mower and Mrs Jelbert, was swept along in the crush until they all found seats a few rows short of the front and the pulpit.

272

As the minister began to speak, to introduce the purpose of the exceptional service, the whispers of the gathering were reduced to silence, a great sense of occasion settling upon everyone present; for, in truth, it was more than a Thanksgiving, it was also a wake, a remembrance for those Falmouth men who would never return home save only in the recollections and enduring dreams of their loved ones. Twenty minutes in and a deeply introspective Pat stared all about him; within many of the pews he could see ladies in tears; even some of the men of his crew, old salts that they were, were similarly afflicted; and his own feelings sank lower until he was entirely gripped by an immobility both of mind and body, something of a trauma.

More minutes passed by, entirely unnoticed by Pat who was consumed within his own slow musings, until the minister paused to assess his congregation, the chapel falling into an expectant silence, the sense of occasion utterly overbearing. From around the hall, from widely separated pews, quiet sobbing could be heard. Subdued that it was or could be, the low weeping remained audible in the general quietude; not everyone's grief could be held at bay. The minister eventually concluded his sweeping inspection to his own satisfaction, all murmurings from the pews gradually falling away, and he spoke up in firm voice, 'Captain O'Connor has been asked if he would like to speak for a brief moment... to offer a few words.' He looked towards Pat, 'If you please and are so inclined, sir.'

Pat, sitting frozen within painful reflections, his sensory perceptions dulled, remained oblivious to the invitation and to the low chorus of 'Hear, Hear,' which flowed around the hall like a gently breaking wave on a gravel beach: muted, soft, arriving slowly as if the wash of the tide was announcing the future, the imminently forthcoming moment. Sitting on his left side, Simon Ferguson gently nudged his elbow and whispered in a voice that was scarcely more than silence, 'Brother, you are called to speak.'

However, Pat could not shake off a mental immobility; nor, seemingly, could he find in that moment the least physical strength or conviction to rise from his seat; and so he sat, frozen in something akin to fear for a near full minute as the gentle calls of endorsement from the congregation faded to a puzzled silence; and still he could not dispel the powerful grip of the two twins of regret and guilt, surging feelings of which coursed through all his thoughts in flashes of recollection and momentary images of lost shipmates; all such struck hard upon his mind in a sea of confusion. An absolute silence now pervaded the hall but heads were turning to stare, and then the merest scintilla of a whisper could be heard from here and there about the hall, until Pat stirred at last; 'I cannot find the draft,' he murmured to Simon in a frightened voice, 'I have lost it.'

Michael Marston leaned over Pat's shoulder, passed a single sheet of paper and whispered, 'Sir, here is my copy, if you will.'

Emblyn Jelbert, sitting at Pat's side - she had observed his distress - squeezed his hand tight, until Pat turned to look at her, his own face the strangest of melds, of both the gratitude which he felt in his heart and the sustained fear that he felt in his mind. His throat and stomach too were both nervously afflicting him, and he could find no words. Gradually, he rose to his feet, clutching the precious paper, and he walked infinitely slowly towards the pulpit, his heart racing, pounding; his mind was all awhirl with the most frightening sensations, ones which he could not formulate as firm thoughts. He reached the pulpit and somehow and without faltering he managed the few steps and stood, gazing all across the hall upon an infinity of silent people all staring back at him, waiting, expectant; and in that moment he felt an enormous weight of responsibility mixed with guilt: guilt that he was here before the families of men who were not returning, could never do so, all of them physically consigned to a watery oblivion. Another minute passed, or ten - *for so it seemed to Pat* - but slowly his thoughts crystallised, the overburden of crushing sentiment was somehow controlled, at least held at bay, as he saw that everyone, everywhere within his vision within the chapel, was waiting on his words in an utterly respectful silence; indeed, Mrs Jelbert was smiling at him. The fleeting thought that struck him in that instant was to wonder whether they could all see plain his distress.

He bit hard on his lip and slowly he began to speak, softly at first but with a rising conviction and volume, 'My dear friends... *all of you*... for more than thirty years I have been a sailor in His Majesty's Royal Navy... For twelve of those years, together with many seafarers of Falmouth, I fought against the tyrant, Bonaparte... to preserve freedom in our own cherished isles... and for these past three years we... that is... my men and I, *we, together*, have fought against another tyrant... to help *another people*, the Greeks... to gain *their* freedom.'

A momentary hesitation and Pat looked up and cast his gaze across the entire hall, and his anxious eyes registered that everyone was receptive, was listening, all were waiting for him in patient silence; and so he resumed, finding a beginning of confidence, 'We have been engaged in a long war, and aboard our home at sea, HMS SURPRISE, we have met a fierce enemy on many an occasion when... to our great dismay... we have lost shipmates... our revered friends; indeed, they were truly *our family at sea*, all of them...'

Pat, emotions on fire once more, could feel his eyes filling, and he blinked rapidly to dispel the liquid before it might begin to flow, before it might be perceived by the hundreds of people attending his words, 'We are gathered here today to remember and respect those stalwart men of this town who devoted and ultimately gave their lives... that freedom might - *will, God willing*, emerge for those peoples in a far distant place of which we know but little...'

He felt for the first time the watery flow down his cheeks, now become an unabated flood, and he struggled to read his words, for they were obscured by his tears, 'We... the living... cannot tend their graves, nor can we consecrate any places where they might lie... at rest, for that is not our way... *cannot be*... aboard ships at sea... but we take great pride... and, too, consolation... that our brothers did not die in vain... for they fought for a cherished cause... one which is so precious to us all... and so they will remain forever in our memories... and in our hearts and minds... as bearers of that true flame... which is *freedom!*'

At last, the end of his brief moment had come, and Pat hoped that the audience could not perceive his now uncontrollable distress, for in the last moments his voice and his hands had begun to shake. With a determination and with difficulty he strived once more for a voice which he hoped might not betray his faltering spirits, and he finished, 'God bless them. God bless you all... Thank you.'

Pat paused, immobile, to gather his breath and his thoughts, for his speech had drained him, utterly. It registered with him that his wounded leg had begun to tremor uncontrollably. For the briefest moment silence reigned in the hall, and then the applause began, vigorous hand-clapping from everyone in the chapel. Within a minute this was followed by loud cheering from all the *Surprise* veterans present, which went on and on, 'HURRAH! HURRAH!' The great tumult of noise was rising as bibles were thumped with determined force on the backs of pews throughout the hall; it was a bedlam never before seen in the chapel, a cacophony of loud applause which, seemingly, would never cease. The minister, succeeding Pat on the pulpit, reluctantly - for so it seemed to all persons watching - slowly raised his arms in the air in supplication, in an appeal for a cessation. Slowly the cheering, the bible-thumping and the hand-clapping drew to a close as an astonished and exhausted Pat stumbled hesitantly the few rows back towards his pew, pressed by all as he passed by to shake their hands. He regained his seat with huge relief, never before had one been so welcome. Mrs Jelbert seized his trembling hand and squeezed it gently, 'God love you, sir; I do.'

A sad evening was drawing to its eventual close, and the mood of the gathering around Pat's table was gloomy. A little of the fading dusk light lingered, offering a weak illumination through the stern panes; it was complemented by the feeble, yellow light of the lamps, already lit by Murphy, one on each side of the cabin. However, neither the darkling light nor the lamps managed to lift the depressing ambience in the cabin. Scarcely a word had been uttered in the mood of introspection, in the doldrums of glum reflection. The lingering small stock of red wine had been most severely depleted until, ultimately, it was succeeded by great depredations inflicted upon the final reserves of brandy and whisky, quite copious quantities of both consumed, greatly to Murphy's dismay, although he persisted with a reluctance which diminished only slowly. To no avail, for the spirits of all persons present were sinking in parallel with their liquid contemporaries, the utter failures of consolation that they proved to be.

Eventually Pat broke the silence, looking up and staring at his companions until all realised that he intended to speak, 'Mr Marston... *Michael*, I thank you for your most estimable words of today. I was a lost man, I was so.' Pat managed a small laugh, 'But you saved me, you did.'

A shocked Murphy, who had scarcely left the cabin save for a few hasty rushes to the liquor store, simply gaped, unaccustomed as he was to hearing such words from his captain.

'Sir, I beg to differ,' declared Marston, 'for those were *your* words, *your spoken words*, and that is the very essence of the matter. On paper, they are a mere feeble device; yet when spoken with conviction, as was the case in the chapel this evening, they gained an importance which far exceeds the written word. I must remind you, sir, that those sentiments were *your thoughts*, and I was only a helper... a mere assistant in their formulation. I doubt there is another man in Falmouth town or in any church of the land who could have spoken as you did this evening, and the success... *the acceptance* of your words was plain to see... and to hear. Your presence, sir, was a most commendable and surely heartfelt consolation to all those people attending. Your words... *your words*... were a great help to all of us, and I include myself, I do.'

'Hear, Hear,' murmured all present.

'Thank you, Michael; thank you all. That is a... a great comfort to me.' A minute of silence passed, all waiting, and Pat spoke again, a little of resolution returned to his voice, 'I am minded that Michael's plan... which I have been thinking about this evening since we returned aboard the barky, is one which we will follow. On the morrow we will set things in train: Mr Reeve will sail the barky to Devonport; Mr Jason will post up to London to report to the First Lord - *my God, I wish I could be there to see that encounter!'* Pat laughed, 'I do beg your pardon, Abel. Duncan, Simon... we will shape our course for Mull... aboard *Mathew Jelbert*... We will depart at the very crack of dawn; yes, we will; and Michael, you are to remain in Falmouth to attend our wounded shipmates...'

'Lord, Marston, I shall miss you,' a visibly dismayed Simon unexpectedly blurted out his anguished interruption.

'As will I miss you, dear colleague,' murmured Marston, visibly much set back; 'But please to set aside all disquietude... and be assured - *for I have no doubt, not the least* - that Our Lord will ever be at your side.'

Simon could find no words of reply and was reduced to simply staring, becoming bewildered by the events all about him, as if overtaken by the swift and imminent change about to beset him.

'Gentlemen,' Pat broke the consequent, hanging silence of the intimate moment, 'Let us take a few minutes in reflection, I beg you will.' Silent nods were offered all about the table and Pat resumed eventually, 'We will await Murphy... I venture he is now about the toasted cheese... has set things in train...' Pat's voice faltered, for he was himself somewhat lost for words. Finding a modicum of fortitude, he continued, 'Perhaps this is the occasion to broach any lingering bottles of the best port wine we may still possess...

the one with the red seal... the precious standby that it always is... *if Murphy ain't drunk it all, the rogue!'* The realisation that the dawn would see a parting of the ways and that it would be a painful one had struck hard; the end of a precious companionship was here before them all, and the prospective but only written bond of a remote, distant friendship was no consolation in the least. Pat, much set back himself, could see that plainly in the dismay on his friends' faces, but he persisted, 'I have always considered a capital port wine to be something of a comforter.'

His words, the straw to clutch that was offered, did not seem to be grasped by anyone, for the table remained silent; introspection had overtaken them all once more; even Murphy hesitated, no move made towards the treasure trove that he considered the liquor store to be. And so, as the twilight faded, all discourse lapsed with it and the evening eventually ended, all energies dissipated and all minds much unsettled as everyone returned to their cots to claim what sleep they could find.

Pat, much disturbed by myriad thoughts, lay awake for hours, listening, but nothing did he hear; the silence was absolute, and although welcome it was uncomfortable at the same time; there was nothing audible of note from the wind in the calm of the night; neither was there the familiar wash of the wake about the rudder, nor anything of the customary creaking of the rigging under strain, and never too the familiar ringing out of the ship's bell every half-hour, for near every man of the crew was ashore and the glass was no longer turned; and so, in his wakefulness, his concerns and anxieties lingered to oppress his thoughts until exhaustion finally claimed him just a few hours before the dawn.

Chapter Eleven

On a clear spring morning, the welcome daylight a warming throw of low rays from the eastern sky, and in the slack water before the ebb of the tide, a tired Pat made passage from the barky to the Greenbank Quay aboard the launch, accompanied by Murphy and Duncan, few words spoken as the six oarsmen pulled across the hundred yards in a mutual ambience of hesitation, as if mere words could not carry the essential meaning, the sense of trepidation, that all felt, every man much aware that it might be the leaving of the dear *Surprise* for the final time. The sun was already rising well above the top of the St Mawes peninsula, offering its bright greeting as Pat hauled himself up the vertical ladder at the sea wall, assisted by Reeve with a hand at the top. 'Good morning, Mr Reeve. Thankfully, it seems that we are blessed with a fine one.'

'Good morning, sir; indeed, it is.'

'It would seem that I am a trifle late. Is *Mathew Jelbert* ready to sail... watered and provisioned?'

'She is, sir; stores for five days were loaded last night from the King's Arms Inn larder. Mr Selley would not take a penny in payment.'

'That is uncommon civil of him,' exclaimed Pat. 'I had thought we were condemned to endure hard tack, the leavings even of the millers.'

'Never in life, sir. Selley has a nephew, George Chard, serving aboard the barky.'

'Chard; yes, a larbowlin, and he serves Bolitho's gun, *Tempest*, if my memory serves me; a capital hand.'

Reeve nodded, 'He has been singing your praise to his uncle, sir, since the service last night.'

'Has he indeed?'

'Dr Ferguson is waiting for you inside the hotel; Mr Jason and Mr Marston are both attending.'

'Very good; let us go in.'

Pat and Duncan, Murphy following, entered the reception hall of the hotel, a quite imposing room, before stepping into the parlour, which offered a sweeping view of the harbour towards a distant Carrick Roads. Pat's eyes lingered on the anchored *Surprise*, a momentary flurry of recollections and regrets flooding his mind; thankfully short-lived as the host, Thomas Selley, escorted his visitors to their seats. 'Sirs, we have fresh coffee and a fine breakfast prepared for you.'

'Thank you, Mr Selley,' murmured Pat, 'but I regret to say that my purse is quite depleted... *finished even.*'

'We will pay that no mind, sir; it's on the house.'

'Most generous, Mr Selley, most civil; you have my best thanks,' Pat, somewhat taken aback, insisted on shaking Selley's hand before he took his seat with all his officers. The attentive waiter poured coffee whilst another swiftly presented plates laden with the finest breakfast that Pat could ever recall, certainly so at sea: a plethora of sausages, bacon, eggs and black pudding in magnificent quantities, and a tray of hot toast was deposited upon the centre of the table.

'Well, gentlemen,' declared Pat with a rising pleasure, 'this is quite the welcome start to our day. Please, do not stand on ceremony; do begin.'

Twenty minutes of determined feasting and the trays were reduced to stark emptiness, bereft of even the least crumb. Murphy too had eaten his fill or at least everything that everyone else had not consumed, and he sat at the side of the room in a state of complete satiation, ignoring the burning indigestion which had already fiercely beset him whilst listening with fascination to the conversation about the table.

'Mr Reeve,' Pat reluctantly returned to the present, 'Mr Prosser has informed me that he will be with you for the voyage to Devonport. I am in fear of what the Master Shipwright will say to you when he espies the damages to the

barky, for Edward Churchill is a man who speaks his mind!'
Pat laughed, a welcome sight for his friends.

'I have fifty men standing ready to depart for the Dock,
sir,' replied Reeve. 'When will you have us leave?'

'I am sure the morrow will serve... or even - will I suggest
- late on Wednesday. Admiral Saumarez will no doubt ask
you a deal of questions when you arrive, *which you will be
obliged to answer truthfully*. Do not venture the least untruth -
no black lies! - for he will most assuredly smoke any evasions,
and I would not care to be chased down by a frigate before I
have rounded the Lizard...' Laughs erupted from all around
the table '... and I am already a month late to begin the
infernal peat cutting!' The ensemble laughed louder, Pat
included, and he paused momentarily for reflection,
wondering if, perhaps, the long-held burden of strain was
lightening just a very little. 'Doubtless too Admiral Pellew
here will remark the state of the barky, and his brother
Samuel, the Excise Collector of the port, will certainly have
his ear to the ground.'

Pat turned to Jason, 'Mr Jason, was you to accompany Mr
Reeve aboard the barky on Wednesday, then - *with a friendly
westerly* - you will surely arrive at Devonport on Thursday
morning. There is a coach which departs the Dock Gate in the
morning for Exeter - *which you will likely be too late for* - and
another from that place to Bristol, and thence to London. If
this weather holds then it will not be too arduous or cold a
journey for those three more days it will take you to reach the
Admiralty; and was you to arrive at the weekend then it would
likely be Monday before you can present yourself to the First
Lord. Mrs O'Donnell at the Feathers tavern in the Liberty of
Westminster will be pleased to accommodate you; she is a
grand friend of mine. Here is a note I have prepared for
Melville. We might hope that he will believe it... else I fear he
will hang you!' Everyone laughed once more, something of a
sense of relief pervading.

'Mr Marston - *Michael* - it is nigh on time to say
goodbye,' Pat's voice dropped to little more than a whisper,

'but allow me to say that... although the future has never seemed less certain than at present... indeed, there is truly an ocean of doubt before us all... I will ever keep in mind those kind words you have offered me in the most difficult... the most dreadful... of times these three years gone... aboard the barky. I am in your debt, I am so; and I will ever be proud to call you friend.'

From all at the table came a rousing round of applause and loud shouts of 'Hear! Hear!' All of Selley's other patrons stared from every table in the lounge as Pat, casting all formality to the wind, embraced Marston in a hug. Everyone rose from their chairs as one, and a great deal of handshaking followed, until Pat signalled a move towards the door.

Simon lingered to speak with Marston, for the two of them had also become the closest of friends; for each had looked to the other for support in many a distressing moment.

In that instant, as the party exited to the reception hall, four men were waiting to present themselves; Prosser, Codrington, Pickering and Mower had all appeared to say goodbye. 'Gentlemen,' Pat joked, 'I begin to think that I will miss my tide!'

Eventually and with halting progress, with heartfelt farewells offered with reluctance, the quay was reached and Simon was carefully assisted down the ladder to gain the deck of *Mathew Jelbert*, anxious eyes following his precarious progress. When all were aboard Duncan called out, 'Cast off for'ard, Barton; cast off aft, Murphy.' The tide demonstrating the increasing flow of its ebb, the cutter was immediately pulled from the quay and so to the channel and away towards the Carrick Roads as Reeve, Marston, Jason, Prosser, Codrington, Pickering and Mower - Thomas Selley too - all waved farewell from the sea wall.

Wednesday 31st May 1826   *12:00*   *Irish Sea*

Noon, Land's End left far astern, and *Mathew Jelbert* was proving her sea-keeping attributes to Pat's immense satisfaction, running at near seven knots within the influence of the steady south-westerly wind on her larboard quarter. The pilot cutter was making a most creditable passage as she dipped into the successive wave troughs of a benign Irish Sea, a constant splash of saltwater flying up and back over the bow and washing aft all along the deck. Pat was revelling in the joyful experience of sailing in a small vessel upon an open sea; no more the organisation of two hundred and fifty men to consider; nothing of the rote of changes of watch, nor the ordained diktat of the ship's bell and its consequent bustle of diverse activities to pay heed to; nothing of the towering heights of three masts with their acres of canvas and miles of rigging to observe, all of which demanded a constant attention, a perpetual flurry of maintenance, much to-ing and fro-ing. No, he was thankful that there was nothing of that ilk to blight his spirits; and his cutter, for she was his personal possession, was doing all that she was built for and more, and with the casual but enthusiastic assistance of only Duncan and Barton; and so Pat delighted in the sense of freedom and immersed himself in an utterly *ad hoc* attention to the wind and the sails, little change ever required in the prevailing wind and weather. All distressing thoughts of Greece, all unwelcome concerns about the Admiralty, were left behind, forgotten, cast aside with joyful abandon as he wrestled with and managed *Mathew Jelbert* with commensurate skill through the strong winds and the chop of the sea, and with an enjoyment which he could not quite recollect feeling for a very long time; indeed, every moment passed in the most exquisite release from that long-held purgatory which had oppressed him for an age in the Greek war.

The sea state had steadily increased in intensity since the rounding of Land's End, building to its present turbulence since the cutter passed by the Gower a few hours after the dawn; so much so that the lee rail was occasionally subsumed within the foam of the wake, at the sight of which Pat marvelled; his pleasure in the predictable motion, in the surety of stability of his vessel, was something of a considerable pride and joy, the feeling so utterly sublime. He breathed

284

deeply as if such by the very action he would further suppress any lingering demons of downcast spirits, and for hour after delightful hour he held firm to the tiller himself, taking huge satisfaction in holding it tight, secure, and only occasionally spelled by an admiring Barton, to whom he conceded the control with reluctance and an enduring smile, few words offered and none necessary between two longstanding shipmates.

Every hour without fail Murphy presented another small satisfaction in the form of a tin cup filled with hot coffee, properly leavened - as Murphy saw things - with a generous tot of rum, and to Pat's silent inquisition after the first taste he offered confirmation only in the form of a nod and a near-toothless grin. A seemingly happy Murphy lingering near the helm, Pat sipped his coffee in a mood of the utmost satisfaction, until after ten minutes or so he ventured a few words to his steward, 'It is quite the glory to be at the helm of this uncommon delightful vessel, Murphy, when she is put to her shifts... so small that she is after the barky.'

'Well, sorr, there be as many good horses in carts as in coaches.'

'Now there's something of a pearl of wisdom from the Old Country, eh?' Pat smiled wide. 'Do you ever have the yearning to get back there, to Ireland, to Galway, to the town itself? I confess I am with child with the thought of tying up at the Cleggan quay. What do you have to say about that?'

'Well, sorr, your feet will bring you to where your heart is.'

'Your grandma again, no doubt!' exclaimed Pat, his own pleasure plain to see in his face; and Murphy too smiled wide; a rare occurrence, thought Pat: *perhaps for him too the oppressive burden was also lifting?* 'I begin to enjoy that rising feeling of certainty that *Mathew Jelbert* really will bring me to where my heart truly is, to Connemara, where my feet may again stride across the peat, where I will gaze from the cliffs upon that *steepe Atlantic stream*, and where I will thank God that I am alive and at home with my beloved family.

Perhaps I am coming it the poet, eh?' Pat beamed with the pleasure of those very thoughts. 'But first we will look to the needs of our friends.'

Simon appeared on deck, much to the consternation of his companions who followed his every stumbling step with apprehension, fearful that he might slip and injure himself or even fall overboard, for such had been known. 'This is quite the refreshing experience, Pat,' he shouted with an enforced enthusiasm immediately before a surge of salt spray caught him full in the face, dousing his enthusiasm completely.

'Indeed, it is! Clap on! One hand for the ship!' Pat seized his arm and held it tight until Simon established a precarious balance near the stern, clinging with a desperate determination to the larboard rail. 'How are you faring... in this chop?'

'I confess to a modicum of unease in the motions,' Simon gasped.

'The motions? I much regret myself that without Wilkins we must endure Murphy's endeavours in the cooking line. Would you care for a biscuit? A dry one might answer. Forgive me if I am coming it the medical man!' Pat laughed before a thoughtful pause, 'Did you mean that you are afflicted - *incommoded* - with something of an indisposition when you attend the head... the seat of ease?'

'Not at all, I beg your pardon for my imprecise turn of phrase. I merely referred to the vigorous swell... the significant rise and fall of the floor in this discommodious - *this more minor* - vessel; a sloop would she be? I will have you know I have learned a great deal about many a variety of vessels these three years gone.'

Pat had considerable doubts about that, well-founded ones, he was sure; but he replied without the least inference of such in his voice, 'Not at all, she is no sloop but a cutter.'

'Yet I counted the masts, and she has but one.'

'Indeed, she does, and so has the sloop; I speak of *the smaller* sloop, the Bermuda, not the ship of war.'

'Then I cannot grasp how you can credibly discountenance my assessment.'

'Why, you were doubtless misled by the rig.'

'Oh, she has a rig too? It is quite the complexity.'

Pat smiled and reconciled himself to an explanation which he was sure his friend would probably not grasp or, more likely, quickly forget; for he was long convinced that Simon's mind ran on quite different lines, 'The sloop differs in that she may, on occasion, boast a square-rigged sail hoisted on a yard at the top, whilst the cutter likely possesses of a larger jib *or even two*. The jib is that sail which the mariner of some experience will generally hoist *forward* of the mast.' Pat made his declaration with a hint of ridicule in his voice and a self-indulgent complacency in his manner, which did not escape Simon's ear or eye.

'I see; and the *inexperienced* mariner - *the relative beginner* - might - *on occasion* - hoist it *behind* the mast?' Simon persisted, deprecating Pat's humour at his expense.

'No, not at all; no sensible soul would be minded to hoist such a sail behind - *aft* - of the mast, *never in life!*'

'Then you suggest that the experience *or lack thereof* of the mariner is irrelevant to the process of hoisting that particular sail - *the jib* - or even two of them; is that not the case?'

'No; that is to say... now you have confused me, old Simon.'

'Indeed, and one might venture that you are *hoisted* by your own petard!' Simon laughed.

'I see you practice upon me,' declared Pat without the least irritation. The two friends settled to a contented silence, Simon gradually becoming accustomed to the wet nature of his clothing, which was not excessively uncomfortable, the top of the day keeping its warmth even in the cold spray splashing from the swell.

'This must be how the world was in the beginning,' declared Simon, ruminating aloud after a half-hour of silence; 'Nothing of a frenetic excitement happening and no man paying the least notion to time, save for the inevitable rise and fall of the sun; and perhaps the day passing with nothing other than a hunger to contemplate, yet firm in the conviction of a sure bounty of fish to catch or an animal to hunt...' Simon's voice tailed off, 'but then came politics and ultimately the dictatorships in all their forms to beset and oppress us.'

'I beg you will forgive me for reminding you that any mention of politics, even of governments - whether dictators or even such enthusiasts as the kipper codlings - will lead to the end of all comfortable talk, and more quickly so aboard this *exceedingly small* vessel - *this cutter.*'

'I beg your pardon, I am forgetting myself. When will we see our first sight of bonny Scotland, the Mull... *the peninsula?*'

'Which one? There are two.'

'Oh, I was not aware.'

'The first is Galloway and the second Kintyre. We have been most favourably blessed since clearing the Gower with a constant wind of ten knots, and I am minded that - blessed weather permitting, *and in June in these parts it generally is* - we might see the Isle of Man in the emerging twilight of the morning, see Galloway after breakfast and shave the Kintyre after dinner.'

'Sure, it is a beatific thought.'

'The sun lingers high for a long day in June - *you have probably remarked it,*' Pat's humour came more readily than it had for a long time but Simon affected not to notice, 'and the sunset is uncommon late; in the last days of May and through June it is nigh on nine o'clock; and so we are blessed with something of a long-enduring twilight and nothing of a total darkness as we navigate the Sound of Jura, skirt the Corryvreckan, find our way past the Slates towards the Sound of Mull, and so to gain Tobermory.'

Simon smiled, 'It is becoming quite the scenic passage and I am much taken by the tranquillity of our voyage; indeed, I believe I have found something of an internal quietude these recent days... in gazing upon this empty sea; such that I wish...' A brief pause, 'I wish we might sail on like this for ever.' Simon smiled again, a long-lingering satisfaction found in the moment, which much pleased Pat to see.

'I wish too that it might be so, old friend, but I am minded that we will likely tie up at the quay mid-morning on Friday.'

'Thank you for your benevolent prophecy, brother.' A long and thoughtful interlude followed, a mutual awareness of a profound satisfaction resting upon both men being recognised, minutes passing, until Simon spoke once more, 'Tell me one thing, if you will.'

'Sure, anything.'

'I have always been minded that the origins of your particular surname, *being O'Connor*, and your home, Connemara, must likely evidence a Catholic origin. If such is the case, how were you able to become a Royal Navy officer? Forgive me if you consider I am become the least bit impertinent... *or leaning towards the political line.*'

'Oh, I will pay that no mind. Yes, I was born a Catholic, to a family of the most modest standing and without influence; but in my early years my grandma pressed my parents to bring me up as a Protestant.'

'And why did she do so, pray tell?' Simon was intrigued, and so he resumed, never before having felt sufficiently comfortable to raise such a delicate subject within the cabin, the prohibition of all political talk being absolute in the past. 'It seems an exceptional diversion from any norm, particularly so in those more distant parts of His Majesty's realm; if you will forgive me for saying so.'

'Indeed, it certainly was. I have always been led to understand that my father once had occasion to resort to moneylenders, and a cousin of his who lived in the King's County, a peat cutter of the Clara Bog - *an uncle I never did meet* - described a man of money, a banker if you will, who lived in Warrenstown.'

'Is that place proximate to Connemara?'

'It is a hundred and fifty miles away, on the long road to distant Dublin, and no mean journey to undertake for a man who worked seven days a week, rarely possessed a spare shilling and owned but a single donkey. My father - *for so the story goes* - was vouched for by his priest, such that he was able to borrow fifteen pounds from that moneylender; but little did he know, until it was remarked when he repaid the capital, that the lender was Admiral Sir Peter Warren, who is something of a legend in those parts. He had himself been born a Catholic but was raised as a Protestant, and some years later he swore the oath and joined the Royal Navy, ultimately to become a renowned admiral... even a Knight of the Bath! What a splendid tale to tell, eh?'

'Most certainly; I am astounded, brother, I am.'

'And so it was my own grandma, the precious dear, who - upon hearing that tale from my mother - made my father swear to raise me as a Protestant; and you are to consider that my grandma was a woman who spoke not a word of English; she only ever used the Gaelic tongue! She coaxed me - *whenever I visited 'Shark* - in the grand tale, such that I might follow the path of Warren; for there was no other prospect for an enterprising young man to be found anywhere in Connemara, save to be a poor fisherman or an impoverished peat cutter. There, old Simon, you have it, my life story.'

'Fascinating!'

'And now I am, myself, to become an impoverished peat cutter when I fetch home... on my twelve acres of bog!' Pat laughed and Simon laughed with him. 'The world surely turns in great circles, does it not?'

'So, I have always understood.'

'Well, sorrs, coffee's up!' declared Murphy, arriving and pleased to see his charges in good humour.

Friday 2nd June 1826   09:00   Tobermory, Mull

Mathew Jelbert near drifted to the end of the pier at Tobermory in the flow of a rising tide, having made slow but uneventful passage through the Sound of Mull since the low light of the dawn in a weak and failing wind. Barton hastened to the ladder before Simon might set foot upon it. He swiftly tied up the mooring ropes thrown by Murphy, and he turned in haste to offer a hand to an enthusiastic man who had reached his home and was already venturing upon the slippery rungs. 'Have a care there, Ferguson!' shouted Pat.

At the top of the pier the Surprises gathered, Simon in a degree of excitement. 'Barton, look to the tide,' declared Pat, 'I venture there may be a want of water here at low tide. You are to take the cutter out and anchor when the ebb begins. We will repair to the Mull Inn at the head of the pier and await news when Dr Ferguson returns from his home.'

'Aye aye, sir.'

'My home is but a short distance away,' declared Simon, walking along the pier in a meld of excitement and anxiety, 'I will be no more than an hour.' Pat and Duncan nodded and proceeded to enter the inn as Simon hastened away.

Quickly reaching his cottage, Simon stared at the bleakest of scenes, for there was no sign of habitation. The door was locked, which was unexpected, for he had never before found cause to lock it; nor would anyone answer his increasingly desperate knocking upon the door with his clenched hand; and his loud shouts at the window were all to no avail. He returned to the door and beat upon it again, striking it with a fury, so hard that it bruised his hand and he had to halt. He stared in bleak dismay, a great tide of disappointment overwhelming him, his anxieties quickly overtaking all rational thought and becoming distress: *where was Flora? Where could her lassies be? Why was the door locked?* And then he remembered the key, secreted in a tiny hole in the wall below the window cill many years ago, and he fell to his knees and groped along the wall until his fingers found it, much encrusted with dirt. He returned to the door and after a minute of fiddling with the rusty key within a reluctant lock the door handle turned and he entered, brushing away the cobwebs which festooned his hair. The room was plainly unlived-in, gloomy, a dismaying vacancy before his anxious eyes, and the air reeked with the twin smells of damp and mould. On the interior window ledge a dozen dead flies and moths lay, unmoving, a testament to a long absence of all life, of warmth, the least thing. He stepped, so very slowly, through the dim light of the cold room, only burned ash remnants remaining in the fire place, an increasing despond consuming him as each minute passed, and a wave of dismay gripped his mind, seized his thoughts, as he recalled the very same feeling, thirteen years previously, when he had returned home from sea to find an empty home, his neighbour informing him of the death of his wife, Agnes; and his spirits sank to a low like never before.

Five minutes of dismaying speculation brought only further distress, until he was reduced to simply standing still, unable to formulate the least idea until, some minutes passing, with reluctance he turning about, to hurry back to the inn: *someone there would surely know what had happened to his beloved and her bairns, for Tobermory was such a tiny settlement, scarcely even a village.*

'Do you know anything of this small place, Duncan?' asked Pat as they awaited their whisky whilst standing in the parlour; 'I can scarcely count a dozen houses.'

'Your whiskies, sirs,' declared the landlord, returning to present two mutchkins in something of an air of small triumph to his Irish guest; 'Will 'ee care for hot water or sugar?'

Pat stared in near disbelief at the glass tumblers, 'Why, I dare say there's three-fourths of a pint in each! Does anyone ever order a second?' Pat laughed. 'No, no water nor any sugar, thank you.'

Duncan chortled too. 'It is the norm in these parts; there isnae any want of whisky here. I doubt the Customs House sees a tenth of what is drunk in the Isles; the King isnae a popular man in Scotland, nor his father before him. No, I havnae ever been here before,' he declared, returning to Pat's question. 'The village is a creation of the Fisheries Society. I have seen similar new settlements for myself in Lochbay and Ullapool after crossings from Harris and Lewis; and sad places they are.'

'Why is this happening, tell?'

'Those lairds of a - will I say - *grasping inclination* are evicting tenants from their crofts to make way for sheep to graze upon their land. Such destitute folk that the former crofters are now become are expected to support themselves as fishermen, though none possess either the knowledge or the boats, and nae capital to build any.'

'Why that is despicable... *monstrous!*' a shocked Pat exclaimed; 'Ireland has never recovered from such similar depredations. Was not Cromwell tyrant enough for all sensible men, for all love?'

'Aye, and it's worse: Ullapool remains quite ruined because the herring has long forsaken the Wester Ross fisheries for the Forth and the Tay; and so too all hopes of a Lochbay fishery are also finished; consequently, those folk who were shifted to the new villages have long been starving, and on account of such destitution each family was gifted half an acre in which to grow potatoes and the right for one cow to graze upon common pasture.'

'On my life, Duncan, that is a sad tale, *the saddest!*'

'Aye. In my own parish of South Harris, the laird is a most profligate wastrel and reputedly in much debt. The good-for-nothing squanderer *that he is* cleared out all the crofters of my own village, Rodel, in the year 'eighteen, a mere seven years after he inherited the estate from his father, a man who did strive to improve the lot of his crofters. Aye, the present dissolute rogue has sent all of them to a barren coast of moss over poor soil, where they are expected to fish and live on the potato; that is to say, if they do not incline to emigration... Canada has oft been suggested; aye, Nova Scotia - *New Scotland indeed!* And now there are but five tenants on Rodel's rich, red soil, which is the best in all of Harris; and all are sheep farmers, one of them being the laird's factor. The world is changing all about us, old friend, and it seems it isnae for the better,' Duncan concluded with a sigh.

'Let us set aside all talk of such lamentable policies,' murmured Pat with sinking feelings, 'about which we can do nothing.'

"Tobermory on the Isle of Mull"   William Daniell 1815   "A Voyage around Great Britain"   The furthermost building is/was the Mull Inn

'Aye, that is surely the case. You may recall that Simon mooted his dissatisfaction with such ill-conceived state and other interventions to Hastings... aboard the barky. They are an abomination to all principled men.'

'I remember the occasion perfectly well,' declared Pat, recovering his equilibrium; 'Another half-hour and I venture we might have resorted to pistols in the cabin!' Pat laughed aloud, for such was the underlying happiness that he felt. 'Thankfully, Hastings was a good-natured soul.' At that moment his ranging gaze fixed upon a solitary man sitting near the fire, his back turned to the servery. 'Upon my word, Duncan, I venture I know that fellow! Good Lord, that is Peddler! Peddler of all people, and in this remote place! I am amazed... *amazed!*'

'If you recall, Simon mentioned that his childhood was spent here and with Peddler; do you not remember?'

'Yes; indeed, he did; you are in the right of things. But the fellow plainly does not care to speak with us... *with me.* Perhaps that is because the rogue owes me a thousand pounds for the twenty percent shareholding he bought in my gold mine venture; indeed, his friend Perkiss also owes me two thousands for his forty percent.'

'Did you not say that any gold was yet to be found, that your wife lamented the great swathes of dross all about your land, that the local folk were unhappy about such developments?'

'Yes, that is the case; but a deal is a deal; at least it is in my book. Wait; here is Simon, returned.'

Simon entered the room in that moment, and to his friends' gaze, their heads turning away from the fire as he approached, he was plainly much set back. 'Landlord, a whisky for my friend, if you please,' declared Duncan swiftly.

'There is not a soul at my home,' Simon spoke in a voice of great dismay, 'Ne'er a one, and no sign of anyone being there for some time, for the curtains were drawn and I could gain entry with my key only with difficulty.' Simon's ranging eyes, an inability to concentrate upon his friends' attentions, focused upon the man seated near the hearth. 'Peddler!' he cried out, 'Benjamin Peddler, is it you?'

The figure turned about, rose from his chair and slowly walked across to the servery. He smiled weakly at Simon, 'It is indeed, old friend; how are you? Why, Captain O'Connor, I bid you good morning... Captain Macleod, you too. Gentlemen, I did not observe you here.'

Pat was speechless, for such an excuse was not credible in the least. Duncan too held his silence, and both men looked upon Peddler with a degree of scepticism that they could not disguise; but an anxious Simon pressed Peddler immediately, in hope of news of his beloved, the village community so very small, 'Benjamin, have you any news of Flora MacDougall, of her bairns? Where are they? Why is my house all locked up, tell? What do you know? What can you tell me?'

'I much regret to say, my dear friend, that I can tell you but little; a small fishing vessel - *the smallest,* an open boat it was - tied up at the pier a week or longer ago, coincidental with the Sheriff attending your house - *and such is a rare event in these parts;* indeed, I have no recollection of the Sheriff ever being in the village before. Mrs MacDougall and her daughters boarded that tiny boat and were gone within the very same hour, gone west, towards the Minch. There is not a soul in the village who knows a single thing more about the matter; I asked in the Customs House; I asked everyone of my acquaintance, but nothing could they tell me, I'm sorry to say.'

'The Sheriff, did you say? Why, I venture that the contemptible rogue - *my landlord, Salmon* - has seized my house; and Flora - *Mrs MacDougall* - has plainly been evicted. I have been in fear of such an eventuality these past three months, I have so... and now it has happened.'

'Mr Peddler,' Pat decided it was time to intervene, to seize the moment before the man in his gaze might conveniently beg leave to disappear, likely never to be seen again. 'Might I ask your attention for a very few minutes?'

Not waiting for any reply, Pat pressed, 'I would speak of your investment in my mine - which, *no doubt*, you do recall.'

'Of course, sir.'

'I have always liked to believe that I am a moderate man and a patient one, but the occasion must come when patience... *like every old stocking I ever possessed...* must wear thin. Do you follow me, sir?'

'If you speak of my purchase of your shareholding, sir, then I beg to tell you of a change in my circumstances.'

'Please, do go on; what do you have to say about that purchase and also that of Edward Perkiss?'

Nothing was heard from Peddler in reply for a long and hesitant minute as rigid faces stared in silent curiosity, until Simon, his nerves already on edge and rising feelings of unwelcome doubt overtaking his shrinking patience, interrupted, 'Benjamin, old friend, to what do you refer?'

A further hesitancy, a reluctance of a particular ilk plain to see, and Peddler spoke in low voice, 'I put my shares in with Edward's.'

'I beg your pardon?' exclaimed Pat in sharp voice. 'There is a want of clarity in your statement, sir; please to explain.'

'I am no longer a shareholder, sir,' Peddler was scarcely whispering, as if loathe to offer his explanation; 'Perkiss now holds - *owns* - all my shares.'

Simon, his attention captured by the exchange, interjected with shock in his voice, 'Upon my life, I am much taken aback; you assured me of your good intentions, that you would never let me down, that you would never countenance Perkiss holding a majority share in Captain O'Connor's venture.'

'I was in fear of the venture failing... no report had ever reached me of any discovery of gold, the least thing, and - *I confess* - my own bank was pressing me for - *admittedly* - a modest sum.'

'I believed in you!' Simon exclaimed in a rising voice, 'Indeed, I would have trusted my last farthing to you, and this is how you repay my trust! I thought I knew you... since we were but six years old and we both came to live in this place. All these years I believed you to be my old friend, *my close friend, the closest.* I was always minded that you would never let me down, *never!* Shame! Shame on you for your lack of fidelity!'

'Mr Peddler,' Pat spoke in grave voice, 'I will not speak further of your want of integrity, for such is plain to see; save only to say that you have sold me down the river - *would you not agree?* But tell me, I have never received a penny piece from Perkiss for his purchase; where is he to be found?'

'I regret to say, Captain O'Connor, that I know not. Of course, there are stories... rumours...'

'Do go on.'

'I speak of the bank failures. It is said that, consequent to the financial panic of last year, near two score of private banks failed. Some speak of seventy.'

Yes, I am familiar with bank failures, Mr Peddler,' declared Pat in caustic voice, 'to my great personal cost. It would seem that they are not the sole preserve of disreputable rogues and fraudsters.'

Peddler continued in a low voice, 'Perkiss's commercial venture - *Peninsula Metal Alloys* - was dragged down in the crash, and - *for so I believe* - it is also the case that his own brother did squander the remainder of what little capital that Perkiss then still possessed upon ill-conceived and expansionary ventures of a speculative nature.'

'Benjamin Peddler, you Judas!' Simon could not restrain his anger, perhaps exacerbated by the dismay he felt upon discovering the loss of his home *and, more particularly, the possibility of losing his intended*; but then he resumed in something of a more moderate voice, 'Do you have no shame? I never would have thought this of you, never in life. If you possess the least part of a conscience - *which I must now deem doubtful* - then this sordid transaction - *this cheap trick, this sell out* - will assuredly haunt you for the rest of your days; and whenever your mind casts back to those memories of those happy days which we spent together in our youth, then I hope you will reflect upon your selfish and despicable lack of scruple in this matter.'

'Come, Simon,' declared Pat, putting his arm around his true friend's shoulder, 'it is best we leave this place; let us return to our cutter. We will put our mind to thinking of Mrs MacDougall, to finding someone *who is truly deserving of your trust and your time*. Come now with me, I beg you will.'

At the door, a greatly agitated Simon turned back and shouted in fierce voice, 'Judas! Shame on you, Peddler! A plague upon your house!'

Chapter Twelve

The Minch was behaving with a perfect grace and *Mathew Jelbert*, having left her Tobermory anchorage shortly after the dawn in the full flood of the ebb tide, had made excellent progress since, a consistent eight knots carrying her beyond the Small Isles' Canna in the early morning and her passage in the clement conditions so accomplished that she passed Skye's Neist Point on the starboard beam under a golden sun at noon. The customary and constant south-westerly wind swept the cutter along with scarcely the least attention called for, and all persons fell back into a comfortable somnolence. Near the helm, the three close friends sat in muted conversation, for the dismay of the prior day's events was ameliorated, at least for Pat and Duncan, by the simple pleasures of a grand day of sailing; so steady a voyage that even Murphy seemed to be in good cheer; which was remarkable for all to see, for there was an absence of liquor aboard the cutter since two days.

'Well, gentlemen, I am broke!' declared Pat out of the blue. 'It seems that I will never see an ounce of gold from my mine venture, nor my promised three thousand pounds.' Pat's unexpected announcement after a half-hour of silence was offered in a tone which carried a world of dismay; 'That's the end of *my* dreams.'

'Well, sorrs,' declared Murphy in ribald voice, having been listening in as he prevaricated over delivering the precious routine which was coffee - but which had cooled - to the helm, 'It's sure that if you lie down with dogs you'll rise with fleas.'

'Why, you are quite the wit this morning, Murphy,' murmured Pat in disgruntled voice; 'Doubtless that was your grandma, eh?' Murphy merely grinned and nodded.

'I can scarcely believe the despicable conduct of Peddler,' declared Simon for the fifth time since departing Tobermory.

'Well, sorr, character is better than wealth,' pronounced Murphy, still grinning and much enjoying his role as sage. Pat scowled at him with undisguised venom.

'I, myself, widnae be averse to some small degree of wealth,' Duncan spoke up for the first time in the rising mood of despondency; 'Would that I might possess such!' He laughed, but Pat simply stared.

'And now I am leaving the home of my youth, the village in which I found my feet as a young man,' lamented Simon, 'The house where I married my wife - *bless her*. I have left that precious place in which I had hopes of making a home once more and with a new-found love, with Flora - *Mrs MacDougall* - and her bairns. It is the rare event when a man is gifted a second chance... but it seems that my ship has not come in; rather, it has foundered, and I am come to the end of *my* dreams, I much regret to say.'

'Simon,' Pat stirred, 'To be sure, we will find Mrs MacDougall in the Uists. Did you not say last night that she has a brother, a fisherman, in the north part of those islands? I well recall you spoke of him at supper... before we were overtaken by the inn's whisky.' Murphy frowned, for of whisky he had enjoyed none.

'Sure, I believe his cottage is somewhere near Lochmaddy; it is a desolate place where there is but a solitary inn for the traveller and little more.'

'We decided last night that we shall sail there when we depart Rodel. We will surely find Mrs MacDougall; for, as you say, there are but few souls residing in the Uists.'

'That's right,' interjected Murphy.

'Hold not to the least doubt, old friend,' added Pat whilst scowling again at his steward.

'Thank you, brother; that is a comfort,' Simon sighed.

'Murphy,' Pat turned towards the unwanted contributor, the rising irritant in his own dissatisfaction, 'Have you nothing of significance to occupy you? Is there not a deal of washing to attend?'

'Well, sorr, rightly no; washing days be Monday and Friday. I done it all yesterday... washed and dried, sorr, *right proper... while 'ee was attending the inn.*' The final element of Murphy's reply was tinged with an exceptional degree of audible emphasis, a discernible touch of envy, even a note of wicked condemnation; and then he added, 'and today it be Saturday... all day, sorr.'

'All day, eh? Well, it would be the rare day were that not the case,' retorted Pat in rising ill-temper; 'Perhaps in your domestic munificence you might light along another pot of *right proper* coffee, *a hot one...* as this hogwash is gone cold, for we possess no whisky with which to slake our disconsolation. Murphy, *you infernal lubber*,' added Pat with a sour scowl, 'did your grandma never tell you that *the mouth that speaks not is sweet to hear?* Now get away below!'

Duncan laughed aloud, as did Barton at the helm, and an admonished Murphy decided that discretion really was the better part of valour. He retired below deck muttering near-silent profanities to himself, many unfavourable comparisons with the essential and familiar parameters of life aboard the barky - including plentiful spirits - included.

Simon looked to his friend, 'Pat, I beg you will forgive me for saying so, but you are become cursed snappish with Murphy, a trifle uncivil even. I only throw out the remark.'

'Eh? Uncivil? Not at all, never; it's become time to clap a stopper over his remarks, the impudent bugger. Why, another day or two at sea and I venture he will become beyond disagreeable, more so than the customary sour curmudgeon which he is; perhaps he will even essay giving *me* orders, and then what will the world be coming to?'

'Are you become so greatly cast down, tell, by - *as seems inevitable* - the loss of your anticipated capital? Are you confounded by such a great deal of unease within your thoughts? For such seems to be the case,' Simon ventured, a degree of sympathy stirring. 'Is there yet any prospect that the valuable vein, *the ore*, might yet be found?'

'It had become something of a dream, *the prospect* of boundless riches to be found from my gold mine, for so it seemed. I dreamed of *boundless wealth* lying there for the taking - *the digging*. To be sure, it was a more greatly appealing prospect than digging the peat! For when you have grown up with the greatest of respect for a copper ha'penny... when the shoes on your feet have thrice been stitched in repair, and when the dinner for the fourth day was no more than a potato with the merest trifle of butter - *if, that is, the cow was not dry* - then, *sure,* such *prospect* holds a glorious appeal, it surely does.'

'No doubt,' concurred Simon with a murmur. Duncan nodded and Barton leaned ever closer to listen.

'And then along came the speculators... akin to the carrion crow... seeking to take advantage and gain their free meal.'

'No doubt you speak of Perkiss and Peddler, but was it not a beneficial transaction *for both parties*; surely so? Was not their capital to be a beneficial influence on your intended development?'

'Their capital? Sure, *had it actually existed*; but I have seen not a penny piece of it - *if it ever did exist*; and now my land is strewn with boundless dross, *great mounds of it*, from the excavations, and my neighbours ain't happy; no, they ain't; not by a very long chalk.'

'But what if there is yet a turnabout, a discovery?'

'No, it is a dream, no more; indeed, it truly is the end of *my* dream, I much regret to say. In fact, I am minded there is a greater prospect of finding the reputed treasure ship of the Armada. Will we return to Tobermory Bay? For that is where she blew up and sank.'

'It is a delightful notion, no doubt,' for the first time Simon smiled, 'but I venture the Duke of Argyll would likely make some claim of priority.'

'Land Ho!' announced Barton, standing at the helm.

Another hour and the interest of everyone was rising as landfall neared, and Duncan assumed command of the cutter in some small state of excitement himself. 'Steer into Loch Rodel there, Barton,' he ordered, pointing; 'The entrance channel to the harbour in this wind, such that it is, is a narrow passage from the west. I venture we have water enough for another hour before the low tide must keep us out, for I dinnae care to await a making tide. Once in, there will be time enough to set us down at the end of the pier, after which you must anchor in the basin without delay. There's two and a half fathoms there.'

And so it was, slack water was already ceding to the ebb tide as *Mathew Jelbert* near drifted out to the centre of the pool; Barton was at the helm and Murphy left aboard to assist. Duncan, Pat and Simon watched from the harbour wall. The three friends took stock for a few minutes, looking all about them in varying states of trepidation as they contemplated the walk to Duncan's home, to what they might find in the matter of Kathleen's health; indeed, Duncan himself was in a state of deep disconsolation, for the relief of returning home could not prevail above his fears for his wife.

'Come on, old friend,' urged Pat, 'we have twelve hours before the tide when Barton will look to the pier. Thankfully, this light wind is a friend for the cutter, and this fine weather - *dry that it is* - is benevolent for our own purposes in this place.'

Few words ventured, none seemingly adequate to the moment, and the trio set off, trudging past the Laird's house. Duncan returned friendly waves of greeting to a gaggle of fishermen, old acquaintances who sat mending nets, but he did not pause to speak, being seized by a tension; and they walked on in silence, along the track and up the hill. For a short distance the church tower peeked over the top of the brow to the right as if deigning to offer a greeting to an old friend before disappearing once more.

Boots ground firm on the dry, dusty track as the swift pace was maintained, breathing became heavy, and few words were spoken; to which nothing was ever offered in reply save for a brief nod of acknowledgement. At the top, at the meeting of the ways, for a second road enveloped the church perimeter, Simon paused to regain his breath, Pat and Duncan halting with him. 'Is your home a deal further?' ventured Simon, gasping; 'I am become unaccustomed to such rapid perambulations.'

'It isnae.' Duncan smiled for what seemed the first time since leaving Tobermory, but it failed to hide his concerns, as was plain to his friends to see. 'Look there, 'tis but thirty yards more.'

'That is a mercy,' declared Simon with relief, staring towards an unexpectedly imposing structure; 'Why, it is quite the splendid house!'

'Not at all, be not deceived; the lower floor is the winter home of the cow and the milking goat... soon to be stocked with plentiful straw for bedding. Also therein, by the end of this month, will be the summer crop of hay for winter fodder, and there is too a plentiful number of casks for the salt herring. In these parts there is but little to eat save for that herring, or a salmon from the sea or a trout from the lake; and a careful family must ever look to their husbandry, most particularly so for the winter. It is uncommon bleak in these parts.'

The distinctive fragrance of burning peat reached them with a strong wind gust as they gained the steps outside the house; a dozen paces up, a cursory knock on the door, and Duncan led the way in. Sunlight flooded into the room as bright arrows from small windows; the air was warm, suffused with aromatic smoke particles rising from the open fire upon which a pile of peat cuttings smouldered. Short, bright flickers of teasing, orange flame erupted from within the black mound, quickly subsiding to be replaced by others spurting and flickering elsewhere; and above the heat a charred black pot was suspended on a hook hung from a horizontal rod, and the rich and distinctive aroma of a fish stew drifted towards the three entrants, reminding them of their hunger.

"Rowadill (Rodel) in Harris" William Daniell "A Voyage around Great Britain" 1815

'Plainly, dinner is near ready,' remarked Pat, pleased, 'but where are Kathleen and Brodie?'

'I doubt they can be far,' replied Duncan with a degree of trepidation, 'for Kathleen with her illness cannae walk any distance... for so she said in her last letter. Perhaps they are milking the animals?' A momentary reflection, 'Yet I didnae hear a sound as we came up the road, so that cannae be.'

'The church perhaps?' suggested Simon in quiet speculation.

'Please to wait here in case they return; I will go and look to the church,' declared Pat without hesitation. He hastened out immediately and set off at a swift pace, his own anxieties rising by every step until his own mind was filled by a disturbing foreboding which he could not shake. Thirty yards on and back at the road junction, he decided to double-time, quickly reaching the low stone wall of the church perimeter and the gate. He rushed through and up the path, not sparing a glance to the gravestones in passing or the wider and splendid panorama in view all around until he gained the rise top and the church door, where he paused briefly to regain his breath. He did not care to exhibit the least alarm were anyone to be inside, and so he forced himself to breathe deeply for a half-minute before he pushed open the heavy door and stepped in. There was no more the sound of the blowing wind, slight that it had been; indeed, there was nothing to disturb an absolute silence as, his eyes adjusting to the lesser light, he stared the length of the small chapel to the far end where he could discern two figures kneeling upon the flagstones of the floor. Neither had heard his entrance, as they did not turn their heads in the least.

Pat swallowed hard and looked harder; recognition registered and he was sure: it was his wife's sister, Kathleen, and her daughter, his niece Brodie. He hesitated for a brief moment and stepped slowly towards them, not wishing to disturb the absolute quietude. As he silently approached, he began to hear the low murmur of their prayers. Another few paces and the creaking of the ageing leather of his sea boots alerted them to his presence; heads turned and wide smiles of a beatific pleasure met his gaze. 'Duncan is here in the house,' he declared quickly.

Rising from the floor, Kathleen seized Pat in a bear hug from which she would not release him for several minutes. 'Our Father has answered our prayers,' she whispered in his ear.

It was a slow plod back to the house, Kathleen unable to walk faster, and it was with relief that Pat opened the door for Kathleen, for the steep steps had been for her something of a struggle. Duncan rushed to the door and hugged his wife, and then came Kathleen's tears, a great convulsion of sobbing which would not cease, which endured for an age, as Pat and Simon stared in silence and with thoughts of the utmost benevolence; until Brodie interposed herself within the cathartic embrace and was in turn swept into the iron grip of Duncan's arms, the trio holding each other tight in a powerful release of heartfelt emotion.

Simon stared at Kathleen as discretely as could be during the dinner, a joyous occasion; and although she did not exert herself in the least - for Brodie served the food - her discomfort was plain to see in his careful scrutiny: the consumption had taken hold and she was visibly not well.

The dinner concluded, a bottle of whisky consumed, and the three friends enjoying a degree of contentment, Simon proposed a walk to the pier, ostensibly to apprise Barton and Murphy of their intentions. The walk was much slower than their arrival, much pleasure taken in the enduring warmth of the late evening; the wind had abated, utterly, and the all-enveloping silence of the natural world all about them bestowed a great satisfaction, in such absolute contrast to recent times.

'I give you joy of your homecoming, Duncan,' declared Pat as they strolled down the hill; 'At least it is not the end of *your* dreams.'

'Aye, but I fear for Kathleen; she isnae well. The precious lass *is my dreams* and I am greatly affrighted that I may lose her.' A momentary and awkward pause for all concerned, a dozen more yards, and Duncan ventured his anxious question, 'Simon, will you care to tell me your thinking on the matter?'

Simon set aside his deep reticence, but it was plain to hear in his voice, 'I cannot speak with the authority that a careful examination will furnish. Perhaps that is an undertaking for the morrow - *if Kathleen will consent.*'

'Aye, she will; there isnae doubt of that, old friend,' Duncan's apprehension was perfectly plain to hear.

'There is a degree of enfeeblement, that is plain to the eye; but we can be grateful that she does not display the more extreme symptoms of the advanced stages... I did not see a deal of coughing; very little, in fact; and there is certainly no cyanosis of the lips.'

'Cyanosis?' Duncan interjected in his acute anxiety.

'A blue tinge; it is a sign of the *latter* stages of the disease; the sufferer is struggling to gain a sufficiency of the vital air; and so we may hold to the view that this is not the case. I will expound further with a clearer view after my examination. I hope that my few words are sufficient for the moment.'

'Thank you, I thank you with all my heart; that is most welcome to hear. I am in your debt, I am; thank you.' That Duncan was much set back was plain to the gaze and the ears of his friends.

The trio ventured a few steps but then Pat halted and his friends paused with him. He seized Duncan about the shoulders and spoke with all the encouragement of the world in his voice, 'Hold fast, hold fast to hope! Michael Marston said that to me in a particularly black moment and I will never forget it. *Hold fast to hope, Duncan.* You are also to consider that here with us - *with Kathleen* - is the medical man of the world, right here; Simon is with you... *with Kathleen.*'

'You do me too much credit, Pat,' Simon smiled and spoke in light voice, seeking to recover something of the prior air of contentment. 'Will we continue now?'

The walk was resumed, the pier soon reached, and *Mathew Jelbert* was sighted at double anchor in the basin outside the tiny harbour. And then came the familiar voice of Murphy, reaching out from the group of fishermen sitting in front of the Laird's house, 'Sorrs! Sorrs!' Murphy ambled across, his gait exhibiting a degree of irregularity; the reason for which was evidenced most clearly as he halted before Pat, for the air itself was immediately suffused with the aroma of whisky; it was very much evident. Barton followed in close attendance. 'Well, sorrs,' declared Murphy in obvious good cheer, 'the lads here - *friendly fellows that they be* - hailed us and fetched us across in a boat... invited us to share a whisky.'

'Or two,' added Pat; 'Perhaps three, or was it four? Or was it a mutchkin you speak of, Murphy?'

'Only the one, sorr,' Murphy lied blatantly and did not elaborate on the precise measure.

'You are quite the grand dissimulator,' declared Pat, for he was neither deceived nor surprised; but it was no matter, for he understood that his own anxieties endured still, and he could never dispel the thought that they might never leave him, the past three years having been so greatly unpleasant; and they must have been similarly so for Murphy. Recalling his own relief of late Pat spoke to his steward in gracious voice, 'We will pay that no mind, a man is surely entitled to seize his moment.' He stared again in close scrutiny of his steward, 'All a-tanto, Murphy?'

'Well, sorr, *every man to his fancy and me to my own fancy*... said the old woman when she kissed her cow.'

Pat stared, speechless, whilst Duncan and Simon both laughed aloud, Barton too. Pat turned to Barton, 'Dr Ferguson and I will take to our cots aboard the cutter overnight. Please to fetch the boat to carry us across.'

Simon stepped a few yards away with Duncan, 'It will much assist my evaluation of the case were you to closely observe Kathleen during the night.' Duncan nodded and Simon resumed, 'Please to take note of any coughing, the least thing, and whether it may seem a particularly hoarse or dry

310

cough. Am I plain?' Duncan nodded again, for he could still find no words, and Simon continued, 'You are to observe the dear soul as she sleeps, in order to see if she exhibits anything of a fever, an excessive perspiration. Allow the fire to go out and do not relight it, the temperature of the air this fine evening will suffice for the household. Be not alarmed, I am speaking as a practised medical man. I will attend her for an examination in the morning. We will look after her; be assured of that, my friend.'

A few words of farewell, and Duncan set off up the hill. Pat and Simon clambered aboard the small boat at the pier, and thanks to Barton's skill with Pat assisting, Murphy being no use at all, they climbed aboard *Mathew Jelbert* as the sun blinked out a farewell as it descended below the hill in the west.

Sitting on the deck near the helm in the subdued dusk light, Murphy somehow having managed to make coffee, Pat and Simon sipped slowly, much appreciating the twilight quietude. 'Will you care to elaborate on your *preliminary* diagnosis of Kathleen, for no doubt that has been in your considerations all day? What is to be done?' Pat could not hold back his concerns.

'My impression, and this is only in the nature of a first or most cursory impression, scarcely that of an examination, is that I am in hope that the affliction is *not* sufficiently advanced such that a long spell of rest, *bed rest*, would assuredly fail - *as far as such a regime might be accommodated*. However, that approach will demand a great deal of nursing, likely more than Duncan and his bairn will be able to provide; and that is the dilemma I find. I am searching for a solution which I might offer in the morning.'

'And if rest alone does not answer the case? What then? What more might be done?' asked Pat, fearful of the answer. 'Is there any other remedy, the least thing?'

A long pause, several minutes passing before Simon replied, a discernible reluctance in his voice, 'As a student at Edinburgh Medical School I became familiar with the surgical

311

dissection of corpses...' Pat shuddered as Simon continued, '...for such was a vital element of the education, and the inspection of *the lung* was ever a matter for close scrutiny. The blight of consumption was nigh on inevitably a fatal affliction, at least at the stage that the poorest of folk presented themselves... sought medical help. Indeed, the majority of the populace could not afford a doctor, yet little could be offered to the sufferer; even an assured palliative was unknown, save for that precious standby, laudanum. Hence that particular disease and the least amelioration of it seemed to me to be a worthy challenge to the physician, a matter most deserving of investigation, and I devoted as much time to it as was feasible; but progress was painstakingly slow; indeed, the practical difficulty was in securing an adequate supply of dead bodies.'

Pat blanched, 'Perhaps you might set aside for the moment the... *the more greatly precise* description of your endeavours?'

'Certainly, and I do apologise; the more *sensitive* attributes of your good nature slipped my mind. To return to the story, the earliest treatise on the subject was actually published by a mariner, Ebenezer Gilchrist, who advocated sea voyages for the treatment of consumption. That was fifty years ago.'

'I was never apprised of such a remedy in all my years at sea,' declared Pat.

'The wheels of medicine do turn exceedingly slowly; and, sadly, it seems that innovation is much frowned upon in all establishment circles. If you recall, I spoke of such lamentable perspectives aboard our vessel, the dear *Surprise*. Were we very near to harsh words, Pat, you and I, in that charged moment?'

'Not above a minute or so, I dare say.'

'I will apologise again, brother; I was carried away by my emotions... I am minded that it was something of a release from a myriad tensions.'

312

'Of course, I do understand. We will pay that no mind. Please, continue.'

'Of the efficacy of Gilchrist's remedy *or otherwise* I cannot say; certainly, his writings evidence a deal of credible research, and we may hope that there may be an underlying foundation for those claimed results which he professed to have found. However, when in Edinburgh I made the acquaintance of another student there, a most engaging man of a particularly devoted and inquisitive inclination, James Carson. He is an Irish compatriot of yours, and together we found a common interest in the study of consumption, in what treatments might be discovered of a medicinal or surgical nature, anything which might aid the case, the least thing; for the ailment was so widespread.'

Pat, his interest much declining, offered only a tentative, 'Did you find any remedy, anything at all which helped?'

'Such marvels of medicine are exceedingly rare, and care is necessary when considering all new proposals of - *will I say* - a *radical* nature... in case of exaggeration - *or worse*. You will be familiar with such wild claims as those made by the proponents of - *for example* - the perpetual motion... or even - *will I mention* - the prospects for the discovery of gold... and in the most unlikely of places!' Simon laughed but Pat scowled. 'However, I digress; our dissections... in Edinburgh... suggested the notion that - *and I am cutting a very long story here short... to the very quick...*'

'I am most grateful,' declared Pat, gratefully.

'Our considerations suggested that a lung which was afforded an opportunity to heal, *in a stasis,* one which halted the least exercise of the organ tissues - a *halt to breathing, if you will* - might achieve a degree of healing, something of a recovery.'

'I think I see the flaw in your case,' offered Pat with a sigh.

Simon frowned, 'Of course, the treatment of a single lung will be advocated before any attempt is made upon the other. In all these years since I have kept in touch with Carson - he is these days practising in Liverpool - and we exchange the occasional letter. In the year 'twenty-two he apprised me of two successful experiments in the line of our thinking of all those years ago when we were in Edinburgh; indeed, he had performed a number of successful experiments of a preliminary nature, compressing the lung in each case.'

'That is quite the achievement,' replied Pat, his attention stirring slightly; for in truth the matter was not to his taste in the least, but he did not care to apprise his friend of such, 'How many people was he able to assist?'

'*Only rabbits*, two of them; not people.' Pat sighed, but Simon continued, 'However, he was determined to progress his endeavours and he subsequently treated two residents of Liverpool who were both suffering from *advanced deteriorations*, whose prognosis was poor... *grim*. It was their last card, their time so short.'

'And did he deliver them anything of a success?'

'They died, sadly. The affliction was too far advanced, as Carson found in the subsequent post-mortems.'

'Perhaps you should incline towards the gentler remedies?' murmured Pat, shocked. 'Will I say that I doubt Duncan will greatly care to hear the whole tale... or, indeed, the least part of it... notwithstanding the... *the fascinating*... *potential* that... that must surely exist...' Pat's voice tailed off as he realised his affirmation was not in the least convincing, neither to himself nor to his friend.

Murphy reappeared in the ensuing silent pause, bringing a tray with a bottle. 'Well, beg pardon, sorrs; here be a tot of whisky, a present from them fine folk on the quay. Will 'ee care for a bite of supper? There be a plentiful bowl of sea pie left over... cold, like.'

'I dare say we could see off a portion,' replied Pat without the least hesitation, quickly adding, 'And might there be a dash of Michael Kelly's sauce left over from yesterday's crubeens?'

'There might be, sorr.'

'With all my heart,' declared Simon emphatically. Raising his glass, he spoke with heartfelt feeling, 'I give you joy of our escape from that place of Hell.'

'My dear, you are to consider that I am in this moment your physician,' declared Simon as he sat with Kathleen, all other persons banished from the house, 'And you are to keep that in mind when you weigh my enquiries; for, to be of the least service to you, I must be assured of the most forthright replies. Hold nothing back; do you follow?'

'Thank you. I understand.'

'I collect - *it pleases me to say* - that you are *not* subject to - *will I say* - night sweats or anything of a persistent, dry cough. Nor have you experienced a weight loss these six months gone. Is that the case?'

'Yes, it is so; but I feel ever a want of air, and there is a soreness about my breathing, in my chest.'

'Please to cough - *hard* - into this handkerchief and to spit out the least mucus persisting in your throat.' A cough. 'Thank you; fortunately, there is nothing of blood in evidence. Now I wish to listen to your lungs. Please to remove your blouse and I will place this simple, wooden device, merely a hearing tube, upon your skin. I ask you to breathe deeply and keep your silence.'

A few minutes and Simon spoke again, 'Thank you. I am not excessively concerned. The affliction is there, sure; but I believe we may hold to the prospect of securing a degree of relief.'

'Thank you. I am much heartened to hear it.'

'Listen *most carefully*, if you please; the lung is an extremely delicate organ; once damaged, the prospects for self-repair, *self-healing* - unlike a wound or a fracture - are greatly less propitious. We practitioners possess not the least medicine suited to the need. Hence the body itself must serve, but it can only recover *exceedingly slowly* in a hard-working organ as is customary for the lung. Hence, you must *not*

315

engage in any physical activity, *the least thing*, nothing which presents a burden to the lung. You must *not* do as much as even to walk to the lavatory outside; *a chamber pot must serve*, and it will be emptied by your nurse. Such *absolute* application is essential. The recovery must be approached exceedingly slowly, *gently*, and with the utmost conviction.'

'My nurse? The least burden? But what of such as milking the cow? Who will grind the oatmeal, pick the potatoes? What of the washing, the cooking, a walk to the church? I am a good Catholic, and it is Sunday, and I am ever there on the sabbath long before this time of day.'

'I am afraid that all such activities must be set aside, my dear, all of them; not a single one can be countenanced.'

'Dear Dr Ferguson...'

'*Simon*; please to call me Simon, for I am your friend as well as your doctor.'

'*Simon*; how can I do nothing, the least thing? My daughter will attend me - for some of the time - but my husband is away more often than not. How can I consider such a strict regime? It is quite impossible.'

'My dear, I cannot labour the point enough; I have seen as many cases of consumption that I, myself, can bear to deal with. It is the greatest affliction to beset us since the great plague, and just as deadly - *over time*. I am entirely decided - *and I will brook not the least protest, let me tell you* - that *together* we will fight back against this insidious blight. Your husband - *be assured of it* - stands ready to attend, *to be with you during this journey*. And when we begin - *and I include myself* - there is no turning back... until we gain the safe haven which is an improvement in your condition.'

Kathleen, shocked and astounded, began to cry.

Simon took her hands, 'Listen, dear Kathleen; I will attend you, I will, and for as long as is necessary. The affliction can be halted; a healing to a very considerable degree is possible, but only with a great deal of time and such care as I describe.'

'How can you be with me, tell?'

'We are going to leave this place - *all of us* - to go where there are more people to nurse you.'

'But what of the cow... and the goat? Where am I to go, tell? I will not go to an asylum, I will not!' Kathleen began to cry again.

'My dear, the animals are not of the least consequence; I dare say a neighbour will look to their care; but *your* care is my concern, not that of the cow or the goat.' Simon laughed for the first time, and for Kathleen the spell of despond was broken; she ceased crying and smiled. Simon resumed, 'You are going to your *earlier* home, to that your sister, to Ireland; and I will be accompanying you. Sinéad and her bairns will aid your care, will be your nurses; for we cannot be assured that staying here, with only Brodie and Duncan to assist you, will be sufficient to answer the case; for I am minded that there will be too many calls on their time. No, we are all going to Claddaghduff... *in the morning*; and, I venture, the voyage, the fresh air, the sea air, will do you good. There will be no more peat fires, nothing of smoke to inflame that *irritation* within your lungs.'

On the pier, Simon walked up and down with Pat and Duncan, Simon recounting his examination of Kathleen and the conversation. 'But how can you accompany us?' asked Duncan, recovering from the initial surprise of his friend's announcement. 'You have yet to find Mrs MacDougall. What of her? What of her prospects, her wishes?'

'I am much mindful of those matters,' replied Simon, 'but you are to consider that she is not ill; and hence my - *and Mrs MacDougall's* - interests must be relegated to a lesser priority.'

'That is uncommon decent of you, old friend,' whispered Duncan, shocked, 'It is so, and I am much set back by your generosity.'

'Let me tell you something, if you please,' Simon spoke in a quiet voice but one which was filled with an absolute conviction, an audible determination all about him; 'You may recall that I lost my beloved wife, Agnes, in the year 'thirteen to the very same affliction... consumption. I was at sea - *we were all at sea, together* - aboard *Tenedos*, and I was helpless... a thousand miles away - *for so it seemed* - and with no news of her decline... to... *to the end*; and I have ever been consumed by guilt for not being there for her... for Agnes.'

The three friends halted, Simon visibly upset, neither Pat nor Duncan able to find the right words for the moment.

In a voice filled with tremors, Simon resumed, 'During our recent voyage - *I speak of the passage from Falmouth to this place* - I remarked upon the emptiness of the sea, a great void, nothing of the least vessel did we espy; and I took a considerable pleasure in that, I did; but later I also thought of the feeling of emptiness in a different light; I recalled those of our shipmates whom we had lost. I speak of such as Hammett and Kitto, and Mathew Jelbert before that; and I recognised another form of void - *an absence, if you will* - of a great many of our people. I was mindful of the loss of many folk who were precious to us in their own way, and I do not care to contemplate the loss of another, of someone who is just - *if not more* - important to all of us standing here. I do not care to allow that to happen, I will not, no. I am henceforth in the service of Kathleen... for as long as I can be of the least help.'

'My dear friend...' but Duncan was all broken up and could find no further words.

'That is the most gentlemanlike gesture,' declared Pat; 'You are a capital shipmate, old Simon; you are so... and the finest of friends; and I am most heartily pleased to hear your thinking. Why, I dare say we can call by the Uists and look to finding Mrs MacDougall when we make passage to Connemara.'

'I am very sensible of your kindness in suggesting such,' murmured Simon quietly, for the significance of his momentous decision was truly beginning to register.

'I am greatly indebted to you,' mumbled Duncan, taking his friend's hand.

'No, that is most certainly not the case, old friend,' replied Simon gently; 'There is no place for debt... in the heart.'

GLOSSARY, for pressed shipmates

Bargeman..................weevil (usually in the bread and biscuit)
Blatteroon................ senseless babbler or boaster
Blunties ....Old Scots term for stupid fellows
Boggart.................... Mythical creature inhabiting marshes
Boggies.....................Irish country folk
Bombard...................Mediterranean two-masted vessel, ketch
Boney....................... Napoleon Bonaparte
Bower.......................bow anchor
Boxty........................traditional Irish potato pancake
Breeks.......................Scots term for trousers or breeches
Browster wife...........a landlady of a public house or who brews beer
Bumbo.....................pirates' drink; rum, water, sugar, and nutmeg
Burgoo.....................oatmeal porridge
Capperbar................ theft of government property
Captains' Thins........Carr's water crackers, a "refined ship's biscuit"
Caudle.....................thickened, sweetened alcoholic drink like eggnog
Clegs........................Scots term for large, biting flies
Commons (short)..... Short rations
Crabbit.....................ill-tempered, disagreeable, crabby
Crubeens..................boiled pig's feet
Dimber-damber...... chief rogue
Dock (the)................ original name for the navy's Devonport base
Dreich......................Old Scots for cold, wet, miserable weather
Drookit....................Scots term for drenched
Dun...........................Bailiff
Dunnage.................. personal baggage
Etesian.....................strong, dry, summer, Aegean north winds
Felucca....................small sailing boat, one or two sails of lateen rig
Fencibles..................the Sea Fencibles, a naval 'home guard' militia
Flat...........................a person interested only in himself
Flux..........................inflammatory dysentery
Forty Thieves.......... a class of ships subject to dockyard pilfering in build
Frumenty..................a pudding made with boiled wheat, eggs and milk
Galway Hooker....... coastal sailing craft (fishing) of western Ireland
Golden Horn (the).... the harbour of Constantinople
Gomerel....................a stupid or foolish person
Groyne (The)............La Coruña in north-west Spain
Gull...........................to deceive
Hallion.....................a scoundrel
Hazing (& starting).. harassment of crew by officers (with canes)
Hockogrockle, Marthambles and Moonpall ... Tufts fictional diseases
Hoy...........................small (e.g. London-Margate passengers) vessel
Jollies.......................Royal Marines
Jollux........................a fat person
Kedgeree..................a dish of flaked fish, rice and eggs

Kentledge..................56lb ingots of pig iron for ship's ballast

Laidron......................loutish, lazy rascal

Letter of marque......an official (legal) document (and ship) to differentiate from   pirates

Larbowlin (and Starbowlin) those of the crew who attended the larboard (and starboard) side guns

Lasking.................... an oblique attacking approach in order to keep the guns   able to fire on an opponent

Laudanum................a liquid opiate, used for medicinal purposes in the Blue pill

Lobscouse...............beef stew, north German in origin

Marchpane...............marzipan

Mark of mouth.........from aged eight a horse's teeth no longer indicate its age

Marshalsea...............19th century London debtors' prison (another London   prison was the Fleet prison)

Mauk.......................Scottish for maggot

Meed..................a person's deserved share of praise

Meltemi....................Greek and Turkish name for the Etesian wind

Millers.....................shipboard rats

Mistico.....................similar to the Felucca sailing vessel

Negus.......................a hot drink of port, sugar, lemon, and spice

Nibby.......................ship's biscuit

Pinchfart...................miser, withholding to the detriment of others

Popinjay....................a vain or conceited person

Porte (the Sublime).. The government in Constantinople (actually the Sultan)

Press (the) .... the Press Gang service to seize unwilling navy recruits

Puling.......................whining in self pity

Rapparee .... a bandit or irregular soldier in Ireland in the 17th century

Receiving Ship........ where new navy entrants were received

Scrovies ....worthless, pressed men

Seventy-four.............a 74-gun ship (a 3rd rate in the hierarchy of warships)

Sick and Hurt (Board).... the governing medical authority of the Royal Navy

Sillery................. a still, dry white wine of NE France

Skillygalee............... a gruel made with oatmeal

Solomongundy..........a stew of leftover meats

Snotties....................midshipmen

Stingo.......................strong ale

Strategic Chess......... Strategichess, 14x14 squares (multiple) chessboard(s)   (game available from the author)

Treacle-dowdy...........a covered pudding of treacle and fruit

Trubs..........................truffles

Truckle..................... interfere with

Vespering..................moving westward; towards the setting sun

Whoreson....................an unpleasant or greatly disliked person
Yellow jack................Yellow fever (or flag signifying outbreak)
Xebec........................ A fore and aft rigged sailing vessel with (galley-like) oars

AFTERWORD - PTSD

If you are a serving military person or a veteran (or a friend or family member of either) who is in difficulty or affected by any form of distress, turmoil or anxiety, don't hesitate to seek help:

in the UK, contact **SSAFA**
the Armed Forces Charity
www.ssafa.org.uk/help-you/veterans
or

Combat Stress for veterans' mental health
www.combatstress.org.uk/helpline
email: helpline@combatstress.org.uk
The free telephone helpline is open 24 hours a day,
365 days a year
0800 138 1619 (veterans and families)
0800 323 4444 (serving personnel and families)

in the US, contact the Department of Veteran's Affairs
The National Centre for PTSD
www.ptsd.va.gov
call 1-800-273-8255
email: ncptsd@va.gov

Elsewhere, do search the web and find your own country's help providers; they will surely help you.

Please do bear in mind that trained, courteous, caring people are standing by to help. There is nothing at all to be lost by calling. There is not the least shame in seeking help. There is no need to struggle on alone with PTSD difficulties. Call: you are not alone.

***

If you have enjoyed this book, I would be most grateful if you would post an Amazon review and also mention it on the social media sites which you enjoy using; other fans of historical (and particularly nautical) fiction may then discover it for their own pleasure. Thank you in anticipation; a glass with you!

Alan Lawrence   *Devon, January 2024*

Printed in Great Britain
by Amazon